Kitty's Torment

by

Rita Wilkinson

Best Wishes
Rita Wilkinson

Published in 2016 by FeedARead.com Publishing

A CIP catalogue record for this title is available from the British Library.

In memory of Mum

She laboured hard for those she loved

A little tribute small and tender

Just to say I'll always remember

Chapter One

Struggling with a large, heavy, rather shabby looking suitcase, Kitty tread very cautiously as she made her way down the steep cold dark dingy staircase. Despite the electric lights being turned on in the entrance hall and first floor landing, both of which lacked the luxury of a pretty lightshade, this part of the house was very dull and uninviting. In the hallway below, a solid wooden front door badly in need of a fresh coat of paint had an engraved glass panel above showing the house name 'Hazeldene' and the number 13 but offered very little in the way of daylight. Its discoloured glass and dust covered cobwebs were evidence that it had been many months since this fine piece of workmanship had been cleaned and polished by the residents within.

Halfway down the stairs Kitty stumbled when suddenly the rusted metal locks burst open scattering the entire contents everywhere. 'Oh bugger it,' she yelled as she flung the suitcase full force to the floor below. Furious, she plonked her bottom on the threadbare stair carpet, her chin resting on her clenched fists, and watched mesmerised as it bounced noisily one step at a time until finally coming to rest with an enormous clatter behind the front door. Disgusted by her actions, she buried her head in her hands and recalled how earlier that morning after locking the suitcase, she had doubted its reliability.

'I knew when I lifted it from the top of the wardrobe that it had seen better days, and those damn locks, well they're neither use nor bloody ornament,' she muttered to herself while staring blankly at the overturned suitcase, concluding it was probably about as much use as a cardboard box. Sadly, with neither the time nor the money to replace it, she gazed in disbelief at the contents which she had packed so carefully and decided the only way to resolve the problem would be to wrap one of Ernie's belts around it. Feeling slightly dejected she remained seated and her thoughts turned to the reason she found herself in this awkward situation, and a more sinister use for a belt came to mind.

'If I'd pulled one tight around his neck before he managed to force himself on me in one of his drunken rages I wouldn't be in this bloody predicament.' Instantly a cold shiver ran the length of her spine. Wrapping her arms around her body, she shook herself vigorously as though to rid her whole being of such an evil thought, and contemplated the terrible consequences of carrying out such a wicked deed.

'With me in prison and no one to look after me precious bairns they would be put into a children's home and this one...,' she paused, gently stroking her hands across her slightly extended belly, '...this one would be born in a prison hospital, taken from me and handed over to strangers. I might never be allowed to see it or Annie and Jack again and they would never know they had another brother or sister.'

In her heart she knew she could never do such an evil

thing. Although Ernie was no longer the loving, caring man she married several years earlier she still loved him and vowed, as long as she had blood running through her veins she'd always be there for him to come home to no matter what kind of a life he put her through. She would carry on in spite of her troubles, protecting the bairns and making sure they never had to suffer as a result of his actions. Regaining her composure she stood up, dusted herself down and made her way downstairs, gathering the scattered contents on the way.

Sitting quietly on the cold black and white tiled floor in the hallway of the mid-terrace Victorian house, clothes tucked under both arms and shoes laid across her lap, she looked around the dingy surroundings she shared with Peggy, the elderly widow who lived alone in the ground floor flat. Hearing Peggy's door open she smiled to herself, knowing only too well that she would be peering from behind, curious to learn what all the commotion was about.

'Oh dear God whatever have you done, Kitty? I heard the banging and wondered what on earth it was. Are you hurt?'

Not waiting to hear her reply she immediately picked up the suitcase, gathered the remaining contents and laid them next to Kitty where, together they repacked them as quickly as possible. With everything neatly back inside they closed the lid and after several attempts, the overweight Peggy crash-landed her rather large posterior on top to make sure it remained shut as they forced the locks back into place.

Kitty's sombre mood lifted when, amused by Peggy's unexpected actions, and the threat that the suitcase looked as though it was about to be completely flattened, she set off into a fit of giggles. Hearing Kitty's infectious laughter, Peggy was unable to control her own and the two sat side by side, tears rolling down their cheeks unable to move.

'If only you… if only you could see yourself.' Kitty struggled to get her words out. Her laughter was uncontrollable as she stared at Peggy's spread-eagled legs. Her stockings were rolled down to her ankles exposing her badly mottled legs, and with her skirt high above her knees the bottoms of her long off-white bloomers were in full view. She looked uncomfortable with her arms folded between her rather distended belly and sagging breasts, and as she continued laughing hysterically the notorious locks burst open once again.

Through her tears of laughter she watched as Kitty forced them back into place then managing to find her voice she firmly suggested, 'I really think you need to fasten something around it, Kitty. Looking at it I reckon it's almost as old and worn out as me and that's saying something. It'll take more than a couple of dodgy locks to keep this thing shut that's for sure.'

'Really, Peggy, I don't think it's quite that old, and I'd already decided that would be the only answer. Now if you can calm yourself down, I'll pop upstairs and get one of Ernie's belts and pick up the keys for the locks. In the meantime I strongly advise you not to move even an inch until I return to make sure it stays shut.'

'Move? You've got to be joking, pet. I couldn't possibly move, and it'll probably take a crane to lift me back onto me feet.' Peggy chuckled to herself as she envisaged the unsightly view poor Kitty had been confronted with.

After rummaging through drawers and wardrobes without success, Kitty assumed Ernie must have taken all his belts with him. Disillusioned, she began to question as she has done so many times before, why he preferred to work away from home rather than helping with the local rebuilding work taking place in his native North East. With the country gradually getting back on its feet following the end of the war, new roads, homes and factories were appearing everywhere, but for reasons best known to himself, Ernie preferred to work further south.

'You know I earn much more money working away. I send money home to you every week, and come back as often as possible to see you and the bairns so why do you keep complaining?' His irate response was always the same whenever she questioned him. Finally she gave up the challenge of asking in fear of another thrashing each time she broached the subject, and eventually accepted being alone with the bairns for weeks at a time. She was thankful he kept his promise to send her money each week but unfortunately she never benefited from the extra money that went into his pay packet and she often wondered how much he kept for himself to spend on beer, cigarettes and dare she even think it... other women?

Before heading back downstairs she popped her head

around the living room door to check on the bairns. They were where she had left them, sitting on the large multicoloured clippy mat, one of several she had made out of clippings from old clothing and blankets. Keeping very quiet she watched Annie who, at four years of age, loved playing a motherly role to Jack her twenty-month-old sibling. She was explaining the words and pictures from her ABC book as he sat patiently listening by her side. An immense feeling of pride warmed Kitty's heart as she gazed in admiration at her two beautiful offspring. 'There's nothing in the world I wouldn't do for either of you,' she muttered under her breath.

'And H is for horse, Jack,' Annie said pointing to the picture when she sensed her Mammy's presence and immediately dropped her book, jumped to her feet and rushed towards her. 'What are you doing, Mammy?' she asked inquisitively, aware that something unusual was happening that morning.

'I just have a little job to finish with Aunty Peggy. You stay here and carry on reading your book to Jack and I won't be long.' After giving her a quick peck she closed the door securely and dashed back downstairs where, as she had hoped, Peggy was still sitting spread-eagled across the suitcase.

'I can't find a belt anywhere, Peggy and I don't even have a length of string long enough to go around so I wondered, is there any chance you might have something suitable?'

'Well, I was about to tell you not to bother looking but you went flying off upstairs before I had a chance to open me mouth. I know I have a couple of Fred's old belts kicking about the house somewhere, and as you've seen from his photographs he was even larger around the middle than me so there's bound to be one big enough to go around. Just give me a few minutes and I'll find one, though I'm only sorry I don't have a decent suitcase I could lend you. Seeing as we never went away anywhere we've not had the need for one, but don't you worry I'll soon have you sorted out. We can't have this thing bursting open while you're on your travels. Can you imagine the embarrassment that would cause you?' Peggy cringed at the thought. 'I can almost picture your face, Kitty, if it did happen… you wouldn't know where to look if Joe Public were to see your undies spread about all over the place.'

'You can say that again!' Kitty responded as she leant over to help Peggy off the suitcase.

Bursts of laughter erupted again when, holding Peggy by the hands, it took Kitty several hazardous attempts before she finally managed to haul her to her feet and swiftly take her place. Pausing for a few seconds to catch her breath, Peggy stuffed her hands inside her pinny pocket then made her way to her flat dragging her feet as she inched across the floor in her old tatty red slippers which, with holes in the toes and worn down at the heels had long since seen better days but she flatly refused to discard them. Her grey hair as always was wound around dinky curlers and partly hidden by a blue flowered headscarf tied in a turban style. She gave the impression that she hadn't a care in the world, but Kitty knew

11

different. She loved this sweet old lady who was worth her weight in gold, caring more for the welfare of others than herself even in her twilight years. On entering her flat, Peggy imagined the scene if the suitcase were to burst open in public and tried to see the funny side of it, but it only emphasised to her the need to save Kitty from possible embarrassment. If it was the last thing she did she would make sure the suitcase was secure enough to see her through to her destination.

Awaiting Peggy's return, Kitty looked solemnly at the shabby brown box that dared to call itself a suitcase and her laughter ceased. She recalled her parents' warning, in particular her father's angry words about marrying Ernie against their wishes but remained steadfast in her decision never to admit to them that she had regrettably accepted they may have been right about him all along.

The sound of Peggy's feet shuffling back across the floor broke her thoughts and she was relieved to see she was carrying a folded black leather belt with a large metal buckle. Without warning she cracked it through the air and Kitty recoiled sharply as though she was about to receive a beating. Amused by her reaction Peggy enlightened her of bygone days. 'I can tell you this much, Kitty, over the years there's a few bairns around this area could have done with a damned good whack on the backside with one of these. I'll always remember a young lad called Johnny Smith, right cheeky little beggar he was yet his parents thought the sun shone out of his backside. If Fred could have got his hands on him I often think he would have done it himself, but the cute little monkey was always too quick for him and was off down the street as fast as his legs could carry him. Fred would be left shaking his fist with nowt else to do but shout after him threatening, 'I'll catch you the next time, you little bugger, you mark my words, lad.' She paused a moment and looked heavenward as she reminisced. 'Of course he never did and Johnny turned out to be a fine upstanding young man who did his family proud in the end... but that's enough of the past, Kitty, it's the present that's important and this belt will certainly be big enough to go round, and before you say anything, I know like the suitcase it does look a little worse for wear but it will serve the purpose and that's all that matters.' Lifting the suitcase from the floor, together they managed to wrap the belt around, pulled it tight and fastened the buckle securely.

'There now, that's fixed it, it can't possibly burst open again but mind you, don't you dare come running down those stairs telling me you have forgotten to put something inside, that case is staying belted until you reach your destination.'

While threatening Kitty, subconsciously she began patting the belt buckle as if it was still fastened around Fred's belly holding up his trousers, along with a pair of worse for wear blue and grey striped braces which he always wore at the same time. 'Just in case,' he would say to Peggy. 'We can't risk having me trousers falling down around me ankles now can we, Peg?' Peg being his pet name for her when he was in good fettle, but when he demanded something urgently it would be 'Peggyyyyyyyy'.

'Now that would be a sight for sore eyes,' she would tell him. 'It's bad enough me being married to you and having to put up with such a sight, I certainly wouldn't wish that on anyone else.'

Pressing her chubby thumbs firmly against the locks ensuring they were properly secured, she felt saddened over her loss. She missed not having Fred around even though once he retired he was rather on the lazy side and always seemed to be under her feet. Secretly though she loved looking after him making sure he was well cared for and now sadly Kitty and the bairns were leaving her as well. How long they would be gone she had no idea and she sounded upset when asking Kitty what time the taxi was arriving to pick them up.

'Taxi, Peggy? I can't afford a taxi.' Kitty gasped; surprised that Peggy would have even thought it remotely possible. 'It's costing me more than enough for the train fare, but I know I can manage alright on the tram; the conductors are more than willing to give a hand and there's always some kind soul helps me with the bairns.'

Peggy shook her head in disbelief. 'Kitty what on earth are you thinking of? You must be mad. You can't possibly manage on the tram with all you have to take with you. Now just you listen to me, young lady, I'm going to put me coat on and pop along to the phone box and order you one. I'll pay for it and there will be no arguments about it either.'

'You're doing no such thing, Peggy Wilson, I couldn't possibly let you do that, and besides I know I can manage. Thank you for being so generous, but I couldn't possibly accept and now I must get back upstairs and finish off the few jobs left to do or I'll be running late for the train and it certainly won't wait for us.'

Not one to take no for an answer Peggy turned a deaf ear to Kitty's refusal. 'Now what time was it you said the train leaves?'

'I didn't,' Kitty replied quite sharply knowing Peggy was cunningly trying to gain information.

'I know very well you didn't but I'm not moving from this spot until you tell me so you might as well accept that as final. If you think for one minute I am going to let you out of that front door with two bairns, a pushchair, a suitcase and goodness knows what else without a taxi waiting for you then you are sadly mistaken. You have been a good neighbour to me ever since you and Ernie moved in upstairs, despite the many times I've listened to the two of you fighting like cat and dog and I've had to race up the stairs and intervene. I'll admit there have been times when I've even threatened to ask the landlord to evict you, and if it hadn't been for my understanding nature and my love for you and those two canny little bairns of yours I would have done.' She hesitated for a moment, her tone softened. 'You know it's been a lonely life since Fred passed away and not having had any bairns me self, your little family has kept me going. You've saved me from feeling sorry for me self and I would really like to help you, Kitty. It's my way of saying thanks.'

Kitty smiled. She knew how much Peggy loved them and equally she knew there were times when she too had been thankful Peggy was there for her when Ernie's heavy drinking and physical abuse began. It was quite early in the marriage when Kitty saw a different side to Ernie and began to live in fear of his drunken states. There had been times when he was drunk and would start an argument which often turned into a beating, and was relieved to hear Peggy thumping at the door threatening him with the police. Once again Peggy was there for her, grasping the opportunity to help and Kitty knew she would not back down. Her determined nature and strong will meant she usually got her way, and Kitty knew she would have little say in the matter. Reluctantly, but gratefully, she accepted.

'It's really very kind of you to offer, Peggy, so I won't be so rude as to throw your kindness back in your face when I, more than anyone, know how much pleasure you get from helping other people. We're catching the eleven-thirty train but I will need to be at the station long before eleven to pick up my ticket and make sure I have time to spare; I don't want to be rushing around at the last minute. I must admit it will be a big help having a taxi to pick us up, it will save me having to struggle, and at the station I'll get a porter to bring me a trolley and with a bit of luck he might even let the bairns have a ride on it. Now then I really must be getting back upstairs. I've one or two things that still need doing before we leave. The bairns are nearly ready but as you can see I'm not and I still have quite a bit of rubbish to take down to the dustbin. I don't want to return home to find unwanted pests running around the kitchen from waste food left lying around. Oh and by the way I've some bread and cake you might as well eat as we can't be throwing good food away with some of it still on ration, and if you run out of coal before the next delivery, use what's left in my coalhouse. It's not much, only a couple of shovels or so, but it will be a bit of extra warmth for you if the weather turns a bit chilly again.'

'There you go, you see, we are quits already. I do something for you and you give me something in return. Now then, just remind me how long you'll be away?'

'I'm not sure yet, Peggy. It will be only a short stay, but don't worry, I'll write to let you know what we are up to. I'm not giving the flat up so you won't be having strangers moving in upstairs, and I don't suppose Ernie will be back again before we return. I'll be sending the landlord his regular Postal Order each week to cover the rent, and I'll make sure he receives it in good time, so there's no way he can possibly call around threatening to re-let the flat.'

Aware that Peggy liked a bit of gossip with the neighbours, Kitty didn't want her to be the one to break the news that she was pregnant again and decided to keep it to herself until a later date. Little did she know but Peggy, who never missed a trick had already suspected the reason for her sudden trip away and wondered if Jean, Kitty's friend who lived opposite, knew anything and they were keeping it a secret between themselves?

'Well I better be getting along, Kitty, I can't dash around like I used to and I've got me stockings to attach to me suspenders, and me coat and shoes to put on. It takes a good five minutes nowadays for me to reach the phone box and I must check me purse to make sure I have enough pennies. If I haven't I know I have a sixpence and I'll pop into the corner shop and Bessie will change it for me. Mind you I bet she will want to know who it is I am going to phone, but I'll just tell her to mind her own business for a change. As soon as I get back I'll pop up to let you know what time the taxi is booked for, and then just before it's due I'll give you a hand with the bairns and any last minute jobs that still need doing.'

'Thanks, Peggy. I don't know how I would have ever managed without you at times, you've been a godsend to me and the bairns while we've lived here and we'll all miss you while we're away. Oh, and just one other thing before you leave the house, I suggest you take a couple of them curlers out of your hair; you know the neighbours love to pull your leg about forgetting to brush your hair in the mornings.'

Unable to raise a smile Peggy began taking the curlers out one by one and with moist eyes told Kitty, 'It won't be the same around here without you. I love having you and the bairns around as it can be lonely at times living here on me own. Aye, I'm going to miss you that's for sure.'

Saddened at seeing Peggy looking so unhappy Kitty assured her, 'We'll be home again before you know it and you've still got Jean if you feel the need for company and think of it this way, at least you won't have to worry about me and me troubles for a while.' Peggy didn't acknowledge her and despondently made her way to her flat quietly closing the door behind her.

Kitty knew her stay would be longer than Peggy w have wished, but chose to leave her guessing, fearing s would worry about living alone in the big old house with an empty flat upstairs and the possibility that Ernie could land home unexpectedly. Climbing the stairs two at a time it had dawned on her that she had left the bairns alone for longer than usual, and although her concerns were always for them first and foremost her thoughts turned once again to her unforgiving parents. She knew what they would be thinking when they heard she was going to Connie's and especially the reason why, and she could almost hear her dad's disapproving words ringing in her ears.

'As if having two bairns by that good-for-nothing isn't bad enough, here she is having another one. Stupid girl, she'll never learn. Well, she'll just have to get on with it, Mary, she never has listened to us, and you know only too well from the minute I set eyes on Ernie Cartwright I knew how her life would turn out if she went ahead and married him, and up to now she hasn't proved us wrong!'

Chapter Two

Kitty's parents had been quick to recognise their daughter had fallen head over heels in love with Ernie Cartwright, and that they faced a long battle trying to discourage the relationship. They immediately suspected he would not make an ideal husband and discreetly made a point of finding out as much about him as possible. When their suspicions were confirmed her father would repeatedly tell her, 'He's not right for you, Kitty, we've met his type before. Yes, he's good looking, immaculately turned out in his smart suits, highly polished shoes and Brylcreemed hair, but believe me it's all a charade. He's very clever, he persuades young girls like you that he's a decent fella with a good upbringing, but your mother and I are not stupid, we can see right through him. Can't you see, girl, you deserve someone much better than him?'

Whenever Kitty mentioned marriage the very thought of Ernie Cartwright ever becoming their son-in-law caused them a great deal of anxiety, and relentlessly they tried to convince her that by marrying him she would live to regret it for the rest of her life, but she would never listen.

Repeatedly her father would ask, 'Why can't you choose someone like Cecil Taylor's son James? You know he is studying at college to become an accountant and is very keen on you. He would provide you with a nice home and a comfortable lifestyle, more than can be said of that young good-for-nothing you prefer to be with.'

Kitty would just blank him every time he mentioned James, and in frustration he would raise his voice to her. 'Ernie Cartwright will never be able to provide you with a secure future, instead he'll drag you down to his level then you'll want to come running back to us when things go wrong, and mark my words, young lady, they will.'

Time and time again they tried to persuade her they were only advising her for her own good, but were beginning to accept that one day they might have to give in, if only to bring an end to their endless squabbling. Allowing their daughter to marry someone from the poorer area of the city would humiliate them amongst their more affluent friends, though Kitty suspected there was a more profound reason behind their disapproval.

The younger of two daughters of highly respected parents, Kitty had a privileged childhood living with her family in their neat semi in a smart residential area on the outskirts of the city. The homes in that area had fortunately escaped the ravages of war, though everyone had still lived in fear of the distant sound of German warplanes approaching. Terrified, they would shelter under the stairs as planes flew overhead on their mission towards the River Tyne where they would drop their deadly weapons on armament factories and local shipyards. Employed by the Local Government, her father worked in the finance department, a position of responsibility which he still holds today, and which in addition to his full-time work he currently acts as spokesman on behalf of the local community. He regularly attends meetings alongside council planning officers regarding improvements needed throughout the area. Her mother, like her father is highly thought of locally for the support she gives her husband and for the amount of hours she gives to the voluntary sector.

Ernie on the other hand lived with his parents and several brothers and sisters in a nineteenth century rented terraced house and despite many properties nearby having been destroyed by enemy bombs, theirs had miraculously survived. Overcrowded, and still in a fairly dilapidated state, their living conditions were very poor, and with very little money about were unlikely to see much improvement in the foreseeable future. Most of the families in that vicinity lacked many of the privileges Kitty's family enjoyed, but she firmly believed Ernie's promise that, though unskilled, once they were married he would find a better job and would provide her with the standard of living she was accustomed to.

Determined to marry him from the moment she met and fell in love with Ernie, no matter what her parents thought of him, neither they nor anyone else were going to stop her. Tall, dark and handsome he was every young girl's idea of the perfect boyfriend and she became the envy of many. He was, without doubt, the man of her dreams; they talked of marriage, raising a family and having a long and happy life together. To Kitty he was perfect in every way and she was determined no other girl would steal him from her by marrying him as soon as possible.

Eventually her parents, following many heated discussions, feared they may have to give their consent, conceding that no matter how long and hard they tried to convince her she was making a big mistake, she was never going to change her mind.

'She's far too headstrong is that one, nothing at all like our Vera, and I don't know where she gets it from,' were her father's stern words to his wife when he was feeling under pressure, but they both agreed there was no point continuing to argue with her any longer. 'All we can do is let them go ahead and marry. It's obvious where it will end, and we can only hope she will learn something from her mistakes. It would be nice to think that in years to come she could prove us wrong but I'm sure you'll agree with me, Mary, I don't think for one minute that will ever happen.'

Mary agreed, there was no sense in them continuing the battle, it was wearing them both down and their daughter being so besotted by Ernie Cartwright, nothing anyone said would change her mind. It was all becoming too much for them, and to save embarrassment amongst their friends they decided it would be better to finally agree to let them go ahead and marry, agreeing, though very reluctantly to attend.

Kitty was just nineteen when the quiet ceremony took place in their local registry office attended by a small group of family and friends. It had been apparent to everyone that this union did not have everyone's blessing, but no one, it seemed, had the courage to speak out against it. Had it been the fear of repercussions by the tough Cartwright family who were well known for all the wrong reasons? Little did Ernie or any of his family realise just how much he was despised by his new in-laws and how determined they were that not one penny of their earnings would ever reach his pockets. They were never going to accept Ernie Cartwright as their son-in-law and to prove it they were even prepared to forsake their daughter soon after the wedding.

It had been only a few weeks following one of Ernie's long weekends at home when Kitty discovered she was pregnant with their third child. 'He's making damn sure I have my hands full while he's away,' had been her immediate reaction when the pregnancy was confirmed. The thought of having three bairns all under five to feed and clothe with very little money and her husband away for weeks at a time caused her some concern. She knew her life would not be easy living in an upstairs two bedroom flat with a front door leading directly onto the busy street, and a hazardous flight of concrete steps to the rear yard which was so dangerous it was an accident waiting to happen. With precious little space in the yard; the bairns had nowhere safe to play and had to spend lots of time indoors.

Weighing up her circumstances she decided to write to her sister Vera, and her best friend Connie, to break the news that she was pregnant again. Her parents still refused to make contact with her even though they knew they had two grandchildren and she decided they did not deserve to be informed at this early stage though she would let them know at some future date.

It came as no surprise to her when, within a couple of days, it was Vera who was the first to reply. She ripped open the envelope eager to read what she had to say. The letter began, My dearest sister, and immediately she became suspicious. Devoted sisters they were not and she knew those words would not be meant in an endearing way. She began reading again.

My dearest sister, I can't believe what you have just told me. I would have thought you had more sense than to get yourself pregnant again especially with Ernie working away most of the time. How on earth you think you will manage on your own with three bairns all under five beats me. Have either of you ever stopped to consider how you would cope should he have a fatal accident, which as you know is highly possible with the type of work he does? There are lots of young widows struggling to bring up bairns alone, with very little to live on and it can't be easy for them, and it wouldn't be any different for you.'

Young widow! The words leapt from the page. Sickened at the very thought of such a dreadful thing happening, her face drained of colour and she felt her heart thumping deep inside her chest. The prospect of being a widow with three children was almost too much to bear. Suddenly she felt quite weak and vulnerable, and wished Ernie was living at home despite the fact she would have to cope with the mental and physical abuse he put her through.

Brushing such shocking thoughts from her mind she returned to Vera's letter fully prepared for further lecturing, including the usual reminder of not heeding Mam and Dad's advice about marrying Ernie, but as she continued down the page she was quite surprised by what she read.

We have given your situation some thought and have decided, albeit a quick decision, that you should come here and stay with us until after the baby is born. We know no one will be be prepared to help you from either family, and we are a little concerned how you will manage on your own especially up and down those dangerous concrete steps with two bairns and carrying a third. I know Mam and Dad wont change how they feel and I agree they are right refusing to help, you knew how much they were against you marrying Ernie and you can't expect anything different. However there is no point looking back; the mistakes have all been made and nothting can be changed.

'There it is! I knew she would have to mention it,' and

she threw the letter to one side. Filled with anger, she made her way to the kitchen where she boiled the kettle to make herself a pot of tea wondering if her sister would ever find it in her heart to try to persuade Mam and Dad to share their lives with her and their grandbairns. She already knew the answer. 'Of course she won't, she prefers things the way they are, the obedient daughter who has done nothing wrong in their eyes, and like our parents dislikes Ernie immensely.'

The whistling kettle broke her angry thoughts, and after pouring boiling water over the tea leaves, she placed the teapot alongside a cup and saucer and a few homemade biscuits onto a tray and returned to the living room. Annie and Jack were as always playing happily together and she handed them each a biscuit, poured her tea and returned nervously to the letter.

We feel we have no other choice than to ask you to come and stay with us. I couldn't leave Kenneth for such a long period of time and he couldn't possibly give up his work; as you know he holds down a very responsible job. We did briefly consider Kenneth asking for a temporary transfer to the North but as you don't have a spare room we will just have to manage somehow to accommodate you here.

'Well, that certainly doesn't sound like a welcoming invitation… we feel we have no other choice but to ask you to stay with us.' She repeated the words vocally causing Annie's head to turn quickly hearing her mam's sudden outburst, but she was too young to understand and carried on playing. 'Well, we'll see about that, dear sister. I have never depended on you before and I am not going to start now.' She knew she wouldn't have to struggle along on her own. Peggy for one would be more than willing to do what she could for her, but she felt it would be wrong to rely on her too much as she was getting well along in years. Also her friend Jean would be more than happy to lend a hand with the bairns, but she still had one slight problem on her mind. She remained determined not to tell Peggy or Jean right away about her news. With gossip spreading like wildfire in the street she was not prepared to be the topic of conversation until she was further along in her pregnancy. Everyone loved a bit of scandal, and Ernie in particular was already the talk of the neighbourhood. He was notorious for his rowdy behaviour when under the influence of a few pints of the brown nectar, and she didn't at this early stage want to give them anything else to talk about. Peggy would always let her know what she heard the neighbours saying about them, so she knew that they would gloat over the news. She could almost hear them, 'the drunken so and so has got her pregnant again', and for that very reason she was determined no one would hear a thing for the time being.

Barely considering Vera and Kenneth's offer of help, she withheld her reply choosing to wait until she heard what Connie had to say. Kitty and Connie had been best friends since childhood. Having attended the same school they grew very close when they were growing up,

28

spending most of their free time together. They discussed music, the latest fashion and hairstyles, their changing bodies, and told each other their secrets when interest in the opposite sex became exciting. They even talked about how many children they would like when they were married, promising that they would always live close by one another and would remain lifelong friends.

Connie had been the first to have a boyfriend, when at the tender age of sixteen she started dating Malcolm who was three years older. Her parents never objected, though Kitty's parents would regularly comment that Connie was far too young to be going about with boys and that she had better not start thinking about having a boyfriend for a few years yet. Although Connie and Malcolm spent a lot of time together, they made sure they never excluded Kitty from their lives. Connie still spent time alone with Kitty but unbeknown to all three, major changes were about to take place in the not too distant future. Connie's dad had been asked to transfer his job to the North West and the family were leaving the area. Kitty was heartbroken, but not as much as Malcolm who said he could not bear to be parted from Connie and, much to everyone's surprise the lovebirds quickly married enabling him to move with her when the family left the North East for their new life. Barely a week would pass without the two friends writing to one another, visiting on occasions and Connie had of course been Matron of Honour at Kitty and Ernie's wedding. Nothing could break the loyalty between the two friends, and in time Connie suspected that Kitty's life with Ernie was not always as she made out in her letters. Still she supported and encouraged her as best she could to draw out her problems when she suspected there was one, and assured her that come what may she would always be there for her in times of need. Connie's sincerity was proven once again when unlike Vera's letter, hers read...

My dearest friend Kitty, how you never fail to surprise me, and how envious I am that you are pregnant again. I'm beginning to think it is never going to happen for us. How often I have wished that you lived closer to us as we promised we would do all those years ago, and that we would always be there for each other. There is nothing Malcolm and I would love more than for you to spend some time with us in Calderthwaite. Come for as long as you like so we can help you with the bairns who we are longing to see again. You'll be able to rest whenever you need to and between us all we can look after Annie and Jack. Our little cottage is big enough for everyone, and with Mam and Dad living only a stone's throw away there are plenty of us to look after the bairns if you need us to. Think seriously about our offer Kitty, as it will give us peace of mind knowing you will have some help. We're sure you will love being here again away from the hustle and bustle of city life, and you're almost certain to enjoy

the peace and quiet when we're out and about
in our beautiful countryside. If you do decide
to come, and we desperately hope you do, as we
 can't wait to see you all again, make it
soon... very soon.

 Hugs from us to Annie and Jack, your ever
loving friends Connie and Malcolm
        Xxxx'

Kitty didn't need to spend hours thinking about it. She accepted their warm invitation immediately and within a couple of days, three letters had been posted. The first was to Ernie though why, she was not sure as he made very little mention of their third child as if it was some phantom pregnancy she was having. Her second was written to Vera and Kenneth thanking them, but turning down their invitation and informing them that she was going to stay with Connie. Her final letter was to her beloved friends Connie and Malcolm, whom she loved dearly. She knew how much it would mean to them to spend time with the bairns, and to help her out during the early stage of her pregnancy, and within a matter of days arrangements were in place for them to travel to the North West.

Chapter Three

Kitty dashed back upstairs, her hands clasped tight against her chest. The excitement of the next few weeks lifted her spirits, and although the reality was that she would have to return to the North East and her unpredictable life with Ernie, she was determined to make the most of her unexpected visit. With lots of love and laughter to look forward to with Connie, Malcolm, and Connie's parents who she affectionately calls Uncle George and Aunty Kath, along with lots of good clean fresh air to fill their lungs, she was feeling completley exhilarated.

She had just finished the last minute jobs in her tiny kitchen and was about to pop the few leftover perishables into a box when she heard Peggy's knock. 'Come in, Peggy, the door's off the latch,' she shouted excitedly, knowing she had come to let her know what time the taxi would arrive. Immediately she stopped what she was doing and as she headed into the living room, it suddenly occurred to her that she hadn't written to inform her parents she was leaving Newcastle. Though not overly concerned about it, she did feel it was only right that they always knew where she was should they ever find it in their hearts to want to get in touch. She had specifically asked Vera not to inform them, saying she would drop them a line before she left, though whether she would respect her wishes was debatable. Vera always seemed to do the opposite of whatever Kitty asked.

'Aunty Peggy, Aunty Peggy,' Annie shouted as she entered the room. Jumping to her feet she raced towards her with outstretched arms knowing she would be picked up immediately for a cuddle. After a bit of a struggle Peggy had her in her arms, stroked her lovely blonde hair and planted a kiss on her cheek, but as she glanced across at Kitty she was taken aback by her troubled expression. 'You're looking a little worried, Kitty, I hope you're not having second thoughts about going after all the trouble we went to over that damned suitcase earlier?'

Kitty smiled. 'That was really funny this morning, Peggy, it did make us laugh, and no I'm certainly not having second thoughts. I'm really looking forward to going only I've just remembered I haven't informed my parents and I feel it is only right that they should know where I am.' In an attempt to avoid confrontation knowing Peggy would blurt out her usual curt remarks about them, she asked her if she would mind popping into the drawer of the sideboard and fetch out the writing paper, envelopes and pen, while she popped back into the kitchen to finish what she was doing,

'Tell me you're kidding me, Kitty. Do you *really* think they deserve to know considering they don't ever get in touch with you?' Her sharp response came as no surprise. Expressing her disgust at the rejection of their daughter was a regular occurrence. She would never understand how they could do such a thing and even more so knowing they were grandparents. Not having had any

33

bairns herself, Peggy was certain she would never ever have abandoned them under any circumstances.

Walking towards the kitchen, Kitty felt relieved to have her back to her as she began to explain. 'I know what you think about my parents, Peggy and I'm inclined to agree with you to a certain extent but…,' she hesitated for a moment in order to choose her words carefully fearing she might let slip her pregnancy being the main reason for her visit to Connie's, '…they might be in poor health for all I know, and in case of an emergency they should know where to find me. You know I try not to feel bitter towards them, after all I insisted on marrying Ernie against their wishes so I can hardly blame them for the way my life is turning out. Besides, Peggy, you must agree, their loss is far greater than mine, never seeing the bairns they are missing out on so much, but who knows maybe one day, just maybe…' Then her voice faded.

'Oh you have such a good heart, Kitty Cartwright, it's no wonder people love you. Well if you insist on sending a letter to them then I'd better find that pen and paper so you can get it written,' and as she crossed the room she glanced at the clock. It was nine-thirty. 'Is the clock showing the right time?' she called to Kitty. 'Because if it is you need to be getting a move on, your taxi will be here at ten-thirty so it's not giving you much time to be sure you have everything ready, it's no good leaving things until the last minute and having to rush around.'

'Yes it's the right time, Peggy, and stop worrying, an hour will be more than enough time. I'm all organised, I've almost finished in here and everywhere else is nice

34

and tidy to come home to. I've just myself to get ready and everything I'm wearing is laid across the bed so it won't take me long.'

Kitty returned to the living room with the box filled with leftovers. 'This is for you, Peggy, it's the few leftovers I mentioned earlier, and now if I dare ask you another favour, would you mind taking the rubbish outside for me while I write this letter? Oh, and by the way you'll be pleased to hear it'll only be very brief so it will only take me a few minutes to write.'

'It had better be!' she snapped at her as she did on rare occasions, then as asked she went to collect the rubbish to take outside.

Kitty sat at the table on one of her three dining chairs, all of which had the padding replaced and recovered several times, and which were once again showing signs of wear and tear. The fourth chair had been so badly damaged, it was unsuitable for sale when they purchased the second hand dining room suite, but it was as much as they could afford at the time. A dark green chenille table covering, one of the few soft furnishings she had bought new for her home hid several large scratch marks, and an empty cut glass vase which rarely held fresh flowers these days was placed in the centre. Rolling the tip of the pen between her fingers, she stared vacantly at the blank sheet of paper muttering quietly. 'Where on earth do I start when they are not in the slightest bit interested in anything we do? It makes it so hard to even think of just a few words to say.' Several seconds later, when the pen finally touched the paper, formalities such as her address and the date were intentionally disregarded reasoning that they knew where she lived, though at times she sometimes wondered, and in her neatest handwriting she began to write.

Dear Mam and Dad,

I am writing to let you know that I'm going to stay with Connie and Malcolm in Calderthwaite for a while. I'm in the early stages of another pregnancy and they have kindly invited us over. They would love to see the bairns and give me a hand with them, rather than me having to on struggle alone when they know Ernie is still working away. I know you won't be happy to hear this news but I feel you should at least kno where I am. Vera has Connie's address should you need to get in touch with me. I hope this letter finds you both in good health.

Kitty

She had just finished sealing the envelope when she heard banging at the front door and ran downstairs having guessed who it would be at the other side. Sure enough as expected after dropping Michael off at school, it was her friend Jean from number 16. Kitty had intentionally kept her departure fairly quiet, but she would never have left without telling Jean who had befriended her when she moved into the street. There were not many young people living nearby and it was easy to see why they formed a close friendship. Jean was about six months pregnant at the time and loved having Kitty popping in and out for cups of tea and a chat. For Kitty it meant having someone of her own age to talk to about the things she couldn't always discuss with Peggy, who being that much older she felt certain subjects were inappropriate for discussion between the younger and older generations. She loved spending time with Jean, especially after Michael was born and she longed for a son or daughter of her own. Little did she know that she was already pregnant, and before Michael reached his first birthday she was the proud mother of a beautiful baby girl she named Annie. Now almost five years on, whoever would have believed that not only does she have Annie, but also Jack and another on the way, while Jean quite happily is still the mother of one.

Unlike Peggy, Jean hadn't suspected the reason behind Kitty's sudden visit to Connie's, but accepted that whatever made her want to disappear all of a sudden she had every right to keep it to herself. There had been odd occasions when she couldn't hold back from voicing her opinion which resulted in them having a disagreement followed by a brief falling out, but on this occasion she decided it was best not to ask questions.

The front door was barely ajar when Jean barged past Kitty and headed straight upstairs, talking as she went. 'I hope you didn't think that you were going to get away without saying ta-ra to me, Kitty Cartwright... I'm here to find out exactly what time you're leaving because I'm going with you to the station. You're kidding yourself if you think you can manage everything on your own.' Halfway up she stopped to take a breath, and shaking her head in disbelief she turned to Kitty. 'I really can't believe you haven't asked me to help you with the bairns.'

Astounded by Jean's strange actions, and with the door still held ajar, Kitty stood speechless for a moment as she watched her taking the stairs two at a time. 'And a very good morning to you too, Mrs Baxter,' she called to her and closed the door with a heavy hand. 'It appears I wasn't going to get the chance, even if I planned to sneak off without anyone knowing.' But they both knew that would never have happened.

On reaching the landing, Jean could hear Peggy talking to the bairns. 'Oh, it's going to be so exciting, the taxi is coming to take you to the railway station and then you are going on the train to Aunty Connie's.' Stopping dead in her tracks, she was taken aback by what she heard, and as she entered the room she asked Peggy outright. 'Did I hear you mention a taxi?'

By this time Kitty was right behind her and answered on Peggy's behalf.

'Yes you did, Jean. Peggy insisted on arranging it this morning, and not only that, before you even ask how I can afford it, she has very kindly offered to pay for it.'

'Oh, Peggy that's typical of you, you're so kind, but I planned to go with her to give her a hand.' She gazed at Kitty with a look of disappointment on her face. 'I didn't tell you because I wanted it to be a surprise so you had someone with you to wave you off.'

'Well that's very nice of you to offer, Jean, but with a taxi coming to pick us up I'll be able to manage and it will save you wasting your morning.'

'Seeing you and the bairns safely onto the train certainly isn't what I would call the waste of a morning.'

Then Jean suggested to Peggy that she could maybe ask the driver if he would allow her to go with them.

'That's okay with me, Jean as long as Kitty is happy about it, but if he says you can go, you do understand I won't be paying for a taxi home for you!'

'Of course I wouldn't expect that, Peggy, but I really would like to be there to wave them off.'

'Now, if you two have quite finished discussing when and where we are going to say our goodbyes, will you listen to me for a second? If the driver says you can come then you are more than welcome, Jean, but right now I need to be doing the last minute finishing off or we won't be going anywhere.' Remembering about the letter she handed it to Peggy. 'Would you mind having a look in my purse, Peggy, I'm sure I have a couple of stamps, and would you mind popping it in the post today?'

Finding the stamps she stuck them on the blank envelope, and looking somewhat bemused gave it back to Kitty. 'It would be helpful if the Post Office knew where to deliver it! It'll never reach your parents, or anyone else for that matter, without an address.'

Slapping her forehead when she saw the blank envelope, Kitty began to laugh. 'How stupid of me, I just dropped everything when I heard the front door then I never gave it a second thought. I'll do it right away then it's finished with. That's if I can remember their address,' she teased, picking up the pen and writing her parents' address. 'Promise me you will post it today, Peggy, and yes I know you think I'm being stupid and they don't deserve this, but it's done now and I want to be sure they receive it as soon as possible then I can leave with a clear conscience.'

'You know you can trust me after all these years, and I won't let you down it'll be in the post before you have even left the railway station. Now, don't you think it's about time you started moving? Before you know it the taxi driver will be banging at the door and he'll not wait if you're not ready.'

Jean had listened inquisitively and when she heard the letter was to Kitty's parents, like Peggy she was shocked. They shared the same views on the subject of Kitty's parents but she said nothing assuming Peggy would have already made several cynical remarks about it before she arrived on the scene.

By this time it had got around to ten o'clock, and Peggy and Jean took it on themselves to see to the bairns, while Kitty disappeared into the bedroom to change ready for the journey ahead. When she returned, she was dressed in a smart two piece light grey suit with a box pleated skirt which still fit comfortably around her waist. A pretty pale pink blouse tucked inside her skirt emphasized her still trim figure, and the loose fitting jacket was left unbuttoned. She was wearing black court shoes, but due to the shortage and high cost of stockings, her legs were bare. Like many other women, she would often draw a line down her legs with an eyebrow pencil to give the appearance that she was wearing stockings, but today, as the spring weather had arrived and she would be sitting most of the time she hoped no one would even notice.

'You look very nice, Kitty, it's a long time since I've seen you dressed in your suit.'

'Well let's be honest I never go anywhere to justify the need to wear a smart outfit do I?'

Peggy ignored her remark, not wanting to agree but knowing it was true. 'Now then, what about the clothes you have just taken off? If you give me whatever dirty washing you have lying around I'll see that it is washed and ironed ready for you when you come home.'

At this point Kitty was feeling guilty about all the help the two women offered. 'I don't know how I'll ever be able to thank you both for everything you have done for me, and I don't just mean today but ever since we moved in here.' She was very emotional and was struggling to hold back her tears, but knew for fear of upsetting the bairns she must.

'We've always helped each other, Kitty,' Jean reminded her. 'Nobody owes anyone anything you should know that by now. We're always here for one another whenever the need arises, so don't you be going away feeling indebted to anyone.'

'You're probably right, Jean, but I need you both to know I've always been grateful for everything you've done, especially the times when Ernie was so drunk I had to flee from the house with the bairns to get away from him. One of you always provided a refuge for us even though time and again he threatened you with trouble, but thank goodness he never carried it through and by the time he sobered up he could never remember anything anyway.'

'He's all mouth and no action,' Peggy retorted. 'By the time he had taken his anger out on you he'd run out of steam and was only capable of crashing out until he slept it off. Anyhow that's enough about him, Kitty, let's get that washing sorted out before your taxi arrives. I'll double check the back door is locked, and make sure all the gas taps and lights are turned off before you leave.'

With so much still to think about, she chose not to argue with her over the washing and calmly gathered the items together and handed them to her. Jean meanwhile tidied up the few toys which were laid around on the floor, but Annie kept her eye on her ABC book. When she saw Jean was about to pick it up she managed to grab it first and clung onto it, determined she was not going to get her hands on it. Jack's favourite blue hand-knitted rabbit, one Peggy made for him from oddments of wool, was sitting on his lap, but Jean knew he would be taking it with him; he carried it with him wherever he went.

No sooner had Peggy returned from taking the washing downstairs, they heard the door again and everyone knew the taxi must have arrived. Jean immediately dashed downstairs to let him know they were ready, at the same time asking if it was possible for her to travel with them.

'Aye no problem, pet, I understand the bairns are only little so there is plenty of room for you all.'

In the meantime Peggy slipped Kitty the taxi fare with a little extra for a treat for the bairns. She could see Kitty was struggling to maintain her composure and half expected the floodgates to open, but she managed to hold back the tears.

By the speed at which Jean dashed back up the stairs, it was obvious she was allowed to travel with them and between them all, they had everything organised within minutes. Kitty locked the door. How long it would stay locked no one could be sure. She handed Peggy a spare key. 'Just in case something unexpected should happen and you need to get into the flat,' she explained. 'Ernie has his own key with him but in case he should return home unexpectedly without it you can let him have this one.'

'He needn't to blooming bother!' The very thought unnerved Peggy and as they began to make their way downstairs she admitted, 'It's to be hoped to God he doesn't turn up, that's the last thing I need. I would hate to be here on me own with that drunken so and so upstairs. Without you to pick on he might decide to have a go at me, and I can well do without that at my time of life.'

'Don't be silly, Peggy, he wouldn't do anything like that. I know he can be trouble at times, but he wouldn't turn on a defensive old lady, and besides there's very little chance of him coming home when I'm not here. He'll have nobody to cook and wash for him and you know he's useless on his own.'

'Aye you're probably right there,' she said a little more enthusiastically.

Jack's pushchair and the notorious brown suitcase were already by the front door, and as Kitty bent down to pick up the suitcase Peggy managed a smile, 'Just you be very careful with that blooming thing. It needs plenty of gentle handling, you know it has a history of doing as it pleases,' then gave her a hug and reassured her it would be fine. She wrapped her arms around Annie and Jack and hugged them tightly. Not wanting them to leave, tears welled up in her eyes, and like Kitty, she didn't want them to see her like that. She kissed them goodbye, then promptly entered her flat preferring to watch them from her living room window where they wouldn't see her tears.

'Leave those where they are, love, they look a bit too heavy for a lovely slim young woman like you to be lifting, and besides it's all a part of the service you're paying for.'

Kitty felt flattered and left him to do his job, then taking Annie by the hand led her to the taxi where Jean and Jack were already seated. She glanced across to Peggy's window. Holding back the lace curtain with one hand she used it to wipe away her tears, with the other she half-heartedly waved them off. Kitty waved back and blew her a kiss. 'She is going to miss us so much,' she told Jean, 'but at least she still has you for company while we're away.'

Chapter Four

As they approached the railway station Annie appeared a little upset. 'Is that man coming with us, Mammy?' she whispered nervously to Kitty.

'No, silly, he's just the driver, he takes people to and from different places in his taxi, it's his job and how he earns his pennies.'

'Oh that's good because I don't want him to,' she said sounding quite relieved. 'Is Aunty Jean coming with us?'

'No, pet, it's just you and me and Jack of course who are going to Aunty Connie's. Aunty Jean has come to help us onto the train then she has to go back to collect Michael from school.'

'Why isn't Daddy coming with us?'

Completely bewildered by Annie's latest question considering Ernie never goes anywhere with them, Kitty pondered a moment to consider her answer.

'Daddy has to go work, just like the taxi driver is doing. They go to work to make the pennies so Mammies can buy food and clothes for their families. Now listen to me for a minute, I want you to be a good girl for Mammy while I pay the driver for bringing us here, then it won't be long and we will be on the train and on our way to Aunty Connie's.'

Taking the fare from her purse, Kitty felt guilty that it was Peggy's money she was spending and vowed she would write the very next day to thank her again, and that some time in the future she would repay her both the money and her kindness. Fare paid and with everyone out of the taxi, she suggested to Jean to wait with the bairns while she nipped inside to find a porter. Jean agreed it was a sensible idea, and with Jack safely in her arms, she gripped Annie's hand making sure she didn't try to follow her. Annie was smiling again, but Jack seemed afraid of all the noise and buried his face into her chest. Still holding onto his rabbit, he covered one ear with his other hand to try to block out the noise while Jean held him tightly and tried her best to reassure him that nothing would harm him.

Several minutes passed before Kitty finally returned with a porter, who was pulling a large empty trolley big enough to hold the luggage and all four of them as well.

'These yours, pet?' he asked Kitty pointing to the pushchair and suitcase.

'They are,' she replied politely and waited while he lifted them onto the trolley, then much to everyone's amusement he picked Annie up and sat her alongside.

'Look, Jack, look and see where Annie is.' Jean spoke excitedly hoping to relieve his fears. Cautiously he lifted his head and looked around to see where she was.

'Are you going to have a ride as well, son?' the porter asked and held his arms out towards him. 'Come on, it won't hurt you. All the bairns love to have a ride on Uncle Dennis's trolley.'

At first he gave him one of his distrustful looks, but seeing Annie's smiling face as she nodded her head to encourage him, he stretched his arms out to the porter who quickly took him from Jean and sat him comfortably between Annie and the suitcase.

'Now what about you two ladies?' He gestured towards the space on the trolley. 'There's plenty of room for you all,' he said with a cheeky smirk and a wink as he observed their startled expressions.

'I reckon we should give it a miss for now Jean!'

'Well, it's free; it might be worth considering as you don't get much for nothing these days.'

Free ride it may be but they chose to maintain their dignity, preferring to walk, one at either side where they could watch the bairns' faces as the metal wheels bounced and clanked noisily across the uneven platform. Jack looked unsure, and again placed his hands over his ears trying to block out the noise but Annie was as ever full of confidence. The noise of trains constantly arriving and departing, doors clashing and banging and whistles blowing didn't faze her at all. She was captivated by her surroundings, watching with interest the comings and goings on the busy station.

'I need to know where you ladies are heading off to so I'm sure to drop your luggage off on the right platform!' the porter enquired.

'We're off to the North West on the eleven-thirty train from platform six,' Kitty said sounding very much like the well seasoned traveller. Having made the same journey several times she knew which platform she needed to be on, but as an afterthought added, 'Of course that's unless they have changed it since the last time I made the journey.'

'You're right, pet, it's still platform six. Now if you'll grab the bairns I'll head off and you'll find your luggage waiting for you, and have a good journey.'

'Thanks a lot, I'm sure we will.' Kitty acknowledged him and handed him a modest tip, being all she could spare. As she was just about to lift Jack off the trolley she was taken aback by Annie's sudden actions. She had spotted a soldier running directly towards them and she began pointing her finger at him and yelling at the top of her voice, 'Daddyyyyyyy…,' much to the delight of some of the other travellers.

Kitty had her back to him and was unaware the man Annie was calling out to was a young soldier. Although it was obvious to Kitty that she must be imagining it to be her Daddy, her heart raced. She feared the worst, surely he hadn't come to stop them going? Her mind was working overtime as she tried to recall whether she had told him the exact date they were leaving. Even if she had, she reasoned, she would not have been so precise as to mention the train times. That being the case, how could he possibly know exactly when they would arrive at the station? A little concerned as to why Jean had turned rather pale and remained silent, she began doubting herself, but knew she must turn and face up to him whatever the consequences.

'Daddyyyyyyyyy…,' Annie yelled a second time, her arms waving frantically in all directions, but Kitty was able to breathe a sigh of relief as the man, who she now discovered was a soldier, ran past them into the arms of a young lady running from the opposite direction. Upset that he hadn't stopped, Annie held out her arms for comfort as the tears began to well up in her eyes.

Holding her tightly Kitty tried to explain. 'It's not your daddy, pet. Daddy is still working away and won't be back for a while, that's why we are able to go to Auntie Connie's for our little holiday, but you will see him again very soon.'

She tried to sound calm but it had left her slightly shaken. Why Annie thought it was him baffled her. She could only assume he must have had a look of Ernie and she thought it was him because he appeared to be running directly towards her. Having managed to settle her down she turned to Jean to enlighten her on just how dreadful she had felt about the entire incident.

'Thank goodness it wasn't him, Jean… I hardly dare to think what might have happened if it had been. To be honest part of me knew it wouldn't be him, but you know as well as I do what Ernie's like, even the impossible seems to be possible with that man!'

'I didn't think it would be him either, but I tell you what, Kitty, I think my heart almost stopped when Annie shouted and I hardly dared take a look in case she was right. God forbid… can you imagine if it had been him what a commotion there would have been in front of all these people?'

'It would have been very embarrassing if it had been that's for sure!'

Throughout the entire incident the bemused porter seemed rooted to the ground as he looked on in silence. Fascinated by their actions, he wisely refrained from asking questions, happy to ponder his own thoughts as to exactly what their bizarre behaviour was all about.

'Well panic over thank goodness!' Kitty sounded relieved as she lifted the bairns from the trolley. 'If you'll hang onto these two I better nip over to the ticket office or we won't be going anywhere.' Despite the station being very busy there were just two ticket windows open with the result that people were queuing for well over five minutes and where, not knowing exactly when she would be making the return journey, Kitty purchased a single ticket. Jean in the meantime had taken Annie and Jack to one of the kiosks for a few sweets as a last minute treat, which she gave to Kitty on her return.

'Oh, Jean, you really shouldn't have, Peggy has already given me money for treats for them.'

'Don't be silly, it's not much and I couldn't let them go away without a little something from me as I've no idea how long it will be before I'll see them again.' She added the latter in the hope that Kitty would give her at least a hint of how long they would be away, but as with Peggy, she too was left guessing.

'Who knows how long we'll be staying? I'm just going to take it a day at a time. Connie and Malcolm might get sick of us after just a few days and send us packing sooner rather than later.'

'You know that'll never happen but one thing I do know, Peggy and me will miss you all, but more important at the minute is my platform ticket. I better pop and get one if I'm to see you safely onto the train and into your seats.' Opening her purse she took out one penny, the price of the ticket that allows none travelling passengers to enter the platform. 'It won't take long and I'll be back before you can say Bob's ya uncle.' She reassured Kitty who was looking a little anxious, but she assumed it was probably reaction from the shock Annie had given her rather than having second thoughts about travelling alone with the bairns.

The constant hustle and bustle of commuters and workers was unnerving Kitty, causing doubts to race through her overactive mind. 'Will the train arrive on time? I don't want Connie to be kept waiting at the other end. Will there be enough seats for everyone and what if there isn't and I have to stand?' Her head was in a spin and she lifted Jack safely into her arms, took Annie by the hand, and tightened her grip on them as her motherly instinct took over. Being so small, she feared they could easily be swept away amongst the ever-increasing crowd, and all she wished for was to be settled on the train and be on their way.

'I'm back,' Jean announced waving her platform ticket at Kitty. 'I told you I wouldn't be long and have you noticed your train has arrived so we better start heading over?' She was doing her best to sound cheerful, but in truth she was not looking forward to saying goodbye to them.

Kitty passed Jack to Jean. 'If you will see to him I'll take care of Annie while we squeeze through the barrier because I have a terrible fear of getting trapped in them.'

'Me too, they're not the easiest of things to get through and just imagine if it was Peggy trying to squeeze through there instead of us!' Jean began to snigger as she pictured the scene which brought a smile to Kitty's face but she refrained from passing a comment.

The queue for platform six was stationary as the ticket collector hadn't arrived and when a couple of young soldiers joined directly behind them Kitty was conscious that Annie continually turned around and stared up at them. She quietly explained to her that it was rude to stare at people, but for some reason she continued to keep having a sneak peep. Looking very smart in their khaki uniforms, highly polished black steel cap boots which you could probably see your face in, they carried large heavy kit bags on their backs. Chatting incessantly they inhaled deeply on cigarettes as though they hadn't had a smoke in years, and their smiling faces gave Kitty the impression they were heading home on leave and were excited about seeing their families again. 'Just like me,' she thought, 'travelling to see loved ones.'

A cool breeze which had wound its way onto the station drifted around Kitty's bare legs causing a shiver to run through her entire body. Rubbing her shins alternatively against her calves to increase the blood flow she gradually warmed through bringing a healthy glow to her cheeks. Feeling more settled knowing she had made the right decision to stay with friends rather than with her sister, she began to look forward to the days ahead.

Eventually the ticket collector arrived and took his place behind the barrier where, as he punched their tickets he welcomed them onto the platform giving Annie a pat on the head and a cheery smile. They found a fairly quiet carriage and Kitty suggested she should board first then Jean could pass the bairns and the luggage to her.

'Would you like us to give you hand with your luggage? It looks a bit too heavy for you to be lifting on your own.' It was a deep male voice. Jean turned to see who it was and immediately recognised the two soldiers Annie had been so fascinated by while they waited in the queue.

'Yes please, that would be a good help. Perhaps one of you wouldn't mind taking the pushchair and the other the suitcase.'

'No trouble, lass, we're more than happy to help a couple of damsels in distress.'

'I wouldn't go as far as to say we're damsels in distress, but yes your help will be appreciated.'

The soldier who made the offer picked up the suitcase leaving his mate to carry the pushchair. Kitty having heard their conversation stepped aside leaving sufficient room for them to pass, then reached across to Jean taking Jack from her.

'There's no need to go too far along.' Kitty raised her voice as she trailed behind. 'And be careful with that suitcase it's very delicate, it's not one of your sturdy kit bags you can just throw around anywhere, you might just forget that for a minute and give it a bit too much manhandling.' She felt slightly guilty seeing them laden down with kit bags and luggage yet she managed to raise a smile as her sense of humour returned.

'Umm I wouldn't mind manhandling you,' were the thoughts of the soldier with the suitcase who suggested that they would be better near the middle of the carriage where it would be a bit warmer.

'Anywhere will do as long as we have seats, and incidentally my friend isn't coming with us she is only here to give me a hand and wave us off.'

'All the more room for you then,' he said as he lifted the suitcase onto the overhead rack. 'Are you travelling far?'

'Yes, we're off to stay with my old school friend in Cumberland, what about yourselves?'

'Same as you, off to Cumberland. It's where we're both from. We're on leave for just over a couple of weeks so we're off back to see our families.'

'They'll be looking forward to seeing you again, and Cumberland with its wonderful scenery is a beautiful part of our country so you'll be glad to be going home.'

'We certainly are…. Now if you need any more help during the journey feel free to ask; we'll be more than willing to lend a hand.'

'I think I'll manage on my own once I have Annie settled into her seat but if it's needed I will ask, and thanks. You have both been very kind.'

Jean and Annie meanwhile waited on the platform to give Kitty plenty of time to settle Jack onto a seat, but Annie was fidgeting and tugging at her hand all the time wanting to be with them. She seemed a little fretful, obviously thinking as her mam and Jack had disappeared from sight they were going to leave without her.

'Don't worry, Annie, they'll not go without you so I think we'll let this lady get on before us.'

Jean could see by the expression on Annie's face she wasn't very pleased with the idea but she said nothing and edged closer to her as the elderly lady moved towards the carriage. With a walking stick in one hand and clutching her handbag in the other, she looked very frail and well into her mid to late eighties, yet she refused Jean's offer to help her board. Watching her as she stepped into the carriage she was so spritely Jean was amazed, the elderly lady had completely fooled her by her appearance.

Next she lifted Annie into the carriage, and her little feet barely touched the floor as she pushed straight past the old lady, she was so desperate to be with her mammy and Jack again. 'Well it might have been better for the poor old soul, if I had left her on the platform rather than have Annie bulldozing straight past her,' she thought, but as she caught up to her thankfully she could see she was unharmed.

The two soldiers chose the seats directly opposite Kitty and when Jean arrived the chatty one came over and offered them a cigarette.

'Oh no thanks neither of us smoke.' Kitty kindly rejected his offer on behalf of them both, knowing she had never seen Jean with a cigarette.

'Well you're more than welcome to try one,' he said before closing the packet and returning it to his pocket. 'By the way I'm Tom and me mate's Bernie,' he said offering Kitty his hand.

'It's nice meeting you, Tom. I'm Kitty, this is my friend Jean, and my bairns are Annie and Jack,' and she offered her hand in return.

'A couple of bonny lasses I have to say,' and he winked at them before pausing for a second to cheekily ask, 'Leaving your husband's behind are you?'

'Not at all, as I said before Jean isn't coming with us but I suppose you could say I'm leaving mine. It's just for a short while as he works away from home, but as soon as he lets me know when he'll be returning we'll be on the first train back home to see him.'

The sudden slamming of carriage doors interrupted their conversation causing them to panic. Kitty grabbed Jean by the arm giving her a gentle shove. 'We should have been keeping an eye on what's going on around us instead of getting carried away chatting to strange men.' She grinned with raised eyebrows and a twinkle in her eye knowing they had both enjoyed their brief encounter.

'Well just make sure you don't get too carried away with them on your journey,' Jean warned her. 'Look after yourself and the bairns, and make sure you drop me a line or send me a postcard to let me know how you are!' She gave Kitty a quick hug, thanked the soldiers for their help then dashed down the aisle jumping off the train just in the nick of time, as the guard was about to slam the carriage door.

'By you've just made it in time, young lady, you were nearly on your way to Cumberland with the rest of the passengers,' he told her and slammed the door shut causing another deafening bang. After making sure everyone had boarded, he blew his whistle signalling the all clear for the engine driver to commence the journey across country.

While Jean waited on the platform Kitty and the bairns watched from the window. As the train pulled away Annie waved excitedly with both hands, while Jack, who seemed rather confused by all the comings and goings, could only manage a little smile. Kitty blew her a kiss and continued waving until she was completely out of view, then turned excitedly to the bairns. 'At last we're on our way and we'll soon be at Aunty Connie and Uncle Malcolm's where you'll be able to play outside all day if you want to.'

Chapter Five

As the train pulled out of the sidings it gradually built up momentum, causimg a trail of thick white vapour from it's coal fired engine to belch into the atmosphere, emerging like cotton wool clouds beneath the clear sky.

The early spring sun shone brightly through the carriage window and with her bairns safely by her side Kitty felt for the first time that morning that she could finally relax. Annie sat opposite her with her head in the pages of her ABC book which she must know off by heart the number of times she has read it, and with Jack snuggled up on her knee, his thumb in his mouth and his eyelids drooping she knew it wouldn't be long before he would be asleep. It had been a long tiring morning for her let alone the bairns, and as she admired them it made her heart swell with pride at their almost faultless behaviour.

'Are you excited about having a ride on the train, Annie?' she asked as she gently stroked Jack's hair..

'Yes, but why can't Jack sit beside me so I can read to him and we can look out of the window together?'

'You can see he's very tired so I think it would be better if he has a little sleep first, but as soon as he wakes up he can come and sit beside you.'

'Alright, but he better not sleep for a long time.'

'He won't I promise,' Kitty said hoping Jack would have just a short nap and not cause her to break her promise.

Across the aisle, Bernie had stretched out across the seat and looked settled down for the journey. Resting his head on his kit bag, his eyes already closed, he seemed determined to catch up on some sleep. Tom on the other hand, deserted by his mate, appeared to be wide awake. Unbeknown to Kitty he was already scheming up how he could get to know her better, and as soon as Jack and Bernie were asleep he made his first move by inviting Annie to read her book to him, but being a little wary of him she immediately looked to her mammy for reassurance.

'You can if you want to,' she told her, but seeing Annie's worried expression as she inched closer to the window she knew she was going nowhere.

'I think she might feel happier if you were to come and join us, but only if you'd like to of course?'

'I'd love to,' he replied. 'Just what I was hoping she would say,' he thought and without hesitation began loosening his jacket as he stepped over his kit bag then sat a comfortable distance from Annie so as not to alarm her. She offered him a cautious smile and Kitty knew she was very unsure of him.

'I think you're a clever girl being able to read all on your own so would you like to read to me for a little while?' He spoke quietly and when she began to slowly edge towards him he knew he had gained her confidence. 'And are you going to tell me how old you are, Annie?'

'I'm four but Jack is still only one so he can't read and that's why I have to read to him,' she informed him with gusto, opened her book and began without hesitation to

59

read from the beginning. 'A is for apple,' followed in detail with her knowledge that the outside is the peel and inside the black things in the middle are the pips that are planted in the soil to grow into big apple trees.

Tom raised his eyebrows at Kitty, who responded with the radiant smile of a very proud mother.

There was no stopping Annie now. 'B is for basket,' she told him and continued in the same way, explaining every picture in detail.

Tom didn't seem to mind and continued to encourage her, while at the same time keeping a keen eye on Kitty who was intrigued by how quickly Annie had warmed to him. 'My word you are very clever, Annie and I think Jack is lucky to have you for a big sister. What about Mammy, I'm sure you'll agree?' he asked offering her not only his charming smile but also a saucy wink.

'I agree, she is very clever for her age,' Kitty responded quickly appreciating how he had recognised her daughter's abilities and thought Jack was not the only lucky one in the present company. To have a charming male accompanying her she felt flattered and wondered what, if anything, he was implying by his saucy wink. She assumed being so handsome he was sure to have either a girlfriend, or a wife back home, but was still enjoying the occasional flirt whenever the opportunity arose.

Annie continued reading and explaining every picture until she reached the letter J, when she finally succumbed to her tiredness. Yawning and rubbing her eyes it was clear she too was in need of sleep which for Kitty came as a relief having heard her read the book so many times she could recite it from Z-A. Tom though seemed to have had the patience of Job as he listened to Annie but Kitty felt sure he too would be feeling relieved.

'Why don't you have a little sleep like Jack and you can finish reading your book to me later?' Tom suggested patting his thigh. 'You can rest your head here if you would like to,' and without a word Annie put her book down, stretched out across the seat and lay her head in his lap to join Jack and Bernie in the land of nod.

Wondering what she could find to talk about now there was just the two of them left to make conversation, Kitty felt a little uncomfortable, but fortunately the words began to flow.

'It's going to be a very long day for the bairns, they've been up since six-thirty as they do every morning,' she said focusing on what she knew to be a safe subject. 'With so much going on today it's no wonder they're worn out, and it's not like Annie to fall asleep on an empty tummy especially since it's several hours since we ate breakfast.' She hesitated for a moment. 'Come to think of it I haven't given food or drink another thought since I made a packed lunch to eat on our travels I was so busy making sure we made it to the train on time.'

'I've a few snacks in my kit bag you're more than welcome to, but it looks like we'll have to wait until Annie wakes up before I can get them for you.'

'Oh don't worry I'm fine, and I would prefer to eat with the bairns anyway.'

An uneasy silence followed.

'Will you...'

'I was just...' Kitty said as they both began to speak at the same time.

'After you.' Tom gestured

'No please, after you.'

'Ladies before gents always,' he insisted.

'It's nothing important, I was just going to ask if either of you are married.'

'Bernie's married, but I'm in no rush, besides I haven't met the right lass yet, but I reckon one day there'll be someone out there who'll be the right one for me.'

Silence fell again as Kitty pondered her previous thoughts. 'Now that does surprise me, I could have sworn he would have been snatched up by now. The girls in Cumberland must be blind letting him slip through their fingers, not only because of his handsome good looks but I reckon he'll know how to treat a woman properly, unlike Ernie who has changed so much over the years and now he is working away from home most of the time he spends very little time with me and the bairns.' The thought left her feeling a little dejected but she knew it didn't give her an excuse to become too friendly with the handsome soldier opposite.

'You say Bernie's married so does he have any bairns?'

'Not any that he knows about,' he answered with a smirk, 'but then again it's a long time since he was home so who knows, he may have a pleasant surprise waiting for him when he gets back.'

Unsure quite what to make of his response she stared blankly at him causing him to quickly assure her. 'I'm pulling your leg, Kitty.'

'Oh I see…. So you like to be a bit of teaser on the quiet then,' she said, raising her eyebrows and giving him a coy, but come on I am enjoying this, look. Since meeting Ernie she had never been interested in any other man but she found she was taking a liking to Tom's gentle calming nature. With little male attention in her life and secretly relishing his company she intended to embrace the occasion, convincing herself that there was no wrong in what she was doing as it was not hurting anyone. Completely oblivious to everything that was going on around them, they were soon chatting away like old friends, even failing to admire the beautiful countryside the train passed through. It was clear to see they had eyes only for each other and it wasn't long before Tom made his first move.

'From the minute I set eyes on you, Kitty, I was determined to get to know you and was hoping you were single, and that the kids were your friend's. I visualised us walking hand in hand into the sunset but… seeing as you're married,' he put on a glum face, 'well I guess it's never going to happen but I hope it's not going to stop me from trying to get to know you better.'

Kitty felt flattered, but quickly reflected on how she had felt when she first set eyes on Ernie. Now several years and two bairns later with a third on the way, things had changed quite considerably and she no longer believed there was such a thing as the perfect couple or a happy ever after. However in spite of the difficulties she had to face at times she vowed never to leave him, hoping that maybe one day their first love might be rekindled.

'You can never be sure of anything in life, Tom. I believed Ernie and I were the perfect couple when we fell in love… and I expected it would be like that forever, but I've learnt the hard way that it's not the case. When a couple of social beers with his mates turned into seven or eight pint sessions that's when things seriously began to change and at times he puts me through not just mental abuse…' Her voice began to fade. 'I don't like to admit it but quite often it turns into physical abuse.' She turned away from him and faced the window shocked by what she had just revealed to him. 'Whatever am I doing? I'm on the way to stay with my best friend accompanied by a dashing soldier and like a fool I'm opening my heart out to him about my marital problems and making myself feel miserable thinking about it.'

Tom could see her mood had changed and wondered just how badly and how often Ernie abused her. Plucking up courage he asked her outright. 'Have you ever thought of walking out on your marriage or are you too afraid because of his aggression of what he might do to you if you were to leave?'

Realising how stupid she had been to talk so openly about her marriage to a complete stranger, she decided to explain her situation to him. 'I don't really have much choice, Tom, you see my parents begged me not to marry him. Ernie was always a real gentleman in their company, but they, unlike me could see he was trying to impress them. They had suspected from the start that he wouldn't make an ideal husband or a good family man. The thing is my parents are quite comfortably off, Dad works for the government and is highly respected locally for the work he does seeing that improvements are carried out in the neighbourhood. He firmly believed Ernie was more interested in improving his living standards by marrying into a respectable family, rather than working hard to achieve a decent job to provide for a wife and family. I never listened to them and we went ahead with the wedding, but little did I know at the time that we were heading for a huge shock. Because I married against their wishes they wouldn't have anything more to do with us, and they have more or less cut us out of their lives altogether. But to be fair my marriage is far from all bad news.' She managed a smile as she gently stroked Jack's cheek with the back of her hand. 'Let's not forget the bairns, I couldn't have asked for anything better to come out of our marriage.' She looked affectionately across at Annie. 'Why would I think about leaving when they are his bairns as well as mine? And even though he sees very little of them, I'm sure he loves them as much as I do.' Although showing a little doubt in her expression she shrugged her shoulders and tried to convince him. 'No, I'll never leave him. We married for better or for worse and the bairns need their daddy.' She could see he was surprised that she was determined to continue living with an abusive man, and thought it best not mention that she was actually carrying his third child and that her pregnancy was the reason she was making the journey to Cumberland.

'Well in my opinion, a man who physically abuses a woman is a coward and I swear to you, Kitty, if you were my sister he wouldn't be getting away with it because I wouldn't stand back and let it happen.'

'That's a very nice thought, Tom. I've never had any of my family challenging him on my behalf, but don't be fooled, I might only be small but I'm pretty tough when it comes to taking care of myself. I don't just sit back and take it. I give him back as much as he gives me.'

'I can imagine you do, Kitty, but it doesn't make it right.'

'If you knew his family you wouldn't even suggest it, you see he has several brothers and sisters. The brothers are all big lads who stick together particularly in times of trouble and are known for being afraid of nothing and no one. I have often asked myself had I known as much about his family as I do now, would I still have been so keen to go out with him?' Rubbing her chin she observed Tom's reaction before continuing. 'Yes I would,' she said decisively. 'I married him, not his family and in spite of everything I really don't have any regrets. Why would I when we have produced two such beautiful bairns who mean the world to me?'

'I'm probably right in saying you must still love him then?' he quizzed.

She didn't answer. Was he trying to put doubts in her mind to suit his own ends?

'I take it you *are* still in love with him then?' he asked again, this time sounding quite gloomy. He had his preferred answer but he doubted it would be the one he would hear.

Determined not to be rushed Kitty weighed up the

unexpected situation she had found herself in. 'A complete stranger has walked into my life, is asking me about my marriage and now I find I'm wondering what my true feelings are for my husband. I must be going crazy,' she decided. 'I would have credited myself with more sense than to be drawn into something so personal.' She knew she didn't have to give him an answer as it was really none of his business, but aware that more often than not her heart ruled her head she mulled over her answer for a little longer. She concluded that whatever she decided to say it didn't really matter as once they arrived at their destination they'd never see each other again. Eventually she took a long deep breath and looked directly into Tom's eyes. 'I don't know what you expect me to say, Tom, and besides it won't make any difference to you what my feelings are for Ernie but I'm going to be honest with you; it can be hard at times to love him as much as when we were first married. He has changed quite a lot but, and I must emphasise this, I do still love him. I admit it's hard to feel passionate about him when he's drunk and knocking me about. It makes my life difficult, but when he is sober believe me he's a completely different person.' She wondered who she was trying to convince the most, herself or Tom, but knew she would never give up on her marriage.

Tom could see it pained her to talk about the difficult times and she was trying desperately to hold back her tears. He leaned towards her, placed her hand in his and squeezed it gently. 'It's terrible that he treats you so badly, Kitty. You're beautiful and I have to admit the thought of him knocking you about sickens me. What do you think it is that changes him from one minute being a loving husband then the next he's turned into a bully? Sorry, Kitty, I shouldn't have said that but to me, that's exactly what he is, a bully!'

The feel of a lover's touch as he held her hand aroused her, but she quickly withdrew; her emotions were all over the place and she was struggling to hold back her tears. In Ernie's defence she snapped at Tom. 'He's not a bully; it's the bloody brown. I'm sorry, I shouldn't swear but I know it's the brown ale to blame. It's only ever after he's had a long session on the beer that his character changes completely, and I'm sure you don't need me to tell you that as the saying goes, when drink's in wit's out and anything can happen.'

He was taken aback by her sharp response. Had he overstepped his mark by taking her hand, or had it been calling Ernie a bully? He couldn't be sure but he hoped it was the latter and tried to calm her. 'I hardly ever touch the stuff myself, Kitty so I couldn't say if a session on it might have that same effect on me, but I know one thing: I don't intend putting it to the test. Besides there's not a pub close to where I live so if I do fancy going out for a drink I have to walk or cycle three miles to the nearest one. You'll know that the rural communities lack a lot of the amenities you have in the towns and cities but I could never swap my rural life for urban living. Rural life is in my bones, and all I really know.'

Grateful that he had unwittingly given her the opportunity to turn the conversation around she asked him about his family.

'I have always worked on the farm with my dad which meant I was exempt from doing National Service. I was disappointed at the time and said when Jim, that's my younger brother, was old enough to take over from me I would join the army for a couple of years. Although farming has always been in my blood I wanted to learn a trade that could be useful on the farm and decided the army would be the best place and I'd be able to see a bit of the wider world at the same time. My parents weren't happy with the idea, as the farm was expanding at the time and didn't think Jim was quite ready to take over from me, but eventually they came to terms with it and of course Jim was totally capable of stepping into my shoes. Unfortunately the army never offered me an overseas posting and I won't be getting one now as I'm finished in a few months but nevertheless, I've thoroughly enjoyed the whole experience and I'm coming out with skills I otherwise wouldn't have had. When I'm back working on the farm I plan to put them to good use by doing all the mechanical repairs to save us having to pay someone else. If word gets around and I can pick up work around the farms in the area then hopefully sometime in the future I can set up my own business.'

'Sounds like you have your future all worked out.'

'Hopefully it will be, if it all goes according to plan.'

'I'm sure it will, Tom, you seem very positive about it.'

'It's been my vision for a long time, but it's still a long way off. I've nearly three weeks leave to enjoy at home first to catch up with my pals and do my bit around the farm then I have to go back. But that's enough about me, and you've not got around to mentioning where you're staying in Cumberland.'

'It's a place called Calderthwaite, a lovely little village you've probably heard of if you have lived in Cumberland all your life.'

'Calderthwaite.' Tom gasped in disbelief knowing his luck was in. 'I don't...'

'It's only a short journey from the railway station,' Kitty continued oblivious to anything Tom had to say. 'I'd say it's about thirty minutes by car, longer of course on the little country bus depending how many pick ups and drop offs there are and...,' but before she could say another word he finally managed to interrupt her.

'I must stop you right there, Kitty,' he said raising his hand. 'I can't believe your friends live in Calderthwaite, the pub in the village, The Dog and Gun, that's the pub I was telling you about.'

'You're kidding me? I do know the pub but of course I've never been in the place.'

'It's quite a small pub with usually just a few locals in at any one time. Maybe I could take you in for a drink sometime during your stay. I would love to, and you would be more than welcome to bring your friend along.' Wanting her friend to join them was an outright lie but he felt it was necessary if he hoped to see her again. 'I'm sure you'd enjoy a night out for a change and you never know, it might even turn out that your friend and I know each other by sight. You'd have no need to worry about Ernie finding out, there's no chance of that ever happening.'

The longer they talked the more she found herself experiencing the same desires she felt when she first met Ernie and it unnerved her. 'What on earth are you doing, Kitty? You're a married woman with two bairns and a third on the way. It's wrong to have these feelings for another man so why are you allowing him to continue talking to you like this?' She knew she was treading on dangerous ground, and decided she must disregard her feelings and do the right thing.

'I'm not sure I can do that, Tom, it certainly wouldn't be right. You seem to forget I'm married with a family and I don't think my friends would be very pleased if I said I was meeting a man I had only just met on the train. It's very nice of you to ask and I admit I'm flattered but it would be wrong so I'm sorry, Tom, but I really must decline.'

'Are you saying you would join me, if your friends approved?'

She blushed, the thought of being alone with him excited her, but her conscience wouldn't allow the excitement of the moment to justify such a wrongdoing. 'That's not what I'm saying at all, Tom, and let's get this quite clear, it wouldn't be right, and if I did accept and Ernie found out he would make my life hell, and probably yours as well. He would track you down and make trouble for you, and that's the last thing I would want to happen.'

'Okay I apologise. I shouldn't be asking you out and I will respect your wishes, Kitty, but if you do change your mind you'll know where to find me.' Seeing she looked a little on edge he tried to make amends. 'Listen, I am really sorry if I've embarrassed you, Kitty, but I never expected for one minute that we would see each other again once we left the train. I had intended to let you know that being with you over these couple of hours has meant so much to me, but then hearing you are staying in Calderthwaite I felt I couldn't let the opportunity of asking you out slip through my fingers.' Not prepared to let her disappear out of his life as quickly as she had entered it, he cunningly tricked her into telling him where Connie lived.

Without thinking she came straight out with it. 'She lives on the green in Rose Cottage almost opposite the pub,' then instantly she realised her mistake. 'Don't you *dare* think about calling while I'm there if that's what you're intending to do'

He didn't reply. Having already come up with the idea that he would call saying he would like to see the bairns again and to meet Kitty's friends, no one he thought would suspect anything different.

'Are you listening to me, Tom? I mean it when I say I don't want you calling while I'm there.' Raising her voice quite significantly disturbed Jack and he woke from his sleep which, much to Tom's delight saved him from having to respond immediately.

'Hello, sleepy head, you've had a nice long sleep,' Kitty said kissing his forehead whilst running her fingers through his ruffled hair.

Still half asleep, he pulled a strange face and after a long stretch, rubbed his eyes. Seeing Tom sitting opposite he gave him a suspicious look as though to say, 'who are you?' but when he realised it was Annie sleeping with her head on his lap, he pointed to her. 'Annie… but…'

'That's Tom, can you remember, Jack? Tom and his friend helped us onto the train, and while you have been asleep, Annie read some of her book to him.' Desperate to finish her conversation with Tom knowing they were fast approaching their destination she turned Jack around so he could watch out of window.

For the most part Kitty had enjoyed their flirting, but with Jack awake she was reminded of where her responsibilities lay, and braced herself ready to give Tom a reality check making sure he understood their brief liaison would end as soon as they left the train.

'Tom,' she said taking a deep breath then hesitating for a moment realising the importance and the effect of what she was about to say. He gazed passionately into her eyes, pulling at her heartstrings and in truth she really didn't want it to end but knew it had to be done.

'It's okay, Kitty, I know what you are about to say, so come on, come straight out with it!' There was a hint of urgency in his voice.

'I've really enjoyed your company, Tom, but it will have to end once we leave the train. Connie will be waiting for us and between us we'll manage the rest of the journey.'

'That's okay, Kitty,' he sounded quite cheerful which somewhat surprised her, 'but you'll still need help with your luggage. Me and Bernie will see to it again. You can't manage everything on your own, but before we say our final goodbye how about introducing me to your friend? I'm sure Annie will be telling her all about the journey so you can hardly exclude me!'

Realising it was another ploy in his little game to stay with her for as long as possible, now more than ever she was convinced he wouldn't walk away from her with a simple goodbye, and she felt obliged to introduce him to Connie after all he had done for her.

'Of course I will. I'm sure she'll be fascinated to hear you live just a couple of miles from her.' With an almost apologetic smile she added, 'I suppose it was quite a coincidence that you joined the queue directly behind us.'

'That wasn't a coincidence, Kitty, it was fate. We were meant to meet each other I'm sure of that.'

She didn't respond, she'd never believed in fate, but rather that life is what you make it yourself.

Meanwhile as Annie and Bernie continued to sleep Tom aimed at befriending Jack in the same way he had Annie, and to Kitty's surprise he was succeeding. Quietly she listened as Jack allowed him to gradually break down his barrier, and she couldn't help imagining what a lovely dad he would make. He had given her bairns more attention than Ernie would ever have done, and she felt sad knowing she couldn't recall any occasions when he would sit one or both of them on his knee to read to them, or tuck them up in bed with a story and a goodnight kiss.

The sound of the train's whistle interrupted her thoughts meaning they were approaching the station. As it began to slow down she was aware it was both the end of the journey and the end of their brief encounter. Once again their eyes met, and it went without saying their parting was not going to be easy. Annie began to stir, the chatter between Tom and Jack had disturbed her though it seemed across the aisle, nothing could arouse Bernie. When the train finally came to an abrupt stop Tom made sure Annie was comfortable before he headed over to waken him.

'Wake up, you lazy beggar.' He shook his friend quite severely to make sure he could revive him as he was in such a deep sleep. 'Come on, Bernie mate, you're almost home. This is our station and we need you to give us a hand with Kitty's luggage.'

It took several minutes before Bernie was back in the land of the living, and he couldn't believe he had slept the entire journey.

'Well I reckon I must have been tired, and don't try and kid me that you've not been in the land of nod as well,' he said sitting up straight and stretching his arms above his head.

'I had a catnap,' he lied not wanting to be deceitful but not intending to fill him in with the truth either. 'I nodded off a couple of times that's all. Jack slept nearly all the way and Annie read her book to me for a little while until she needed a sleep. Fortunately for Kitty she was able to have a quiet spell with them both asleep, and I do believe she's the only one who managed to stay awake throughout the entire journey!'

Bernie didn't doubt him and prepared to be of assistance. 'I think we should let the other passengers off first. It will be easier for everyone and there will be no chance of the little ones getting knocked about.'

'Good idea, Bernie.' Kitty acknowledged him and remained seated until their carriage was empty. The lads headed off leaving Kitty to follow with Jack in her arms and Annie clinging onto the back of her skirt fearing she might be left behind.

'Pass the kids to me, Kitty, then I will help you off.' Tom gestured, his arms outstretched ready to take Jack first. He passed both the bairns to Bernie before holding out his hand and taking Kitty's in his to see her safely onto the platform. Gripping her hand firmly, he pulled her close and once again their eyes locked, and they stood motionless for several seconds. The passion between them was electric, and her legs weakened, but when she heard the sound of her name being called, she was quickly brought back to reality.

'Kitty, Kitty. I'm here, over here.' Connie's arms were waving frantically as she ran towards the barrier her arms so widely outstretched she almost knocked over the elderly lady Jean had seen onto the train earlier. She had spotted the two soldiers, one holding onto the bairns while the other was quite clearly holding Kitty's hand but shrugged it off assuming they had simply been helping her off the train.

Tom squeezed Kitty's hand again, this time more firmly, and instinctively she knew he did not want her to leave. Reluctantly as he saw Connie getting closer he slowly released her hand, picked up the suitcase and together they all made their way towards the ticket barrier where an excited Connie waited at the other side. With everyone safely through, the two friends embraced then Connie hugged the bairns.

'My little darlings, I can't wait to take you home and...' She spotted Kitty's luggage. 'How on earth you managed on your own with all this lot I'll never know.'

'Well actually I haven't had to thanks to several very kind people. I'll start with Peggy who arranged for a taxi to take us to the station, and my friend Jean came along and helped me with the bairns while I bought my ticket, and finally these two handsome soldiers offered to see to the heavy luggage. Believe me they've been knights in shining armour helping me throughout the entire journey. I've been very lucky, Connie. I couldn't have had any more help had I begged for it. I must have looked a real damsel in distress, and believe me I have appreciated everyone's help.'

'You certainly have been very lucky, because from where I'm standing there is no way in the world you could have made it here without help.'

'I realise that now, but not at the time I was so excited about coming, but I must admit I did feel sad leaving poor Peggy. She was in tears when we left but Jean has promised to pop in to make sure she's okay. I know she is going to miss us but it won't be for long.'

It suddenly occurred to her that she hadn't introduced Tom and Bernie. Tom was playing safe by preferring to keep a short distance between them. She turned to Bernie, 'This is Bernie,' then nodding in Tom's direction, 'and his mate Tom who helped with the suitcase.'

Whilst shaking Connie's hand, Bernie's eyes scanned the platform looking for his wife. When it became obvious he had spotted her, joy was written all over his face. 'You'll have to excuse me but I've just seen my wife so I'm off.' He sped away shouting back to Tom, 'I'll see you back here in a couple of weeks,' and he was gone in a flash leaving Tom alone with the two friends, the two bairns, and the notorious but still intact, suitcase at his feet.

Chapter Six

'Hello, Tom nice to meet you.' Connie greeted him warmly. 'Unfortunately I didn't get a chance to thank your mate properly, he disappeared so fast, but it was very kind of you both to give Kitty a hand. How she ever thought she could manage the bairns and *that great big suitcase,* beggars belief!'

'Pleased to meet you too Connie, and I can assure you it was our pleasure. Like you, Bernie and I thought it was very brave of her to attempt to travel alone with two kids and so much luggage but she obviously thought she could manage or she wouldn't have set off in the first place.'

'Believe me, if you knew Kitty as well as I do you'd understand, if someone asked her to move a mountain, mark my words she would have a try.'

'I wouldn't doubt that for a minute, we did chat quite a lot on the train coming over and from some of the things she told me I'd already worked out she's one very determined young lady.'

'She's that alright, and you'd have had no problem making conversation with her, she loves chatting to people, and with her husband working away I'm sure she will have enjoyed your company for a change. She only has the bairns to talk to most of the time and it'll have been a nice change for her to have someone of the opposite sex rather than just chatting to Peggy and Jean her close neighbours.'

'She did mention her husband works away and she spends weeks at a time bringing her two kids up on her own.'

'And she does a wonderful job with them, it can't be easy for her at times but you'll have noticed they are very well behaved.'

Just out of earshot, Kitty waited nervously wondering what on earth they found to talk about. She expected a brief handshake and nothing more but for some reason they appeared to be rooted to the spot.

'Can we go now, Mammy? I want to go to Auntie Connie's house,' Annie pleaded tugging impatiently at Kitty's sleeve.

'In minute, pet, we're just waiting for Aunty Connie and Tom to finish talking then we'll be on our way.' Little did Annie know that was exactly what she wished herself, but so deep in conversation it didn't look like they were in a rush to go anywhere.

Tom glanced across at the waiting family and noticed Annie seemed a little agitated. 'I suggest we make a move, Annie's tugging at her Mammy's sleeve so it looks like she wants to be on her way.' He picked up the suitcase and they carried on chatting as though they had known each other for years.

'Kitty tells me you've been friends since your school days.'

'Yes, we've been best friends for most of our lives haven't we, Kitty?' Connie nudged her gently in the ribs having finally caught up to her. 'And there's nothing we like better than to see each other again so we can

80

reminisce about some of the daft things we did when we were young, and some of the even dafter things we've done since.'

'You're right there, Connie, and when we do, there's no nicer place than Calderthwaite to catch up. Letters are great for keeping in touch but they're nothing compared to being together having a good old natter and a giggle over a brew.'

'And we'll be doing plenty of that during your stay, but what about you, Tom? I'm guessing from your accent you must come from around here?'

'You've guessed right; born and bred in Cumberland, Little Ellerton in fact. Kitty did say she would be staying in Calderthwaite so you're sure to know it well.'

'Little Ellerton, of course I know it…. My word it certainly is a small world.' Turning to Kitty she shook her head in disbelief. 'Whoever would believe it? The chance of you meeting someone on the train who lives only a couple of mile away from us… well you must admit it's quite a coincidence.'

'It certainly is,' was all Kitty could bring herself to say as she listened nervously to the friendly interaction between the two new acquaintances. Afraid Tom might mention something she had foolishly confessed to him, something which she perhaps had not even discussed in depth with Connie, she felt she should intervene. The last thing she wanted was for Connie or Tom for that matter to suspect how much she enjoyed his company. Afraid it could happen she decided to step in quickly and break up their conversation. It wouldn't be easy asking Tom to leave but she felt it had to be done, and done convincingly. She hesitated for a moment, drew in a long deep breath, exhaled slowly and managed to speak.

'I guess this is where we say our goodbyes, Tom. Connie and I will be able to manage the rest of the way. I can't thank you enough for all your help and thank Bernie again for me when you see him and be sure to enjoy your leave.' Swallowing the large lump lodged in her throat which felt the size of a golf ball, she hoped she sounded convincing. He looked slightly dejected which quite frankly didn't surprise her, but felt pleased with herself that she had wisely though maybe a tiny bit regretfully allowed her head to overrule her heart.

Tom knew it wasn't what either of them would want. Their meeting had been far more than a brief encounter, but for reasons best known to Kitty, she chose to be in denial, and barely had her parting words left her lips when, in her innocence Connie played directly into Tom's hands.

'Is someone coming to pick you up, Tom?'

'No, I'm taking the bus, everyone will be too busy working to spare the time, and you'll probably agree the bus will be far quicker and more comfortable than the alternative which is on the back of our old Fergie tractor,' he joked. 'Come to think of it I bet Annie and Jack would love to have a ride on it,' he said ruffling Jack's hair. 'It's just as easy for me to take the bus as it stops right outside the farm gates so there's no need for me to trouble anyone. I'm hoping there's still one at three as the next one won't be for another couple of hours after that making it a long wait. The three o'clock will get me home in good time to join Mum in the kitchen where she'll have spent most of the day cooking an extra special meal for my homecoming.'

'They're expecting you home today then?' Connie asked, then assured him there was a bus leaving just after three and that they planned to be on it too.

'Yes they know exactly when I'm due to arrive home, and I bet there's an air of excitement at Low Ellerton Farm today as it's about ten months since we were all together. To be honest I'm expecting they've killed the fatted calf and laid on a huge banquet in celebration of the return of their first born.' He sniggered knowing only too well that the nearest the fatted calf would be to the oven, would be in the cattle wagon as it passed the farmhouse on its way to market. He was certain of one thing though, the delicious food his mother served far exceeded his army meals, and just the mention of them was already whetting his appetite.

'Well seeing as we are all travelling on the same bus you may as well stay with us, Tom, that's if you would like to of course.'

The very thought of him spending more time in their company unnerved Kitty, her stomach muscles contracted and she felt nauseous. 'I know exactly where this will be heading... with Connie having more time to get to know him better I can guarantee she will invite him over to meet the rest of her family.' It seemed everything was going in Tom's favour which presented a problem for Kitty and she was regretting she ever set eyes on him.

'Like a fool,' she thought, 'I've succumbed to his irresistible charm just as I did when I first set eyes on Ernie, I must be getting dafter as I get older!' Knowing he wouldn't refuse an invitation to visit Connie's meant she had no choice but to go along with it. She would have to give a reason for him not to call and she couldn't do that without giving something away, now that Connie had befriended him, and she must be prepared to face the outcome as there would be no escaping him now.

Annie thankfully interrupted her troubled thoughts when she once again began tugging at her sleeve. 'When are we going to Aunty Connie's? And I'm *really* hungry, Mammy.'

Her request came as no surprise as they hadn't eaten since breakfast. 'I'm sorry, pet, what an awful Mammy you have. We'll be going to Aunty Connie's soon but we'll have something to eat before we get on the bus.' She felt ashamed that she had not given food a thought, but with plenty of time to spare before the bus was due she suggested to Connie they make their way over to the waiting room where they could sit down to eat before leaving the station.

'What a good idea and I take it you will be joining us, Tom?'

'I'd love to if Kitty doesn't mind, but she is probably sick of the sight of me by now, even if the kids aren't!'

'Of course I don't mind, Tom, and I know the bairns would love you to stay.' She looked at him nervously, thinking he may be fooling Connie into believing they were the real motive for him to stay but he isn't fooling

84

me!'

'If that's the case, then I'll pop over to the snack bar and get a sandwich and a cup of tea, so if there is anything I can get anyone while I'm there just say the word.'

'Nothing for me thanks, Tom, I've brought sandwiches for us, a flask of tea for me and cold drinks for the bairns which as you know we intended to have on the train, but what about you, Connie? No doubt a cup of tea will go down well?'

'You're right it won't go amiss but what about yourself? Surely you would prefer a nice fresh cup rather than one that has stewed in a flask for hours?'

'I agree, it never tastes the same out of a flask as it does fresh from the pot, so I guess that will be three teas if you're sure you don't mind?'

'Milk and sugar in both?' he asked.

'Milk and one sugar for me please, but what about you, Kitty?'

'No sugar for me and just a little bit of milk.'

'Of course you don't need sugar, you're sweet enough,' Tom thought, his mind focused more on Kitty and his plan that she wouldn't disappear out of his life as quickly as she entered it, than the job he had in hand.

'We'll meet you at the waiting room. I must go and feed the bairns or they'll be passing out from lack of food and then I'll be branded as a really bad mother.'

'I'm sure you won't, Kitty, if they had both stayed awake you would have fed them on the train. Now, I'll be off and get the refreshments which I think everyone could do with.' Suddenly remembering the suitcase just as Connie was about to pick it up, he stopped her in her tracks. 'Leave that to me, Connie, I'll carry it to the waiting room. I'm not having you lasses lugging it around when I'm here to help, and while I'm over there, it would make more sense if I drop my kit bag off as well.'

'He's so considerate,' Kitty thought, comparing him to Ernie who never joined her on a visit to Connie's. She struggled to find something negative to say about him as he hadn't done or said anything that could make her dislike him, and as he was going to be around her for a while longer, she feared she might let her feelings towards him show. Still not understanding what on earth had possessed her to behave the way she had, having never shown any interest in another man since she met Ernie, she knew she must keep her emotions in check, but also knew it wasn't going to be easy. Her world had been turned upside down since stepping out of bed that morning, and she could hardly believe that so many unexpected events could take place in such a short time.

Entering the waiting room they almost stumbled over an elderly couple sitting right by the door which left very little room for anyone to pass, but neither of them attempted to move. They had no luggage with them so it was hard to know whether they would be taking a train somewhere or were perhaps waiting to meet someone off later arrivals. They seemed oblivious to the world around them, both sitting in silence with vacant expressions on their wrinkled weather beaten faces. The old man was dressed in a shabby looking raincoat and flat cap which was cocked to one side of his head and which looked as if he had plonked it there quite unconcerned as to where it landed. Holding a cigarette between his nicotine-stained fingers he dragged on it as though it was his last. Sitting next to him, the old lady, presumably his wife, wore a rather heavy thick tweed coat and a headscarf which was tied tightly under her chin, both of which seemed rather out of place on such a beautiful spring day. She appeared a little edgy, her eyes shifting suspiciously from side to side as though afraid of something.

Having cautiously squeezed past them, Kitty was saddened by their unhappy appearance, and hoped their silent thoughts were pleasant ones, but sadly they did look as though they were carrying the worries of the world on their shoulders. Secretly she wished she could help them, but with plenty of concerns of her own at the minute, she resisted the temptation to offer.

Further along, a middle-aged man was reading his morning newspaper. Looking up he acknowledged Tom as he placed the suitcase and kit bag in a corner, then gave Kitty and Connie a friendly smile before returning to what looked to be the sports pages of his newspaper. Unlike the elderly couple he seemed content and at peace with the world. Connie attended to Annie, leaving Kitty to see to Jack and the shopping bag containing their lunch, and once everyone was seated, Tom headed off to the snack bar flatly refusing to take money from them for their refreshments.

'Where's Tom going?' Annie asked sounding quite upset to see him disappearing from the waiting room.

'He's just going to get something to eat and a cup of tea and then he's coming back,' Kitty assured her, surprised that she seemed upset to see him leaving.

'I rather think your daughter has taken quite a liking to Tom!' Connie remarked as she too was surprised by her reaction.

'Well considering they sat together on the train while he listened to her reading her book, including explaining colours and shapes and anything else she could think of, then I'm not surprised. When she eventually tired herself out, she was so at ease with him she put her head on his knee and was asleep in no time. Poor Tom, he was stuck with her for the rest of the journey, but I don't think he minded, and we chatted to each other to help pass the time while the bairns slept.

'Well from what I've seen of him up to now, and knowing what you are like, I don't think either of you would have been stuck for words.'

'We weren't, but it did seem strange, we probably looked to the other passengers like a happy little family when in truth we were complete strangers!'

'It must have been nice for you though having a bit of company, but I can't help wondering what Jack thought when he woke up and saw a strange man sitting with you.'

'He seemed a bit unsure at first, and gave him one of his suspicious looks which as you know he is quite renowned for, but once he saw Annie with him he decided it was okay.'

'I hope you didn't mind me asking him to stay with us, Kitty? I just thought it was silly for him to wander off on his own when we are all heading for the same bus. I must admit it never really occurred to me about how the bairns, Annie especially, would feel as they are bound to be wondering why he is coming with us.'

Unsure as to where this conversation might be leading, Kitty began rummaging around inside her shopping bag for the lunch box in the hope that she might change the subject. From what she had already told her surely there was nothing else she needed to know. Was she becoming suspicious or had Tom innocently let something slip when they were talking to each other?

'It would have been silly not to have asked him, and you have already seen how upset Annie was when she thought he was leaving. She did after all spend quite a long time reading to him on the train so she is used to him being with us and Jack well... if he sees Annie happy then he's happy.'

'I would have thought of the two of them Annie would have been more wary of him when he just suddenly appeared out of nowhere. We both know Jack hasn't spent a lot of time with Ernie as he's hardly ever at home so he probably wouldn't think anything of it, but Annie, well she certainly knows who her daddy is!'

'Of course she does, and I'm sure Jack does as well!' she snapped, shocked by Connie's unexpected comment which brought to mind the incident on the railway station that morning. 'That reminds me, Connie, I must tell you about what happened while we were on the railway station this morning. There was an incident when a soldier was running towards us, his wife or sweetheart, or might even have been sister who knows, was close by and for some reason, Annie thought it was Ernie and began shouting Daddy at the poor fella. When he ran straight past you can imagine what she was like, she was so sure it was him and it took a while before I managed to convince her otherwise. Bless her she was upset but I think she did eventually understand when I explained that he wouldn't be coming home until after our holiday.'

'Tea up, everyone.' Tom's cheerful voice brought Kitty's tale to an abrupt end. With both hands full he pushed the door open with his bottom until it was just wide enough for him to squeeze through, and edged his way carefully past the elderly couple who were still sitting in exactly the same position and hadn't spoken a word to anyone.

'Thanks, Tom, I can't tell you how much I'm ready for this cup of tea,' Kitty said taking one of the cups out of his hand and making sure not to spill its hot contents anywhere near the bairns. Once everyone was tucking into their late lunch Tom seemed to be relishing every mouthful of his sandwich as though he was sitting down to a royal banquet. She thought he was looking relatively paler than when they had met earlier and wondered like themselves how long it had been since he had eaten. Annie, sitting quite ladylike eating her sandwich, fussed over Jack by constantly sweeping crumbs from his lap onto to the waiting room floor, muttering to him that he was making too much mess.

'I reckon she's is going to take after you, Kitty. Just look at her, she's a proper little mother and wants everything spick and span just the same as you.'

'You're probably right, she tidies up after him all the time, sometimes even putting his toys away before the poor bairn has even finished playing with them.'

'Bless her, I guess it's not her fault though, she'll just be copying what you do and likes to act grown up by helping, and...,' she raised her voice slightly, '...you are after all Jack's big sister aren't you, Annie?' But she wasn't listening. Tom had bought Chocolate Wagon Wheel biscuits as a treat for them and she was too busy helping Jack to remove his wrapper.

Connie checked the time. It was nearly half past two. 'We have barely half an hour before the bus is due so I suggest we get a move on. I think we could do with filling our lungs with some good clean fresh air before we get on the bus rather than the unpleasant smokey atmosphere we're inhaling in here.'

'Good idea, Connie,' Kitty agreed and made the first move. 'Come on, Jack, let's get you back into your pushchair and Annie, will you pick up your book and Jack's rabbit? Look,' she pointed to them, 'they've fallen under the seats,' and immediately Annie was on her hands and knees retrieving their two most precious possessions.

'Got it, Jack. I've got your rabbit for you,' Annie told him excitedly and quickly rammed it into his hand. With her book in one hand she went to take Tom's hand with the other. The expression on the faces of the three adults was priceless, they glanced at one another in amazement but neither Kitty nor Connie said a word until after Tom had left the waiting room.

'It looks to me like you've lost your daughter,' Connie said as they watched Tom laden down with his kit bag on his back, the suitcase in one hand and Annie in the other. They were astounded to see how happy she was to walk away hand in hand with a man she hardly knew.

'It certainly looks that way, but to be honest I would have thought he would have had enough of her for one day. Look at the poor fella, Connie, he's laden down with luggage and now Annie is pestering him!'

As they began following them, Kitty couldn't stop herself from smirking at the unprecedented scene before her eyes. 'Poor soul, he looks as though he is serving a punishment for bad behaviour rather than heading home on leave.'

Feeling slightly guilty she called to him. 'Send Annie back to us, Tom, there's no need for you to be struggling along with her as well as the luggage.'

'Leave her if she's happy to stay with me, besides we're best friends now and I don't mind,' he called back. He smiled at Annie and suggested they wait for the others to catch them up.

Annie glanced round at her mam. She was looking rather smug after hearing Tom say that they were best friends. 'You are my new best friend aren't you, Tom?'

'Of course I am, Annie, yours and Jack's as well.'

'I give up, Connie, there's no the point interfering, if she's happy to stay with him and especially now as he's travelling with us to Calderthwaite I may as well just leave them to it. I do think though, that perhaps we should take Jack out of his pushchair and put Tom's kit bag there instead. I really can't stand back and watch him laden down like that.'

The swap was done and Tom led the way to the exit, with Annie talking nonstop to him as though he had always been a part of her young life.

'It's hard to decide who is the happiest between the two of them. Do you think it's because she doesn't see Ernie very often that she is enjoying having a father figure around?'

'It probably is, Connie, and not having grandparents as well, they must both be missing out a lot, but there's nothing I can do to change things, I've tried in the past without success. To be honest I'm wondering what she will be like when we get off the bus without him, she's probably thinking by now that he is coming with us. I've never seen her so relaxed with a stranger as she is with Tom, but he'll soon be forgotten when she has her Uncle Malcolm and Uncle George giving her lots of love and attention, and who knows, maybe when we go home, with a bit of luck Ernie will find a job locally and they'll have their mammy and daddy at home with them all the time.'

'Let's hope so, but for now I think it might be nice if Tom were to meet Malcolm, and Mam and Dad as his name is bound to crop up now and again. We could maybe invite him over for a meal one night. He's been such a huge help to you it would a kind of thank you and I'm sure the bairns would love to see him again, especially Annie.'

'I wasn't wrong,' Kitty thought. 'I know her like the

93

back of my hand. She's the same as Peggy, always doing good for others, totally unselfish the pair of them, but to invite Tom over, well I'm not sure how I feel about that.' The warm air lifted her spirits as she walked out of the station, and she paused for a moment, lifted her face towards the sun and soaked up its warm rays. She decided there and then that she must put her worries to one side and make the most of the time she would spend in Calderthwaite.

'Are you still okay with Annie or would you like us to take her for while?' she called to Tom who looked a bit hot under the collar in his heavy khaki uniform.

'She's fine, stop worrying. We are having fun and it's not for much longer, before we know it we'll all have arrived home.'

'Do you know, Connie, I really can't believe Tom. He has only known us for about three or four hours and you would think he had known us years. It's odd isn't it how you can take to some people straight away and that's exactly what the bairns have done with him, yet normally they are very wary of strangers, especially men.'

'It doesn't surprise me that they like him, Kitty. He's a gentle giant with lots of patience, it's no wonder they've warmed to him. I felt at ease with him the minute I shook his hand and dare I say it… he's just the opposite of Ernie.' She realised Kitty appeared a little taken aback by her remark. It was too late, it had been said but she did feel that she might have overstepped the mark.

'Don't worry, Connie, you've said it now and we both know Ernie has changed but you have to admit he was much the same as Tom when I first met him; the same handsome good looks, which he still has of course, and he was always generous, polite and very affectionate. No one would have guessed it was all a facade, except of course for my parents but the least said about them the better. Who knows, it might turn out that Tom is a bit of Jekyll and Hyde as well. Men are very clever at turning on the charm to get what they want.'

'Oh you can be so pessimistic at times, Kitty Cartwright and be honest, how many people have you met that live their lives that way? Anyhow we'll no doubt find out if he accepts my invitation to come and meet Malcolm and Mam and Dad.'

'Come on, you three, you're lagging behind and the bus will be here pretty soon,' Tom shouted, as they strolled along seemingly without a care in the world.

When they did eventually catch up they had already joined the queue, and to Kitty's horror Annie was sitting on the suitcase swinging her legs and kicking hard with her heels. Instantly she lifted her down, still not convinced it was strong enough to remain intact before their journey was over.

'If you only knew the trouble I had earlier this morning with that suitcase, Tom, you would probably have refused to carry it let alone let Annie sit on it.' She recalled the morning's antics and shaking her head from side to side she began chuckling so loudly she had to place her hand over her mouth to muffle the sound. 'Don't ask me to explain now, it's too long a story but me and Peggy did have such a laugh with it this morning.'

Before anything more was said, the bus pulled into the stop. The short queue began to move and Tom prepared to board with the infamous suitcase, and insisting the pushchair was also left to him so they could see to the bairns.

'Come on, everyone, step on board the Cumberland Express.' The driver welcomed them onto his bus with a cheery smile.

'I see you're still in good fettle,' Connie greeted him as he was the same driver who had brought her into town.

'Always the same, lass, you know that. No good being any different, and with spring in the air we couldn't ask for more.'

They took their seats near the front of the bus, where the conductor, who was equally as cheerful as the driver, also welcomed them on board.

Being the driver's regular route, though the queue had boarded, he waited for a few minutes for two elderly ladies who make the same journey every week to arrive. In the meantime a young teenage boy dressed in school uniform, with his tie hanging loose under his shirt collar and his satchel slung over his shoulder boarded, and typical of most young lads, he headed straight to the back and stretched out full length across the seat.

'Here they are,' the driver shouted so all on board could hear as he watched the two women, one with a slight limp and aided by a walking stick, as they made their way slowly but surely along the pavement to the waiting bus. 'I knew they'd turn up sooner or later, I've never known them to miss their weekly trip out as long as

I've been working this route, and that's a lot of years now.'

The conductor assisted them onto the bus and helped them into their seats right opposite Kitty and Connie. He already had their tickets ready for them, knowing the exact fare they required to take them home.

Doors closed, the driver shouted again. 'Everybody's sitting down so we're off.' He revved the engine, released the handbrake and filtered into the traffic, ready to make his way out of town and onto the narrow winding roads leading to the rural communities.

The conductor began collecting the rest of the fares. 'Two to Calderthwaite and one to Low Ellerton please.' Connie jumped in before Tom had time to ask for his fare.

'I'm paying my own fare, don't you listen to her,' he quickly jumped in, offering the conductor the money he had ready in his hand.

'No, this is on me, Tom and no arguing, you bought the teas remember.'

The conductor smiled and waited while they settled their little difference. 'You two sort it out between yourselves,' he said, 'it makes no difference to me who pays as long as I get the money for three fares.'

Tom insisted again but Connie refused to take no for answer.

Dispute settled, the conductor happily took their fares from Connie then handed her the three tickets, two to Calderthwaite and a third to Low Ellerton Farm, Little Ellerton.

Annie was sitting quietly on Connie's knee, but she didn't intend to stay there for long. 'Can I go and sit with Tom again please?'

'Me want to as well, Mammy,' Jack said waving his hands frantically in the air.

Tom had heard them and agreed they could both join him, causing the two women to once again look at one another in amazement, but they happily let them go then settled down to enjoy a peaceful scenic journey to Calderthwaite without any interruptions.

'You don't know how lucky you are to live in a lovely place like this,' Kitty said as she gazed out of the window at the rolling fields and hills which seemed to stretch for mile after mile. 'Your dad certainly knew what he was doing when he accepted the job transfer to this part of the country.' She felt a little envious, but appreciated she was very lucky being able to come and stay for as long as she wanted, as without their move she would never have had the privilege of visiting such a beautiful part of the country.

'I do know, Kitty… and cheer up. You're here as well now so enjoy it for as long as you want to. It won't be long now before we're home and you can put your feet up and take a well earned rest, you must be feeling a little worn out by now.'

'I'm not too bad but it will be nice to know we have finally arrived.'

'I'm so looking forward to tonight after everyone has gone to bed when we can sit around the fire and have a good old chin wag… we might even swap teacups for sherry glasses to celebrate, what do ya reckon?'

'I can hardly wait,' Kitty said, slipping her arm through Connie's and resting her head on her shoulder.

They looked and sounded so excited, and they had every good reason to; today was the first day of many happy times they would share in the coming days.

Chapter Seven

Much to Annie's disappointment Jack won the battle for Tom's knee, but she soon got over it when Tom sat her nearest to the window and they played name the animals in the fields. Crossing the Lune River by means of a very narrow humpback bridge Tom pointed to a couple of men fishing on the riverbank and asked Annie if she knew how the water got there.

'I don't know, Tom. Will you tell me?'

'The rainwater runs down the hills and mountains and trickles down in little streams. Some of the water runs all the way down to the very bottom and turns into rivers.'

'But why don't they get full because it rains a lot?'

'That's because they are flowing all the time. They flow all the way right down to the sea.'

'So does that mean one day the sea will get full?'

Tom wondered what he had let himself in for. 'It will take too long for me to explain now but when you start school you will learn all about things like where the rain comes from and about the sun, the moon and the stars. You'll love school, Annie, because you learn about all sorts of things.'

He could see how much she was enjoying learning but Jack was unsettled and he handed him back to Kitty. Moving to the window seat, he sat Annie on his knee so she could see better and seeing a field of dairy cows in the distance, he pointed to them. 'You see those cows over there, Annie, well I live on a farm and we have lots of cows just like them.'

'Can me and Jack come to see your cows?'

'Of course, but only if Mammy says you can.'

Within seconds she was up on her feet leaning over Tom's shoulder pleading with Kitty. 'Mammy, Tom has a farm and he says me and Jack can go and see his cows. Can we, Mammy, please, please?'

'We'll have to see about that, pet. We don't know what Aunty Connie and Uncle Malcolm have planned for us but I promise you I will think about it.'

Sitting back down in her usual confident manner, her eyes glaring into Tom's she nodded excitedly. 'We can, Tom. I know Mammy will let us, she likes us to learn about things and we've *never ever* been to a farm.' Fascinated by the delightful little character sitting happily on his knee as though she had known him all her short life, Tom could only smile.

With Jack wanting Kitty's attention Connie took the opportunity to sit with Tom and invite him to meet her family. 'I know where their conversation will eventually lead to,' Kitty thought nervously, but there was nothing she could do. about it.

'Has she not worn you out by now, Tom?' Connie asked as she listened to Annie chattering on about visiting the farm. 'I reckon she has her heart set on a visit but I don't think she will be disappointed, Kitty's nearly sure to agree and if you were to visit us at home first, then you'll get to know the bairns even better before you whisk them away to the farm.'

'Sounds like a good idea to me and it'll be nice to meet your husband and see everyone again, especially this little character,' he said bouncing Annie gently up and down on his knee making her giggle.

'Good. We'll look forward to a visit from you after you have spent some time at home with your family. Pop over whenever you like, we're nearly sure to be at home. Oh and by the way, it's Rose Cottage on the green right opposite the pub so you'll easily find us.'

'Kitty did mention where you live when I'd told her I had the occasional drink in the Dog and Gun.'

'Perhaps Malcolm and me could pop over and join you for a drink some time. We very rarely go into the place but we could make a special effort while Kitty's here. I'll see if I can tempt her to join us as Mam and Dad will be more than happy to babysit. Mind you if she does we'd need to be very careful, you know what village folk are like for barking up the wrong tree, and she wouldn't like people getting the wrong idea especially being married with two bairns and you being a local lad.'

'You'll never stop people talking, Connie. You know as well as I do that most people love a little bit of gossip but there would be no need to worry as we wouldn't be on our own to set tongues wagging.' He paused and thought for a moment. 'If only we were... there's nothing would please me more, but dream on, Tom Watson, you know it will never happen.' Without sounding too enthusiastic about the possibility of Kitty joining them he went on. 'There's some real characters pop in for the odd drink and I'm sure Kitty would enjoy having a bit of crack with them, but all you can do is ask, who knows she might surprise everyone and say yes.'

'She has met quite a few of the village folk on previous visits but never in the pub, and you're right, we can only ask then it's up to her what she wants to do. I'll suggest it to her once you have met Malcolm and she's settled in but I warn you, she will only do what she wants to, if she thinks that it wouldn't be right then she won't even consider it.'

'I wouldn't doubt that for a minute, she has already proved to be very strong-willed but who knows she might look forward to a night out as I'm sure she must be tied in most nights with her husband working away.'

'She is, but it's because he is away that Kitty can have a little holiday with us every now and then and my parents do love her, she's like a second daughter to them and it's an opportunity for us all to spend time together.'

Their seemingly endless conversation had again unnerved Kitty and she decided she couldn't hold back any longer. She had tried to listen in, but with Jack wanting her attention all the time she had found it impossible. Leaning forward she enquired jokingly, 'I don't know what you two find to talk about all the time but I'm wondering if I'm might be missing out on something exciting!'

'I was just asking Tom if he'd like to come and visit us while you're here. I thought after all he has done for you and the bairns it would be nice for him to see you all again, and I'm sure Malcolm and Mam and Dad would like to meet him being a local lad.'

103

'I'm sure he'd prefer to spend time with his own family and friends considering he hasn't seen them in months, so don't you be putting pressure on him, and besides I'm sure he'll have had enough of my two by the time we arrive in Calderthwaite!'

Tom was quick to clear matters up between the two friends and he popped his head over the back of the seat so he could see Kitty's expression and speak directly to her.

'I've already accepted Connie's invitation to meet her family and I'd love you all to come and visit the farm while you're here. The kids will enjoy seeing the different animals and maybe they will see the cows being brought in for milking. Annie especially will love it as she's so keen to learn and I guess like today her questions will be nonstop.'

'Next stop Calderthwaite,' the conductor announced taking everyone by surprise.

Changing down the gears, the driver very carefully manoeuvred the single decker bus around the last few long winding bends, before finally braking gently as he drove down the steep hill leading into the village. They were the only passengers for Calderthwaite and Tom was first off carrying the suitcase. 'I'll be back for the pushchair in a tick,' he shouted to the driver, 'and don't forget my stop is Little Ellerton so don't you be driving off without me!'

'No need, lad, the conductor's right behind you, and don't you worry I haven't forgotten. I know exactly which stop is yours; I've covered this route for so many years I just about know where everyone lives.'

With all four safely off it was time to say their goodbyes. Kitty stood back, a little hesitant knowing Tom had got his wish that their parting would not be final. He explained to the bairns that he had to get back on the bus as he still had a little further to go, and promised them he would be back soon to take them to visit the farm. Finally he turned to shake the hands of his two new acquaintances.

Connie was first to accept. 'Thanks again, Tom, for all the help you've given Kitty and don't forget your invite. We'll all be looking out for you.'

'Yes, thanks for everything.' Kitty acknowledged him, and then panicked fearing he would take *everything* as literal. She sounded slightly nervous as she took his hand. 'It seems we'll be meeting you again after all, Tom and I'm sure the bairns will be looking forward to a visit to the farm.'

'They will, Kitty. You'll see I'll keep my promise to them; I won't let them down.'

His cheeky grin and glint in his eye, which she had now become familiar with, convinced her that the chances of him not turning up was indisputable. Turning to the bairns he gave each a gentle cuff on the chin. 'See you soon, kids,' and he boarded the bus giving them the thumbs up. 'I won't break my promise,' he shouted as he made his way back to his seat to the sound of the bairns shouting 'Ta-ra, Tom' and waving continually with both hands until they lost sight of him.

As the bus pulled away the driver honked the horn and

the conductor gave the smiling quartet a friendly wave.

Tom had placed the suitcase onto the pushchair saying it would be easier for them to manage rather than trying to carry it, and Kitty insisted she would push it for the final stage of the journey. Heading towards Rose Cottage she was struggling and finally admitted to herself that she would never have managed without all the help she had received. Carrying Jack and Kitty's bag, Connie kept a close eye on Annie who was trailing behind, happy to be alone in her own little world.

Spotting Connie's mam waiting at the door to greet them, Kitty instantly abandoned the pushchair which promptly tipped backwards from the weight of the suitcase, but unconcerned she ran, arms outstretched and they embraced with the affection of a loving mother and daughter.

'Aunty Kath what a lovely surprise. I didn't expect to see you so soon.'

'Oh you might have known I wouldn't stay away. It's such a long time since you were here and you know it means the world to us having you visit. Now come on let's get you indoors. I can't wait to have a proper look at you and to see how much the bairns have grown.'

Kitty didn't need telling twice and entered the cottage empty handed. Oblivious to everything going on around them neither had heard Connie shouting to them.

'It's fine, you two, don't worry, I'll manage. I'm used to lugging two bairns and all the family's personal belongings around.' Putting Jack and the bag down on the grass, she chuckled as she struggled to drag the suitcase off the pushchair. Apart from it being so heavy, her arms were tired from all the carrying she had done but eventually she succeeded and began pushing it along the ground towards the front door. 'Have you put the kitchen sink in here, Kitty Cartwright? Going by the weight of this thing I think you must have!' she shouted a little louder this time hoping to be heard.

'We're coming, Connie,' Kitty called to her but couldn't help laughing when she saw her almost level with the ground as she pushed and shoved with all her might. Seeing the bairns standing alone, Aunty Kath rushed over to them giving each a huge bear hug then took them indoors, leaving Kitty and Connie jostling with the suitcase.

'It's no wonder Tom wouldn't let us try to carry this thing,' Connie remarked almost out of breath, as she mustered up her last remaining bit of strength and gave it one final push over the threshold. Finally the pushchair was brought inside and Connie closed the door behind them. They were both exhausted, especially Kitty who collapsed in a heap at the bottom of the stairs. Kicking off her shoes, she stretched her legs and stared blankly at the suitcase. The earlier events of the day came flooding back and she burst into laughter.

'If that suitcase could talk, it would tell you... it would tell you a tale you would never believe...' Her voice trailed off, she could hardly speak for laughing. Eventually she managed to control herself. 'I can't tell you right now, it's too long a story but as I'm sitting now is precisely how at Hazeldene today's crazy events began.'

Aunty Kath popped her head around the living room door to see what all the laughter was about, and mother and daughter looked at one another dumbfounded, wondering what on earth could be so funny about sitting on a staircase with a suitcase. Seeing Kitty so happy, which is the opposite of how she often interpreted her letters, Connie joined in her laughter until the two didn't even know what they were laughing about. When they finally managed to stop and could talk sensibly again, Kitty naively told Connie, 'I'll leave it here for now and take it upstairs later.'

'Don't you even think about trying to lift it, Kitty. It took two of us to manage to get it through the door so how on earth do you think you're going to carry it upstairs on your own? Don't you dare even attempt it in your condition, and I can't imagine you will need anything out of it before Malcolm and Dad are home and one of them will carry it upstairs for you.'

'Your condition.' Connie's words brought her back to reality with a jolt. She had almost forgotten through all the excitement that she was pregnant, and it came as a stark warning that she must slow down or she would be losing the baby.

'How on earth you have managed with all that on your own, Kitty, is beyond me!' Aunty Kath commented when she realised the amount of luggage she had with her.

'The truth is, Aunty Kath, I didn't have to thanks to all the help I've had throughout the day. First of all friends and neighbours helped me with everything this morning and then a couple of young soldiers who, fortunately for me were travelling on the same train, helped with the suitcase and pushchair. But wait till you hear this…,' she hesitated for a second, '…you're never going to believe it but one of them only lives in Little Ellerton.'

'Do you know Kitty, I thought I saw a soldier standing beside you but when the bus pulled away and there were just the four of you left, I decided it must have been a figment of my imagination.'

'Well you'll be pleased to hear that you're not going mad, Mam. There was a solider with us for a few minutes; the one from Little Ellerton that Kitty's just mentioned. He's called Tom and you'll really like him. He turned out to be a blessing in disguise for Kitty because there was absolutely no way in the world could she have ever managed to carry everything on her own. How she ever thought she could completely dumbfounds me, but then we all know what she's like, don't we? I reckon it was her sheer determination to come to us rather than have Kenneth pick her up and take her to stay with him and that awful sister of hers in Yorkshire.'

'Well you're all here safe and sound and that's all that matters, but to be honest, Kitty, looking at you, I suggest we find you a comfortable chair to put your feet up on with a nice cup of tea. The kettle's already been boiled once so it won't take long and I've baked some fruit scones for us and gingerbread men for the bairns as you must all be feeling a bit peckish by now. As we're not eating dinner until late tonight you'll need something to keep you going until then otherwise you will be passing out on us.'

As ever Aunty Kath was already spoiling them, but she didn't want to disappoint her by telling her it had not been that long since they had eaten, so they weren't really hungry, but the minute the kitchen door was opened, the aroma of her home baking reached her nostrils, and it went without saying, no one refused to partake of her delicious offering.

Rose Cottage, like most properties in and around Calderthwaite is rented from Crowther Estates. Robert G Crowther, great, great-grandson of Charles R Crowther inherited the land and properties from his family, and remaines one of the richest land owners in the area. Connie's parents also rent their cottage from Crowther Estates and it is where Connie and Malcolm lived until another property became vacant in the village.

It was through the sudden death of old Mr Lambton, better known in the village as 'Loner Lambie' due to his independent and quiet nature, that Rose Cottage became available for rent. He had been a widower for several years following his wife's premature death, and firmly refused help from his neighbours saying he was quite capable of looking after himself. Rarely seen out and about, when he did leave his cottage, which was more often than not early morning or on the very rare occasion, an evening, he appeared to be a very sad, lonely figure and many of the villagers were concerned for his welfare. Aware that it had only ever been Mrs Lambton who participated in village events they respected his wishes for privacy but secretly kept an eye out for him. Often the victims of village gossip as visitors were never seen entering or leaving their cottage, many people had felt sorry for them but Mrs Lambton refused to have a wrong word said about her husband. Both regular church goers they attended Matins every Sunday but immediately the service was over Mr Lambton would leave with his head bowed and make straight for home and the potting shed, leaving his wife to exchange pleasantries with the vicar and his flock.

Sadly Mr Lambton never got over the loss of his wife and became more and more of a recluse, only seen when he made a quick dash to the village store and back, or on an occasional Sunday morning when he attended church. When no one had seen him for well over a week the village postmistress had a word with the vicar who took it upon himself to check and see if he was okay. With no response at the cottage he immediately contacted the police who broke in to find the elderly man lying face down just inside the back door where he had collapsed from a massive heart attack.

Fortunately, following his wife's death he had very wisely given both the vicar and Crowther Estates details of a distant relative no one knew existed and who in the event of his death, and he had emphasised... *only* in the event of his death, was to be contacted. The villagers gave him a good send off but his anonymous relative, like Mr Lambton shared very few words with his mourners.

Shortly after his funeral Connie and Malcolm contacted Crowther Estates to express their interest in taking over the tenancy and were accepted immediately. As expected, the cottage was in a state of disrepair leaving the owners little choice but to make a few necessary renovations before it could be re-let and within a couple of months Mr & Mrs M Ferguson became the proud new tenants.

Overlooking the village green Rose Cottage is accessed through a small garden gate, painted cornflower blue with the name plate attached, both of which were handmade by Malcolm. Following a short winding path with gardens on both sides offering an abundance of colour when the various flowers come into bloom, you arrive at the front door which is painted the same shade of blue as the gate. A black door-knocker and letterbox contrast nicely against the paler shade and a small oblong window offers a little daylight into the entrance beyond. A yellow rambling rose when in full bloom winds its way through a trellis around the door, adding even more colour and fragrance to the wonderful floral display throughout the summer months. To the rear, a long rectangular garden has a well trodden path down the centre running its entire length. One side is cultivated for growing vegetables while the other is lawned with a couple of small flower borders and a section is fenced off to accommodate half a dozen bantam hens. A rabbit hutch is the most recent addition, made especially in time for Annie and Jack's arrival, houses a white Netherland Dwarf rabbit. At the bottom of the garden the sound of a trickling stream can be heard flowing gently through the thick undergrowth as it makes its journey into the unknown.

Indoors, the living room runs from front to back with windows at both ends. The kitchen and bathroom take up the remaining ground floor at the rear of the cottage. Directly opposite the front door a narrow staircase leads to the first floor with its tiny landing leading to two good sized bedrooms. One overlooks the picturesque village green, the other the rear garden and dense woodland and hills far away on the horizon. The larger of the two bedrooms and the one Malcolm and Connie share is at the rear, while the other, comfortably furnished, is kept neat and tidy as a guest room.

Working together Connie and Malcolm have spent many happy hours turning Rose Cottage into the cosy home they had grown to love. They renovated one or two items left in the cottage when Mr Lambton passed away, along with some second hand furniture they bought and cleverly redesigned. Connie being a gifted needlewoman worked hard at her old Singer sewing machine, altering curtains and making quilted bedcovers and other soft furnishings. She also collected oddments of wool from friends and neighbours, spending many a happy hour knitting squares which she sewed together to use as chair coverings and blankets, many in the most amazing array of patterns and colours which enhance their decor or, as is often the case, raises money for the village hall as she donates them to the craft stalls. Over a period of time they have transformed the interior into a beautiful cosy cottage, one where many special occasions have been celebrated.

Resting in the comfort of the big armchair, Kitty admired the hard work they had both put into turning their quaint cottage into the beautiful cosy comfortable home it is now. She has never envied Connie and her family their peaceful country life, yet secretly she wishes she could live here alongside them but is well aware that it is an impossible dream, Ernie would never contemplate a move to the countryside as city life is in his blood and what he loves.

Having left Kitty to rest up for a little while, Connie and Aunty Kath spent time in the garden with Annie and Jack. They were delighted to be able to offer the family a peaceful haven, one where Kitty could enjoy some relaxation away from the hustle and bustle of her busy city life, and where they could breathe some good clean healthy air into their lungs.

'Are you coming to join us, Kitty? There's a cup of tea out here for you that is getting cold and the bairns have something they want to show you,' Connie asked popping her head around the living room door eager for Kitty to come outside and see the expressions on the faces of the two bairns with their new furry friend.

Dragging herself from the comfort of the armchair she made her way down the garden path to the delightful sounds, mainly coming from Annie as Connie lifted the rabbit out of its hutch and onto her lap.

'What did you say you call it, Aunty Connie? Is it your

rabbit? Will it scratch me?' Her questions were unrelenting while Connie held onto the rabbit as Annie began to stroke him.

'We've bought him for you and Jack, and thought Snowball would be a nice name for him as he's small and round just like a snowball, but if you and Jack would like to choose a different name for him we wouldn't mind.'

'Do you think that's a nice name for him, Jack?' Annie asked wanting to include him in the decision.

'Not bovered really,' he shrugged, 'but me want to hold bunny as well,' and he sat on the grass next to her where she very reluctantly with some help from Connie passed Snowball to him.

Connie was sitting beside them showing them both the correct way to stroke him so that he wouldn't want to make an immediate dash for freedom, when they were distracted by a male voice.

'Hi, everyone, we're home.' It was Malcolm followed by Uncle George. They had finished work early in order to spend time with the bairns before their evening meal and, no doubt an early bedtime as they would surely be worn out after travelling most of the day.

'Malcolm, Uncle George.' Kitty raced towards them, arms outstretched, not sure which one she should fling herself around first. The decision was made for her as the two men approached, side by side enabling her to wrap an arm around each of them at the same time. 'Oh I can't tell you how happy I am for us all to be together again. I have only been here a short while and already I feel as though I've never been away.'

'And we're happy to have you. I don't have to tell you how much we would love it if you and the bairns were living near us… and just look at the smiles on their faces, it seems they are really pleased with the rabbit,' Malcolm said as all three made their way towards them.

'It's a lovely gesture you buying them the rabbit, but as you know they have never had one before so we will need to keep an eye on them. There's every chance they might kill the poor little thing with kindness if we don't!'

'They'll be fine, Kitty, once they get used to handling him properly, you'll see,' George assured her. 'Now then how about one of you ladies making the workers a nice cup of tea?'

'I'll see to that,' Kath butted in. 'I'll make us all a nice fresh brew while you get to know the bairns, but be careful with Jack, you two. He may be a little wary until he gets used to you both, he's still only a baby you know,' and she headed for the kitchen conscious that no one was heeding a word she was saying; they were all too busy enjoying themselves.

With the refreshment over, Connie asked Malcolm to carry Kitty's suitcase up to the bedroom. Kitty followed him a few minutes later to unpack, and on entering the room she immediately smelt the flowers Connie had picked earlier and placed in a vase alongside a glass dressing table set comprising of a tray, ring dish, perfume bottle with stopper and matching candlesticks. Pulling the stopper from the perfume bottle the familiar fragrance of Coty L'aimant perfume which, over the years had been a favourite of Connie's reached her nostrils, instantly bringing back memories of their teenage years. Not having the time to ponder over bygone days, she turned to look out of the window. She had to stretch over a small camp bed which Connie had most likely made up for Annie, and her eyes immediately caught sight of the Dog and Gun. Tom came to mind in an instant but she forced herself to brush him aside and turned back to admire the cosy bedroom Connie had prepared for their short stay.

One of Connie's hand knitted blankets was used as a covering over the flannelette sheets and thick green army type blankets, making the camp bed look very warm and welcoming. A beautiful quilted bedspread which Kitty knew would have been sewn by Connie's skilful hands was so big it reached the floor at both sides of the double bed. The cream coloured walls perfectly matched the background shade of the brightly coloured floral bedspread. 'That's enough admiring for now.' Kitty checked herself and turned her attention to the job of unpacking. Kneeling down to undo the belt buckle around the suitcase her thoughts turned to Peggy, and she hoped she would not feel too lonely while they were away. She knew Jean would keep her promise to pop over every day to make sure she was okay, and with the days getting longer Peggy would probably be on the doorstep hoping to catch a neighbour or passer-by who could spare the time for a bit of a natter.

She pulled the belt from around the suitcase and as she expected the locks opened with just the lightest touch of her finger. She began emptying it placing their clothing

117

neatly into drawers and a small wardrobe, feeling relieved that it had made it here intact, just as Peggy had assured her it would. Whether it would survive a return journey though, she was very doubtful!

Out in the garden, Jack panicked when he realised his mam had gone missing and Connie decided to take both of them up to her and show them where they would be sleeping. On entering the bedroom Annie excitedly made a dash for the camp bed. 'Can I sleep here, Mammy?' she asked already stretched out full length whilst making her claim.

'I think you had better ask Aunty Connie who is sleeping where; she might have made that bed up for me to sleep on so you and Jack can sleep together in the big bed,' she joked as Connie entered the room with Jack.

'Please can I, Aunty Connie? Jack can sleep in the big bed with Mammy, he'll like that best.'

'If that's where you want to sleep of course you can.' Then she slipped her hands beneath the blankets and pulled out a hot water bottle with a red hand-knitted cover. She took another from the double bed saying she would refill them then left them to settle into their room.

'I like it here, Mammy. Do you?' Annie asked in an almost adult tone which seemed more to reassure her mam everything would be okay.

'I love it here, pet and we can stay here until Daddy lets us know when he will be back at home, so we'll make sure we have lots of fun playing outside in the fresh air.'

'I know we will because Tom said he is coming to take us to his farm to see the cows.'

Without answering she lifted her from the camp bed, threw her gently onto the bed then lay between them cuddling them in close. 'My two precious bairns,' she said as she snuggled them in even tighter then all went quiet. All three, not surprisingly, were worn out after their long tiring day.

In the silence her thoughts turned to Tom. She was unsure what to make of him and the unexpected events of the day that had left her somewhat bewildered. Even if she had wanted to forget about him, it was obvious this wouldn't happen in the immediate future as he would most likely be around whenever he could make it throughout their stay.

Then there was Ernie, what about him? She never knew exactly when he would be coming home, as it could be anywhere between four to eight weeks, but she was secretly hoping this time it would be the latter. Excited about her stay in Calderthwaite the longer he was away the better for all of them. They would have lots of time with Connie and her family, and Kitty could mentally and physically prepare herself for the unplanned new arrival before returning.

Determined to try and put the two men out of her mind, though she doubted if she could, she left Annie and Jack to rest while she finished unpacking, and thought about the happy days that lay ahead at Rose Cottage with her beloved friends.

Chapter Eight

With a cool breeze blowing in from the north and the evening sun beginning to fade, a unanimous decision was made to go indoors. Annie and Jack would have been happier to stay in the garden with their new animal friends, but as Annie was already asking if she could collect the eggs after discovering them in the nesting box Kitty insisted they'd had sufficient fresh air and excitement for one day. Once inside, their appetites were whetted by the delicious aroma coming from Aunty Kath's home cooking and the welcoming coal fire roaring up the chimney, warming the living room. Its dancing orange and red flames immediately drew the men to the comfort of the armchairs positioned one at each side of the hearth.

'That almost smells good enough to eat,' George called to his wife as he pulled his armchair closer to the fire.

'We'll have less of your cheek, George Swainstone, much more of it and you won't be getting any dinner tonight.'

Connie and Kath had been putting the finishing touches to the evening meal and while Kath prepared to serve up in the kitchen, Connie laid the dining table for the extended family.

'What would you like me to do?' Kitty offered feeling guilty that she had done very little in the way of helping out since she arrived.

'Nothing thanks, Kitty, you can give me hand when Mam's not here and don't even suggest wanting to help with the washing up. As far as the rest of today goes you're not doing anything other than tucking the bairns up in bed after dinner.' Connie as always was concerned for her friend's wellbeing, convinced that she must surely be ready for a well earned rest.

'Okay, but that rule only applies for today!'

'Well we'll see about that. At the minute the only thing you need to think about is yourself and the bairns.'

'Talking about the bairns I'm beginning to wonder if Jack will last until after dinner. He's already showing signs of needing his bed and he's not one to go much past his usual bedtime. No doubt Annie will be feeling the same very soon, but hopefully they'll manage to last out until we've eaten.'

Kitty collapsed onto the sofa stretching out full length, only to have the bairns climbing on top of her battling to see who could get the closest for a cuddle. Malcolm, who thought she was looking quite weary managed to entice them to sit with him by talking about the hens and rabbit, and asking what they would like to do tomorrow.

'We'll play with Snowball first then I'll get the eggs in for Aunty Connie if she will let me, and oh I nearly forgot we're going to see Tom at his farm, aren't we, Jack?'

Malcolm and George's eyes made instant contact, their furrowed brows and vague expressions proof that they were of the same mind, but it was Malcolm who raised the question.

'Come on then, Kitty, are you going to tell us who this

Tom is that Annie is talking about?' but as she was so relaxed and with her eyes closed she was oblivious to their conversation.

'Tom was on the train *and* on the bus with us wasn't he, Jack?' Annie explained excitably.

Neither of the men responded choosing instead to await Kitty's explanation about the mystery traveller. Unsure whether she had intentionally ignored his question or she hadn't heard him, Malcolm approached her again in a louder, more persuasive tone.

'Come on, Kitty, are you going to put us in the picture as to who this Tom is that Annie is talking about or not?'

'Oh, are you talking to me, Malcolm? I'm sorry, I must have dozed off for a minute.'

'I was asking you who Tom is that Annie is talking about. Some bloke she says was with you on the train and something about going to a farm.'

Annie, bright as a button as usual was just about to speak when Kitty stopped her in her tracks.

'It's alright, Annie. I'll explain to Uncle Malcolm and Uncle George who Tom is.'

She obeyed knowing her mam's tone meant she had to remain silent, but her face displayed disappointment as she was eager to tell them all about their new friend. Kitty on the other hand seeing the puzzled expressions on the men's faces felt she was about to be interrogated and acted quickly. Swinging her legs off the sofa, she sat upright, put on an innocent smile and proceeded cautiously to enlighten them.

'Don't look so worried, I haven't a strange man hidden

122

away somewhere,' she said raising her hands as if to brush it aside as unimportant. 'All will be revealed soon enough, but to put you briefly in the picture, Tom is a soldier we met at the station but he is also a farmer. Him and his mate Bernie helped us onto the train and sat near us and well… you're not going to believe this, but it turns out Tom only lives at Low Ellerton Farm which apparently is just along the road from here, so he has invited the bairns to visit the farm while we're here. Now I'm pretty sure you'll both agree, if I'd left it up to Annie to do the explaining we might have been here all night!'

They were both naturally surprised, and George with a look of approval on his face turned to his son-in-law. 'Well that's a relief, Malcolm. I thought for a minute she had herself a fancy farmer friend over here she had been keeping secret all these years, but as that's not the case we have to agree with her, it is quite a coincidence that she met someone living just a couple of miles away. I'm not sure which is Low Ellerton Farm, but I rather suspect it could be the dairy farm with the gate quite near the roadside. You know the one, Malcolm. It has a long drive up to the farmhouse and you can just see the farm buildings in the distance. Anyway I'm sure we'll find out sooner or later as it seems the bairns have already set their hearts on a visit.'

Thankfully the subject of Tom ended when Kath invited everyone to the table which was positioned near the window overlooking the rear garden. Covered with a pretty floral hand embroidered tablecloth which had been worked by Kath's own hands many years earlier, it was

123

testimony to who Connie inherited her sewing skills from. A variety of dinner plates in different shapes, sizes, colours and patterns were used as with most families they didn't own a dinner service big enough to serve seven people, but nothing as trivial as mismatched crockery could blight this blissfully happy gathering. Aunty Kath's mouth-watering homemade meat pie, with a variety of vegetables tantalised everyone's taste buds and they were soon tucking into her delicious meal, and with so much to catch up on not having seen each other for a long time, the conversation was lively with everyone in high spirits throughout the entire meal. Eventually Jack began rubbing his eyes, finally giving up his fight to stay awake and everyone left the table, their bellies full to almost bursting and thanked the women for their delicious meal. While Connie and Kath cleared everything away, as agreed, Kitty attended to the bairns.

The chill of the evening incited George to leave ahead of his wife in order to light their fire so the house would be warming up for her when she returned prompting Malcolm to add a log and another large shovel of coal to keep the fire burning. After assuring Kitty and the bairns he would see them again the next day, George bid everyone goodnight. Malcolm settled back into the comfort of his favourite armchair, picked up his morning newspaper, a small Collins Dictionary and his pen in preparation to finish the crossword, part of his regular evening routine.

The long day was finally catching up on the Cartwright family. With so much excitement and the fresh country air contributing to their tiredness Annie and Jack were finally taken up to bed. It was after eight which was well past their normal bedtime and much to Kitty's relief while reading them a story they both fell asleep before she had turned to the third page. For her, the exciting evening ahead which she wouldn't miss for the world encouraged her to drag her tired body from the bed where she could quite happily have crawled beneath the covers and slept until morning.

'Well that didn't take long, Kitty. They must have gone out like a light,' Malcolm remarked, shocked she had returned so quickly.

'They took no rocking tonight though I wasn't too sure how Jack would settle in a strange room but he was probably too tired to even notice.'

'Talking about going out like a light, Kitty, I hope you've left one on for them,' Connie asked as she entered the room carrying a tray of freshly made tea.

'I've left the landing light on for them with the staircase being accessible unlike at home, where the flat door sperates ours from the downstairs, but I don't want them to start getting used to sleeping with a light on. I was afraid to leave them in complete darkness so I've left the bedroom door ajar and I've locked the safety gate across the top of the stairs… I remember it well,' she reminisced giving Malcolm a warm smile, 'it's the one you originally made for Annie when she was tiny, long before Jack arrived on the scene.'

'I'm just glad we kept it and don't worry about them, Kitty, they'll be fine. With all the fresh air they've had today they'll be absolutely worn out and unlikely to waken early.'

Aunty Kath eventually finished her long day's work in the kitchen and when she finally returned to the living room she looked quite weary, but like everyone else said she had thoroughly enjoyed the day.

'I'm going to grab my coat, Connie and get back to your dad so I will say goodnight to everyone, and listen to me, you two, don't you be sitting up talking until the early hours of the morning. Remember, Connie, Kitty will be very tired and there are two bairns upstairs who will be full of beans as soon as they wake up which you're not used to.' Her eyes dropped to the floor, the words pained her deep inside, knowing how much Connie and Malcolm longed to have bairns of their own running around the house all day and how much George and her would love to be grandparents. With a slight hint of sorrow in her voice she hastily wished them goodnight quietly closing the door behind her.

'Say goodnight to Dad, I can't remember whether I did or not with so much going on here,' Connie shouted after her but it was too late, she was gone.

'Goodnight, Mam,' Malcolm said peering over the top his paper but, like Connie he too realised she had disappeared rather quickly.

'Well she disappeared all of a sudden,' Connie commented.

'She's probably keen to get home and put her feet up with your dad for a couple of hours before bedtime,' Malcolm suggested and went straight back to his

126

crossword.

'And who can blame her, after all the hard work she put into that lovely meal tonight?' Kitty added.

Kath's thoughts were with Connie and Malcolm as she steadily made her way home across the dimly lit village green. They longed to become parents and she suspected having Annie and Jack around Connie would start to feel broody again, but on a more positive note seeing the loyal friends spending time together again she was more than happy for them both.

'Did anyone think to lock the hens up and feed the rabbit?' Malcolm asked, aware that there was every possibility they could have been forgotten about during the excitement of the evening.

'Oh good heavens I haven't!' Connie sounded shocked that they had been left out, especially as recently the occasional fox had been spotted prowling around in the vicinity. 'I did put some more hay in for Snowball but I've not heard anyone mention anything about locking the hens up.'

'Don't worry, they'll have most likely gone inside to roost but I'll go out and check and lock them in for the night, and while I'm out there I think it might be a good idea to fill the coalscuttle.'

'Good thinking, Malcolm!'

'Well you'll need to keep a decent fire burning tonight as knowing you two you will be up until fairly late.' He turned to Kitty. 'Has she told you she has already sorted out a good book for me to make sure I head off to bed early? It's obvious she doesn't want me around listening to all your girlie talk!'

'There won't be anything said that's not suitable for your ears, Malcolm and you're more than welcome to stay up with us,' Kitty assured him. Malcolm knew as it was their first night together in a very long time they would have lots to talk about and he would be better off out of the way.

'I don't mind at all, Kitty, in fact an early night will do me good. I know it's difficult to have long conversations when the bairns are around so make the most of it while they're asleep.' He folded his paper in half adding it to a pile of old newspapers stored in the corner of the room for fire lighting, picked up the empty coalscuttle and headed out to finish the chores.

'Don't spend too much time outside, your tea will go cold,' Connie advised him as she was about to add a few grains of sugar to his teacup, the meagre amount she allows him as it's still on ration.

'I'll do my best, I'm pretty sure the hens will have gone to roost but you know what old Henrietta is like. I usually have to chase her in and I don't suppose tonight will be any different. I may be a while, so I suggest you don't sugar my tea yet. You know I won't drink it if it's cold.' He disappeared from the room whistling a tune that neither of the women could identify but it did make them both smile.

When he returned they had nicely settled down in the armchairs for the night and he decided against his cup of tea instead heading for the bathroom for a wash and shave then made himself a cup of hot cocoa. With his drink in one hand and his book in the other he was off to bed after a quick reminder from Connie that he needed to go quietly so as not to wake the bairns.

'Goodnight, girls, see you in the morning, and remember by the time you two call it a night I'll be fast asleep so try not to disturb me as you get into bed, Connie.' Then he was gone leaving the two friends inching their chairs closer to the fire and knowing that within a matter of minutes their marathon chat-a-long would begin.

Pulling up at Low Ellerton Farm, the driver had a few words with Tom. 'Make the most of your leave, lad and enjoy all that good home cooking your ma will have ready for you, I'm sure it'll be better than that army grub you've been having.'

'It will that's for sure. I can't wait to get stuck into Mam's cooking; she's the tops when it comes to feeding us and it'll be nice to sit around the table eating with the family again.'

'Aye she'll be looking forward to seeing you, lad, and I bet she's waiting at the door with open arms.'

'She's nearly sure to be as she is expecting me off this bus.'

'See you, lad, look after yourself.'

'I will, and I'll no doubt be seeing you again during the next couple of weeks. I'll be out and about and needing your services from time to time.' He leapt off the bus, flung his kit bag over his shoulder and headed straight for the farm gate.

After waving him off, the driver, still in first gear, took his foot off the brake, accelerated slowly and set off down the narrow road to the next village, a journey so familiar to him, he knew every twist and turn like the back of his hand.

As soon as Tom's mam spotted him she began waving frantically. Never wanting him to join the army in the first place, she was overjoyed to see her first born returning home for his final leave before coming home for good and she took to her heels like a young spring chicken to meet him.

Leaping over the wooden five bar gate leading up the track to the farmhouse Tom's heart was pounding; he was so pleased to see her and his home surroundings again. Running towards her, his kit bag looked almost weightless as he raced up the track.

'Tom,' she was shouting at the top of her voice.

'Mam, how are you?' he asked, wrapping his arms around her hugging her tight.

'I'm fine, son, how are you? I can't believe you're home at last, it seems so long since we last saw you,' and like young lovers they slowly made their way arm in arm towards the farmhouse.

'It's great to be home, Mam and I can't wait to see Dad and Jim again. Are they both okay?'

'Aye they're fine as well, son. Working hard as usual, they'll be busy fetching the cows in for milking soon which means you probably won't see them until they've finished unless you want to pop over before then.'

He was about to answer when Blade, their German Shepherd who joined the family as an eight week old pup over seven years ago came charging towards them. He immediately recognised Tom and began jumping up and down and running rings around him almost knocking him off his feet.

'Settle down, Blade and give him a chance to get up to the house,' his mam shouted at the dog. 'I guess he's like the rest of us, Tom, pleased to see you again and at least he hasn't forgotten you.'

'He's alright, Mam, he'll never forget me will you, lad? He knows who it was who trained him as a pup and fed and watered him,' Tom said ruffling his thick coat. 'Now then I expect you've already had the kettle on the boil, I'm desperately looking forward to a good cup of your home brew and changing into something more comfortable then I'll take me self off to see Dad and Jim and have a feel of a cow's warm soft udder in the palm of me hand… you know how much I love milking those animals.'

'Really, Tom!' his mam retorted at his choice of words.

'Well you have to admit it, Mam, I have been brought up milking cows, and they are a lot warmer on the hands than the cold metal tools I have to work with when I'm repairing and servicing all the different types of army vehicles especially in winter when I'm working outside in the rain and snow.'

'Aye you're probably right, lad. Now come on, let's have you up to your room and out of that uniform. You must be sweltering and weighed down with it the number

131

of hours you'll have been stuck in it today.'

'Now don't you start fussing over me already, but I must admit it will be nice to be without it for the next couple of weeks and remember it won't be for much longer after that.' He winked at her knowing how much she was looking forward to the day when he would be home to stay.

'Believe me, son, I can't wait for that day to arrive. I never ever wanted you to join up in the first place and neither did Alice Armstrong. You do realise you broke that lass's heart when you said you were leaving to join the army...? Anyway you'll be pleased to hear I was only talking to her last week so I told her you were due home. She seemed excited and bless her, she blushed from head to toe, she did seem a bit embarrassed when I mentioned it. She must still be carrying a torch for you, Tom, as I've not heard if she has found herself another young man, and you know how word would have got around if she had. I expect she'll be paying you a visit as soon as she hears you're home.' She paused, her head nodding slightly as she spoke. 'Aye I reckon she must be saving herself for you, Tom, and I will say this about her, she obviously knows a good man when she meets one.'

'Well she's wasting her time, and I don't want her calling here so don't you go encouraging her. I've told her so many times there has never been anything between us, and since I never replied to any of the letters you forwarded on from her, she must surely have got the message by now... either that or she is even more stupid than I thought she was.'

132

'Now that's not a very nice thing to say about her, Tom, and with no other lass in your life the least you could do is give her a chance after waiting all this time for you to come home.'

'Now just you listen to me for a minute, Mrs Watson, you don't know whether there is a special lass in my life or not,' he said giving her one of his 'I'll keep you guessing' winks. 'I don't tell you everything and you know what my plans are when I finish the army and it hasn't changed. I still intend to take advantage of the trade I've learned by starting up my own farm machinery repair business so I won't have time for lasses for a while. Anyway enough of this stupid talk, nobody knows what the future holds for any of us, only time will tell.'

'You're right there, son, but every good man needs a good woman behind him and I don't think you'll find a nicer lass around here than Alice Armstrong. Anyway, if she doesn't call at the farm to see you before next week you're bound to bump into her at Calderthwaite Village dance which is being held while you're home.'

'Oh, the dance, when's it on?' he asked excitedly.

'A week this Saturday.'

'That's great news, there's always a good turnout for it so I'm nearly sure to catch up with everyone before I go back and before you say anything else, I won't be dancing the night away with Alice Armstrong if she is there. I will be keeping her at arm's length in case she starts getting stupid ideas about us again.'

'You're a hard nut to crack, Tom Watson, but I know you'll only do what you want and if she's not the one for you then so be it. I can't pick your lass for ya.'

'Like I said, I intend to concentrate on working hard to start up my own business, so lasses will be on the back burner for a while. I'm planning on securing a good future for myself not having to slave on like Dad has to almost eighteen hours a day sometimes even twenty-four, seven days a week.'

'Yeah, your dad's had to work long hard hours to keep a roof over our heads all these years but he still looks well on it and you always have had a mind of your own, Tom, so good luck to you if that's what you plan to do. I can't say I blame you. Now off you go and get out of that heavy uniform and I will have a nice strong brew ready for you in no time.'

With that he happily disappeared to his bedroom, eager to settle back into country life for a couple of weeks but already scheming up how soon he could see Kitty not knowing how long she would be staying at Connie's. Hearing the village dance was to be held next week was the best news he could have had. Almost certainly she would still be here and he was already planning to ask her to join him. Dancing together he decided, was probably the only way he could get close enough to explain his feelings for her.

Stripped of his uniform he crashed onto the bed. 'Home sweet home,' he thought as he lay, legs spread-eagled with his hands behind his head, but the second he closed his eyes, a vision of Kitty appeared arousing feelings he'd not experienced before. He knew the right thing to do would be to try and forget about her

134

altogether, but he couldn't get her out of his mind. He tossed and turned, it was impossible, the harder he tried the more she appeared before him. Her beautiful face was right there in front of him, so much so that he felt he could reach out and touch her delicate velvety skin. He tried reproaching himself. 'She's a married woman with two kids who you have only known for a few hours. If anyone knew how you felt about her they would think you had gone mad and lost all sense of morality.' But he knew his feelings for her wouldn't change; she was the woman of his dreams but unfortunately she was already married.

Searching the familiar surroundings of his bedroom in the hope that she would fade from his mind, he picked up his old school photograph and after a fleeting glance tried to recall the name of his form teacher sitting in the middle of the front row, but for the life of him nothing came to mind. It was fully occupied with thoughts of Kitty. Had she entertained him during their journey because she was attracted to him, or had he been an easy target to offload her problems about her life with an abusive husband and uncaring parents? Knowing she would be returning to her husband as soon as she received word to say he would be home, the likelihood of him ever seeing her again seemed pretty slim, yet for some reason he didn't feel troubled. Instead he felt quite the opposite; a feeling of excitement flowed through his body, he was so convinced that in the not too distant future he would play a major role in her life doing all he could to improve her unhappy situation. He lay still, his spirits soared, only to be broken when his mam called from the bottom of the stairs.

'Tea's ready, Tom.'

Reluctantly he rose from the bed, grabbed suitable clothing to wear around the farm and made his way downstairs to join her before heading off across the farmyard to the all too familiar sounds and smells of the farming life that flows through his veins.

Chapter Nine

Connie checked the time on the alarm clock by the bed. It read 6.45 a.m. Not wanting to disturb her guests with the noise of the clanking metal bells which were timed to ring at 7.00 a.m. and were loud enough to waken an entire household, she stretched across and slid the on/off button to the off positive before gently nudging Malcolm to waken him.

'Wakey wakey, Malcolm. Nearly time for you to get up for work,' she said tugging at the bedcovers. 'It's Friday morning so you've only today to work then we have the weekend to look forward to with Kitty and the bairns.'

Slowly his head appeared from beneath the covers as he tried to make sense of what his wife was saying. 'I think I'm going deaf, Connie, I never heard the alarm go off and what's that you're saying, something about the weekend? Oh I don't know I hardly caught a word of what you said.'

'Don't be silly, Malcolm, you're not going deaf. The reason you didn't hear the alarm is because I switched it off before it had chance to ring. I didn't want it to waken Kitty and the bairns as they were all quite late to bed last night and will probably want to sleep a little later than usual.'

'Do you know, Connie, for a minute I'd forgotten about them being here? I slept so soundly last night it's going to take some time for me to return to the land of the living.'

'Well you better give yourself a good shake because I was trying to tell you it's Friday and... are you listening to me, Malcolm?' she snapped at him when she caught him sliding back under the covers.

'Yes I'm listening, it's just I seem to be exceptionally tired this morning even though I slept well.'

'Right I'll start again and make sure you are listening to me this time. It's Friday morning, so you've only today to work then we can both look forward to the weekend with our guests and you'll be pleased to hear... it's not quite time to get up so you can lie for another ten minutes to waken yourself up properly while I go down and start the breakfast.'

After giving him a peck she quickly dressed then drew back the curtains and opened the window wide allowing the crisp early morning air to drift into the room. Tiptoeing downstairs to avoid the creaking stairs she was so familiar with, she was totally unaware that her well meaning efforts were in vain. Her guests, though still in bed, were wide awake. Kitty insisted they snuggled up together in the double bed where they were quietly whispering beneath the covers about what they would like to do during their stay.

Although he was never one to leap out of bed the minute he heard the alarm, Malcolm willingly sacrificed his extra ten minutes in the hope their guests would appear before it was time to leave for work. 'Good morning, Connie,' he cheerfully greeted his wife as he took his seat at the breakfast table. 'I'm quite surprised to see you looking so fresh after the long tiring day you had yesterday. Now tell me the truth… what time did you and Kitty make it up to bed last night, or I should I say this morning as it wouldn't shock me if you had sat up talking until well after the stroke of midnight?' He had heard the hum of their constant chit-chat whilst reading his book but it hadn't been for long. Once his eyelids began to droop he closed his book, switched off the bedside lamp, and knew nothing more until Connie had woken him that morning.

A little surprised that he had suspected the two of them might sit up talking until the early hours of the morning, Connie assured him it was well before midnight when they finally decided to go to bed. 'Kitty popped up a couple of times to check on the bairns and as they were both fast asleep we decided it might be a nice idea to open a bottle of sherry seeing as we hadn't seen each other for such a long time. We talked until the fire had little more to offer than a few dying embers and it began to feel a bit chilly, it was then that we decided it was time to call it a day and head off to bed.'

'And how many glasses of sherry did you manage to have before the pair of you fell about laughing like a couple of young schoolgirls?'

'We did manage a couple of glasses each, only small ones I hasten to add, but not being used to alcohol it soon went to our heads and you're right, we did finish up in fits of laughter when reminiscing about some of the silly things we have done in the past. How we didn't waken the bairns I'll never know, but just as Kitty said, they've slept like logs. Poor things, they must have been worn out with all the excitement they had yesterday as they are still asleep.'

'I never heard a thing once I put my book down and turned the light off, but whatever you got up to, I'm pleased you had a good night without any interruptions.'

Throughout breakfast all remained very quiet upstairs and they assumed everyone was still sleeping. As Kitty had insisted they stay in bed until Malcolm left for work it resulted in Connie waving goodbye to her disappointed husband for not having seen them before he left.

'Shush a minute,' Kitty said placing her index finger over her lips. 'I think I heard the front door closing, but don't get too excited it might just be Aunty Connie collecting the milk from the doorstep.' She crept out of bed and crossed to the window where she spotted Malcolm heading towards the bus stop. 'Okay you can get up now, it was Uncle Malcolm leaving for work.' They didn't need telling twice, and within seconds they were out of bed and Annie had the bedroom door wide open. Not wanting to keep them tied upstairs any longer, she watched nervously from the top of the stairs after agreeing Annie could take Jack down if she was very careful.

Giggling, they made their way hand in hand to the kitchen where Connie was busy working and when Annie popped her head around the door shouting 'Boo' she acted completely surprised.

'It's just me and Jack, Aunty Connie. Did we frighten you'?

'Oh you did give me such a shock,' she said placing her hands across her chest in pretence. 'I was just thinking what a right pair of sleepyheads you were and here you are out of bed and full of the joys of spring.'

'Sleepyheads they certainly are not,' Kitty interrupted. 'They've both been awake for ages.'

'So you must be the one who didn't want to get out of bed this morning and I'm accusing the bairns.' She smirked though she wouldn't have blamed her considering the unearthly hour they had gone to bed last night.

'You really don't think for one minute that they would let me sleep once they have opened their eyes? They've been wide awake for ages but I warned them last night that they were to stay in bed and be very quiet until Uncle Malcolm had left for work.'

'Well we never heard as much as a squeak out of anyone and assumed you were all still fast asleep.'

'There's no chance of that ever happening and I'm sure Malcolm would prefer to enjoy his breakfast in peace especially when he is going to work so I'm not going to allow them to come down early. Believe me, you can do without these two lively monkeys bothering you in the mornings.'

'Listen, Kitty, there's nothing Malcolm would have enjoyed more this morning than to have seen the bairns before he left. I know he was a little disappointed that he hadn't, so in future don't stop them; let them come downstairs if they want to. We want to see them enjoying their freedom while they're here not spending it cooped up upstairs in the bedroom and think about it, there are no dangerous steps or steep staircases here where you need to keep an eye on them twenty-four hours a day. You have to agree, Kitty, they're fairly safe here so it's very unlikely either of them will to come to any harm.'

'You're probably right but I won't have them running around and upsetting you by getting under your feet, especially Malcolm's when he has to leave on time to catch the bus.'

'You don't need to worry about that, it's always the same people who take the early morning bus and it never leaves until they're sure all the regulars have made it. It's not like town and city transport in the morning rush hour where, if you're not there on time you've missed it because they have to run to a strict timetable and won't wait for latecomers.'

'Okay, I give in, but I won't let them get away with murder while they're here. They must learn how to behave properly and have respect for other people's property.'

'Oh you are such an old fusspot, Kitty. Just look at them, they are very well behaved,' she said drawing them into her arms. 'Now let's see about getting them some breakfast, they must be starving by now.'

Feeling refreshed as the cool morning breeze brushed against his face, Malcolm made his way to the bus stop still feeling disappointed he hadn't seen the bairns. After joining his father-in-law who was already amongst the queue of regular morning commuters setting off to their various workplaces, together they boarded the bus and made their way to the rear seats. As they passed the seated passengers they offered a friendly 'good morning' to most, but to the couple of 'I hate mornings' people who they knew better than to risk speaking to, they acknowledged them with a simple nod of the head.

Meanwhile back at Rose Cottage Kitty had opened the door leading to the garden; something she was never able to do at home. If she were ever to risk it and turned her back for a second, the bairns could be out of the door in a flash and the possible consequences too shocking to bear thinking about. Whilst preparing breakfast she politely stressed to Connie, who had already put the kettle on to boil, re-laid the table and poured milk into cups, that she didn't want her running around after them. 'This isn't a hotel,' she said, 'and I don't intend to treat it as one. We're not here to be waited on and I don't want you tiring yourself out when you're not used to having two active bairns running around all day.'

'Listen, you're not here for long, Kitty and we asked you to come so we could help you with the bairns particularly in the mornings. I'm only working a few hours a week for Mrs Parkinson so it's not like I'm working my fingers to the bone and I remember how badly you suffered morning sickness during the early stages of your first two pregnancies. Don't forget you have two bairns to look after this time not just one and if you don't slow down and take things easy during these early months you might finish up losing this one.'

'I'm fine, Connie, every pregnancy is different and thankfully I've hardly had any morning sickness this time

143

so I feel really well. Anyway let's forget about me for a minute, what's all this about you having a job? I don't remember you ever saying anything about going out to work.'

'Oh I must have done.' Connie frowned and shook her head unable to believe that she hadn't mentioned anything about it before today. 'You're saying I've *never* mentioned Mr and Mrs Parkinson to you?'

'Well maybe you have but I certainly don't recall the name.'

'I really find that hard to believe, but anyway Mrs Parkinson needed some extra help around the house and advertised in the village shop so I applied for the job, but that was ages ago, long before we moved into Rose Cottage. Anyway I'm only there twice a week and the bit of extra money never comes in wrong. While we were still living at Mam and Dad's we were able to put most of it to one side and it came in very handy when we moved into here.' She still looked puzzled. 'I must say, Kitty, it does seem strange to me that I haven't mentioned it to you before now, it's not like I've been keeping it a secret. Why would I when you know we tell each other everything?'

'Well, maybe you have told me and for some reason I've forgotten but I know for sure that you've never gone out to work when I have stayed here before.'

'That would be because I took the time off to spend with you when you were only here for a short stay but as you're staying for longer this time, I didn't want to let Mrs Parkinson down indefinitely. They are both getting along in years, Mrs Parkinson is quite frail now and Mr

Parkinson who is a retired chartered surveyor is very unsteady on his legs so he can't do much these days in the way of helping her. He spends most of his day sitting in his large leather armchair by the window watching the birds and other wildlife enjoying the fruits of his garden which is kept well maintained. Frank Kelly, a keen gardener, does it for them along with a couple of other gardens in the village for people who can no longer manage. Mrs Parkinson, bless her, does try to manage as best she can but finds it hard going, so being comfortably off they are more than willing to pay others to help with the work in and around the house. It makes their life a lot easier and the money comes in very handy, especially now as there are always things we are looking to change around the cottage.'

'I'm guessing they live in the village then?'

'Yes, they live in the big detached house just off the main road as you head down the hill. It sits in its own grounds behind the large wooden gates. I'm sure you'll know where I mean, we pass it on the bus as it comes into the village. It's really handy for me and it only takes me five minutes or so to walk there and this week seeing as I've already worked Monday and Wednesday I don't need to go again until after the weekend…. I'll maybe go in on Monday if you're nicely settled in by then, we'll see.'

'Well after hearing that news, I guess you'll have to agree with me; I think you have more than enough work to do and believe me, Connie, just being here is relaxing itself. I don't have to plan meals or clean rooms as much as I do at home so let's not fall out over me wanting to do my little bit to help out. You can see I'm feeling really well this time and being pregnant isn't an illness, life carries on as normal, and just you watch, in a couple of days or so, you'll find Annie is wanting to help as well. Once she has got used to everyone, she'll be there busying herself like she does at home. She loves playing at being mother and tidying up especially after Jack, she's such an old fashioned little thing and I hate to admit it but I rather fancy she's going to take after me.'

'I was just about to say I know where she gets it from,' Connie responded with a smile. 'With three women in one house, umm… well I guess I'm going to have to give in this time, and seeing as we've never had a major disagreement in all the years we've been friends I don't think we should start now!'

'You're right we haven't and not many friends can say that. It's what makes our friendship extra special.'

'That's settled then so after breakfast seeing it's such a beautiful morning the first thing we'll do is get the bairns dressed so they can go outside to play. We'll let them get Snowball out for a while and let the hens out, then maybe, just maybe, I'll let Annie collect the eggs, though that might have to be open for discussion. Once I've finished tidying through we'll take them for a little walk around the village, then we'll pop in and see Mam for a quick cuppa. That's if she hasn't turned up here first!'

'Excuse me, after who's tidied up? Haven't we just come to an agreement?' Kitty shook her head, raising her eyebrows in disbelief. 'There is just one thing I would like to do before we go out, if you could you spare me a couple of sheets of writing paper and a couple of envelopes. I promised to let Peggy and Jean know straightaway that we arrived safe and after all the carry on we had with the suitcase yesterday morning, Peggy will be desperate to hear if it survived the journey in one piece.'

'I bet she is having seen it for myself, and you must keep your promise, especially to Peggy. I don't know her that well but I know she will worry until she hears from you as she does seem to cherish you and the bairns like you were her own flesh and blood.'

'She does love us bless her, and I know she won't settle until she knows we have arrived safe and sound.'

'I'll pop the writing pad and envelopes on the table for you, and when you're ready I'll entertain the bairns in the garden so you can sit down and write without them interrupting.'

'Thanks, Connie, but I'll just be writing them a few short lines so you don't need to worry about the bairns. They'll be fine on their own for a little while if you want to be getting on with something else.'

Breakfast over and cleared away, beds made and everything in its place, Connie, as she said she would, took the bairns into the garden while Kitty sat down quietly to write her letters. She debated whether she should write to Ernie at the same time but after reasoning that he probably wouldn't be that concerned about them it didn't take her long to decide against it. Any correspondence to him would be better left until later in their holiday.

She began by writing Connie's address at the top of

the sheet of blue unlined writing paper. Starting with Peggy's letter, as on this occasion it would be shorter than Jean's, she said how happy she was to see everyone again but very little about the journey other than how people had been more than willing to offer a helping hand. After telling her briefly about the bairns and their new furry friend, she thanked her for all the help she had given her yesterday, assuring her that the suitcase survived the journey intact and again promising that she would one day repay her for her kindness. She concluded her letter by saying she would be grateful if she would pass Jean's letter on to her as it would save money on postage, and promised to write again to let her know how they were and what they had been up to.

She pondered for a while over Jean's letter wondering just how much she should tell her about her journey with Tom. How he had deliberately used Annie as an excuse to get to know her better and how both the bairns had taken to him as though they had known him for years. Then of course the biggest surprise of all, that as he lived just a couple of miles from Connie and Malcolm and there was every chance she might see him again.

'Oh stop being so stupid for heaven's sake,' she reprimanded herself. 'What on earth do you think she's going to read into it?' Still hesitant, she realised that she was the one who was reading too much into the events of yesterday and she only needed to tell her what a good help the soldiers had been. Eventually she put pen to paper, saying very little about Tom other than that he lives on a farm nearby and has invited the bairns over for a visit. Finally she asked again if she would keep an eye on Peggy as she was worried she might feel lonely in the big house all on her own. Folding the letter in half she placed it inside an envelope, sealed it and wrote her name on the front. Along with Peggy's letter she placed them into a second envelope and addressed it to 'Hazeldene'. With the letters ready for posting all that was needed was a stamp which she could buy from the village Post Office while they were out walking.

The Post Office and general store is tucked away in a quiet corner overlooking the village green but can quite easily go unnoticed. For that reason, several years ago a meeting of the parish council agreed that it should be signposted at both ends of the village, in order that passing traffic might bring extra business for the owner Gwen Chapman.

Gwen, a spinster now in her early sixties is often referred to as Postie Gwen, there being another lady of the same name living nearby. She has run her business for many years mainly single handed, bringing her experience of the postal service from her younger days to a much needed service in the village. Her hard work is much appreciated by the residents of Calderthwaite and surrounding villages who regularly use the store, not only for essentials but as a place where they can catch up on a bit of local gossip. An active member of the 12th Century St. Mary's Church, Gwen is the regular organist, still teaches at Sunday school and is a member of the Women's Institute which holds its meetings in a tiny wooden purpose-built hut close to the church. The reason she never married, she would tell everyone, was because she could never find the time for boys, and if she had married, her husband would hardly ever see her as she is always so busy. Totally dedicated to serving the small community; she is spoken of very highly for her endless commitment to please others.

It was Gwen who, when Connie's family first moved into the village and were finding it hard to feel part of the community, took it on herself to make sure they were soon made welcome and it wasn't long before they were all participating in village activities. Connie and Kath joined the Women's Institute and help out with the events in the village. Connie willingly turns her hand wherever help is needed and kindly volunteered to alter a pair of large thick brocade curtains which were donated for the WI hut when the old ones were looking well past their best. George attempted bell ringing but much to his disappointment was unable to master it, but still helps out where he can, while Malcolm contributes to the village by volunteering to keep it free of litter after the previous elderly gentleman found it a little too much for him. With the entire family active volunteers in the village, they have found life in Calderthwaite so friendly and peaceful that none of them have ever regretted their move from the city.

Staring blankly at the address she had written on the envelope, which of course is the same as her own apart from Flat A and Flat B; Kitty began imagining an envelope addressed to Mr and Mrs E Cartwright, The Green, Calderthwaite, but she knows that a family move to the village for them is completely out of the question. Country life would never appeal to Ernie, particularly with only one public house in the village which only opened when it suited the landlord, and without his regular boozy pals to join him, it would soon drive him back to the city.

Outside Connie lifted Snowball from his hutch and as she watched the bairns playing with him she recalled some of the promises she and Kitty had made to each other during their teenage years. They vowed they would remain lifelong friends and live near each another when they married so they could raise their children to become firm friends like themselves. Saddened not only by the fact it hadn't worked out that way, Connie often wondered what kind of life Kitty really had with Ernie. She had a vague idea that he treated her badly at times, and believed it was the one thing Kitty kept close to her chest. If that was the case, Malcolm would tell her then there was nothing she could do about it. If Kitty wanted her to know then she would only tell her in her own time.

'How much longer will Mammy be?' Annie interrupted her thoughts.

'She shouldn't be long now, pet, and as soon as she has finished writing her letters we'll pop out to post them, then we'll go for a little walk so I think we'd better put Snowball back into his hutch and start getting ready.'

'Alright,' she said seeming happy enough on this occasion to hand him back to Connie.

Comparing her life to Kitty's, the only possessions Connie envies her for is of course Annie and Jack.

Married longer than Kitty and still without a young family saddens her, but she lives in hope that one day she too will be the proud mother of a son or daughter.

While getting Annie and Jack ready for their walk, she refuses to allow her own disappointment to spoil their time together and is determined to enjoy every minute she can with them, making sure when they leave Calderthwaite, they will have lots of happy memories to take away with them.

Chapter Ten

By Sunday evening both families decided to retire early having spent a fun packed weekend outside in the fresh air. The highlight for Annie and Jack had been a trip into the nearby woods which they accessed through a gate at the bottom of the garden. The narrow stream which flowed through the undergrowth was carefully crossed by means of a few strategically placed stepping stones leading them on to a path that led directly into the woods. Annie was spellbound by the density of the woodland with its carpet of spring flowers and trees of all shapes and sizes with enormous protruding roots which she said looked like giant's fingers crawling out of the ground. Jack, being so much younger, and much to the amusement of the adults, wasn't impressed by the beauty of nature preferring to play hide and seek amongst the vast number of huge tree trunks.

Their first weekend passed quickly and as she lay snuggled up in bed with her beloved bairns Kitty could hardly believe it was Monday morning already. It seemed like it was only yesterday when they arrived and she realised how quickly the days would pass. Leaping out of her comfy bed she drew back the curtains, flung the window open to embrace the beautiful morning and, inhaling the cool spring air, filled her lungs until they felt they were about to burst. As the sun rose in an almost cloudless sky the early morning chorus could be heard high up in the treetops. May blossom already out in full bloom trickled to the ground like snowflakes as it floated on the gentle breeze, and everywhere she looked an abundance of spring flowers produced a glorious display of nature's colours. Gazing out of the window she was captivated by the beautiful panoramic view; a picture postcard scene of the village and the surrounding countryside stretching far into the distance. With warmer weather and longer days to look forward to her spirits soared to an almost record high. She hadn't felt this happy in a long time and like a young teenager she bounced onto the bed wrapping her arms around Annie and Jack. She held them close hoping they could sense the happiness that enveloped her entire being but unfortunately they had other ideas. Confident in their new surroundings, wide awake and bursting with energy they wanted to be up and running around with the result all three were soon out of bed, dressed and looking forward to another exciting day.

Downstairs Connie was preparing to go to work as she had suggested she may do. Her guests were nicely settled in and as Kitty intended to do some washing that morning she thought it would be better if she was out of her way so she had the kitchen to herself. To her amusement, Kitty had expressed how excited she was to be able to hang her washing out in the garden rather than in the small enclosed yard at home. The relief at not having to tread cautiously up and down a flight of concrete steps, risking life and limb with two bairns, and a basket full of washing to the yard below had her feeling

154

naturally overwhelmed as sadly, the last time she had experienced what now seemed to be a luxury was whilst still unmarried and living at home with her parents. Connie understood how Kitty must be feeling having always had the good fortune of living in a house with a garden and how happy she must be seeing how much Annie and Jack were enjoying their freedom to run around outdoors.

'Just look how much those two are loving being outside, Kitty, so I suggest as soon as you get home you go and put your name on the council list for a house with a garden on one of the nice new estates.'

'I have already considered it, Connie. I know with three bairns to look after it will be almost impossible to manage in the flat and I intend to discuss it with Ernie when he's next at home.'

Home was the last thing she wanted to be thinking about right now with so many reasons to feel happy and relaxed and after Connie left for work she was tempted to dance up and down the garden path with the bairns, but abandoned the idea fearing the neighbours might see her. Refusing Connie's kind offer to use her new electric washing machine, whilst hand washing at the kitchen sink memories of her younger days when she lived at home with her parents and sister came flooding back. Instantly her mood changed; they weren't all happy memories and she felt agitated. Numerous times she had wished they had accepted Ernie as their son-in-law then Annie and Jack would not be deprived of grandparents. For a brief moment she felt downhearted, but quickly brushed away her negative thoughts knowing there was no point dwelling on something she knew she could never change. Knowing that her bairns were happy and healthy was the most important thing in her life and the last thing she wanted was for them ever to see her looking sad. With the washing finished, it wasn't long before it was hung on the line swaying in the breeze, and she was back in the kitchen preparing a light lunch. Sandwiches and drinks were enjoyed in the garden under the warmth of the late morning sun then it was a quick dash upstairs to tidy up leaving her just enough time for a short walk before Connie would be due home from work.

They raced each other up to the bedroom, and by letting the bairns win they made an instant dash for the camp bed beneath the open window. Annie seemed to be full of mischief, and putting her finger to her lips she indicated to Jack to keep quiet. When she knew her mammy wasn't looking, she placed her hands on the windowsill, stood on her tiptoes and hauled herself up, leaving Jack looking at her in utter amazement.

'Mammy, Mammy look what Annie's doing,' he shouted.

'Shush, Jack, don't tell.' But of course it was too late. Kitty turned round instantly and was shocked to see her climbing on to the sill. Her heart skipped a beat, and the colour drained from her face as she watched her succeed before she had time to reach her.

'Annie, come down from there this minute,' she yelled at her, terrified she would fall through the open window. Shuffling about for a comfortable position she showed no sign of fear and completely ignored Kitty's command, not even attempting to turn around as she clung on to the window frame with one hand then with the other began waving excitedly to someone outside. Kitty assumed it must be Connie returning home a little earlier than expected, but she was soon to learn she was wrong. Before there was time to grab hold of her, Annie had already enlightened her.

'It's Tom, Mammy, its Tom,' she said gasping for breath through her excitement. 'He's coming to see us, look, Jack, it really is Tom.' Unable to see out of the window he raised his arms for Kitty to lift him up so he could see for himself.

'Don't be so silly, Annie, it can't possibly be Tom,' she snapped at her sharply, while taking Jack into her arms and grabbing hold of her at the same time.

'It is him, Mammy, I know it is.' Her voice sounded almost defiant, and her expression was of disbelief that her mammy would doubt her and she began banging on the glass.

'Stop it, Annie, stop that right this minute, you'll break the glass and cut your hand.' But all she did was tap more gently as she continued trying to attract his attention.

Pulling the camp bed to one side in order to reach far enough out Kitty closed the window, sat Jack next to Annie on the window sill then plucked up the courage to have a proper look herself. Sure enough there was Tom pushing his bike across the green in the direction of the cottage. When he was close enough to hear Annie's tapping he glanced up at the window and was shocked to see them both sitting with broad smiles on their faces and immediately he began waving to them.

By this time, Jack was also excited having recognised Tom and like Annie his expression was priceless. Kitty was completely taken aback by their reactions as she hadn't seen them acting so excited in a long time, not even when their Daddy returned home. How they had become so fond of Tom in such a short time was beyond her and she could only put it down to the time he spent with them during the journey, and of course his promise to take them to visit the farm.

'For goodness' sake will you two settle down,' she said crossly as she lifted them from the sill on to the bed. Struggling to compose herself she couldn't resist having another fleeting glance from a position where she knew Tom wouldn't be able to see her. She stared at him in disbelief as his pace quickened. Her emotions now in utter turmoil, her heart rate increased, her head spun, and she felt as though she was losing control. 'Stop being so stupid,' her inner voice screamed at her as she watched him getting closer and knowing Connie had invited him she had no choice, she must go down and invite him in.

Dressed in the latest fashion of denim jeans and an open neck blue and red checked shirt he was even more handsome and broader set than she had remembered. Moving away from the window fearing he may catch a glimpse of her watching him, she glanced at herself in the mirror. Shocked by her dishevelled appearance she quickly began to smarten herself up. Lifting her skirt she tugged at her petticoat then tucked her blouse inside in an effort to emphasise her still slim figure. Unfortunately it felt a little uncomfortable due to her slightly expanded waistline, giving her a sharp reminder that she was pregnant which, through all the excitement she seemed to keep forgetting.

Taking a sideways look in the mirror, she stroked her hands over her slightly swollen abdomen and immediately pulled her blouse outside of her skirt for comfort. Untying her hair, she took a brush through it and let it fall loose to her shoulders. It had been her intention to look her best when she knew they were to meet again, and she was disappointed that he had caught her unawares by arriving days earlier than anyone expected. To make matters even worse, calling when Connie wasn't home to welcome him further unsettled her. She had butterflies in her stomach and debated over the best way to greet him so as not to appear pleased to see him. Perspiring slightly, she grabbed her nightdress from the bed using it to wipe away the sweat that began to trickle down her brow, then taking Jack in her arms with Annie following close by she was just about to make her way to the top of the stairs, but paused again to check her appearance. Her mind was working overtime; she was unsure what she should say to him, and after taking a long deep breath braced herself for what was about to take place. Steadily they made their way downstairs and the second the door was even barely ajar Annie was squeezing her way through the narrow gap repeatedly calling Tom's name. Very warily she opened the door wider coming face to face with her admirer who was standing only a few feet away. Tom's handsome good looks and charismatic smile brought back memories of when she first set eyes on Ernie, who, at that time she swore was the most handsome man she would ever meet. Today, directly before her stood his equal rival. She knew instantly this wasn't a good idea, but with Annie already pulling at his hand, she knew she couldn't refuse him entry. Having been officially invited to Rose Cottage, she knew had Connie been at home she would have welcomed him in with open arms, oblivious to the real reason for his visit and where he hoped it would lead.

'Now what have you all been up to since I last saw you?' Tom asked Annie with a smile, whilst gently cuffing Jack on the chin. 'And your lovely mammy…. How are you?' he asked, turning to Kitty. 'It's nice to see you again.'

'And you, Tom, but you have taken me completely by surprise so you'll have to excuse my appearance. I've been busy washing most of the morning and wasn't expecting visitors. Had I been, I would have dressed more appropriately. Feeling uneasy she tugged at her blouse and ran her fingers nervously through her neatly brushed hair, unsure whether it was the shock of his unexpected arrival or her guilt at feeling she would have liked him to take her in his arms?

'Is Tom coming in, Mammy?' Annie interrupted her thoughts. Completely love-struck by the handsome stranger she had met only days earlier, she remained silent and made no attempt to move towards him or invite him in. Annie looked puzzled, and glancing up from one to the other she asked, 'Mammy, why isn't Tom coming in?'

Her voice expressed utter disappointment that he had been left standing on the doorstep.

'Oh I'm really sorry, Tom.' Kitty finally found her voice again and gestured for him to enter. 'Connie's out at the minute but as she did invite you over I had better ask you in. She'll be home anytime now so you won't have long to wait to see her again.'

He knew Kitty was well aware who he had really come to see and as he stepped indoors close enough to slide his arm around her waist he whispered, 'You look perfect to me, Kitty,' but not wanting to overstep the mark so soon, he turned his attention to Annie who was still slightly puzzled by her mammy's actions.

'So are you going to tell me what you and Jack have been up to since I last saw you, and…'

'We've got something really special to show you, Tom.' He hadn't finished his sentence before in her excitement Annie was dragging him through the living room and out into the garden to show him Snowball, leaving a dumbfounded Kitty trailing behind with Jack still in her arms. Finding it hard to take everything in, especially the motive behind Tom's earlier-than-expected visit, she held Jack securely in her arms afraid to let go of him as though he was shielding her in some way. He had other ideas though and was wrestling with her to be put down so he could run outside and join in the fun. On reaching the back door she paused for a while observing Annie and Tom until finally giving in to Jack so he could toddle off to join them. With Snowball already out of his hutch Annie was showing off to Tom how confidently she could handle him. Eventually making her way slowly down the garden path to join them, it went through Kitty's mind that Tom was completely unaware that his life was about to be taken over by two very lively bairns. If, as she suspected the real motive behind his visit was to be with her, then he was going to be bitterly disappointed!

'While you're busy entertaining or perhaps should I say being entertained by the bairns I'll just pop back upstairs and finish the job I was doing when you arrived. It will only take me a few minutes and I'll be straight back and make us a nice pot of tea.'

'There's no need for you to go rushing around, Kitty. I have all day and I'm sure the kids won't mind if you're missing for a while, it seems they have lots to tell me so they probably won't even notice you've gone.'

'You're probably right,' she agreed, then left them to it and made her way back upstairs. Her thoughts turned to what he might have told his family that morning before he left, but on entering the bedroom she seemed to not have a care in the world and once again bounced on to the bed like a young teenager experiencing her first crush. With her pregnancy the last thing on her mind she wrapped her arms around her body squeezing herself tightly indicating the joy she was experiencing, but wondered what the real reason was for her unprecedented behaviour. Was it the joy of spending time in Calderthwaite with her lifelong friend, or could it have more to do with seeing Tom again? It was probably both she convinced herself as she lay there for a few minutes relishing the moment. She hadn't felt like this in years, yet deep down she knew that it wouldn't last.

'If only my life could be more like Connie's, how much happier I would be but I know it will never change. If only Ernie was still the same as the day I married him. If only Mam and Dad would welcome me back home with open arms. If only... if only, with so many if onlys I can't ever imagine my life being as contented as Connie's.' Comparing her life to Connie's seemed wrong. She had chosen to marry Ernie against her parents' wishes and, annoyed with herself, she leapt from the bed to finish the job she came upstairs to do. Exchanging unpleasant memories of Ernie and her acrimonious family for much happier ones of the present, she once again checked her appearance. Brushing her auburn shoulder length hair until it almost shone, she tucked it behind her ears, holding it in place with two tortoiseshell combs to reveal her attractive profile and long slender neck. Whilst straightening her clothes she reminded herself why she was here in Calderthwaite and as it certainly had nothing to do with meeting someone of the opposite sex, then why was she so concerned about her appearance? In her heart of heart she yearned for the passion of her first love to be rekindled, and would never give up on Ernie, hoping that one day he would return to his old ways, and become once again the loving, caring man she married. With that thought in mind she reprimanded herself.

'Just remember, Kitty Cartwright, not only are you a married woman but you're pregnant with your third child so no matter how flattered Tom Watson makes you feel you mustn't encourage him.' Convinced his visit was more to do with coming to see her rather than anyone else, she was determined to keep him at arm's length, even contemplating whether she should tell him about the baby thinking it could possibly be the best way to stop him in his tracks.

Arriving back in the kitchen she was surprised to find he had made himself at home, the kettle was already boiling and he was just about to lift the teacups from the cupboard.

'I've left Annie and Jack to play on their own for a while as... well I thought you looked rather tired and would be ready for a cup of tea.' He sounded a little subdued and looked down at the floor. Seconds later he raised his eyes to engage with hers before confessing, 'That's not exactly true, Kitty. I wanted to catch you on your own for a few minutes... you see... look, I know you will think this sounds stupid but I've never been in love before, in fact I'm not even sure what love is, but I haven't been able to get you out of my mind since we met and I couldn't put off any longer coming to see you. There's a dance in the village hall this Saturday night and I'd love you to join me...,' then hastily added, '...and of course to make arrangements for Annie and Jack to visit the farm.' It was obvious to them both which of the two arrangements took precedence.

Shocked and slightly embarrassed, she felt a sudden rush of blood turning her face scarlet and her palms sticky. Considering her lesson on morality moments earlier how could she even think about going with him, and as Connie and Malcolm hadn't mentioned anything

164

about a dance she assumed they weren't planning to attend and decided it would not be a good idea to mention his invitation. She knew they wouldn't agree to her going to a dance with another man, particularly in Calderthwaite where they could quite easily be implicated in the arrangement which, if Ernie ever found out could spell trouble for them. She pondered for a moment, needing to choose her words carefully.

'It goes without saying, Tom, being married, it just wouldn't be right. Connie and Malcolm, the whole family in fact would be outraged, and though this might sound quite a feeble excuse, I don't have anything to wear for a dance as that's the last place I would have expected to be going during my visit. As a matter of interest I couldn't tell you the last time I went to a dance, it was certainly long before Annie was born, so I'm sorry, Tom, it is completely out of the question and once again it's a definite no.'

'You make it sound like I am asking you to commit adultery, Kitty. I'm not even asking for the two of us to go out somewhere alone, it's the village dance and we'll be surrounded by people. I'm sure you'd enjoy it especially since you say you haven't been dancing in years, and have you thought about this, maybe Connie and Malcolm have made plans to go but just haven't got around to mentioning it yet?'

'You're not listening to me, Tom, I've said no and that's final so let's just leave it at that.'

Not one to give up easily he refused to close the subject. 'I promise you, Kitty, it's always a great night.

165

You'd really enjoy it, a night out will do you good. From what you have told me about your life at home you could do with one.'

'That might be so, but the answer is still no.'

'There's even food and a bar on along with a bit of the old ballroom, always the barn dance and of course a bit of swing.' He smiled as he attempted a few dance moves and held out his arms for her to join him. It wasn't easy but she didn't allow herself to be tempted and remained firm in her resolve to keep him at a distance.

'I very much doubt if Connie and the family will be going. They would surely have mentioned something by now and I hardly think they will have arranged to go leaving me at home with the bairns when we hardly see each other. I can assure you, Tom, they are far too caring a family to do such a thing, but if by any chance they are going then I wouldn't be upset about it. It's their local dance and it must be nice for them when everyone gets together to have a good night out.'

For several minutes their eyes were transfixed, their blank expressions giving nothing away as they gazed at each other not knowing what the other was truly thinking, and completely unaware that any second now the awkward silence that had transpired was about to be broken.

'I'm home,' Connie shouted, having arrived much earlier than expected, and dashed straight through to the rear of the cottage, inquisitive to find out if she had guessed correctly who the bicycle's rightful owner would be.

'Ah, Tom, I guessed it might be you. Lovely to see you again. Have you been here long?'

'About half an hour or so I would say, I'm not sure, not much longer than that. To be honest I don't pay too much attention to time when I'm on leave, it's just so good to be home and be free to come and go as I please.'

'I'm sure it must be, but whatever has happened to you, Kitty? You're looking very pale. Are you feeling unwell or has our friendly ghost paid you a visit?' She could see Kitty was not amused. 'Don't look so frightened, Kitty. I'm only joking; we don't have a ghost!'

Connie catching them together worried her. 'Had she been in the house long enough to have heard any of their conversation?' she wondered. The very thought filled her with guilt, yet she knew she had done nothing wrong. 'If I had seen a ghost it probably wouldn't have shocked me as much as you turning up and catching us alone in the kitchen,' she thought as the colour slowly returned to her cheeks thanks to Tom who quickly stepped in to ease the situation.

'I think I'm to blame, Connie, though why she seems so shocked I don't know. All I've done is to ask her to arrange a visit to the farm and, as you probably know, the village dance is on this Saturday night, so I have asked her to join me.' He shrugged his shoulders, and held open his palms in an attempt to make his actions sound completely innocent. 'She seems completely taken aback that I've asked, and now I'm thinking it's probably not such a good idea after all.'

'Well I could tell from the colour and expression on

her face when I first walked in that something was wrong so that explains it. Mind you that's exactly the reaction I would expect from her after all being married with bairns, and I have known her long enough now to know that since the day she met and fell in love with Ernie she would always be true to him.'

'Err excuse me,' Kitty butted in quite abruptly. Discussing her as though she wasn't in the same room annoyed her. 'If you wouldn't mind letting me get a word in, I'll do some explaining. You're right, Connie, I was naturally shocked because I would never have expected to be invited to a dance and especially not by another man, and besides I didn't even...' but before she could say another word Connie interrupted her.

'I really must stop you there, Kitty, so I can let you both into our little secret. Malcolm and I have already bought three tickets for the dance on Saturday night and we have everything arranged for Mam and Dad to babysit. We kept it as a nice surprise until the weekend was over but seeing as Tom has asked to take you as well, there is no point in keeping it quiet any longer.' Looking grim faced and sounding very serious she turned directly to Tom. 'Well by a rather strange coincidence, it looks like you are going to get your wish after all but there is just one other thing you need to know...,' she hesitated intentionally to keep them both in suspense, '...I'm really sorry, Tom, but you're going to have to buy your own ticket.'

Chuckling as she said it, her sense of humour gave Kitty some light relief which brought a welcome smile to her face. Though still reeling from the unexpected events of the past hour or so which had completely bewildered her, she tried her best to relax and to appreciate that everyone was doing their utmost to make her stay a memorable one.

'Well that's good news, Kitty. I'll be seeing you at the dance after all.' Tom's voice sounded almost cock-a-hoop, having got his wish in spite of her turning down his invitation, and of course being very grateful to Connie who without her realising it, had just made his day.

'There is just one other thing, Tom. I don't advise you to call here first, you know what village gossip is like. We don't want anyone accusing you of going out with a married woman or even worse, thinking Kitty is behaving like a single woman when in fact she has already exchanged her marriage vows with Ernie.'

Kitty listened with bated breath as they again conversed as though she wasn't present. Everything it seemed was going in Tom's favour and she couldn't believe how Connie was being a little controlling, even she thought, overdramatic to say the least. For her to mention marriage vows when she knew Ernie's commitment to her and the bairns sadly left a little to be desired surprised her. She was, she thought, going a little overboard, and it made her wonder if she suspected what Tom was up to and it was her way of warning him off. She couldn't be sure but one thing was certain, she was going to have to be very careful how she handled the entire situation.

'That's fine by me, Connie. We can all meet at the

dance where I'm sure we'll have a great night out but I'm thinking, it might be nice to meet Malcolm before then if that's possible?'

'Oh of course you can. You could stay and have dinner with us tonight unless of course you have already made other plans, then we can arrange it for another night. Come to think of it, it would be nice for you to meet Mam and Dad at the same time so why don't we arrange dinner here say on Wednesday night which will give me time to plan a nice meal. I've promised Mrs Parkinson I will go in to work on Thursday to help her prepare a meal for friends she has visiting that evening so Thursday night is out of the question and I don't want to have to ask Mam to come over to help. It will be nice for her to sit down and have a meal served to her for a change.'

'Any night is fine by me, Connie, it's what's best for you. But let's not forget about Annie and Jack; they've already been asking about going to the farm they're so excited about it.'

'Oh don't you worry about the bairns, Tom.' Kitty reassured him they could find lots of things to keep them occupied. 'We are nearly sure to be here for another week or so, so there is plenty of time for them to visit before we go home.'

She was concerned what Tom's parents would think about him taking a married woman and her young family to the farm having only just met them a few days earlier and asked him, 'Have you mentioned anything to your parents about us going to the farm?'

'Yes the day I arrived home, over dinner I told them all

170

about us meeting at the railway station and Bernie and me helping with your luggage. Mam was fascinated when I said you were visiting a friend in Calderthwaite, and she thought it was very nice of Connie to invite me over to meet the family, and now my family are looking forward to meeting you all.'

'Okay, as long as I know they don't mind and we won't be in the way,' Kitty said sounding a little more cheerful though still unconvinced that the plans they were making were a good idea.

'I'll leave you two for a few minutes while I pop upstairs and change, then over a nice cup of tea we can make arrangements when it would be best for us to visit.' Connie was eager as always to have plans in place, and disappeared out of the kitchen only to return seconds later. 'By the way, Tom, in case I forget to mention it, dinner will be around six-thirty on Wednesday,' then she quickly vanished again much to Kitty's relief. Hopefully she hadn't spotted Tom winking at her as he made his move towards her the minute she left the room.

Alone again he was hell bent on making sure she knew he wasn't going to give up easily. Sidling close enough to caress her face he whispered, 'I can't help how I feel about you, Kitty, and it's not as though I'm a young teenager having a stupid crush on you. I still say we were destined to meet and I'm sure you feel the same about us but you won't admit it!'

'Stop all this stupid nonsense right now and don't you dare refer to us as though we were about to become a couple,' she snapped at him, pushing him aside and

171

shaking her index finger at him. She was beginning to think he seriously believed they had a future together.

'Stop what?' he responded abruptly, his expression like that of an innocent child who never said anything wrong written all over his face.

'You know exactly what. Stop talking about *us* like that, Tom and... well I'm sure you didn't need Connie to remind you that I happen to be married with two bairns.' Again she avoided mentioning the child she was carrying. 'Anything even bordering on romance is out of the question between us. I'll be going home to Ernie in a couple of weeks and who knows, it could be a few years before I return to Calderthwaite.' Turning her back on him fearing Connie's return she tried her best to ignore him and began making the pot of tea. She was desperate to get him out of the kitchen and asked him to go and see what Annie and Jack would like to drink.

All this stupid talk was getting too much for her. Determined once and for all to nip it in the bud before he foolishly started thinking he could take things between them a stage further, she needed a few moments alone. Connie would be back any minute and the conversation would return to making more arrangements which included him. Why, she wondered, when there were so many single girls out there who she was sure would love to date him, was he wasting his time on her?

She began to shake. Had she brought all this upon herself by being too open with him? Trying to recall some of their conversation had she, she wondered, given him reason to believe that one day she might leave Ernie?

172

Surely not! She'd soon have three bairns to him and despite their problems and the lack of passion they had shared in the early years, as far as she was concerned her marriage was far from over and Tom needed to be made aware of it.

Making him understand wasn't going to be easy and with the dance just a few days away her hopes weren't high. Her gut reaction was that he'd be determined to get her on to the dance floor, the only place he knew he could hold her in his arms.

'Will I have the courage to refuse him or will his irresistible charm be too intoxicating for me to say no?' Admiring his fine physique as she secretly watched him make his way down the garden she had a good idea what her answer would be.

Chapter Eleven

By evening Kitty was feeling mentally and physically exhausted and took the bairns up to bed a little earlier than usual. Once they were asleep she joined Connie and Malcolm around the roaring fire where, desperately in need of a catnap, she curled up on the sofa leaving Connie to enlighten Malcolm about the unexpected events of the day. He was pleased to hear she had invited Tom to dinner on Wednesday after having heard so much about him and was looking forward to putting a face to the name of the local lad who so kindly assisted Kitty during her journey.

'I wonder if he'll be going to the dance on Saturday.'

'Oh he's going alright!'

'You sound very sure of yourself. Has he said he is?'

'You're not going to believe this, Malcolm, but he has actually asked Kitty to go with him. Isn't that right, Kitty?' she asked but got no response. 'She's not listening to us, Malcolm, I suspect she's so worn out she's just having a little rest. It's been quite a tiring day for her what with the amount of washing she did, the unexpected visit from Tom and then the shock of him asking to take her to the dance.' She lowered her voice to an almost whisper just in case Kitty was able to catch what they were saying. 'I think the shock of Tom's invite knocked her sideways, and I must admit when I heard about it even I thought it was rather strange, but to be honest I don't think he's flirting with her. I really believe he's just such a nice lad who mustn't have a girl to take and thought it would be nice to invite her as they seem to have struck up a bit of a friendship. I'm sure it's all perfectly innocent and of course I had to let them both know that we were going and that's the reason I arranged for you to meet him before we go.'

'Well we had intended to let Kitty into our little secret tonight so nothing's been spoilt, but I do feel a little bit like you…. I find it strange that he would ask to take Kitty when he hardly knows her and obviously knows she's married. Ah well, never mind, the more the merrier they say.' Not knowing anything about him he was prepared to wait until he met him before forming an opinion but his unspoken guess was that he had an eye for Kitty. 'If he has I can't say I blame him,' he thought. 'Men have always been attracted to her, but he'll be wasting his time if he thinks he has any chance with Kitty, she has always been faithful to Ernie.'

Back in the land of the living, Kitty planned to spend the rest of the evening listening to music and hopefully having a game of cards but it turned out Connie had other ideas. Lifting her sewing basket and a large brown paper bag from the sideboard Connie carried them across to her treadle sewing machine, one of her most precious possessions. The green hand painted clay plant pot containing a beautiful deep pink geranium atop a cream crocheted doily was removed and placed next to the table lamp and a framed photograph of their wedding on a

175

small occasional table. Feeling excited she opened the extending table top and lifted the machine from underneath, finally removing the contents of the paper bag. Her movements had gone completely unnoticed by Kitty who had seized the opportunity to glance at the daily newspaper before Malcolm set about tackling the crossword. With her head in the pages of the newspaper she was in a world of her own and had no idea what was going on around her until Connie, after several attempts finally managed to gain her attention.

'Kitty would you like to come and see what I'm busy making?'

'I'll be with you in a second,' she answered and finished the article she was reading before handing the paper to Malcolm who was sitting patiently in his armchair rolling his pen between his fingers in readiness to do the crossword. From the other side of the room Connie gave him a wink. They were both anticipating Kitty's reaction as she was about to be pleasantly surprised.

Before Kitty arrived, Connie and her mam shopped for a pattern and fabric which Connie was to turn into a beautiful dress; a special treat for Kitty to wear to the dance. They had chosen cotton fabric with red cherries on a white background and Connie had already done quite a lot of work on it. Although clothes rationing had ended, the family thought it highly unlikely that Kitty would have brought with her a dress that she would feel happy to wear for such an occasion, and between them the family agreed a new dress would be a well deserved luxury for her. It had been a unanimous decision knowing how hard Kitty worked bringing up the bairns mainly single handed for weeks on end. A night out dancing wearing a beautiful new dress would be a deserving treat; something she rarely experienced these days being a busy mother with a husband who never appeared to treat her to anything.

Eager to see what Connie was making knowing what a wonderful dressmaker she is, Kitty jumped up and joined her. Not for a minute would she ever have imagined the surprise that awaited her. Her eyes lit up when she saw the unfinished dress and she gently stroked the fabric while at the same time admiring the style shown on the front of the Simplicity Pattern. The sleeveless bodice had a slash neck and was attached to a fully gathered knee length skirt and accessorised with an optional two inch wide elastic belt with metal fastener and a net underskirt. Handling the fabric as though it was pure silk or a priceless piece of china which she would never own in her lifetime, she picked up the bodice and brushed it gently across her cheek. Not having a jealous bone in her body and naturally assuming that Connie was making the dress for herself, she pictured in her mind's eye how beautiful she would look when suddenly it occurred to her that she hadn't brought anything suitable to wear to a dance. She brushed the thought aside not wanting to trouble Connie with the problem when she was so busy working on her own dress.

'Oh, Connie, I love it. You'll look absolutely gorgeous and I'm guessing you'll want to get it finished in time for the dance on Saturday night?"

'That's my intention but it needs a fitting before I can do any more to it.' Taking the unfinished bodice from her she explained, 'As you can see I've only tacked the side seams as I need to be sure it fits properly before I machine stitch it ready to attach to the skirt.'

'Would you like me to pin it for you when you try it on? I know I'm no good at sewing but I reckon I can't go far wrong sticking a few pins in.'

Connie, touched by her unselfish nature glanced across at Malcolm who appeared deep in his crossword, but was in fact listening intently to their conversation. He didn't want to miss Kitty's reaction when she learnt the truth.

'By the way on the subject of the Saturday night I hope neither of you will be disappointed if I don't make it on to the dance floor, it's that long since I went out dancing I've probably got two left feet by now.'

'You'll be on the dance floor, Kitty, we'll make sure of that. It's going to be one of the best nights out you'll have had in years. Your feet will be tapping away to the music just like all the rest of us and you'll be raring to go. It's going to be a great night and having Tom with us as well it will be just like old times when we used to get dressed up and go out to meet the lads at the dances.'

Malcolm lowered his newspaper. 'I'm listening to everything you two are saying and I'd prefer not to hear what you got up to in your early teenage years. I might learn something I would rather not know about.'

They had been very popular with the lads both in and out of school but they had been well behaved girls and it was Kitty who was sharp to respond.

Well it goes without saying my days of flirting with the opposite sex are long gone. A married woman with two bairns and another one on the way, there's no chance of anybody giving me a second glance, and as for Tom asking me to join him, well he's in for a shock if he thinks for one minute I am going to spend most of the night dancing with him. People are only too keen to pick up on a bit of gossip especially in these places and I'm certainly not having anyone thinking there is something going on between us, but I promise you both I'm going to make sure I thoroughly enjoy myself because goodness knows when the next time will be.'

She was beginning to feel a little excited about her first night out to a dance in years, but with nothing suitable to wear she decided she must share her concern with Connie.

'There's just one thing troubling me, Connie. What on earth am I going to wear? As you can imagine I've not brought anything suitable as a dance would be the last place on earth I would expect to be going. I guess I'm going to have to borrow something of yours if that's okay? Maybe even if it's just a piece of jewellery; a necklace or brooch or something that will dress up a blouse, anything that will glam it up a bit so I won't look dull and uninteresting. At the minute I'm beginning to feel a bit like Cinderella with nothing to wear to the ball and before you say it, no, you are not one of the ugly sisters!'

'Oh I'm pleased about that and you have never looked

dull in your life, Kitty. What are you talking about? With your figure and good looks you were always the first one the lads looked at when we were out, and I hardly got a look in. Now stop worrying, you know I'll be your fairy godmother and have you looking like the belle of the ball once again,' and tapped her fingers on the sewing machine as though she was thinking about what she could come up with. 'I think a new dress would be nice for the occasion rather than borrowing something of mine.'

'Now you are talking rubbish. Where am I going to get the money for a new dress? I only just managed to raise the train fare to come here so that throws your crazy idea straight out of the window. I've no choice, Connie, it has to be something from your wardrobe or my birthday suit. The choice is yours!'

'Now we are talking.' Malcolm sounded excited by the thought.

'And that's quite enough of that from you, Malcolm Ferguson. Since when did you start showing an interest in naked women?' Connie objected sharply to his unexpected response.

'I haven't but I might find myself starting to on Saturday night if Kitty's going in her birthday suit. I just hope there's not a chill in the air like tonight for your sake, Kitty.' He laughed, shook his head and returned to his crossword muttering, 'Kitty going out in her birthday suit... I've more chance of winning the football pools.'

'Well it's not going to be the birthday suit so it's got to be something from your wardrobe, Connie. All the clothes you have there's bound to be something in there that will fit me seeing as I've not put on that much weight.' She patted her tummy and looked across to Connie who nodded in agreement but didn't respond. Instead she held the bodice against herself. 'Be honest with me, Kitty. Do you really like the style and the fabric, or do you just like one and not the other?'

Again Kitty picked up the dress pattern, her eyes shifted between the pattern, the bodice and the probing expression on Connie's face.

'D'ya know what, Connie? I love the style, the fabric, everything about it. The bright red cherries stand out so boldly on the white background, and red really suits your fair complexion. I'd add the belt to finish it off just as it is on the pattern then you'll really stand out from the crowd.'

'Well that's my intention but I'm not the person who will be wearing it, Kitty. You are, so you're the one who will be standing out from the crowd. What do you think, Malcolm? I reckon we're going to have to keep our beady eyes on her. There's sure to be a few red blooded males lining up for a dance when they spot the beautiful stranger in the red and white dress.'

'What's that, Connie? Men queuing up to dance with the beautiful Kitty in her birthday suit? There'll be more than a few that's for sure.'

Kitty was dumbstruck. The colour drained from her face until she was almost as white as when Connie had caught her with Tom earlier in the day. Shock turned to embarrassment and the colour slowly returned to her cheeks. Feeling undeserving of all the kindness she had received over the past few days she wondered how she would ever be able to repay everyone. 'Surely the dress isn't for me,' she thought, 'but if she isn't kidding me and I'm going to look as nice as they say the last thing I need is male attention. It's enough trying to come to terms with Tom's constant flirting.'

'Tell me you're kidding, Connie. You have done more than enough already just having us here without doing anything else.' But from the look of pure joy on her friend's face she knew she wasn't bluffing. Momentarily lost for words and on the verge of tears she stared blankly at the floor.

'It really is for you, Kitty, honestly. You know I wouldn't be as cruel as to kid you about something like that. It was originally Mam and Dad's idea when we heard that the dance was to be held while you were here, they kindly offered to babysit and to buy the fabric if I could find the time to start making the dress before you arrived so there'll be no arguing, Kitty. It is for you and I just hope you are going to like it when it is finished.'

Struggling to hold back her tears Kitty took Connie in her arms and hugged her tightly. 'Like it, I'm going to absolutely love it. You're the best friend and family I could have ever wished for and I love you all dearly.'

'We love you too, Kitty. That's why we agreed we would like to give you a nice surprise. We know only too well that you do without things for yourself to put the bairns' needs first, and it can't be easy for you with Ernie working away and having to manage everything on your own.' Thinking they were becoming a little too sentimental she altered her tone. 'Let's stop all this soppy talk before we both finish up in tears. There's still a lot of work to be done on the dress if it's to be finished on time, so let's have you up the stairs for your first fitting.'

Carefully laying the bodice over her arm she handed Kitty a yellow felt pin cushion in the shape of a hedgehog which appeared to hold more pins than a hedgehog would have spines. With their mood lightened, they giggled like two young teenagers. Forgetting in their excitement that the bairns were sleeping, they made their way noisily upstairs.

Shaking his head in amazement Malcolm could hear the noisy chatter going on in the room above. He knew it meant a lot to Connie having Kitty to stay and he was willing to take a back seat knowing how much the friendship meant to both of them.

With the fitting done, while Connie machined the bodice Malcolm suggested they play some records to get them in the mood for the dance. Browsing through their collection of vinyls Kitty chose songs that they could all sing along to as well as some big band music, which set her feet tapping and her body swaying just as Connie had predicted she would. With the machine work to the bodice completed, a second fitting was needed to be sure of a perfect fit, but Malcolm gave them a gentle reminder that it was getting rather late and there were two early risers upstairs. Not to be hindered by something as trivial as the late hour, they made a quick dash upstairs. The bodice fitted perfectly and on returning to the room much to Malcolm's delight Connie put the dress and sewing machine away for the night. The music was turned off and Kitty nipped into the kitchen to make each of them a warm bedtime drink which they enjoyed while chatting quietly as the few remaining coals turned to ash.

Kitty was first to head upstairs leaving Connie and Malcolm to spend a little time alone. Checking Annie was well tucked in and fast asleep beneath the blankets she quietly undressed and as she snuggled up to Jack she laid her head on the pillow and began to recall the day's events and what a day it had been. 'I don't think I could handle too many of these in any one week,' she thought, but in no time at all sleep triumphed over her thoughts to restore her energies ready for what could possibly be another day of surprises.

The following morning she planned to visit Aunty Kath to thank her personally for the dress and the kind offer to babysit so she could go to the dance. Leaving Annie and Jack with Connie who said she would like to spend more time on her own with them, she was really looking forward to an uninterrupted and friendly chat over a nice hot brew. With a spring in her step she headed off across the green, but barely two minutes into her travels she almost stopped in her tracks when she spotted Tom once again making his way towards the cottage. She pretended she hadn't seen him, but accepted it was going to be nigh on impossible when the sound of him whistling to draw her attention reached her ears. She decided to ignore it, but after a second louder whistle she knew there was no chance of that happening, and knowing how determined he could be she guessed he wouldn't give up until she acknowledged him. She turned around and acting surprised she gave a hesitant wave.

'Morning, Tom. I didn't expect to see you before Wednesday.' She greeted him rather abruptly when he caught up to her.

'Well you should know by now I am a man of many surprises.'

'You can certainly say that again,' she said raising her eyebrows. 'You have without any doubt proved that to me a few times already.'

'Might I ask where you are off too on this lovely sunny morning all on your own?' He paused. 'I'm sure you would prefer it if you had a nice young man to accompany you?'

'No I wouldn't thank you very much and I don't think your presence would be acceptable where I'm going.'

'By they are harsh words coming from such a sweet young lady.' He smirked. 'And where might that be may I ask?'

'By you are being very nosey this morning, but if you must know I'm just popping over to Aunty Kath's. I want to thank her and Uncle George for offering to babysit on Saturday night and to let her know they're invited to dinner tomorrow night and that's when you'll meet them both and not before.' Her tone was firm but she knew she couldn't keep it up for very long; his charming smile could win her over every time. 'When I said I was going to Aunty Kath's, Connie asked if she could spend some time on her own with the bairns and I could have time on my own without any interruptions, then along comes this

185

strange man and stops me in my tracks.' She was mellowing, she knew he could tell she was pleased to see him but insisted he wait at the cottage until she returned.

As she turned to leave Tom grabbed her gently her by the arm.

'How long are you going to be, Kitty? I've come to see if you would all like to come to the farm today.' He waited a second anticipating her response, but she remained silent. Confident she would accept he continued. 'The bus leaves the village in just over an hour and the next one's not for another couple of hours and I think it might be a little bit too far for you to walk with the bairns if you miss it.'

She immediately became suspicious. Had he suspected she was pregnant and thought it would be too far for her to walk? She quickly brushed the thought aside remembering Connie had agreed she was hardly showing and that there was no way anyone would ever guess she was pregnant.

'I had hoped to spend at least an hour with Aunty Kath but if you like I'll make sure I am back in good time just in case everyone else would like to go today, but I insist before you mention one word to the bairns you check with Connie to see what she wants to do as she may have made other arrangements. We haven't discussed today's plans yet but there has been talk of us going into town sometime this week, so don't build your hopes up until you have spoken to her about it.'

'Don't worry I promise I'll confirm everything with Connie before I say anything to Annie or Jack. Let's hope you can make it today. I can't wait to see the kids' faces when they see a real farm for the first time.'

'Well we'll just have to see won't we?' She sounded hesitant but in her heart she knew it was very kind of Tom's family to allow them to visit when they were obviously always very busy. Finally going their separate ways she wondered why he seemed so keen for them to visit so soon, and as she continued on her way her thoughts turned to Saturday night. What will he expect from her, will he show his feelings for her in front of others? Fearing he might be stupid enough to do so her mind was once again in turmoil, not only afraid of what he might do but of her own feelings towards him. She hated to admit it, but each time they met her feelings for him grew stronger.

Chapter Twelve

Back at 'Hazeldene' the house was very quiet without Kitty and the bairns. Peggy had spent two miserable days since they left, refusing to leave the flat and asking Jean if she would pick up her shopping for her when she did her own. Normally very independent she would never rely on others for anything, and made a point of popping out every day for a breath of fresh air and a friendly chat to anyone who could spare her the time of day. It was so unlike her to remain indoors, and though Jean knew she would be missing the family she firmly believed that was all the more reason she should be going out and mixing with people. Wondering if there could be something else troubling her she made a point of finding out.

'I'm alright, Jean. The house is just so quiet without the bairns but I'll soon get used to it. Kitty promised me they won't be away for long so with a bit of luck they'll be home next week.' Her voice, very weak and unconvincing made Jean all the more determined to get to the bottom of what the problem was.

'Are you sure that's all that's bothering you, Peggy, or are you not feeling well and refusing to call the doctor?'

'Oh there's nowt wrong with me health that I can't handle. What's worrying me is I have a horrible gut feeling about Ernie... don't ask me to explain why, but something keeps telling me he's going to land back here while Kitty's away and that's the last thing I need. You know what he's like when he's been out on the beer all day. I know I've stepped in at times when he has been having a go at her but I couldn't risk challenging him on me own. I'm far too old for that game now.'

'Oh don't you go worrying yourself about Ernie Cartwright. He'll not show his face around here while Kitty's away. Mark my words, Peggy that man needs a woman to look after him. From what she tells me he's useless around the house and I dare bet he doesn't even know how to boil an egg. His mother probably did everything for him when he was a bairn and now he thinks it's every woman's duty to do the same.'

'You're right there, Jean. I've never seen him doing anything, not even taking the bairns out for a few hours to give Kitty a little break while he's at home. I thought my Fred was a lazy bugger at times, pardon my language, but he would do things like filling the coal scuttle and clearing the table after we'd eaten. Not much else mind you but if I did ask for his help he was always willing. Ernie thinks about nobody but himself… aye he's a bit of a waster is that one and she's such a good woman she deserves someone much better than him. Mind you I'd never dare say that to her. You know as well as I do she'll hardly have a wrong word said against him.'

'I know she won't. I've had a go at her a couple of times when he's been treating her badly but she'll defend him through thick and thin. You know what, Peggy? I may be speaking out of turn here but I sometimes wonder if she really does love him as much she says she does or if it is more to do with the fact that she defied her parents that she sticks by him. I know she'll never give

189

them the satisfaction of being able to throw everything back in her face by saying they had been right about him all along.'

The very mention of Kitty's parents made the hair stand up on the back of Peggy's neck. 'The least said about those two the better, they're even worse than him when it comes to Kitty and them two lovely bairns. How they have the nerve to call themselves good parents when they have disowned her yet worship that other daughter of theirs, Vida is it or Vera oh I'm not sure.' She tutted and waved her arms in sheer frustration; the very thought of them sickened her.

'I do believe the sisters keep in touch but very rarely, and Vida, no come to think of it I'm sure it is Vera, well she never puts herself out to come and give Kitty a hand or take the bairns over to meet their grandparents. I'll never understand why she doesn't try to reunite the family and I'll say this much, Jean, if I had daughters or sons for that matter... well I don't have to say it, you know exactly what I'm thinking. That family really have no idea what they are missing. Not wanting to see your daughter beggars belief but to never want to see your grandbairns either well that really takes the biscuit. They might not like the bairns' father but they can't get away with the fact that their own blood runs through those bairns' veins.' Her voice was slowly fading, how they could treat their beautiful family in such a cruel way pained her immensely.

'I think enough has been said about them, Peggy. You're getting yourself all upset and they're not worth even talking about. Listen, unfortunately I have to leave now but promise me this, the next time I pop in you'll be looking a lot brighter and remember what I said about Ernie; he'll not turn up here before Kitty comes back so you can stop worrying yourself about him.'

'Aye, you're maybe right, Jean,' she said half-heartedly, her wrinkled face looking ashen and gaunt, evidence of how she was feeling and the result of the long hard life she, like so many of her generation, had experienced. The absence of Kitty and the bairns had left a void in her often solitary life and she was finding it hard to fill.

Keeping her promise to Kitty, Jean popped in to see Peggy as often as she could but having Michael to look after when he was not in school and husband Colin at home evenings and weekends she knew she could only spare her so much of her time. Peggy knowing Jean was only a couple of minutes away if she needed her insisted she must spend the entire weekend with her family.

At barely first light next morning Peggy dragged a dining chair across to the window to watch out for the postman. She was on to her second cup of tea when she finally spotted him at the house opposite, he turned to cross the road raising her hopes that he would be delivering a letter from Kitty as she had promised to write to her straightaway but for some reason he changed his mind and carried on down the same side. Waiting anxiously, her eyes followed his every move but he seemed to quickly disappear out of sight. Feeling a little downhearted but admitting she was probably expecting too much too soon, she wandered into the kitchen to tidy away the few breakfast dishes she'd left on the draining board. Job done she returned to the window and her eyes lit up when she was sure she spotted him again. Excitedly she pulled the net curtain to one side and peered out, sure enough there he was and he appeared to be heading in the direction of 'Hazeldene'. Dashing to the flat door she placed her ear against it. Crossing her fingers she listened in anticipation for the sound of the heavy metal letterbox flap banging and echoing through the hollow hallway. Sure enough the sound reached her ears and excited though apprehensive, she unlocked the door in the hope that the mail was for her and not Kitty. A single envelope lay face up and as she bent to pick it up she recognised Kitty's handwriting which brought a long overdue smile to her solemn face as she shuffled as fast as her legs would carry her back into the flat. With a small penknife she took from the sideboard drawer she eagerly slit the envelope open and was rather taken aback to see Kitty had included a letter for Jean. Laying it to one side she fumbled impatiently, her arthritic fingers paining her as she tried to take out her own letter almost tearing it before she had the chance to read it. Choosing the comfort of her old armchair she opened out the piece of paper and ran her eyes quickly over the page. Reading about the notorious suitcase she chuckled quite loudly as she recalled the scenes the morning Kitty left and felt relieved to learn that just as she promised it would, it had reached its destination intact. Her eyes had scanned the words at such rapid speed she needed to take a breather before reading through it again, this time more thoroughly before deciding what would be the best thing to do with Jean's unexpected letter. In two minds whether to pop over with it straight away after having agreed the previous evening that she must put Colin and Michael first over the weekend she decided against it. Assuming Jean wouldn't be expecting to hear from her so soon she concluded that nothing was spoiling by hanging on to it until Monday and placed it behind a tall highly polished brass candlestick, one of a pair which stood at either end of the mantelshelf alongside a solid mahogany clock, a brass bell with a wooden handle and a small framed photograph of Fred. She vowed it would remain there until Monday morning even though her curiosity was already getting the better of her as to why Kitty would write to them both at the same time.

She added a few coals to the fire, puffed up the cushions and with the letter in her hand sat down again to absorb Kitty's news. After rereading it her thoughts turned to the reason Kitty had left with little advance warning and she was pretty certain in her own mind that it was because she was pregnant again and didn't want anyone to know just yet. 'One thing's for sure time will tell,' she muttered under her breath, 'and if she is, I only hope this time Ernie will do the right thing by her and come back here for work.' Gazing into the flickering flames she seemed almost mesmerised, her eyelids began to droop and she nodded off still holding on to the letter.

Jean managed to stay away over the weekend to spend the time with her own family, knowing Peggy had sufficient food to last a few days, but she couldn't resist the temptation to peer out several times to see if she could spot her. Nowhere to be seen she hoped she wasn't locking herself away moping over Kitty and the bairns.

The entire weekend had dragged for Peggy and Monday morning couldn't come soon enough. She could hardly wait for Jean to arrive after taking Michael to school which she knew wouldn't take long as it was only a few streets away. Watching out of the window she spotted them disappearing around the corner. Barely ten minutes had passed and she was already waiting on the doorstep for her to return. With the warm morning sun on her face and looking forward to seeing Jean, she was more like the Peggy everyone loved, bidding a cheery good morning to passers-by whether she was on familiar terms with them or not. While she waited, not wanting to be the instigator of gossip, she debated whether she should mention to Jean that she suspected Kitty was pregnant. If she was right and Jean already knew, then it would hurt her deeply; treating her like a daughter she felt she should be the first to know.

Thirty minutes passed and Jean still hadn't returned. Growing impatient and desperate to hear what was said in her letter she assumed she must have taken a trip into town after dropping Michael into school. 'Damn it,' she snapped, muttering away to herself. 'That's just typical when I wanted to catch her first thing. I can't wait to find out if Kitty has said anything different in her letter, and now I'm wishing I'd taken it straight over on Saturday morning.'

Deciding to go back indoors she closed the main door

behind her but left her flat door ajar and went to the kitchen and set up a tray knowing Jean wouldn't let her down and would eventually turn up. Pacing the floor like an expectant father, her patience was running out. When she finally heard the long awaited knock on the front door it was turned ten-thirty.

'Morning, Jean, you're very late. I expected you to call as soon as you had dropped Michael off at school.' Although pleased to see her she sounded rather brusque.

'I'm really sorry about that, Peggy, but I couldn't get here any earlier, I meant to mention to you before I left on Friday night, that I had a doctor's appointment this morning but for some reason I forgot; probably too many things on my mind at once!'

'Never mind you're here now so you had better come in. I've had the kettle boiled a couple of times ready for you coming so you wouldn't have long to wait for a cuppa.'

Following Jean into the flat she schemed up how best to mention her suspicions about Kitty. Unwittingly Jean had just given her the perfect opportunity and before she had even closed the flat door she blurted out, 'Are you about to tell me that you've been to the doctors because you are pregnant as well?'

'As well as who?' Jean responded quickly. 'I don't know anyone who is pregnant, so who have you been gossiping to over the weekend?'

Peggy clamped her hand across her mouth in an attempt to make out the words had slipped out accidently, but she knew exactly what she was doing,

195

having just been given the perfect opportunity to broach the subject.

'Come on, Peggy, spit it out. Who do you know that's pregnant around here? There's not that many young people in the street to start with.' Then she paused, the penny had dropped. 'You don't mean… not Kitty… not again, and do you think that's why she's gone to Connie's for a while?

'Now, Jean, you know I'm not one for starting gossip. I like to know what's going on but I'm never the first person to set off a rumour, especially about Kitty. There's enough bad mouthing goes on around here about her and Ernie without me starting any more. To be honest I'm not sure whether she is or not, but you know us older women seem to have a knack for noticing these things and I just think she has had that look about her lately, then with her suddenly taking off at such short notice makes me think I could be right. If she is, then she obviously hasn't said anything to you?'

'She's never mentioned a word to me about being pregnant again,' Jean said shaking her head in disbelief. 'Listen, Peggy, I think it would be a good idea if you keep your suspicions between the two of us. You know you could be completely wrong and Kitty would be really upset if she thought you were talking about her behind her back. I think I need to find you something to occupy your mind while they're away, what with you thinking Ernie is going to arrive home unexpectedly and you've got poor Kitty pregnant again. It seems you've got far too much time on your hands and you're letting your imagination run away with you.'

'Aye I could be but mark my words, Jean, I wasn't wrong with her other two. I had suspected she was pregnant long before she got around to telling me.'

Satisfied Jean was telling the truth, she wandered into the kitchen. 'You'll be ready for a nice cup of tea by now. I've already boiled the kettle and set out a tray so I'll only be a couple of minutes.' The relief of knowing Kitty hadn't said anything to Jean before she left showed in Peggy's face, but it didn't completely satisfy her. She was still very curious to find out why Kitty had written to them both at same time. Was she going to break the news to Jean in writing and that's why she sent it in a separate sealed envelope? She couldn't wait to find out.

Whilst making the tea, it did occur to her that through all her scheming she hadn't thought to mention why Jean had been to the doctors but as she seemed to have chosen not to say she decided against asking. 'Like Kitty I guess she will only tell me what she wants me to know and in her own time.'

'I've got a nice surprise for you this morning, Jean,' she said returning from the kitchen with the tray of tea and biscuits.

Jean frowned, puzzled at what kind of a surprise Peggy could possibly give her. 'You have a surprise for me, Peggy? What on earth *have* you been up to over the weekend?'

'Nothing that would shame an old lady I can assure you. I've not crossed the doors, just sat here gazing out of the window watching the world go by. Mind you I have

197

noticed the better weather is bringing more and more people outdoors, there were a lot more families dressed in their Sunday best and heading off to church yesterday morning. Well I'm taking it most of them were heading off to the church but you can never be sure these days. It was the same thing this morning when I was looking out for you, the street seemed a lot busier than usual especially for a Monday morning which we all know is usually washing day for us women. I reckon everyone must have been up with the larks and had an early start so they can enjoy the nice weather.'

'If you're about finished talking about passers-by and the weather do you think you could tell me about the surprise you have for me? Seeing as you've never been across the doors since Kitty left on Thursday I can't begin to imagine what it is so don't keep me in suspense any longer!'

'Be patient, Jean, there's no rush,' but she didn't hesitate and immediately picked the envelope up from behind the candlestick. Not wanting to give her a hint as to how eager she was to find out what was in the letter she calmly told her, 'This came with my letter from Kitty this morning,' she lied and handed her the envelope.

'Oh already. I didn't expect to hear from her so soon. I understand she would want to let you know they had arrived safe, but I didn't expect her to write to me at the same time.'

'Well she has. She would know that I would be seeing you and would pass it on to you straight away and of course it will have saved her money on postage. She doesn't have a lot to say, she's probably still tired after the journey, but I was pleased to hear they arrived safe and in particular that the suitcase remained intact. I still can't believe she took that tatty old thing with her, but then again I suppose she had no choice and at least it did manage to make it to its destination, though whether it will make the return journey… let's just say I wouldn't like to put a bet on it!'

To Peggy's dismay Jean slipped the letter inside her handbag without even looking at it. 'I'll read it when I get home. She's probably not said anything different in mine seeing as they've hardly been gone long enough to have lots to talk about.' Hearing from her so soon had quite surprised Jean and she was guessing that maybe Kitty had something to tell her about the two soldiers, but with Peggy being so old fashioned and acting like her adoptive mother, she decided the least she knew about them the better.

Trying hard to hide her disappointment by cunningly inviting her to read the letter there and then Peggy suggested, 'I'll pop through to the kitchen if you want to sit and read it straightaway.'

'No it's fine, Peggy. I'm here to give you a bit of company and see if there is anything you need. There'll be nothing in the letter needing an urgent reply so it can wait until I go home, but before I go, I would like you to explain what makes you so sure Kitty is pregnant again.'

'Oh I didn't say I'm sure, Jean. But she does have that certain look about her again and you must admit it's strange that she suddenly took off at such short notice. I

199

know Connie is her closet friend and the one she confides in about most things. Who knows? Maybe I'm wrong and like the rest of us she is just desperately in need of a change of scenery but if she is, then we'll find out eventually.'

'You know as well as I do Peggy that she keeps things close to her chest until she's ready to talk. I do know one thing though, she is going to have her hands full if she is pregnant because I can't see Ernie coming back here to work for a while. Between you and me he seems to enjoy being away from her and the bairns because, let's face it, it's not as if he has to work away from home. He could easily find work up here, there's plenty of it around with all these new housing estates shooting up everywhere needing new roads and all sorts of jobs doing before they can start on the buildings themselves. I don't know about you, Peggy, but I just hope he's not messing about with other women, because I have noticed he does seem to stay away for longer after each visit home. Let's be honest, with so many war widows in the country, there's plenty of opportunity out there for the fellas and one thing we can't deny about Ernie Cartwright: he is a damn good looking bloke.'

Peggy listened in silence taken aback that Jean had such thoughts about Ernie. She had very little if any respect for the man, but she would never have suspected him of going with other women.

'He'll not be rushing back home for a few weeks so Kitty might as well enjoy the short break and I can't say I blame her. She's pretty tough is our Kitty, what with her family not bothering with her and him being away most of the time. I tell you what, I often marvel at how she copes so well on her own. I don't think I could manage the way she seems to, so let's just hope they all have a lovely time. They deserve to, what do you say, Peggy?'

'They do that, and from what she said in my letter they seem to be enjoying themselves.' She didn't dwell too much on what was in her own letter believing much the same would be written in Jean's, apart from maybe some breaking news!

'I'll have that cup of tea topped up, Peggy and then I'll head off home to read me letter. Before I know it, it'll be time to go and pick Michael up and if you don't mind me saying, I think you should pop out and get your own shopping today. The fresh air will do you the world of good.'

'That's a good idea, Jean, I might just do that,' she agreed filling their cups up and resigning herself to the fact that Jean wasn't going to open her letter until later.

'I reckon there'll be lots of folk in the park on a lovely day like this so why don't you have a little walk in there then pick up what you need on the way home? It will put some colour back in your cheeks. You need to get out and about as much as you can when the weather's nice. The time will come soon enough when you might not be able to get about as well as you do now.' Checking the time she realised she was running late, and gulped down her tea. 'It's time I was going to get Michael's dinner prepared before I have to collect him from school.'

Peggy watched disappointed as Jean prepared to leave

and finally gave up all hope of her reading Kitty's letter in her presence. Being more interested to hear if she knew the truth behind Kitty's sudden trip to Connie's Peggy never did find out why Jean attended the doctors that morning. She was however feeling more content since she'd learnt that Kitty hadn't revealed anything to her that she felt she had the right to be the first to know. If there was any breaking news in Jeans' letter, then she was sure she would return at the first opportunity eager to tell her she had been right all along.

Chapter Thirteen

Once again an unexpected caller arrived at Rose Cottage. Hearing the knock on the front door Connie went to answer it and just as Kitty had been a few minutes earlier, she was completely taken aback to find Tom Watson smiling at her from the other side.

'Well this is a surprise… no one expected to see you until tomorrow night but as you're here you had better come in.' Closing the door behind him Connie wondered what had brought him back again so soon. 'There's just me and the bairns at home at the minute. Kitty has popped over to see Mam for a little while and as I've not spent any time alone with them I suggested she left them with me, but now you've arrived it looks like I will miss out again!'

He wasn't quite sure if, by the tone of her voice, she was annoyed that he had turned up unexpectedly and hesitated briefly before explaining his visit. 'I've come especially to see Annie and Jack but I'm sorry if it's not convenient. I thought it might be nice to take them to the farm for an hour or two today. I bumped into Kitty on the way over so I've already mentioned it to her and she agreed that as long as you haven't made any plans for today it would probably be okay. She did emphasise though that we're not to mention anything to them before she has discussed it with you.'

Connie didn't respond immediately and he wondered if

he had really upset her by calling again so soon, or was she perhaps becoming suspicious? Not wanting to make matters worse, he rambled on about the good weather being his reason for his early return. 'I thought it's the perfect time to take them as the land is nice and dry and once the rains arrive which they're bound to sooner or later, the farmyard will be a quagmire of muck and mud and I don't think Kitty or yourself for that matter, would appreciate them being up to their knees in it.'

'Well...,' she pondered stroking her chin, '...I had thought about taking them to the woods again today as they had so much fun in there over the weekend, but as we've nothing definite planned I suppose the farm visit is a possibility.'

She sounded more optimistic. His spirits lifted but just when he thought it was going his way she warned him, 'You do realise of course that it's up to Kitty what we do as it's her holiday and she'll only want to do what's best for her bairns. We'll see what she has to say when she returns so have a seat for now and I'll shout and tell the bairns you're here.'

'I don't think there's any need to shout for them; I can see them running up the garden. They'll have heard our voices and are curious to see who you are talking to.'

'More like they will have recognised your voice and have come rushing up to see you,' she said and watched them racing each other up the garden path. Annie as usual was a few steps ahead with Jack trailing behind shouting for her to wait but she took no notice. 'I don't know what it is with those two but for whatever reason they have certainly taken a liking to you, Tom.'

'It beats me as well as I've not had very much to do with kids, well not two legged ones anyway,' he joked feeling the tension was easing. 'Plenty of animals with…' but before he had finished speaking Annie and Jack were pleading with him to take them to the farm. 'Oh I'm not sure about that,' he told them shaking his head. 'It's up to your mammy to say what you're doing today.'

'She's only at Aunty Kath's so Aunty Connie can we go and get her?' Annie asked already taking her by the hand and pulling her in the direction of the front door. In her own little mind the only reason Tom had called must surely be to take them to the farm and like Tom, Connie could only shake her head in disbelief. The sheer determination she showed when she really wanted something made her smile, but not wanting to build their hopes up in case Kitty decided against it, she suggested they go another day.

'Mammy wants to spend a little time with Aunty Kath this morning and maybe Tom has other things he needs to do this afternoon but I promise when she comes back we'll discuss it.'

As expected she sulked for a minute, let go of Connie's hand in favour of Tom's and needless to say he allowed her to drag him into the garden.

'Off you go then.' Connie waved both hands in the direction of the door and shooed them outside. 'I'll fetch us all a cold drink in a few minutes.'

Annie and Jack were at their happiest when they were playing outside in the fresh air and like everyone Connie was overjoyed seeing them looking so excited. As she watched and listened to their shrieks of delight she felt a tinge of regret that they were Kitty's bairns and not her own. She was beginning to resign herself to the fact that she might never have any bairns and the first opportunity she had to be alone with Annie and Jack had been interrupted by Tom. Not completely disillusioned, she knew there was still plenty of time for her to make the most of every precious moment she could spend with them throughout their stay.

Across at George and Kath's, Kitty was enjoying a nice uninterrupted chat. Aunty Kath was delighted to hear how excited she was about the new dress and having a night out at a dance for the first time in years.

'It's our pleasure, Kitty,' she told her. 'Having you with us is wonderful and then for the dance to fall during your stay it gave us the perfect opportunity to give you an extra special treat you deserve.'

'Everyone has been so kind, I was just saying to Connie earlier I don't know how I will ever repay everyone both here and back at home.' The mention of home brought unhappy thoughts of her parents to mind. 'It's just a pity my own family aren't as thoughtful as my friends and their families. Not that I ever expect anything from anyone, Aunty Kath, you know that, but the love I receive and knowing you are always there for me and the bairns means so much to me.' She hesitated for a moment. 'Would you think it awful of me if I told you I'm so used to not having them in my life any more that I rarely give them a second thought? In fact it's that long since I last saw them you could say I have almost forgotten what they look like.' For a second she almost sounded as hard hearted as them but Kath knew that it was not in Kitty's nature to be like them. 'Has being here in Calderthwaite with a family who adore her opened up old wounds?' she wondered.

'It's a sad situation, Kitty, but one thing is certain; you have at least proved to them that you are capable of managing on your own by not running back for help which must really annoy them at times. I have known your parents since long before Vera and you were born and I know that they would have expected you to go crawling back begging for their help and especially when the bairns came along, but good for you, you've proved to everyone that you can manage without them.'

Although she had praised her for her independence Kath did actually wonder if she ever wished they could be reunited especially now with a third bairn coming along when she could do with some extra help and who better than her very own parents? 'It's such a shame we're not still living nearby, Kitty, but as you know George couldn't turn down the chance of a better job, and now that we've all settled into the country way of life none of us would like to go back to living in the city.'

'And I don't blame you. There's nothing I would like better than to live here in the country near to you all, but the chances of us ever moving to Calderthwaite are absolutely out of the question. I know for a fact Ernie would never make a country bumpkin, he's a townie through and through as you well know.' Her vision of

207

Ernie ever living in this type of environment amused her. 'Could you ever see him setting up home here, pottering around in the garden, taking the bairns for walks through the country lanes and into the woods, and what about taking part in village activities?' She flung her head back in laughter. 'I can just imagine what he would be like say on May Day for example. Under the influence of alcohol he would probably make a complete fool of himself dancing round the maypole but, then again the pub opening hours in the village wouldn't be long enough to satisfy his intake and he would probably take the bus into town. If that was the case the celebrations would likely be over by the time he made it back home saving himself and everyone else embarrassment… no you certainly wouldn't like a man like Ernie Cartwright living here upsetting the tranquillity of the village.'

'Don't be fooled, Kitty, there are the odd one or two living in the village who like to partake of their fair share of alcohol and are seen quite regularly staggering out the doorway of the Dog and Gun. While on the subject of Ernie, do you think he will look for work in the Newcastle area so he can be at home to help you out when the next bairn arrives?'

'I've no idea, but for what help he gives me with Annie and Jack which is none, I can't see him ever coming home especially when there is another mouth to feed and look after. No I think I can prepare myself for much of the same old Ernie, and do you know what, Aunty Kath? Sometimes it can be a relief when he is away, because he always drinks far too much when he's at home. He's usually okay for the first day or two then once he meets up again with his old cronies in the city centre he changes completely because he's out every day before dinner and rarely comes home before closing time. I tell you it's a good job I have Peggy downstairs on the occasions when he comes home fighting fit. If she hears him starting on me she is up those stairs in a shot, banging on the door and threatening him with the police.'

Kath was appalled by what she had just heard. 'You're surely not telling me that he has started hitting you?'

Kitty panicked. Had she let the cat out of the bag after she had tried to hide it from them these past few years? 'Oh he has had a go at me a couple of times, but that was ages ago,' she lied hoping her expression didn't reveal her deceit.

'Well I would never in God's name have expected Ernie Cartwright to be a man who would physically abuse a woman, a man yes but never a woman. If he ever does it to you again just let us know and you come here out of his way whenever you want.' Kath really meant what she was saying but in view of the fact that Kitty said it hadn't happened for a long time the likelihood of her having to escape from him seemed unlikely. 'And what about this next bairn, do you think you will be able to manage in the flat with three of them under the age of five or are you going to try and get a house with a garden? There are lots of new housing estates going up all over the place so don't you think it would be a good idea to go and put your name on the list for one?' Kath playing the role of her caring mother feared for the bairns' safety and wouldn't feel happy until Kitty was living somewhere more suitable for raising a young family.

'I've already discussed that subject with Connie. I have thought about it but as I'm only a few weeks into my pregnancy I've got plenty of time to sort it out. Peggy's a great help to me especially with the bairns, she loves having them and Jean my friend from across the street is good to me as well. Now talking about having plenty of time I should be thinking about getting back. I met Tom on the way over, he has called to ask if he can take the bairns to visit the farm today, and I said I wouldn't be long and we could decide between the three of us so I best be on my way.'

'I must say, Kitty, he does rather puzzle me a bit does this Tom. I know I've not met him but it seems to me he is very keen to be involved with you all. Are you sure he is just doing this for the bairns or...,' she raised her eyebrows and in a more suspecting tone added, '...or do you think he's taken a bit of a fancy for the bairns' mother?'

'Oh don't be so silly, Aunty Kath, the bairns took to him straightaway for some reason and he couldn't shake them off if he wanted to. He has been absolutely great with them and as their own dad doesn't bother much with them when he's home you can understand why. My poor bairns would love to have their dad and a granddad in their lives but unfortunately they only have me most of the time. Even Peggy has lost her husband so there's no man there for them either. Wait until you see them together tomorrow night, you'll be amazed.'

210

'Well I must admit George and I are looking forward to meeting him after all we have heard about him and especially as he's a local lad, but we'll see tomorrow, perhaps I'm wrong and should judge him then and not before.'

Kitty was taken aback by her suspicion as it wasn't like Kath to question people's motives, but having always been very protective towards her she put it all down to her motherly instinct. She hoped she had sounded convincing and decided she'd need to have a serious word with Tom before they met if only to make sure he didn't do anything so stupid as to pay her too much attention in front of the family.

'Thanks for the cuppa and the chat, Aunty Kath. You'll never believe how excited I am about wearing my new dress for the dance,' she said spinning around and hugging herself in the way she so often did. 'It's all very exciting and it makes me feel like a teenager again going out to my first dance.' They both smiled as memories of those youthful years came to mind. Giving Aunty Kath a big hug, she thanked her again for their generosity. 'Now I best be getting on my way and see what's happening over at Rose Cottage. Until tomorrow say hello to Uncle George and take care,' and she was off once again with a skip in her step.

'I'm back,' she called out as she made her way through the living room and headed straight for the garden where she knew she would find everyone enjoying the fresh air being such a beautiful warm spring morning. Annie had heard her call and almost dropped Snowball as she

211

handed him to Jack. She ran towards the house desperate for her mam to say yes to her still unanswered question. 'Mammy, Mammy, Tom's here,' she shouted and held open her arms to be picked up. 'Can we go to the farm today, Mammy? Please… please?'

Kitty held her arms out in front of her to stop her in her tracks. 'Whoa slow down, Annie and let me get through the door before you start asking questions.'

'But can we pleaseeeeee?' she pleaded.

'Give me a minute or two to think about it,' she answered then lifted her into her arms. Her heart yearned to say yes immediately but deep down she was angry with Tom. Had he already spoken to the bairns about it even though she had specifically asked him not to?

Wrapping her arms tightly around her mam's neck Annie was persistent. 'Can we, Mammy, pleaseeeeee? Jack *really* wants to go as well.'

'Just hold your horses for a second, Annie… has Tom said he has come to take you to the farm today?' she shrewdly quizzed her, yet she knew if he had gone against her wishes then Annie's pleading was to be expected.

'No… he hasn't,' she replied defiantly with an expression on her face saying you're not listening to me at all. Cupping Kitty's face in her hands, she kissed her several times then looked directly into her eyes. 'I know he will want to take us because he promised to let us see the cows.'

Kitty wasn't totally convinced that Tom hadn't revealed the purpose of his visit but she felt deeply moved by her daughter's loving gestures and sheer outright determination to get what she wanted. 'I know exactly where she gets that from… her grandfather,' she thought, but still refused to give in to her. 'We'll have to wait and see, Annie, if Tom hasn't invited you to go today, then it's not up to me to ask him when to take us. You must understand people who work on farms are very busy all the time and you might get in the way.' Her voice mellowed as her anger subsided; she felt guilty. Had she wrongly suspected Tom of ignoring her wishes?

Once again her emotions were all over the place. She wanted to believe that it would have been better if she had never set eyes on Tom Watson however, her innermost feelings refused to deny her the truth. She was flattered by the attention she received but sadly that attention was now her cause for concern. With Aunty Kath already becoming suspicious, she wondered if perhaps Connie and Malcolm were too and what they would think if they knew the truth. She put Annie down, took a handkerchief from her pocket and wiped the sweat from her brow, then after a deep intake of breath she braced herself to face Tom once more.

'I take it everything is okay across at Mam's?' Connie asked as Kitty took her place alongside her on the grass. Grateful that she had interrupted her train of thought she intentionally tried to ignore Tom's presence.

'Yes she's fine, we've had a good old natter about one thing and another, and she said how much they are looking forward to tomorrow night. We all know how much she loves a family gathering around the dinner table…' Then Kitty hesitated for a moment. 'She did say it would be nice to meet Tom as they had heard so much about him.' As hard as she tried it was impossible, she couldn't bring herself to ignore him after all he had done for her and with a simple nod of the head she gestured to reassure him he would be welcomed by them. Still very much aware that she must warn him of Aunty Kath's suspicions and that he needed to be very careful not to give her or, anyone else for that matter the slightest hint that he would love them to be more than just friends, she must somehow speak to him alone. Her only chance she reckoned would be if the farm visit took place. Once there she was nearly sure to manage to catch him on his own and she crossed her fingers hoping Connie would agree to go.

'I agree, everyone's looking forward to tomorrow night's meal but I think we need to decide what we are going to do today?' Connie raised her eyebrows and gave Annie an optimistic smile. 'I think Tom has something he would like to ask,' she announced directing her words at Annie and leaving the way open for Tom to fulfil everyone's wishes.

Annie's eyes were almost popping out of her head as she excitedly looked from one adult to another having already anticipated what Tom was about to ask. Kitty knowing her only too well suspected she would interrupt him before he had even finished speaking and promptly cupped her hand gently over her mouth to silence her. 'Keep quiet, Annie and let us hear what it is that Tom has to say.'

'Hands up anyone who would like to go the farm

214

today?' he asked raising both hands at the same time. Annie immediately pushed her mam's hand aside, grabbed both of Jack's almost pulling his arms out of their sockets and stuck hers in the air at the same time shouting, 'Me and Jack, me and Jack,' then jumped to her feet dancing around with excitement.

'Three out of five is good enough for me.' Tom grinned as he waited for Kitty's response. He knew Connie had already agreed they could go but she delayed joining in. She was playing a little game with them, but seeing the disappointment on their faces she couldn't leave them in suspense any longer and she too raised both her hands. Everyone knew that the final decision remained entirely with Kitty and they waited anxiously for her response.

'You as well, Mammy.' Jack's voice was sad and his bottom lip quivered.

Kitty couldn't bear to keep quiet any longer and with no need to raise her arms she announced to everyone's relief, 'Of course we can go today.' Instantly Jack was on his feet, Annie hugged him so tightly she almost squeezed him to death yelling at the top of her voice, 'Hurrah we're going to the farm! Hurrah we're going to the farm! Come on, Jack, let's go.' Her excitement was so overwhelming it was possible the entire neighbourhood could hear her.

'Er before we go anywhere don't you think you ought to remember your manners and say thank you to Tom?' Kitty scolded them, and not having to be told twice they thanked him, though their radiant smiles alone spoke a multitude of words.

With so much going on, the morning was passing very quickly and they were too late to catch the mid-morning bus. The temperature though higher than usual for the time of the year was quite comfortable so they decided it would be nice to walk in the spring sunshine and take the bus back home. Putting a couple of snacks and cold drinks into a bag to eat on the way, they set off with Jack in his pushchair and, which came as no surprise to Kitty or Connie, Annie walking hand in hand with Tom.

The couple of miles to Low Ellerton was a bit too far for her little legs and Tom finished up carrying her part of the way on his shoulders. As the lunchtime temperature rose the walk proved quite tiring and they agreed to take a short break and tuck into their refreshments to restore their energy. They stopped at an old wooden bench which by its worn appearance had been the resting place for many a passer-by over the years. Overwhelmed by the stunning scenery Kitty commented, 'Whoever it was who thought to put a seat here had an excellent eye for a panoramic view.' Surrounded by fields, woods, the little stream which was just visible and hills far away in the distance it was breathtaking. Tom pointed out which of the fields were their farming land and explained to Annie and Jack that the cows grazing nearby belonged to their farm and had to be brought inside every day for milking.

'How does the milk get there, and how does it come out?' Annie asked, directing her question mainly at Tom. Kitty and Connie exchanged glances; they had read each other's minds and it was obvious they were thinking the same. 'I think we'll leave the answer in your capable hands,' Kitty said, 'you'll be able to explain to her better than we possibly could!'

He looked at the two women and frowned as though to say, 'I might have to choose my words carefully,' then turning to Annie he began to explain. 'The cows are brought in from the fields into sheds which are called milking sheds, then my dad and my brother Jim and me when I'm at home take the milk from the cow.' Listening intently the two women were smiling wondering if he would attempt to explain the entire procedure. 'The milk goes into buckets then from the buckets it is put into big milk churns, then they are collected and taken away for the milk to be bottled, and that's how the milkman delivers it to your door every morning.'

'Well done,' Kitty thought appreciating his discretion but waited in anticipation for the ever inquisitive Annie to ask more questions.

'Right….' Annie placed her finger on her chin and everyone knew she was contemplating her next question. 'But, Tom, you didn't tell me how the milk gets into the cow!'

Kitty knew she needed to step in and end their conversation before Tom became stuck for words. 'That's enough questions for now, Annie. We need to set off walking again or we won't have time to look around the farm.'

Tom gave her a wink. 'You'll be pleased to know that you'll have probably left for home before milking starts.'

'Okay let's make a move,' Connie said taking control of the situation and they set off for the ten minute walk

Tom said it would still take them to reach the farm.

As soon as they arrived Blade could be heard barking incessantly, a warning that someone was heading up the track. Tom's mam was busy in the kitchen and knew when she heard him that it would probably be Tom returning and immediately went outside to check.

'Be quiet, Blade, it'll only be Tom,' she shouted at him then seeing he was not alone a broad smile lit up her face. Keen to find out what was so special about the new friends he had hardly stopped talking about since he arrived home, she could hardly wait to meet them.

'Hi, Mam, come and meet my new friends,' he called to her.

Olive Watson was in her late forties. A short stout lady with a weathered face and greying hair; signs of a woman who had spent many years working hard around the home and farm whilst raising her two boys. She greeted them warmly. 'I'm pleased you've managed to make it today it's such lovely weather for the time of year, and with everywhere being nice and dry especially underfoot it's a perfect day for you to take a stroll around the farm.'

Tom introduced them whilst keeping a watchful eye on his mam's expressions. 'Meet Connie and Kitty, and her two kids Annie and Jack.'

'You lasses look worn out to me… I'm guessing you must have walked here seeing as the last bus passed through a good hour or so ago.'

'We have,' Tom answered on their behalf, 'and they're glad they did because Kitty has enjoyed admiring the wonderful views that we often take for granted.'

218

His mam offered Kitty her hand. 'You'll be Connie,' she said assuming that because Connie was holding on to the pushchair she must be the young mother. 'I'm Olive, proud mother of Tom and Jim his younger brother, the two best looking lads around these parts I can tell you.' Giving Tom a sharp dig in the ribs she looked at him with an assured grin on her face. 'It's no wonder Alice Armstrong is prepared to wait to get her hands on you as soon as you've finished with the army.'

'Enough of that, Mam, you know very well she makes up things she would like to happen but never will. There's never been anything going on between me and *her*,' he said refusing to even say her name. 'There never has been and never will be no matter what rubbish she tells you. It's all lies and I can't believe you're stupid enough to believe everything she says.' He was both angry and embarrassed and looked to see Kitty's reaction.

Trying to ignore what had been said between mother and son, Kitty had to admit she felt a hint of jealousy at the mention of Alice, and to avoid further confrontation between them she introduced herself to Olive.

'It's nice to meet you, Olive,' she said with a smile, 'but I'm Kitty not Connie.'

Puzzled, Olive asked pointing at Connie. 'Now let me get this right, she's Kitty, so you must be Connie!'

'That's right, and I presume Tom will have told you that I'm the one who lives in Calderthwaite with husband Malcolm. We're originally from the North East where of course you'll already have guessed is where Kitty still lives, and where we grew up together.'

'Tom has told us such a lot about you all, especially you, Kitty. Travelling alone with *two* little ones and I understand a rather large suitcase and a pushchair.'

Kitty wasn't sure if she could detect a hint of cynicism in her tone having specifically mentioned her name and immediately went on the defence. 'Looking back I don't know how I would have managed without Tom and Bernie's help. How I thought I could cope on my own I don't know, it can only have been the sheer determination to see Connie again… and I was very grateful to the lads for their help, especially Tom. He was so kind and even helped to keep the bairns entertained.'

'Oh I'm sure you were, dear, but that's enough talking for now. You'll no doubt be ready for a nice cup of tea so I'll pop inside and put the kettle on and bring us out a tray of sandwiches. You'll find a couple of old benches further along the yard which Samuel…,' she began to chuckle, '…why I'm giving him his Sunday name when I always call him Sam I don't know… anyway Sam knocked them up many years ago and to be honest I'm surprised they've lasted this long. Hammer and nails aren't his strong point; he'd never make a carpenter I can tell you. Now if you care to take a seat I'll be back in no time and with the warm sun on our faces we can all get to know each other better.'

'There's really no need to go putting yourself out for us, you'll have enough to do working hard looking after the big farmhouse and with three men to feed you must be on the go all day,' Connie said, feeling guilty and looked at Kitty as though to say there's no way we are going stop her.

'It's no trouble, lass, in fact I have a tray laid out ready just in case you did arrive, and it'll only take a couple of minutes to knock up a sandwich each,' and she was gone before anyone could say another word.

'It's very kind of her, Tom, but she really shouldn't. We didn't come here to be treated as guests.'

'She wouldn't dream of not offering you at least a cup of tea. She doesn't get many visitors so when she does she likes to make them feel welcome.'

Throughout the introductions Annie and Jack were well behaved, but Annie was beginning to get a little impatient.

'When can we go and see the cows being milked?' she asked Tom tugging at his trouser leg.

'You won't be able to see them today, Annie, they're still out in the fields, remember I showed you where they were on the way here, but if you like I will show you where they go to be milked when they are brought inside.'

Looking a little disappointed she dropped her eyes to the floor.

'Cheer up, Annie, there's plenty of other animals to see and maybe you and Jack can tell me what they are.'

That's all it took to put a smile back on her face. 'Have all the animals got a name?'

'Not all of them. We have some that don't have names.' He had barely finished speaking when several hens which were being chased by a rather scruffy looking ginger tom came charging towards them. At first glance it looked as though it didn't know whether it wanted to carry on scaring the hens away or come to play. 'That's Archie. He lives outside all the time with our other cat Smudge. Sometimes he likes to chase the hens and other times he is just playing. You needn't be frightened of him, he won't hurt you. If we go and sit down he'll probably follow us and you can stroke him.'

Minutes later Olive arrived with the tray of drinks and sandwiches. Thickly sliced homemade bread with cured ham and pickle and a large pot of tea for the adults, and small thinly sliced bread filled with chopped hard boiled eggs and a glass of milk each for the bairns.

'Came straight from the cow this morning did that milk,' she told Annie as she handed her a glass.

'Thank you,' she said taking it from her, but looked at it suspiciously afraid it wouldn't taste anything like what her mammy gave her to drink out of a bottle.

'They'll not get milk any fresher than this,' she assured Kitty. 'I'll give you a couple of bottles to take back with you. If they drink plenty it'll help them grow healthy teeth and bones.'

Kitty was amused. Did she think they didn't have fresh milk to drink back home? 'That's very kind of you, Olive, and I'm sure it will taste much creamier than what we get out of the bottle.' She doubted Annie and Jack would think the same and just hoped they would empty their glasses. While she tended to the bairns, Connie and Olive chatted away like they had known each other for years rather than just minutes.

'Why don't you and Kitty take the little ones and show them around?' Olive suggested to Tom, waving the back of her hand in the direction of the farm buildings. 'Perhaps you'd like to stay and keep me company, Connie? They won't be gone long and when Kitty returns home you can come again with your husband and Sam and Jim will show you around.'

'That's very nice of you to ask, Olive. Of course I'll stay and keep you company and yes… thank you. I'm sure we'll take you up on that at some time in the future.'

Kitty, shocked by Olive's suggestion, felt nauseous and sat nervously twiddling with her wedding ring. Was going alone with Tom a good idea or not? Yes she needed to speak with him privately but it would only take a minute or two and unfortunately without anyone realising it, they had once again played right into his hands.

'Come on then let's go,' Tom said, followed sternly with, 'Down, Blade, stay,' as the dog instinctively jumped up expecting to be joining his master. As they set off Blade obeyed. Tom had been the one who had trained him from being a pup and he knew by Tom's tone when he meant it.

The rising temperature was taking its toll and Kitty decided to make Jack walk as to take the heavy pushchair across the bumpy farmyard would have been far too difficult. They were soon trailing several steps behind Tom and Annie who seemed totally engrossed in everything he was pointing out to her, but she would occasionally remember about them and give a half-hearted shout for them to hurry up.

With plenty to see they arrived at a large pig pen where a lone pig ignored their presence and continued rutting

223

around for food and thankfully Tom was tactful enough to refrain from telling them it was being fattened for the dining table. The hens and a couple of geese were running free which the bairns and even Kitty weren't too sure of so she lifted Jack into her arms out of harm's way. Finally they reached the cowsheds where the most unpleasant smell reached their nostrils but it didn't deter Annie. She still wanted Tom to show her where the cows were milked but Kitty refused to enter, instead she found a shaded area where she happily sat and waited with Jack. She knew this was the most exciting day Annie had experienced; her face was a picture of sheer delight yet Tom had more surprises in store for them both.

'Would you and Jack like to go and see some baby cows?' Tom asked knowing what her answer would be. 'Because they are still very young they are called calves,' he explained to her as though he was a school teacher educating his class.

'Ooh yes please.' Clapping her hands with excitement she ran outside almost knocking into Jack.

'We're going to see some baby cows, Jack... no that's not right, Tom says they are called calves when they are still babies,' she corrected herself. As they were approaching the cowshed their loud mooing scared them but once Tom reassured them that they couldn't get out of the stalls they were happy to get up close to see them properly. 'Have the calves got names?' she asked Tom.

'Only the cows who are their mammies and that's why they are in there with them, so would you and Jack like to pick your favourite calf and give it a name?'

Annie's face lit up. 'Oh yes which one can I have and which one can Jack have?'

'You can choose whichever one you like.'

She walked up and down, stood on tiptoe and even crouched down to try to choose but she was not very sure and asked her mammy to help.

'What about that one over there, it must like you by the way it keeps watching you, and Jack you can pick a name for this one here,' she said pointing out the two calves. After lots of giggling and with a little help from the adults they finally chose the names, with the result that Low Ellerton Farm now has two calves named Buttercup and Betsy.

It had been nearly an hour since they began their tour and Kitty was beginning to feel weary. The trailing around added to the tension she was already feeling fearing she was not going to manage to speak to Tom to alone.

'I think it's about time we made our way back to the others. I'm sure you two have had enough excitement for one day.'

'But, Mammy!'

'No buts, Annie, it has been a long day and I'm sure Tom will ask us back again before we have to go home.'

'I think Mammy's probably right. There's not much more for you to see and I promise the next time you come I'll take you to watch the cows being milked.'

By a stroke of luck the cats appeared from nowhere and Annie asked if they could stop and play with them giving Kitty the perfect opportunity to speak to Tom alone. Taking him to one side out of view of Connie and Olive she breathed a sigh of relief. 'At long last I've managed to get you on your own. I must talk to you about…'

'Whatever's the matter, Kitty? You look worried sick.'

'I must talk to you about tomorrow night, it's Aunty Kath she…'

'What about Aunty Kath?'

Running her sweaty palms through her hair she nervously took a deep breath wondering how best to explain. 'She really worried me this morning while we were chatting. She suspects your interests are nothing to do with the bairns or meeting Connie's family but more… and I hasten to add these were her exact words… that you have taken a bit of a fancy for the bairns' mother.'

'That's ridiculous, she couldn't possibly suspect anything, Kitty. She hasn't even met me let alone seen us together.'

'I know that, but it's called women's intuition, and one thing is certain she will be keeping her beady eyes on you so I don't want you paying me too much attention allowing her to fill her head with stupid ideas about us and…'

'Admit it, Kitty, we both know she's right.' He interrupted her, looking rather smug as he drew her towards him and placed a finger over her lips to silence her.

She knocked his hand away but he grabbed her wrist.

'I really mean it, Tom,' she snapped at him, bringing a

rush of colour to her cheeks. 'I'm asking you to stop all this stupid nonsense… you're trying to take things too far and nothing is ever going to happen between us.'

'We'll see,' he thought but as she sounded genuinely upset he didn't dare say it. 'Stop worrying. I'll do as you ask, I promise. The last thing I want is to cause you any embarrassment.' He sounded sincere. 'I've still got Saturday night to look forward to where we can get up close on the dance floor, and where no one will suspect a thing,' he thought. Still holding on to her he stroked her cheek with the back of his hand but she was not amused and brushed his hand from her face.

'Much more of this and…' She was just about to threaten that if he didn't stop she wouldn't turn up on Saturday night when she heard footsteps coming towards them. 'Are you planning to stay here all day?' Connie called to them. 'If we don't get moving soon we will miss the bus home and I don't know about you but I certainly couldn't walk back in this heat.'

'We're on our way, just as soon as we can drag the bairns away from the cats.' She knew Connie would see she was flustered and brushed herself down hoping the heat of the day would turn out to be her saviour.

Reasonably satisfied that no one had seen them she thanked Olive for her hospitality and they set off for home. Tom walked with them to the gate where Annie and Jack thanked him for their visit saying they would come back tomorrow to see Buttercup and Betsy, which put a smile on everyone's face. They had had a lovely day, one they'd never forget.

It was around four o'clock when Connie turned the key in the front door. Kitty and the bairns were worn out but as Connie had spent a lot of the time soaking up the warm spring sun whilst chatting to Olive she had managed to restore some of her burned up energy.

'I don't think I mentioned that Malcolm and Dad are doing a couple of extra hours today so they can leave a little earlier tomorrow. Dinner is going to be a bit later so maybe we should feed the bairns at their usual time. Looking at them I think they'll be in bed long before we sit down to eat, and I think it might be a good idea for us all to head off to bed for an early night. It's been quite a tiring today and with a lot to do tomorrow, it's going to be much the same and we'll need to make an early start in the morning.'

Kitty agreed and by ten o'clock not a sound could be heard in Rose Cottage.

Chapter Fourteen

Everyone was up bright and early next morning. Around the breakfast table the adults chatted quietly about the day ahead over tea and toast, while Annie and Jack tucked into fresh lightly boiled eggs which Connie had collected especially for them that morning, but Annie as usual was not silent for long.

'Mammy can we go to the farm again today and can Uncle Malcolm come with us this time?' she asked as she dunked her bread soldier deep into the runny yolk of her boiled egg causing some of it to spill out over the shell.

'Here we go again,' Kitty thought before answering. 'Not today, Annie. We are going into town with Aunty Connie to do some shopping and Uncle Malcolm has to go to work.'

'Annie I would have loved to spend the day with you and Jack but I have to go to work and earn some pennies.'

'Alright… but will you come with us the next time we go?' she asked as she licked the golden yoke from her bread soldier as though she was licking a lollipop.

'We'll have to wait and see if I am invited first!'

'Mammy will invite you,' came her quick response as she dunked another bread soldier into what little was left of the egg yolk.

'Annie, please be quiet and finish your egg before it gets cold. I don't know how many times I have to tell you

229

not to talk so much while you're eating. Look at Jack he's already finished his and that's because he doesn't talk all the time, and if I hear you mention the farm once more I might stop you from ever going again.'

Kitty's tone was quite abrupt. She was annoyed with her for continually asking to go the farm, yet from the mischievous expression on her face she could see that she was quite undeterred and was already thinking about what she could say next.

Several seconds passed and much to everyone's amusement she remained silent, bringing about an exchange of smiles among the adults. They all adored Annie, she was so cute and they found it very hard to be angry with her, but they were also very aware that she was clever enough to realise it!

'Poor Jack he doesn't have a lot to say does he?' Connie said in a whisper. 'He's so much quieter than Annie was at that age and I'm wondering if it's because she does most of the talking and it's holding him back!'

Kitty wasn't offended by Connie's perception of Jack as there were occasions when she was of the same opinion. Ever since she found her voice Annie had always been a little chatterbox but Jack was the complete opposite, and there had been times when she wondered if he would grow up a little too timid for a boy. One thing she did know for sure, if Ernie were to notice, though she doubted he would as he hardly spent any time with him anyway, he would soon set about toughening him up as he'd expect any males bearing the Cartwright name to be strong and fearless like all the men in his family.

'I'm sure once Annie starts school in the autumn and with the Cartwright blood in his veins we'll see a change in him. Another year or so and we could see him putting her in her place when she tries to control him.'

'Mammy I want Jack to…'

'Annie please be quiet and don't interrupt when we are talking!'

'I think you're probably right there, Kitty. He's still only a baby but what I have noticed is when Annie is talking he does listen so he is taking everything in and learning from her. There are no softies in either of your families that's for sure. You'll see he'll open out when he's ready and probably shock everyone.' Malcolm tried to reassure her as he left the table to collect his bait box before heading off to join the queue for their early morning bus journey into work.

During a second cup of tea the two women planned the evening menu and by combining their food coupons they had sufficient to serve up a substantial treat for the extended family and a shopping list was compiled fearing something might be forgotten. Kitty convinced Connie that she felt well and was looking forward to her first trip into town where they hoped to spend the first hour or so browsing the various shops, in particular the large department store. Although unable to afford to buy any of the beautiful things she would admire throughout the store, it never stopped Kitty dreaming that one day she would be able to replace their old second-hand furniture with new.

Connie hadn't realised Kitty was feigning the truth and

that she actually felt anxious about the long day ahead. Disturbing thoughts had kept her awake most of the night and with very little sleep she felt quite weary. Completely torn between believing Tom would do as she asked mindful of the fact that he never did, or deliberately ignoring her request, she feared the outcome if he were to carry on the same in front of everyone. Surely he's not that stupid, she kept telling herself but she wasn't convinced. During the short time she had know him she was sure she had worked out his personality, but had to admit to being wrong about Ernie so how could she possibly be right this time?

Tom and Ernie were very much alike in as much as they were both very handsome with physical attributes that could turn a woman's eye in an instant, but despite Tom's masculine physique he was more of a gentle giant whereas Ernie always liked to act the tough guy. She had no doubts that one day Tom would succeed in fulfilling his ambition to run his own business as he appeared to have the confidence, determination and ability to achieve whatever he aspired to. Strangely enough those were the very attributes in his genetic make-up that worried her the most. Would his ability to always get what he wanted lure her into his arms? Afraid to admit she might surrender had a lot to do with the amount of sleep she lost last night.

Breakfast over, Kitty and the bairns returned to the bedroom where she had left the window wide open as it was another beautiful morning. The air outside was still and the only movement in the trees was caused by the birds as they flew amongst the branches, their mating call a sure sign that spring was in the air. While getting the bairns ready to go to town it was clear Annie's mind was elsewhere when yet again she raised the question of going to the farm.

'Can we go to the farm when we come back from town?' she asked sheepishly.

'Annie, we are not going to the farm today and I won't tell you again so that's the end of it, and definitely not when you're wearing your best dress,' she said as she helped her into the beautiful cream dress with a flocked bodice of colourful rows of embroidered daises, the skilful handiwork of person or persons unknown. She had spotted the dress at a church jumble sale when Annie was still quite small and loved it the second she set eyes on it. Visualising how beautiful she would look in it she bought it even though she could barely afford it at the time. Washed, ironed and carefully wrapped in tissue paper the dress was stored away in a drawer until Annie grew enough to fit into it, and just as Kitty had foreseen she looked as pretty as a picture.

'We're going into the town to look around the shops then we're going to take you to the park for a little while and we won't be leaving the house again once we get home.' She decided to break the news that Aunty Kath and Uncle George were coming for dinner that night and they were going to cook a special meal but she intentionally didn't mention Tom was joining them.

'Oh goody I like Aunty Kath and Uncle George so can we go to the farm tomorrow then? Can we please?' She hesitated for a moment then looked directly into Kitty's eyes. 'Please say yes, Mammy,' she pleaded in the hope of hearing the answer she wanted.

'Maybe, Annie, we'll have to see.' She succumbed to her constant pestering, but was still not prepared to say either way as she knew she would be either jumping for joy or questioning why not if the answer had been a definitive '*no*'.

Finally ready for their trip out she suggested to Connie that they leave the pushchair at home as it was such a heavy thing to hump about and that it would be much easier without it. 'I'm sure we can we manage the bairns and the shopping between us?'

'Oh I'm sure we can, Kitty. The only heavy shopping we have to do will be the food shopping in the market just before we head for the bus home, and I agree it would be far better without it especially as it's going to be another hot day. Lugging it on and off buses won't be easy and we've not got Tom there to do it for us this time. So if that's decided and we are all ready then we need to start making tracks. If we have to wait for the next one then we'll have to miss either browsing the shops or going to the park and I think we'd be disappointed if we had to miss out on one of them.'

'Yes we're ready so come on, you two, let's be off,' she said taking Jack's hand and tucking his toy rabbit under her arm. She had noticed that he had not been quite so obsessed about it since they arrived, only asking for it during the day if he was very tired then again at bedtime, but for some reason he asked if he could take it with him.

Just as they were about to leave, it suddenly occurred to Kitty to check with Connie that she had picked up the all important shopping list.

'Oh stupid me. Do you know, Kitty, it's a good job you mentioned it because guess what? It's still sitting on the table where I left it,' and laughing as she went, she dashed back into the living room and popped it into her purse to make sure she wouldn't lose it.

'So I'm not the only one who takes the trouble to write a shopping list and then forgets to take it, but I have a good excuse with two bairns to think about every time I go out…. So tell me what is your excuse?'

'I don't really have one, but as Malcolm often tells me I would even forget my head at times if it wasn't screwed on. The number of times I have gone upstairs for something, only to get there and then come back down to ask him what it was I went up for.'

'You're beginning to sound old before your time!' Kitty mocked as Connie locked the door then suggested she put the key somewhere for safe keeping seeing as she was so forgetful.

'Problem with me, Kitty, I'm always trying to do too many things at once, instead of one thing at a time. You would expect life in a quiet country village to be fairly relaxed but believe me there is always lots going on, what with WI meetings and the church which generally has something going on a couple of times a week other than the Sunday services and which I hasten to add, I can't see us managing to attend again this Sunday unless we make it to Evensong. Then of course there's working for Mr &

Mrs Parkinson where I do far more than they ask of me, but as they are getting along in years I like to do a little bit extra for them now and again.'

'Here's the bus,' Annie interrupted excitedly pointing towards it and then began pulling Connie's hand encouraging her to move a bit faster.

'It's alright, Annie, there's a couple of ladies waiting at the bus stop so don't worry we've plenty of time and it won't go without us,' she assured her but to keep her happy she increased her speed.

The bus was fairly quiet when they boarded and it stayed much the same for most of the journey, not even having to stop to pick anyone up in a couple of the villages. On arrival they made their way straight to the department store where they browsed around the various departments. Arriving at dress fabrics Connie couldn't resist stopping to admire the large display but had to resist the temptation to treat herself as like Kitty she couldn't afford to pay the high prices. The fabrics she bought came at a much lower price from the stall in the Indoor Market Hall which, when made up looked equally as beautiful. It wasn't a day for fabric shopping anyway she contended, more important was the purchase of a belt to complete Kitty's dress and again, after looking at the store prices they were out of their price range. Unable to indulge in such expensive luxuries they left for the less affluent shops and headed off first to Woolworths where they treated Jack to a spinning top and Annie a book of her choice. She chose a Peter and Jane Key Words reading book from the Ladybird collection which Kitty and Connie thought was a good idea as she could begin to learn to read some simple words before starting school. Soft drinks and snacks were also purchased before they finally made their way to the park to enjoy their refreshments and visit the play area.

The heat of the day was quite tiring and as they strolled towards the magnificent bowling green, setting out the bowls ready to play were a mixture of middle-aged men and women dressed all in white and wearing special shoes to protect the perfectly rolled grass. With plenty of seating all around the green they chose to stay and enjoy their light refreshments while hopefully watching them play. However some of the players seemed to spend most of time walking from end to end in preparation of the game and with time fast running short, a little disappointed, they left for the children's playing area. As promised they spent quite some time amusing Annie and Jack on the swings and roundabouts until it was time for them to head off to complete their shopping at the Indoor Market which was bustling with shoppers searching for bargains from food and drink, clothing and shoes, bric-a-brac, household items and just about everything imaginable all at reasonable prices compared to the high street.

'First things first, Kitty and that is to find you a nice belt to wear with your dress,' Connie advised her and pointed in the direction of the stall where she bought all of her dress patterns and fabrics. Madge the middle-aged lady who owned the stall and with whom Connie and her mam had become well acquainted sold all the necessary haberdashery supplies from pins and needles, threads and zips to fancy trimmings, buttons and ribbons alongside her wide range of fabrics. Recently she had added a few extras such as a wide variety of belts, hair accessories and some reasonably priced pieces of costume jewellery which some women were confidently wearing to compliment even their day wear.

'Hello, Connie, nice to see you again and am I right in guessing this is your friend from the North East you have been telling me all about and these I take it will be her two little ones?' Madge asked with a smile as she acknowledged them at the same time rubbing her hands together to try to keep them warm. The Market Hall, a cold uninviting place had a stone floor and a very high roof with just a few skylights allowing only the minimal amount of daylight through, resulting in the majority of stallholders having to wear extra clothing whatever the season to keep warm. Even the fishmongers, butchers and greengrocers were well wrapped up beneath their protective overalls and aprons but always managed a cheerful smile and an exchange of friendly banter with their customers.

'Yes, you're right, Madge. This is my best friend Kitty from the North East and this is Annie and of course Jack,' she introduced them patting Jack lightly on his head.

'Well you've certainly brought some lovely weather with you. We've not had it this warm in the early months for years and it does help to bring the people out of their homes and back into the town centre to do their shopping. So what are you after today, Connie or have you just brought your friend over to meet me while you're out and about in town?'

'A bit of both, Madge, but we are after either a red or white belt to finish Kitty's dress off… you'll remember the one,' and pointed to the fabric which must be selling fast as there looked to be very little left on the roll. 'You'll remember, Mam was with me when we chose the fabric and pattern as a surprise for Kitty?'

'Of course I remember. It took the pair of you half a day to decide and you wouldn't be rushed. You kept telling me it was for someone very special and for a special occasion, and I commented that I could have had one made in the time it took you to choose and you know what else,' she said turning to Kitty, 'I had a queue almost stretching to the market entrance it took them that long, but I must admit it turned out good for business. A long queue always draws attention and with all these lovely new fabrics arriving I had a good day's trading that day. I'm assuming you'll have the dress finished by now and are after making something for yourself next time.'

'It's not quite finished but I'm almost there which is just as well because it has to be ready to wear by the weekend so we must find a belt that will go with it today, and I know you have started selling them so we'll take a look.'

At the back of the stall Madge rummaged through a pile of inexpensive belts in various colours, and sizes. 'Would you like one of the wide elastic ones with the clip-in buckle?' Madge asked Kitty knowing she would be the

239

one wearing it. 'They're all the rage at the minute or would you prefer a narrower plastic one?'

'I'll try one of each if you have them.'

Madge brought a red elasticated one and a white plastic one. Trying the red one first Kitty loved it but felt it would probably make her feel a bit restricted and although there was not a mirror where she could she herself, she was sure it would emphasize her tiny bump and asked Connie what she thought. 'I think the white one might be better, it will be more comfortable and with that one you can adjust it to suit.'

'I also have that one in red if you would prefer it, and some nice red clip-on earrings which would look nice as well,' Madge suggested picking up various pairs clipped on to card as she discreetly touted for more business.

'I'll have a look at them both,' Kitty said. 'It's not often I treat myself these days so I might just go mad and get a pair to finish off my outfit.' Choosing the red belt and saying she would also take a pair of red earrings she went to get her purse from her bag when Connie intervened.

'I'm paying for those and no arguing, Kitty. Remember this is our treat and the belt's needed to complete the dress, and as we weren't sure which style you would like we didn't want to choose for you.'

'Okay I give in about the belt but I insist on paying for the earrings myself.'

After thanking Madge for her help it was on to the greengrocers and the butchers where they tried to barter down the prices but without success, however, the greengrocer kindly gave Annie and Jack a few grapes each without charge.

'Carry, Mammy,' a weary Jack asked after eating his grapes and she lifted him into her arms leaving Connie to carry the shopping.

They just made it back in time to catch the bus home and they couldn't have been in their seats more than five minutes when Jack nodded off in his mam's arms.

'I'll put him up to bed for a sleep when we get back. Walking has completely worn him out but he did manage to walk a lot further than I would have expected.' Kitty spoke proudly of his efforts.

'I think we'll all be ready for a catnap when we get home,' Connie mumbled trying to talk and yawn at the same time.

'Well there won't be too much time for napping if we are to have the meal ready in time for our guests.'

'I'm really looking forward to it, Kitty and it will be nice for Mam and Dad to meet Tom.'

'Oh it will be… I just hope they get on together,' Kitty added remembering Aunty Kath's suspicions about him and still fearing that he would get up to his old tricks, but of course she had to keep those thoughts to herself.

'Well I can't see any reason why they won't,' Connie said convincingly but Kitty didn't respond.

6.00 p.m. and the first knock on the door was heard. Connie was just about to make her way to answer it when her mam greeted her at the kitchen door. 'It's just us, Connie, so there's no need to stop what you are doing.'

241

'Hi, Mam, hi Dad. We're just about ready for our guests. Malcolm is outside with the bairns putting the animals away for the night and then the bairns will need to wash their hands and faces and brush up before dinner. Kitty's upstairs; she decided to change into something more comfortable but she's been up there quite a while and I am beginning to wonder if she has fallen asleep. Mind you it wouldn't surprise me it's been quite a long day for her and she's hardly sat down since we arrived home insisting she helped with the dinner.'

'Is there anything I can do, Connie? Mind you I must admit looking around it seems you two have everything under control.'

'No nothing, Mam, thanks. Everything's ready, we were just waiting for our guests to arrive.'

George made a direct beeline for the garden keeping out of the way of his wife and daughter in the busy kitchen. 'Too many cooks spoil the broth,' he remarked as he darted through the back door to be greeted by Jack running to meet him, eager to show him his new spinning top which he had hardly put down since he woke from his nap.

Kitty eventually made her way to the kitchen wearing a pale blue button through shirt dress and gently stroking her tummy, 'Oh I feel much better now I've changed,' she said looking quite refreshed after adding a touch of makeup to her face and letting her hair hang loose, apart from the sides which were held in place with a couple of side combs, but subtle enough so as to not set tongues wagging.

'How are you tonight, Aunty Kath and what have you been doing with yourself today?' she asked cheerfully.

'I'm fine. I've had a lovely day thanks, Kitty. I decided to have a lazy one seeing as I hadn't to cook a meal for George and me tonight so I've had my feet up for a change and read a few chapters of my book, glanced through a couple of old magazines and very little else to be honest.'

'Good for you.' Kitty nodded and smiled in agreement.

'But what about you, Kitty, are you feeling up to tonight?' Aunty Kath grimaced, apparently thinking she didn't look quite her radiant self. 'You look a little worn out to me so I hope you haven't been doing too much. I sometimes think you forget that you are pregnant the way you are on the go all the time, and I'm sure it can't be as easy for you even though you have Connie to give you a hand with the bairns.'

'Oh I don't forget, I just like to pretend it's not happening so I can enjoy myself while I'm here. I'll have plenty of time to think about it when I'm back home, and I'm not lying when I say I feel really well this time. I'm probably looking half asleep because I grabbed a few minutes shuteye,' she lied, 'so can we forget *all* about babies for tonight and just look forward to us all being together?' She offered up a silent prayer; the last thing she wanted was for Tom to find out she was pregnant.

If she did appear to look worn out, she knew it was over worrying more about how Tom would conduct himself rather than anything to do with her present condition. While alone upstairs it ran through her mind

243

what could happen if the worst came to the worst and decided the only thing she could do, would be to keep him at arm's length knowing only too well that Aunty Kath would be keeping a close eye on him to see if her suspicions were correct.

The time got round to 6.30 p.m. and Tom still hadn't arrived. Everyone was settled indoors eager to partake of the evening meal which smelt delicious, all that was except for Kitty who couldn't decide whether she felt relieved or disappointed by Tom's absence and as for eating, food was the last thing she felt she could stomach right now.

Uncle George was on the floor still spinning the top with Jack, Malcolm was adding extra fuel to the fire, and Aunty Kath and Annie were counting the number of place settings at the table. One, two, three, four, five, six, seven… eight! Annie stopped and began to count how many people were in the house. One, two, three, four, five, six… and me that's seven,' she said prodding her finger into her chest and looking confused. 'Silly, Aunty Connie, she can't count properly?' and immediately began to remove the extra place setting.

'Maybe we should leave it where it is, Annie, just in case someone else is coming to dinner and Aunty Connie has forgotten to tell us.'

'Well it won't by my daddy because he works a long way away.'

Kath was a little taken aback by Annie's immediate reaction. Her daddy would have been the last person she would have expected her to think might be the

244

unsuspecting guest as she had never heard her mention his name once.

'I know it won't be your daddy, silly, so why don't you go and ask Aunty Connie who it is?'

Kitty had overheard their conversation and was just entering the room when the long awaited knock came which stopped her in her tracks.

'I think you should answer that, Connie, seeing as he's your guest.' She quickly handed her the honour knowing it was bound to be Tom and she didn't want to greet him alone.

'Sure I'll get it, Kitty,' she said removing her pinny as she left the kitchen then flung it over the back of a dining chair and made her way to the front door.

'I wonder who that can be?' Kitty teased as the bairns watched closely to see who was about to enter the room.

'Oh don't worry, Tom, it can't be helped,' Connie said after he had apologised for being a little late due to helping at the farm all day and not realising the time.

'Tom!' Annie shouted out, her face a picture of sheer delight the minute she heard his name mentioned but she remained close by Aunty Kath. Not sure whether it was because she couldn't squeeze past Kath or by choice, Kitty thought it strange that she hadn't made her usual mad dash towards him.

Connie carried out the formal introductions, first to Malcolm and then her parents adding with a smirk that he had of course already met their resident guests, Kitty and her two bairns Annie and Jack.

'I do believe I have met them somewhere before but

245

I'm not quite sure where,' he joked.

'We were at your farm yesterday.' Annie popped up from behind a dining chair giving him a disappointed look that he could have forgotten so quickly.

'Oh of course you were. It was you and Jack who named two of the calves wasn't it?'

'Yes it was us,' she answered excitedly and managed to finally squeeze past Aunty Kath. 'We called them Buttercup and Betsy and we have drawn a picture of them, well I have but Jack's is just a silly scribble.'

'I'm sure Mammy will let me see them just now.'

'I will,' Kitty replied in a rather dull, expressionless tone.

'Would anyone like a sherry?' Connie interrupted lifting six small sherry glasses out of the sideboard along with a bottle of Croft Original. Everyone accepted and with glasses in hand she invited them to take their place at the table. Kitty made a quick dash to ensure she sat between Annie and Jack so Tom couldn't sit next to her. Connie and Malcolm were to sit at either end of the table and Tom, Kath and George opposite Kitty and the bairns. Tom was opposite Annie, with Uncle George next to him then finally Aunty Kath sat opposite Jack. Happy with the seating arrangements Kitty left to give Connie a hand to serve the meal, leaving the others to get to know each other. The food was served directly on to the plates due to the lack of both serving dishes and table space, but Connie did make a point of asking Tom if he had any preferences among the choice of vegetables she had cooked.

'I eat everything that's put in front of me,' he said. 'As kids we were made to eat everything Mam cooked for us, no ifs or buts. Mind you, we've always had good appetites with being out in the fresh air most of the day. Dad would always remind us that Mam worked hard to bring us two lads up and with food on ration and kids in other countries starving, we were taught to appreciate all our meals, and on top of that he was always very strict making sure nothing ever went to waste. If there were any leftovers, which was very rare, they were fed to the cats and dogs.'

'That's how it had to be, Tom, especially during the war. We brought Connie up to do the same, with the result that she's never been picky with her food and she hardly ever turns her nose up at anything... I was just saying to Tom that you always ate everything that was put on a plate for you,' Kath informed her as she entered the room carrying a tray with three meals to the table.

'Might have been a lot to do with you being such a good cook, Mam, but I have to admit it's just a pity I didn't follow in your footsteps.'

'Well looking at the meal I can assure you that you have.' George complimented his daughter on the delicious meal she placed before him.

Everyone was served but Kitty's stomach was still turning over. She felt so tense but knew she would have to try and force her dinner down. Thankfully with so much chattering going on and in between helping Jack and Annie it went unnoticed or so she thought. Connie was aware that she was eating very little.

'You're eating very slow tonight, Kitty, are you okay?'

'I'm just keeping an eye on these two and making sure they don't make a mess especially when we have guests for dinner, but don't worry I'll be tucking into mine just now.'

'Just leave them to manage on their own, Kitty. They can't spoil anything; enjoy your meal while it's still hot, we've not had a lot to eat today so you must be hungry.'

'I guess you're right,' she said and picked up her knife and fork and began to force her meal down hoping no one would suspect anything.

It had turned 8.00 p.m. when they finished their meal and the men who were getting along like they had known Tom for years helped to keep Annie and a very tired Jack occupied, while the three women set about clearing away in the kitchen.

'Well I must say there isn't anything I don't like about Tom from what I have seen up to now,' Kath said as she dried the plates and passed them to Kitty to put away. Kitty didn't acknowledge her fearing it might bring back to her mind their previous conversation.

'There's nothing to dislike about him, Mam, all he has done for Kitty and the bairns over the past week, and you just have to look at their little faces to see how much they have taken to him which is understandable in a way when they hardly see their dad. They're bound to take to any man who gives them so much time and attention, and I also reckon it was fate that they were travelling on the same train, not only because of the help he gave Kitty but for the sheer pleasure those bairns have had when they

248

are around him. I wish you could have seen them at the farm yesterday; they loved every minute of it and can't wait to go back again.'

'Thank you, Connie…' A relieved Kitty thought, 'If only you knew how you have probably saved me from any further embarrassing remarks from your mam.' Tom had also pleased her by paying her very little attention, focusing mainly on getting to know his new acquaintances and the occasional moments when as usual, Annie or Jack craved his attention which he never refused.

'Well I will go as far as to say this, that young man will one day make a good husband and father and I hope he meets the right girl soon.'

Kitty chipped in quickly. The way the conversation was going Tom was being painted as Mr Perfect. 'Let's not forget, Aunty Kath, I thought Ernie would be the perfect husband and father, he always talked about us having bairns but look how things are turning out!'

'I dare say you could be right. You have proved that you can never be too sure about anything, and first impressions can often be mistaken as we know only too well.'

'Well I'm inclined to agree with Mam about him but let's be honest we could well be jumping the gun. Who knows? Maybe he's not interested in getting married and having bairns of his own.'

Much to Kitty's relief the discussion of Tom Watson's future ended.

By now it was nearly 9.00 p.m. and Kitty decided it

was well past bedtime for the bairns. Jack had taken to cuddling his rabbit which was a sure sign that he needed his bed and Annie surprisingly was happy to go up with him. After they gave everyone a goodnight kiss, she took two very weary bairns upstairs. Annie had wanted her to read her Peter and Jane book but she refused telling her that it was far too late and tucked her up for the night, then found herself fighting the temptation to fall asleep as she lay next to Jack to make sure they were both asleep before she left the room.

'One for the road, everyone,' Connie suggested as she began to pour another sherry.

'Don't forget I have to pedal a few miles along unlit country lanes to get home, so don't you be getting me drunk, I've promised Dad I'll make an early start on the farm tomorrow and I can't let him down.'

Returning to the living room Kitty caught the tail end of the conversation and feared that with another sherry inside of him he might loosen up and spoil what had turned into a perfect evening. 'I wouldn't have thought you would meet many people on the road at this time of night. By the time you've had another drink it will be getting quite late.'

'Aye that's true. Time's getting on and we all have things we need to do in the morning. As you know I've promised to go and help Mrs Parkinson prepare the meal for their friends. They are entertaining tomorrow night and I couldn't possibly let them down either, but a quick one to finish off a lovely night will be nice,' Connie said handing everyone a glass.

Malcolm unexpectedly rose from his chair and raised his glass. 'Let's offer a toast to friends and family and to thank Connie and Kitty for all their hard work in serving us such a delicious meal tonight.'

A thoroughly lovely evening had been enjoyed by all and Kitty, though worn out both physically and mentally was delighted that everyone seemed to like Tom and she was more than grateful that he had carried out her wishes. No one, she believed, could have suspected that Tom secretly longed to take her in his arms and tenderly kiss her goodnight.

Chapter Fifteen

The following morning the bairns slept later than usual, which came as no surprise as the previous day had been very tiring for them. Annie did waken at her usual time, but immediately crept into bed with Kitty and Jack and was fast asleep again within minutes. With her two beloved bairns snuggled up one on each side of her, Kitty reminisced about the unexpected events which had taken place since leaving 'Hazeldene' a week ago, and she could hardly take in how much their lives had changed since waving goodbye to Peggy. Concerned how lonely Peggy would be without them, she decided there and then that she must write again that day to let her know they were all well, having a wonderful time and assure her that it would not be long before they would be home again.

She had so much she could write about this time, walks in the woods, the visit to the farm, naming the calves, the trip into town with its lovely park, and of course the beautiful new dress Connie was making for her to wear at the village dance on Saturday night. Thinking of the dress she pictured the completed garment with the matching accessories and wondered how nice she would look in it and her heart suddenly raced with excitement. She held her breath for a moment wondering was it the dress, going to a dance for the first time in years, or was it her prospective dancing partner that excited her the most? She couldn't be sure and concluded it was most likely a combination of all three which triggered off a warm feeling which flowed throughout her entire body. Already she could feel Tom's strong arms around her as they took to the dance floor and she suspected her feelings for him would intensify once he held her closer, and she began to wonder whether it would be wise to mention him in Peggy's letter or not. He had become so much a part of their holiday she knew the bairns would be bursting to tell her all about him and the farm and therefore even on their return he would not disappear from their lives and Peggy would want to know all about him. Fortunately Annie began to stir, breaking her line of thought. She snuggled her up tight hoping she might sleep a little longer but as usual she was as bright as a button and as soon as her eyes were open she began waking Jack and tugging at the bedclothes asking to get up.

'Yes, Annie, we must as we have been real sleepyheads this morning. Aunty Connie will be going out to work soon and she will be disappointed if she doesn't see you both before she leaves.'

'Will you still take us out somewhere while Aunty Connie's at work?' Annie asked having come to expect to be taken out every day as compared to being at home where they spent most days locked indoors even when the sun was shining. Life here was so much more fun for them. With fresh air and freedom to run around outside, Kitty had two exceptionally happy bairns.

'We'll not be going very far today, Annie. I'm going to write to Aunty Peggy this morning then we can pop out and post it and perhaps we will have a little walk around the village.'

'Will you tell Aunty Peggy about Tom and the farm and the baby cows?'

'Maybe, we'll see.'

'She *will* want to know, Mammy.' She sounded surprised that she would think otherwise. 'Aunty Peggy *always* wants to know where we've been when you take us out so you will have to tell her.'

'You're right she does, but don't you think it would be nice if we were to keep it secret for now so you and Jack can tell her all about it when we go home?'

'We will but you still have to tell her about Tom and the farm *before* we go home because she knows we've *never ever* been to a farm and that will make her feel happy.'

Kitty gave her a big hug. Annie was always very expressive and direct, and what she said was quite right but it still amazed her how mature she acted for her years.

'Alright I will tell her but only if you promise to be a good girl and look after Jack while I sit down and write to her. I bet every day she will have been watching out for the postman to deliver her another letter so we don't want to keep her waiting any longer do we? Now both of you out of bed this minute or Aunty Connie will have to leave without seeing you and she will not be very happy if that were to happen.'

'I'm going to beat you, Jack.' Annie laughed holding him back so she could reach the floor first.

As expected Connie was almost ready to leave by the time they made it downstairs. 'Morning, you three lazy bones.' She greeted them with a smile.

'Morning, Connie. Sorry we're up so late,' Kitty said feeling a little guilty that they had stayed in bed much later than usual but trusted she would understand.

'Don't be sorry. You were all in need of a good night's sleep after such a hectic day yesterday, and if you don't mind me saying, Kitty, I think it would be a good idea if you were to take things a little bit easier today. You do realise you haven't had much rest since you arrived and that was one of the main reasons we invited you here!'

'I know but I'm feeling fine and things are much easier for me having your help rather than struggling on my own with the bairns at home. All that running up and down stairs would have taken its toll but don't worry I've already made my mind up to have a nice quiet day. After yesterday I agree with you I feel I need to put my feet up for a while, but if there is anything I can do for you while you're at work…'

'No nothing,' Connie interrupted sharply. 'Just see to the bairns and yourself today and take things a little easier. There's nothing that can't wait until tomorrow.'

'I'm going to drop a few lines to Peggy again this morning and pop it straight in the post but other than that if you're sure there is nothing you want me to do then I'll take it easy, I promise.'

'Well make sure you stick to your word. If you want to enjoy the dance on Saturday night you need to conserve some energy otherwise you'll be sitting on the sidelines watching everyone dancing the night away and I promise you I haven't made that dress for you to just sit around looking pretty. Which, by the way I must get down to finishing tonight. Leaving it until tomorrow is a bit too risky and we would both be bitterly disappointed if Cinderella hadn't her new dress to wear to the ball.'

'Nothing will go wrong, Connie, you're such a professional when it comes to dressmaking and one thing is certain, I can't see me piling on the pounds in the next two days so everything will be fine you'll see. I can hardly wait to see what it will look like with the lovely accessories we bought yesterday, and I just hope you will all like it as much as I know I'm going to.'

'Of course we will, silly. Now I must be getting off to work or poor Mrs Parkinson will be thinking I have forgotten all about her entertaining guests tonight. I'll be home as soon as I can but it could be well into the afternoon and don't you forget what I said you must do!'

Kitty twitched her nose at her with a smile. 'I won't, now be off with you,' and with a gentle hand gesture shooed her away.

It was mid morning by the time she settled down to write her letter. With the bairns playing happily close by where she could keep an eye on them she promised they would go out later to post Aunty Peggy's letter as soon as it was finished. Pulling a chair out from under the table she sat down and began to write, determined that Tom Watson's name would not be mentioned. She would tell her about the visit to the farm and how much the bairns had enjoyed it but knew there was no need at this stage for her to know anything about the farmer's son who had taken a fancy for their mother. She smiled to herself. It was a long time since a man had made a pass at her and

256

she felt secretly flattered, and as for Peggy she would probably just assume that the farmer was a friend of Connie and Malcolm and would think nothing of it.

After writing about most of the things they had enjoyed doing since they arrived excluding of course Tom and her pregnancy, she did feel a little guilty. Peggy took a great deal of interest not only in the bairns' wellbeing but also hers and it seemed an unkind thing to do but she remained steadfast in her decision. She was actually finding it much easier to not break the news of her pregnancy than not mentioning Tom's unexpected arrival into their lives and she felt quite deceitful. He had after all been a major part of their lives from the moment they met on the railway station and most probably would be for the remainder of their holiday. She suspected if she were to tell Peggy, with having so much time on her hands she might well start reading far too much into it, and being of the old school, the very idea of Kitty entertaining a young man would border on being a scandal in her eyes. Kitty knew her well enough to know that it would be highly unlikely that she would be able to keep it to herself and wary of planting a seed in her mind which would grow so fast that gossip would spread like wildfire, she knew no matter how guilty she felt about keeping secrets, she was certain she made the right decision on both counts.

'Would you like to come and put some kisses on Aunty Peggy's letter?' she asked Annie when she finally finished writing.

She jumped up to the table and three large crosses

257

were placed on the page almost covering some of Kitty's neat handwriting. 'One from me, one from Jack and one from Mammy,' she explained.

'Very good, Aunty Peggy will be delighted with those,' she said and folded the letter in half, placed it inside an envelope and neatly addressed it. 'Right, shoes on now and then we'll go out and post it so that she will get it in a day or two.'

'Have you told her all about Tom and the farm, Mammy?'

'I have.' Kitty felt she had no choice but to lie to her about Tom and it was just a little white lie to save upsetting her.

'Jack would you like to walk to the post-box?' she asked quickly changing the subject.

'Want to walk,' he said which was no surprise as it had not gone unnoticed that he was enjoying walking rather than being in his pushchair, and with very little traffic through the village it was perfectly safe for him to run about freely. Taking a few pennies for treats and a postage stamp from her purse, Kitty gave the stamp to Annie to stick on the right hand corner of the envelope which made her feel very important and which, not surprisingly resulted in the stamp ending up rather lopsided.

As they dashed out of the gate, Annie with Peggy's letter in her hand and Jack doing his best to keep up, Kitty felt completely exhilarated. Her radiant glow had returned and with a spring in her step, she gazed adoringly at her two excited bairns as they headed towards the post-box and she almost had to pinch herself. Apart from Tom causing her problems she had never felt so happy in years.

'They're having such a wonderful time,' she thought, 'if only they had the same love and freedom at home as they have here then they would grow up to be happier and healthier children.'

Strolling leisurely behind them her mind flashed back as it so often did to her own childhood. How lucky she had been having parents who loved each other and their two daughters dearly. With their father working in finance earning a respectable salary and their mother at home most of the time there was very little they had to do without compared to many families in the area, with the result that they had a very happy childhood. It saddened her to think as she listened to the shrieks of excitement coming from the bairns, that she could never offer them what she had been so privileged to have as a child, but was thankful that she had such loyal friends as Connie and Malcolm. To give them this wonderful opportunity of visiting the countryside, breathing in lovely clean fresh air and feeling the grass under their feet was something they would never forget. Watching them running around without the fear of seriously hurting themselves was more than she could ever have hoped for, though next year she knew would be very different, with three bairns to look after a further invite would be too much to expect and therefore she was determined to make the best of every day they were here.

It was around 2.00 p.m. when a weary Connie returned

home following the few hours she had spent helping Mrs Parkinson prepare for her guests who were due to arrive in the early evening. She had helped with the food preparation and the laying of the dining table where she had placed their finest bone china dinner service, crystal glasses and silverware atop a beautiful white damask tablecloth. Connie often admired the beauty of their many treasured possessions but was never envious, just grateful that she had been given the opportunity to work for this distinguished and well respected couple. They cared for her like their own daughter and were generous almost to a fault, with the result that at times she felt almost embarrassed by their overwhelming generosity.

Creeping quietly past Jack who was having an afternoon nap on the settee she could hear Kitty in the garden teaching Annie the words from her new book, and as she listened she was amazed at how quickly she was learning.

'Shall I put the kettle on for a cuppa?' she called to Kitty.

'Oh you're home, I didn't hear you come in, and it's me who should be offering to put it on and making you a cuppa seeing as it's you who has been out working hard, but go ahead if you're ready for one. If I'm sounding a little hoarse it's because I've been helping Annie to read her new book, and she doesn't want to put it down.'

'I've been listening at the door for a minute or two and mark my words, Kitty, she'll be reading before she even starts school at this rate, and she's going to be top of the class that's for sure.'

'Oh I wouldn't go as far as to say that, literacy isn't something the Cartwright side of the family can boast about as you well know. Brawn yes but brains never and they're still too young for us to know what they have inherited from that side of the family.'

'I can see Annie has inherited the Donaldson intelligence from your dad's side so you have nothing to worry about on that score, and I suspect Jack will turn out just the same. Incidentally did you manage to write to Peggy?'

'Yes, it's already in the post and should reach her before the weekend. She'll be delighted to hear from us again as she'll be feeling pretty miserable not having us around for company.'

'Did you mention anything about Tom?'

'No why?'

'Nothing in particular I was just wondering.' Then she disappeared indoors to put the kettle on.

Kitty was relieved when she vanished without further questions fearing Annie might pick up on her little white lie.

Several fluffy white clouds appeared blocking out the afternoon sun and a refreshed Connie suggested they take a walk into the woods, which had turned out to be Annie and Jack's favourite place to play. Once inside they rushed ahead to play hide and seek, attempted to climb trees and picked wild flowers which they would put into jam jars at various places around the cottage. Kitty and Connie encouraged them to listen for the different sound of the birds singing their spring chorus high up in the tree-tops but being 'townies' the two women had to confess they were never very good at identifying which type of bird they could hear.

'I have learnt to recognise some of them,' Connie proudly boasted, 'but very few I have to admit so I'm not going to pretend I've become an expert by trying to name any.'

Kitty linked her arm and smiled. 'I must have said this to you dozens of times, Connie but I'm going say it again anyway. You are so lucky to live here surrounded by the wonder of nature which we see so very little of in the big city.'

'I know I am, Kitty, and if I had my way I would have you living here right next door to me, but I guess that will never happen. You'd never get Ernie to move to the country in a million years.'

'You're dead right, he won't ever change so it will never happen, but at least the bairns can always say they have had the pleasure of having holidays in the countryside where they have seen and learnt so much.'

'Well you know there will always be a place with us or with Mam and Dad whenever you want to come and stay so don't you ever forget that. The countryside will always be a part of your life as long as we have anything to do it.'

'You're so kind, Connie. I don't know what I would ever do without you,' she said and squeezed her arm tightly.

'You would manage but as you'll never be without me as your friend you don't even have to think along those lines.'

When the bairns came running towards them with armfuls of wild flowers, they smiled at one another and agreed they better head for home before they stripped the ground bare.

Leaving the density of the woods they noticed the air felt much cooler and for the first time since their arrival the weather looked to be taking a turn for the worse. The white clouds had turned darkish grey threatening a heavy downpour and they made a dash for home taking care not to slip into the stream as they jumped over the stepping stones. They arrived home just in time to hear someone knocking rather loudly on the front door.

'Oh good you are in. I've knocked several times and with no answer I thought I was going to have to head off back home without seeing any of you,' Kath said relieved to find they were at home.

'Well we've just this minute come back in from the woods so it's a good job you didn't come any sooner.' Then she called to the bairns, 'Come and see who's here.' Annie was first to arrive still clutching her bunch of wild flowers and immediately thrust them into Aunty Kath's hands.

'You can have these, Aunty Kath,' she said excitedly. 'Jack has a big bunch as well so Aunty Connie can have his.'

'That's very kind of you, Annie and as I've come over to see if you and Jack would like to come and have tea with Uncle George and me tonight perhaps you can put the flowers in a vase for me?'

'Oh can I?'

'Only if Mammy agrees then yes that's what we'll do.'

Feeling excited she dashed into the kitchen. 'Aunty Kath says Jack and me can go to her house for tea tonight, Mammy, so can we?' Her eyes were wide open pleading for her to agree.

'Are you sure about that?'

'She's right, Kitty,' Kath assured her having followed her through to the kitchen. 'George and I thought it might be a nice if we spent a few hours alone with the bairns. Let's be honest they don't really know us that well, especially Jack. He's still very young and if he were to waken up on Saturday night and find you missing he might start fretting and the last thing we would want to happen would be to call you home early from the dance.'

'Oh I'm sure they'll be fine and it won't hurt them or me for that matter to spend a little bit of time apart.'

'Well I think it's a good idea, Kitty and I'm sure they'll enjoy it,' Connie assured her.

'Please, Mammy, can we? I promise me and Jack will be very good.'

Kitty smiled. She adored how her daughter had such a winning way about her whenever she desperately wanted something. 'I would love to say yes, Annie, but only if Jack would really like to go as he's never very far away from me as you know. If he says yes then I'll agree.' She turned to Aunty Kath. 'I'm pretty sure he won't be a problem, seeing as he's not shied away from anyone since we got here.'

Some fifteen minutes later Annie was still carrying her bunch of wild flowers. Aunty Kath with one bairn in each hand headed home for their unexpected visit leaving the two women hopefully to spend a couple of peaceful hours together.

'I think it might be a good idea to set up the sewing machine and I'll do some more work on your dress while there's just the two of us here. There's no rush to start the dinner. Malcolm never complains about what time we eat and if you don't mind eating a little later we may get it finished tonight.'

'What a good idea and while you are busy at the sewing machine I'd like to make the dinner for the three of us if you tell me what you are planning for tonight and we'll have no arguments about it.'

'That's very nice of you, Kitty, but before we start thinking about dinner let's get the final fitting over with. I can't wait to see you in the finished dress; you're going to look lovely in it.'

'Oh I wouldn't go as far as to say that but I do know I will look nicer than I have done in a long time and I know this may sound silly, but I'm beginning to feel like a teenager attending her first dance.'

'Well considering how long it must be since you did go out dancing that doesn't surprise me, so let's make it a night for you to remember by having you looking a million dollars.'

'Now that is asking a little too much; I never was the prettiest girl in the school.'

'Of course you were, Kitty. I know you were the envy of lots of girls.' Connie complimented her friend, and handed her the dress for the final fitting.

While Connie worked on finishing the dress Kitty busied herself in the kitchen making dinner. Malcolm arrived home just before the heavens opened and as soon as he entered the living room he immediately noticed how quiet the house was.

'I must say, Connie, it's not the same without the bairns being here to welcome me home. Even though your dad did say they were planning to have them over there for tea tonight I half expected them not to go.'

'Oh they toddled off with Mam no bother and like you I'm finding it hard to believe how we have already become so used to having them around that the minute they're gone we're missing them. I don't know what we will do when they have to return home. They're going to be a huge miss.'

'My sentiments too, Connie, my sentiments too, but Kitty knows they're welcome to stay with us for as long as they like.'

She looked up at him and when their eyes met it was apparent they were both feeling the pain of not having had bairns of their own.

Chapter Sixteen

Afraid of overstepping his mark with Kitty and jeopardising any chance he might have to win her over Tom decided to give Rose Cottage a miss on Thursday choosing the safer option of spending the day working at the farm. Dad and Jim were delighted with the extra pair of hands which were always welcome whatever the season, and with Tom's first week already over, they were aware that he would soon be heading off again and that would be the last they would see of him until he completed his military service.

After helping out with the milking and hosing out the storage sheds in preparation for stockpiling hay for winter silage later in the year, he was crossing the yard when he spotted his mam dashing towards him frantically waving her arms in the air to attract his attention.

'She's here at last, Tom. I thought she was never going to turn up and I'll never understand why it has taken her so long. She must have only just heard you're home otherwise I'm sure she would have been here before now.'

'Calm down, Mam. Who on earth are you talking about?' he asked even though he had his suspicions.

'Alice, Alice of course.'

'Oh not Alice again… I'm sick of telling you, Mam. I don't want to see her so why don't you just go and tell her I am out in the fields for the day and won't be back until late.'

'You know me, Tom, I'm never one to lie and definitely not for my sons.'

'So where is she?'

'I left her in the house while I came out to find you.'

'Well go back in and tell her I'm tied up for the rest of the day and that I might bump into her before I go back. With a bit of luck she'll believe you and go.'

'I can't do that to her, Tom. I could see by the colour in her cheeks it has taken all the courage she could muster to come here to see you. The poor lass seemed so embarrassed when I answered her knock and she just stood looking at the floor. She didn't say a word until I invited her in.'

'You should never have invited her in. I've already told you I didn't want anything to do with her.'

'You'll have to speak to her Tom, I can't possibly send her away when I've already told her that you were busy around the yard. Once you see her and speak to her again you will probably feel differently…. She is such a pretty little thing you know, so shy and innocent. I can't understand what it is that you don't find attractive about her.'

'She's not pretty for goodness' sake. I've seen better looking…'

'Don't you dare say what I think you are about to say!'

'And besides we don't know what she might have been up to while I've been away which she is quite entitled to do as she *isn't* my girlfriend, *never* has been and *never* will be so the sooner you understand that, Mam, the better it will be for us all.'

'That's enough of that kind of talk, Tom Watson. I never brought you up to speak badly about people and as the poor lass must have walked here because there wasn't a bus due when she called, you must do the decent thing and go and speak to her. I'll go back and tell her you're here then I'll keep well out of your way, and if you care to think back for just a minute, Tom, you'll remember I did tell you when you first arrived home that the lass still carried a torch for you.'

'Well I'll extinguish it once and for all because I'll be sending her packing you, mark my words.' He spoke defiantly pointing angrily towards the farm gate.

'I'm beginning to think the army has changed you, Tom, because you certainly don't sound like the son that left here a happy-go-lucky lad who would do anything for anyone.'

'I still will, and surely I've already proved that with Kitty and her bairns. The army hasn't changed me at all and I've told you time and again there isn't and never has been anything remotely romantic between me and Alice. Now if you don't mind let's get this over and done with. Send her out here and I'll explain to her… and I promise you I won't be nasty but I'll do whatever it takes to make her understand once and for all that she will never be my lass.'

Olive suspected Alice was in for a tough time after watching him storm off to the old homemade bench farthest from the farmhouse and nervously headed indoors where she knew Alice would be waiting anxiously for her to return.

'I've finally caught up with him, Alice and he's waiting outside in the yard. If you would like to go straight out and meet him I think you'll find he's looking forward to seeing you.'

Immediately she felt guilty. Had she not just told Tom that she would never lie and that's exactly what she had just done! She pardoned herself on this occasion as she could not bring herself to shatter Alice's dreams.

Fearing he might be angry with her in spite of what Olive had said, Alice's mouth was dry as she went over and over in her mind what to say to him. The nearer she got to him the more her pulse raced. He looked even more handsome than she had remembered despite him being in his work clothes. When he didn't make any attempt to approach her, she suspected he was annoyed but she remained determined to see the purpose of her visit through to the end.

'Hi, Tom. I hope you don't mind me coming here to see you, but I've been looking out for you at all your regular haunts since I heard you were home but whenever I've asked no one seems to have seen you anywhere.' She tried her best to sound apologetic as she slowly edged closer towards him, and only occasionally gave him a fleeting glance to test his reaction.

He had no regular haunts as she put it other than the Dog and Gun in Calderthwaite and he knew she would never go in there on her own looking for him. 'Well I must say this is a turn up for the books, you're the last person I would expect to call here and what gives you the right to think you can just turn up here unexpectedly beats me! I'm really shocked to see you, and for your information you won't have seen me around as I've not been far since I came home.'

Deciding there was no point in beating about the bush she swallowed hard, and nervously ran her now sweaty palms through her hair. She brazenly inched closer towards him, at which point he immediately jumped to his feet, but nothing was going to deter her and she blurted out the reason for her visit.

'I don't know whether you have heard or not, Tom, but it's Calderthwaite village dance this Saturday and I knew you would still be on leave so I thought it would be nice if we could go together seeing as we have not seen each other for such a long time?'

This was the last thing Tom wanted to hear. He was furious, but for Alice to ask him outright he knew must have taken some courage. He had always considered her to be quite reserved, however he was seeing another side to her today and he leant over staring directly in her face. There was a strange steely determination in her expression which he read as, 'I will make you come with me if it's the last thing I do.' Shocked by her bold request he knew he had to tell her the truth about the dance, while at the same time making sure once and for all that she understood nothing remotely romantic would ever transpire between them.

Digging his hands deep inside his pockets he began to pace up and down. For someone who was about to simply refuse an invitation which he felt the recipient may well be expecting, he seemed a little irritated. Finally

271

taking the bull by the horns he loomed over her and began as politely as he could under the circumstances to explain.

'I just don't understand you at all, Alice. I would have thought when I didn't reply to any of your letters you would have realised that was my way of telling you that I want nothing to do with you. I really don't know how I am ever going to get this into your thick head once and for all.'

'But, Tom you… you have always made me feel special. Something none of the other lads around here have ever done.'

'That's because I like you as a friend, the same way I like all my friends and I've never once given you reason to think you are any different. Be honest, we've not even held hands and that's because as far as I am concerned there is no chemistry between us. Listen, do yourself a big favour Alice and face up to the truth because you are only fooling yourself by carrying on like this and because of it you're probably missing out on the chance of meeting someone else. You are a nice enough lass, Alice and I know there will be someone out there who is right for you. Who knows, even now he might be waiting to ask you out but won't because you like to make people think you're my lass. Everyone around here knows you fantasise about us all the time and for whatever their reasons, no one seems to have the courage to tell you what a fool you're being.'

He began to pace up and down again, this time rubbing his chin as he planned what to say next. Finally he sat next to her and without thinking he took her hand in his. Her heart skipped a beat, and her smile said it all. She was convinced he had changed his mind and had finally admitted defeat.

'Oh, Tom.' She almost swooned and placed her other hand on top of his. Instantly he jumped up in rage.

'For goodness' sake, are you listening to me or not? Either you do or you can head straight for home right now.'

'But, Tom…'

'No "but, Tom" anything.' He stopped her in her tracks. 'I'm telling you for the last time, Alice, there will *never*, are you listening, *never* be anything between us other than friends, and even that will end if you don't come to your senses and forget all this absolute nonsense once and for all. And while we're on, I might as well tell you, I will be at the dance on Saturday night but it certainly won't be with you. I've accepted an invitation to go with someone, someone you don't even know!'

'Is it another girl, Tom? Have you got another girlfriend?'

'I've never had a girlfriend!' This time he yelled at her. 'And never mind who it is, it's none of your business and you'll find out soon enough if you still intend going to the dance without me.'

'Oh I couldn't do that, Tom. If you won't go with me then I won't be going.'

'There's no reason for you not to go. You'll know almost everyone who'll be there so it's not like you will be on your own. Anyway your sister has always gone with

273

you in the past so you can go with her if she's going.'

'She is but she has a new boyfriend and he is taking her.'

'But that's no reason for you not to go and surely they could take you along with them?'

'I don't want to go with them. I want to go with you.'

'Okay, Alice, I've heard enough now and for goodness' sake grow up will you? My patience has run out so if you don't mind will you please go as we have nothing more to say to each other.'

She didn't attempt to move and took a handkerchief from her pocket as though to wipe away a tear.

'And crocodile tears won't change my mind.'

Tom was almost at the end of his tether and knew he couldn't put up with all this nonsense much longer.

'I'll go up to the house and check the time and get some money so you can take the bus home. I think there could be one due very soon.' He stormed off and as she watched him disappearing she knew she had to finally accept that her dream of ever being Mrs Alice Watson was gone forever.

Returning with sixpence Tom offered it to her saying the bus was due in about eight minutes so she had time to pull herself together before leaving. He hoped he had got through to her and that it would be the last time she would ever visit the farm again.

Accepting the coin Alice put it in her pocket alongside her dry handkerchief. 'Thanks, Tom, I'll go now and I promise I will never trouble you again. I hope you enjoy the dance but without me I doubt it!' she said sarcastically

274

and headed off without even saying goodbye. Rejected but not dejected she had been determined to have the final word and was already scheming how to get back at him.

Tom watched as she disappeared out of the gate, then making sure she had got on the bus he went down and secured it, then headed indoors knowing his mam would be waiting anxiously to hear what had taken place.

'You look a bit chewed up with yourself. I hope you haven't been nasty to the poor lass; she's such a sweet little thing.'

'Don't you be so sure of yourself, Mam because sweet she certainly is not! She's gone but she did manage to very sarcastically have the last dig.'

'Had she come to see if you were going to the dance on Saturday?'

'She had, and I told her in no uncertain terms that I would be there but not with her.'

'That sounds hurtful, Tom. She has always gone and you always have a dance together.'

'Yes but never as my girlfriend. Us lads dance with all the lasses, not anyone in particular. Now will everyone get that into their heads once and for all that there is not, nor ever has there been any romance between me and Alice Armstrong and I don't want to hear her name mentioned in this house again.'

She knew Tom meant it this time and she would have to accept Alice Armstrong would never be her daughter-in-law no matter how much she liked her, and she was beginning to accept that the army had not changed Tom, it had actually matured him. He was no longer a young farm lad nor was he a boy soldier, he was a man now who could stand up for himself and make his own decisions in life. Secretly she felt very proud of what he had achieved and accepted that the army had been good for him even though she had never wanted him to join in the first place.

'How about putting the kettle on and we'll sit down and have a cuppa and one of your delicious homemade biscuits and forget all about this stupid incident?'

'Aye good idea, son. No good dwelling on what's just happened. What will be, will be, and I know Alice will...'

'What have I just said,' he reminded her with a smile as she clasped her hand over her mouth to stop herself from saying any more.

Chapter Seventeen

Kitty's letter had arrived the following morning but not expecting to hear from her again until after the weekend at the very earliest Peggy hadn't bothered watching out for the postman. As a result the letter was left untouched until late morning when as she locked her flat door on her way out to do some shopping she spotted it lying on the doormat. As she had done so many times before she again vowed to get the landlord to put a wire basket behind the letterbox to hold the mail and save her the painful task of bending down to pick it up when Kitty hadn't got there first. 'I'm getting far too old and fat for all this bending up and down,' she muttered to herself as quite breathless she picked the letter up with one hand and eventually after a great deal of effort managed to straighten herself up rubbing her back as she made her way to her flat.

With the shopping immediately put on hold she could hardly wait to sit down to find out what they had been up to. She unlocked the flat, took her coat off and flung it over the back of a dining chair then made straight for the comfort of her old armchair, where she clumsily ripped open the envelope to withdraw the letter. The first thing she noticed were Annie's three large crosses and she placed the letter to her lips returning what she knew were kisses. Wishing she was holding her physically and kissing her soft tender cheeks rather than the cold sheet of writing paper, she accepted that if this was all she was able to have at the present moment at least it was better than nothing and begun to unfold the pages.

'Dear Peggy,

Can you believe it? A week has already passed since we left Hazeldene for our short stay in Cumberland.'

'Only a week!' She shouted so loudly the words almost rebounded off the walls. 'Feels more like a month to me.' Suspecting Kitty would never understand how much they were missed she hoped the words 'short stay' would actually be just that!

Reading on she began to feel a little selfish wanting them back home so soon, knowing this would mean denying them more of the wonderful time they were having. She could hardly believe all the exciting things they had done in such a short time and it turned out just as Annie had said, when she read the bairns had visited a real farm and named a couple of calves, tears of joy trickled down her cheek. 'They would never have that experience living here in the city and I can just imagine how excited they must have been. What a joy for Kitty to watch their little faces, I only wish I could have been there with them to capture the moment.' She paused for a second and thought about Connie and Malcolm, how kind it was to invite them to stay and share their home. It was apparent by the letter that they were all having a wonderful time living as one big happy family.

Continuing to read, her heart was warmed by the sheer

joy expressed in the words Kitty had written and she questioned why she would ever want them to cut short their little holiday when they were having such a lovely time. 'They'll only come home when they're ready,' she thought, 'and not before and who can blame them, but it'll not come soon enough for me.'

Nearing the end of the letter she came to the news about the dance and the new dress which Kitty had intentionally left until last. 'My word I bet she is absolutely over the moon and it will do her the world of good; it must be years since she had such a treat.' She knew for a fact that Ernie had never taken her out anywhere let alone a night out dancing since they had moved into the upstairs flat and she was delighted for her. 'Well bless her heart I hope she's having a lovely time because she deserves it, the amount of hard work she puts into looking after the bairns single handed week in and week out and dare I say it, I bet while he's away that bloody so and so Ernie Cartwright won't be missing out on his share of fun.' After some of the things Jean had said about him she began to wonder if she could be right about him but vowed never to mention it to Kitty. 'I can tell by just looking at him Cartwright's not a man for all work and no play and he probably is bit of a ladies' man, when the cat's away…!'

Completely carried away with her thoughts she checked herself. 'Why am I wasting my time thinking about that nasty piece of work?' Then with a smile on her face which had rarely been seen since she waved goodbye on that sad Thursday morning, she finished reading the letter. Folding it neatly she very carefully put it back inside the ripped envelope then placed it behind the candlestick on the mantelshelf, the usual place all her mail seemed to finish up. With no letter inside for Jean this time she secretly hoped Kitty had not sent one direct, then acting like a child she tossed her head in the air, pulled her shoulders back and convinced herself that she played a more important role in Kitty's life than Jean therefore she was bound to receive all of their news first. Little did she know, Kitty had withheld personal information which would not be revealed to either of them until after she returned home.

Grabbing her coat she locked the door to her flat for the second time, locked the main door of the building and headed straight across the road in the direction of Number 16. She was so eager to find out whether Jean had received a letter she stepped out into the road without looking to see if anything was coming causing a young cyclist to swerve sharply to avoid hitting her. He shouted something abusive at her but quite unperturbed she ignored him, continued on her way and arriving at Jean's banged her fist three times heavily on the front door. There was no reply which was probably just as well as had Jean been at home the noise Peggy generated would have probably scared her out of her wits. Had she only thought about it, she should have taken the trouble to check the time then she would have realised that it was almost lunchtime and Jean would have left to collect Michael from school. She turned away from the unanswered door feeling a little disappointed and headed in the direction she knew Jean would take to return home. Fortunately it would take her past Bessie's shop where she had originally set out that morning to pick up a few items.

Nearing the shop Jean was still nowhere to be seen. 'Just my luck,' she thought and guessed that she must have decided to head off somewhere instead of coming straight home. 'Ah well I best pop and get me bit of shopping,' but with all the excitement she couldn't remember everything she needed but decided Bessie, who asked every time she went in if she had heard any more from Kitty, would still be pleased to see her and hear she'd had another letter. 'This'll please her and give her something else to chat about to her customers,' she thought, 'and at least it's happy news she can pass on as many are the days it's bad news she is conveying about someone or something.'

As she pushed open the heavy door, the overhead bell warning Bessie that someone had entered the shop should she have to disappear into the back room for some reason, clanked noisily. Much to Peggy's delight she immediately spotted Jean with Michael by her side. She was already being served and directly behind her were two other women forming a queue. One was Olga Walker a regular customer at Bessie's and well known by almost everyone in the street. The other woman who was standing right behind Jean was a younger woman who Peggy had never seen before and who she thought looked to be possibly in her early 40s. Ignoring them both she edged past making a beeline straight for Jean. 'So this is

281

where you are, it's no wonder there was no answer when I knocked on your door. I gave a couple of loud bangs but when you didn't answer I did wonder where you had gone.'

'Well, Peggy, it's not like you to not know what time of the day it is. You mustn't have realised that it's lunchtime and you know very well that I have to go out to pick Michael up from school just before twelve.'

'Suffering from short term memory loss are we?' the unknown woman commented rather sarcastically. From her stance and stern expression along with the loud tutting and shaking of her head she was obviously more than just a little disgruntled by Peggy's intrusion. The normally placid Peggy was vexed by her remark and swiftly retaliated.

'I most certainly am not, and seeing as you don't even know me I find your remark quite offensive.'

'And I find the way you just barge past people and move straight to the front of the queue even more offensive so I suggest you go where you should be, at the back of the queue.'

Bessie stepped in quickly to appease the situation. Not knowing the temperament of the unknown customer she was unsure how it might develop even though she knew Peggy was the least likely person in the world who would want to cause a scene. 'Now, now, ladies, settle down. There is no need for all of this. Peggy wouldn't be queue jumping, as you can see she's only come to have a quick word with this lady.'

'Well she should have waited until she had finished

being served. We don't all have the time to waste standing in queues while people gossip instead of getting on with what they've come in for then clearing off.'

'If it's of any interest to you, my dear, though I doubt if it will be, my shop happens to be a place where neighbours can call in for a friendly chat as they pass even if they don't want to buy anything. It's not a place of conflict which is what you have caused. Now if you wish I will be more than happy to serve you before I finish serving Jean.'

'No thank you. I'll wait my turn like everyone else should be doing.'

'Well that's your choice but I am more than willing to serve you straight away.' Then turning to Jean she continued placing the items from her shopping list on to the counter.

'I best get back to my rightful place,' Peggy mumbled quietly to Jean. Although a little shaken by the sudden outburst she had a smirk on her face as she glanced slyly at the woman who completely ignored her as she passed.

With the shopping in her bag, Jean paid for her goods and left the counter to let the disgruntled customer take her place. Stopping by to speak to Peggy, she invited her over for a cuppa when she had done her shopping and of course as would be expected to gossip about the unexpected outburst.

'Now what would you like me to get for you?' Bessie asked very politely in the hope that she might suppress the mystery woman's anger.

'Nothing thanks,' she replied abruptly but then must

have had second thoughts about her attitude. Speaking a little more politely while at the same time keeping an eye on Peggy to see if she was listening she continued. 'I only came in to have a look around the shop and to ask what the neighbours are like around here as I have the chance to take over the tenancy of number 28.'

'Well as you can see the neighbours around here are all very nice so I suggest that if you are thinking of moving in it would be nice if you were to apologise to Peggy for your outburst as you will most definitely bump into each other on a regular basis. She only lives a few doors down from there on the opposite side of the street so you'll not be able to avoid one another, and another thing you need to know, you will struggle to find anyone more helpful than Peggy Wilson around these parts. Isn't that true what I'm telling her, Olga?' Olga had remained silent throughout and was taken aback when Bessie suddenly dragged her into the conversation.

'Aye everyone around here loves Peggy so if you are going to move in then I agree with Bessie a decent apology and Peggy could turn out to be a good friend to you.'

From what Bessie and Olga had told her it was clear she was feeling a little humiliated and turning away from the counter she cautiously approached Peggy. 'I'm sorry if I upset you. I didn't really mean to be so rude to you. Trouble is I'm living on a knife edge at the moment as I'm having serious problems with my husband who has suddenly turned quite violent so I'm looking for somewhere nice to live so I can clear off and leave him.

With my nerves almost at breaking point I don't want to jump from the frying pan into the fire by moving where there is a lot of trouble in the neighbourhood. I've had enough of that where I live now what with him and the neighbours going hammer and tongs at each other all the time. If he's not knocking ten bells out of me he's having a go at someone else. I don't know what has got into him all of a sudden, but I'm not prepared to stay around any longer. I need somewhere quiet to live where the neighbours all get along together.'

Typical of her, Peggy's heart began to melt and immediately she thought of Kitty who faced similar circumstances with Ernie. 'I'm sorry to hear you are going through difficult times but you're not alone. There are quite a few women having the same problem with the men in their lives but if you do decide to move in I would suggest you think before you speak and don't go around upsetting people. Treat us right and we'll treat you the same, everyone helps each other around here and we all pull in the same direction. Times are still quite difficult for many of the families around here and it's reassuring knowing that we all help each other when it's needed.'

'Listen my name is Rosie Mullen and as it's a canny little place that I could manage on my own I'm off to go and think about it and if I do decide to take it I'll remember what you have told me.' Then she left the three locals somewhat bemused yet saddened by her unhappy story.

Peggy was the first to comment. 'Well I tell you what, you two, I don't know about having Rosie Mullen for a

285

name she sounds more like Rosie Sullen to me. I don't know where she's come from but I think she best look for a flat somewhere else if that is going to be her attitude living around here. Still I suppose if she does decide to take it we can only see what happens, after all everyone deserves a chance, and we don't know how bad her life is with her husband and neighbours. No one knows what goes on behind closed doors do they? Now I'd best get me self off to Jean's for that cuppa or she'll be wondering where I am, and I'll pop back in later for me shopping and a natter.'

'That's not a problem, Peggy, off you go. You'll be ready for a cuppa after that little incident and I'll see you later. Now what can I get you, Olga?'

Chapter Eighteen

Kitty was looking out of the bedroom window, but it was not the beautiful view she was admiring, she was rapidly scanning the village hoping Tom might be heading towards the cottage but there was no one in sight. Disappointed she turned away and questioned what on earth she was doing allowing feelings for another man to constantly enter her head, further complicating her life which it seemed was forever dictated by men, and wondered where this latest unforeseen episode was heading.

She knew only too well that her feelings for Tom were morally wrong but was finding it impossible to direct her thoughts elsewhere and he remained constantly at the forefront of her mind. Crossing the room she decided to rest on the edge of the bed. With closed eyes she buried her face in her hands and allowed her confused mind to wander into the realms of fantasy.

'Slowly the bedroom door opens and Tom enters. He immediately closes it behind him. Their eyes meet, and he reaches out and takes her into his arms steering her towards the bed and in a moment's reckless passion he has them both undressed.'

Without realising what she was doing she stretched herself across the bed as though he were actually there beside her in the flesh.

'Manoeuvring her on to the bed he wraps his muscular arms around her receptive body tenderly kissing her lips, her neck. His

warm hands seductively caress her slim naked body and she feels weak with desire. In a complete state of ecstasy he transports her to sexual heights she has never experienced before and she longs for the moment to last forever.'

'Mammy, Aunty Connie says you have to come down because she has made you a cup of tea,' Annie called to her.

'Damn you!' she muttered under her breath in sheer frustration, fully aware that the brief thrill would never become reality. She lay for several moments still immersed in her fantasy with the handsome soldier who walked into her life several days ago and who she suspects she is falling in love with, but who regrettably must walk right out of it again at the earliest opportunity.

'Okay, pet,' she said struggling to compose herself, 'I'll be down in a couple of minutes I'm just making the beds.' Another white lie she regretted telling. Annie's bed was all neat and tidy as was her own before she began her fantasy love affair in the arms of the irresistible Tom Watson.

'What on earth is happening to me?' she asked herself as she reluctantly rose from the dishevelled bed, straightening both it and herself. She vowed there and then that Tom must very soon be erased from her mind forever.

Kitty knew it was inevitable that they would spend a lot of time together at the dance but once the night was over in order to bring closure to this unprecedented episode and avoid the situation getting any further out of hand, she decided though very reluctantly that she would make plans to return home next week. How she would explain her early departure to Connie and Malcolm she couldn't be sure but she would have to devise the perfect excuse to avoid too many questions. Thinking it may well be another year or so before she returned to Calderthwaite and by then Tom would have most certainly moved on with his life, probably even seeing precious little of Connie and Malcolm, the likelihood of them ever finding out about the prospective relationship that was taking place right before their eyes was highly unlikely.

'What on earth have you been doing up there? I thought you must have gone back to bed,' Connie asked smiling at Kitty as she nervously made her way into the kitchen.

'I've not been up there that long surely?' she challenged her trying to cover up her feelings of guilt.

'Long enough to have gone back to sleep I'd say.'

'Well I can assure you I haven't been sleeping, I've been making the beds and tidying around a little… perhaps this pregnancy is slowing me down a bit though I can't say I feel any different than I did before I was pregnant.' Quickly she conjured up the excuse and gently stroked her tummy knowing only too well that the innocent child growing inside her was not responsible.

Handing her a cup of tea Connie agreed that she did seem exceptionally well this time and suggested they have a comfortable seat in the living room and discuss plans for the rest of the day.

'I had thought, why don't we… that's if you're sure you are feeling up to it of course, pop into town again

289

and take the bairns to the park for a couple of hours then we could do some shopping in the food market for the weekend where there are far more choices than Gwen has to offer. Mind you we don't want to be tiring you out too much, you need to save as much energy as possible for tomorrow night!'

Kitty's heart skipped a beat at the thought of the dance, though whether it was with excitement or trepidation she wasn't sure but managed to disguise her shock reminder by ignoring it.

'Sounds like a good idea to me, the bairns will love to go again and I'm feeling fine so let me know how much time I have before the next bus is due then I can change into something more suitable for town and get the bairns ready.'

'It's only ten o'clock and the bus isn't due for about an hour which gives us plenty of time so we'll take a little picnic with us to eat in the park.'

Taking her cup of tea into the kitchen Kitty shouted down the garden to Annie and Jack. 'Would you like to go to the park again today?'

Annie immediately came running to her with Jack in close pursuit.

'The one we went to last time, Mammy?' Annie asked needing to know the full facts as usual.

'Yes and we'll take a little picnic with us as well.'

'Oh yes please. Jack do you want to go to the park?' She turned to him taking his hands in hers and, almost rubbing noses, she glared into his eyes pleading for him to agree. 'We will have a ride on the bus again, Jack and we'll be able to go on the swings and roundabouts and Aunty Connie can take us on the seesaw!'

Jack's face lit up, he drew his hands away from hers and began to clap excitedly. There was no need for him to answer, his actions told everyone he was more than happy to go, and he began skipping around shouting, 'Yippee, park, yippee.'

'I guess that's you and me on the seesaw as well.' Connie motioned moving her arms up and down before taking a couple of hard boiled eggs from the pantry shelf and shelling them. 'We'll make egg and tomato sandwiches. The bairns love them and with a biscuit and a bit of cake, that should be enough to last them both until dinner tonight... well perhaps with a little treat in between.' She winked at Kitty.

'You're spoiling them, Connie, all these extra sweets aren't good for them you know!'

'Listen you're only here for two or three weeks so a few extra treats now and again won't do them any harm and you know how much I love having them here. You also know I'd give the world to have a couple of bairns of my own to spoil and have running around the house all day.'

'I know you would, Connie, and I pray that one day you will. You're still only very young so there is plenty of time for it to happen but in the meantime if you would like to I can always let you borrow my two for a couple of weeks while I stroll off into the sunset for a long peaceful rest before number three arrives.'

'I wouldn't mind that in the slightest if that's what you

would like to do, but I think I know you better than that.'

Kitty smiled. She knew Connie meant what she said but that it would never happen. She loved nothing more than having her bairns around her all the time.

The picnic was soon packed and with everyone ready they set off for their day out. As they left the cottage they noticed the bus was stationary at the stop but on hearing the driver suddenly revving up in order to pull away they panicked. Connie gripped Annie's hand tight almost lifting her off her feet as she rushed towards it leaving Kitty struggling behind with Jack, but doing her best to keep up with them.

'Phew that was lucky.' Connie was out of breath and struggled to speak but she did manage to thank the driver for waiting as she helped Annie on to the bus.

'Don't thank me, thank the young man at the back, if it hadn't been that he spotted you heading this way and shouted for me to wait I'd have been on my way without you.'

Immediately she looked to see who had saved the day, and sitting there beaming on the back seat was none other than Tom Watson. She waved to him at the same time indicating that they would be sitting in the seats nearest to the front and it was obvious he wouldn't waste much time before making his move to join them. The minute Annie realised who it was she began shouting his name which almost stopped Kitty in her tracks. Having been out of earshot she hadn't heard what the bus driver had said to Connie, and reeling from shock she chose not to look to see where Tom was sitting, knowing only too well that he would soon accompany them.

Sitting directly behind Connie and Annie, Tom had the perfect opportunity to come and sit next to Kitty and in no time at all he was by her side making polite conversation such as how coincidental it was that they all decided to take the same bus into town. Thankfully Annie peered over the back of her seat wanting to talk to him.

'We're going to the park for a picnic, Tom, do you want come with us?'

'I can't, not today, Annie, I have some shopping to do and then I have to get an early bus home as they need me back at the farm.'

'Why? Is there something wrong with Buttercup and Betsy?' she asked looking a little unsure as she awaited his reply.

'No, Buttercup and Betsy are both fine and you can come over with Mammy to see them whenever you want, and talking of Mammy you haven't said what you have been up to since I last saw you?' nudging her gently in her side, desperate to continue their conversation.

'Well considering it was only Wednesday night when I last saw you I haven't had time to get up to very much, but I did write to Peggy yesterday,' then lowering her voice in order to avoid Connie hearing she continued, 'to tell her that we will be home early next week.'

Instantly disappointment was written all over his face but he didn't pursue the setback, instead he began to talk about the dance, the one place he knew where he would learn the reason for her sudden decision to go home so soon. Acting as though he was not troubled by the

293

shattering news he continued light-heartedly informing her of the reason for his trip into town.

'I'm actually off to treat myself to a new outfit for the dance. I have to look my best for the ladies you know!' He gave her one of his mischievous smirks and she knew exactly what he was implying but didn't respond deciding instead to play along with him.

'So you're out to charm the ladies tomorrow night then?' Connie turned around having caught snippets of their conversation.

'I'll certainly be trying my best, it's quite a while since I swept a pretty girl off her feet and on to the dance floor and if I'm not looking my best I might be faced with a few refusals.'

'I can't imagine that happening, can you, Kitty?'

'Who knows? It may depend on how many other handsome young men are there that he will be competing against. I remember how choosey we were about who we would dance with and I don't imagine things will be any different today.'

'Shall we tell him what we got up to when we went to the dances in our younger days, Kitty?' Connie asked appearing very keen to confess. 'I know it seems a long time ago but it's not really when you think about it. We used to love getting dolled up, Tom, and it was always in something made from old clothes from our mothers' wardrobes or jumble sales which we would modify so it looked like the latest fashion. Then we'd do our hair up in the latest style.'

'You're right but it was all thanks to you being a dab

hand on the sewing machine. You were able to make something out of nothing. Our outfits were always quite unique which used to annoy lots of our friends as we turned up in something different every time we went out dancing.'

'Yeah you could see some of them were green with envy but let's be honest about this, Kitty, we both loved stealing the show by being centre of attention with the lads.'

'I wouldn't doubt that for one minute,' Tom interrupted, 'and I bet I'm not wrong when I say you would have encouraged them.'

'A little bit of that as well.' Connie chirped up as she recalled the fun nights out they had when they were younger.

Kitty for the main part chose to remain a little more discreet on the subject of what they got up to when out dancing. She didn't want to give Tom the idea that she may be a little more receptive when the atmosphere of the dance hall relaxed her, putting her in the mood for a bit of devilish behaviour.

'Aye those were the days, Connie, but I guess we have to behave more mature now we are both married and me with two bairns. Let's be honest I can hardly go out skipping the light fantastic like I did in those days.'

'Yes but you are still going out to enjoy yourself tomorrow night because Malcolm and I will make sure of that!'

'Me too,' Tom added swiftly, 'and one thing's for...' but Annie interrupted him. She was growing quite impatient at being ignored by the adults.

'Are we nearly there yet?'

'Not yet but it's not far to go now and we'll head straight to the park. By then it will be nearly lunchtime and you'll be ready for something to eat.'

'That's good,' she said and she sat back in her seat with her arms folded as though in protest about something.

Jack was quiet as usual so Tom asked him what he had been doing since he last saw him.

'Me and Annie went somewhere without Mammy.'

'Really, and are you going to tell me where?'

Jack looked to Kitty for reassurance before answering him as though he were about to reveal a well kept secret.

'It's alright, Jack, you can tell him!'

'We went to Aunty Kath's and we stayed for tea.' His little face beamed with delight.

'Did you like going out without Mammy?'

'Yes because Mammy says that makes me a big boy now.'

Ruffling his hair Tom smiled at him. 'Of course you're a big boy Jack, and if you would like to, you and Annie can come to the farm without Mammy. I'll come and get you then take you home again.'

'But Mammy likes to come to the farm with us.'

'Oh I know she does, and of course you must bring Aunty Connie as well.'

By this time the bus had reached its destination and the bairns were sad Tom wasn't going with them but told him they would see him at the farm tomorrow.

'Okay I'll let Buttercup and Betsy know you're coming.

I'm sure they will love to see you again.' He smiled then reminded the ladies as though they needed it, 'Don't forget the dance tomorrow night, and before all the ladies make a beeline for me I want the first dance with you, Kitty and I won't take no for an answer.'

She didn't reply.

'We'll just have to wait and see what tomorrow night brings, tomorrow is a whole new day, no doubt another day mixed with joy and laughter, doubts and fears.'

Not prepared to make any promises she kept her thoughts to herself as they went their separate ways.

Chapter Nineteen

Rays of golden sunshine shone through a gap in the curtains. The singing of birds could be heard through the open window and with her two precious offspring snuggled up close beside her Kitty should never have felt happier. It was the morning of the dance yet barely had she opened her eyes and already she was beginning to worry how the day would end. Cuddled up to Annie and Jack it was Tom's parting words spoken only yesterday that were foremost in her mind. Her pulse began to race and she felt lightheaded.

She recalled the uncertainty she had felt when Tom insisted her first dance was to be with him. 'We'll see… tomorrow is a whole new day,' she'd told herself and now tomorrow had arrived and already she feared the outcome. A vision of Tom looking even more handsome than ever in his stylish new outfit as he strolled towards her, his hand reaching out to her insisting she take to the dance floor with him, caused her to feel nauseous but she knew it had nothing to with morning sickness.

'It's going to be very hard to refuse him,' she thought, 'but if I don't, once he holds me close how will we both feel?' Deep inside her heart felt as though it was being ripped apart and once again she was wishing she had never set eyes on the handsome soldier who it seems has fallen in love with her, and dare she admit it, possibly her with him! Thankfully the bairns asking to be taken downstairs relieved her troubled mind and she flung back the bedclothes desperate for her day to begin as it should, looking after their needs. As she rose, she pushed all thoughts of Tom Watson into the darkest corners of her mind.

The day ahead was already planned. Malcolm and Uncle George had kindly arranged to take the bairns for a trip into the woods in the late afternoon hoping it would tire them out. In their absence Kitty and Connie were to spend the time pampering themselves before it was time to dress for their exciting night out together for the first time in years. Aunty Kath had kindly offered to come over earlier than planned to give the bairns their supper and get them ready for bed so Kitty could dress without interruptions, but it seemed it hadn't occurred to her that if Jack didn't settle without his mam the evening could turn out to be far more demanding than she might expect. After several discussions between herself and Kitty it was agreed she should have an easy day ensuring she would have plenty of energy to keep him entertained should he not settle.

The day passed quickly, and before they knew it Kitty and Connie were dashing upstairs and as usual were giggling like a couple of teenagers. It was hard to say which of the two was most excited about the imminent hair styling and dress rehearsal. As they entered Connie's bedroom Kitty suddenly stopped dead in her tracks, and took a step backwards looking extremely guilty.

'What's happened, Kitty? Are you alright?'

'Really, Connie, how selfish am I? It never occurred to

299

me to ask you what you'll be wearing tonight.'

'Well I shouldn't worry about it because I've been keeping it a secret anyway. Mam is the only one who knows as she was with me when I chose my dress pattern and fabric...' She hesitated for a moment and standing with her hands on her hips added, 'Come to think of it, Kitty, Malcolm hasn't bothered to ask me either even though I've shown him his new shirt I bought especially for tonight.'

'You mean he knows what I'm wearing but not what his own wife will be wearing?'

'That's it in a nutshell, Kitty, but I know he won't be disappointed when he does see it.'

'Well you better let me take a look before I can agree with you!'

Opening her wardrobe door Connie lifted Kitty's red and white dress from the rail and laid it carefully across the bed smoothing it out so it wouldn't crease. Returning to the clothes rail she pushed several hangers along then lifted out another beautiful dress this time with tiny blue butterflies on a cream background. The style, unlike Kitty's had a square neck, cap sleeves, and a flared skirt. A narrow buckled belt in a plain fabric the identical shade of the blue butterflies complimented the dress perfectly.

'I take it by the smile on your face you like it then?' Connie asked.

'Like it? I love it but not as much as mine of course... and besides blue doesn't really suit me,' she added the latter as an afterthought so as not to offend Connie in any way.

'Well that's a relief because that's what I hoped you would say. Mam and me purposely picked red for you knowing it's one of your favourite colours so we knew we couldn't go wrong with it, and well we really want you to stand out as the Belle of the Ball tonight.'

'Belle of the Ball, Connie, you must be joking. I'll be hiding away in a corner somewhere as hardly anyone will know me and you know how people react when there is a stranger in their midst.'

'Don't be silly, you'll soon get to know a few people and there's no way you will be spending the night tucked away in a corner. Let's be honest it must be ages since you had a night out and we really want to see you enjoying yourself. I bet when you see how beautiful you look in your new dress and modern hairstyle you'll feel so good about yourself you'll think differently.'

'Well you have certainly gone out of your way to try and make sure I do and you were definitely right in the choice of colour. You really are so clever, Connie and I have to admit I do envy you being so gifted with a needle and thread.'

'Well you could learn to sew yourself, you know, it's not that difficult.'

'Me, never. It's not a gift everyone has and I'm so ham-fisted even when I have to do a bit of mending it takes me ages to get started because you would think it was a piece of string I'm trying to thread through the needle. I know I would never make a dressmaker and besides I'm always too busy running the home and looking after the bairns.'

'That's true but you could find the time if you really set you mind to it,' Connie said trying though probably unsuccessfully to convince her as she slipped out of her clothes then carefully undid the zip of her new dress. Stepping into it she turned her back towards Kitty and asked her to zip it up for her.

'It looks absolutely beautiful.' Kitty praised her handiwork and stepped to one side for a better look. 'Oh you look stunning, Connie. Now come on you must give me a twirl.'

As Connie spun around the skirt swung outwards showing its fullness and the beaming smile on her face expressed how delighted she was with her own handiwork.

'Now let's see you in your dress with the accessories we bought the other day and then we'll decide how to style your hair.'

'Not before I've seen your complete outfit with the shoes and jewellery you'll be wearing.'

'Okay if I must.' From her jewellery box she took out a blue rhinestone necklace with matching clip-on earrings, then from the bottom of the wardrobe she lifted out a pair of cream peep-toe shoes with two inch heels. Holding them up to Kitty in the manner a shoe shop assistant would hoping to encourage a sale she asked, 'So what do you think about these, do you like them?'

'Very smart I must say and the perfect match with your dress.'

Connie had a smirk on her face. 'Well just listen to this… they only cost me a few pennies at a church jumble

302

sale in town. A real bargain you must agree.'

'I'll say they were. You don't happen to have any more bargains hidden away somewhere?'

'Well it just so happens...' and she lifted out a second pair. 'What about these then? When I remembered we both take the same shoe size I got this pair of white slingbacks at the same time. I thought they would be perfect for you to wear with your dress if they're comfortable. I reckon they belonged to the same lady as there were several expensive looking pairs and all hardly worn so I guess it must have been someone with a bit of money who was having a clear out.'

'Well good for her whoever she is and thanks to her kind generosity we'll both have lovely shoes to wear with our new dresses so let's hope they're comfortable enough to dance in.'

Like Cinderella the shoes fit her perfectly, but carried away with all the excitement she hadn't realised what she had just owned up to, but Connie was quick to latch on.

'Ah so you will be dancing tonight after all.' She smiled.

'Well I am beginning to feel quite guilty with all everyone has done to make my evening special so it would be rude of me not to get up for at least a couple of dances.'

'And Tom, don't forget about him! I can't see you getting away without having a couple with him. Remember what he said to you yesterday when he left us?'

'We'll have to see, won't we? I know he had invited me

to join him before we learnt about your tickets, but I've not made him any promises. I only agreed that he could join us out of politeness but I'm actually hoping there will be a lovely young local girl he'll take a shine to and will want to spend the night with. Think about it, Connie, what does he want hanging around an old married woman like me for anyway? There will be plenty of young single girls going who are sure to fancy him because let's admit it, he is such a good looking fellow.'

'*Old* you certainly are not, married yes but let's be honest, Kitty, you can hardly refuse to dance with him after all he has done for you and the bairns... and you can't deny it he is such a nice lad and he's taken them bairns to his heart like they were his own.'

'Umm that's true but not just them, their mother as well,' Kitty thought secretly before she blurted out, 'Right I've heard enough about Tom Watson for now and if we don't get cracking we'll not even make it to the dance, and I won't be dancing with anyone.'

'Ooh hark at you, bossy boots.' Connie elbowed her lightly. 'Okay how about we go into your bedroom and play about with your hair to see which style we think will look best.'

After several variations they finally agreed that her shoulder length hair should hang loose, but to allow her red clip-on earrings to be seen they decided one side should be tucked slightly behind her ear and held in place with a hair clip to which Connie said she would add a tiny red bow.

'Well that's you sorted, Kitty so I suggest you go first

for your bath and hair wash before the bairns come bursting through the door wanting to tell you all about their visit to the woods.'

'Good idea. It's not often I get to soak in the bath without at least one of them running in and out so I'll take you up on that one.'

Malcolm and Uncle George returned with two excited but weary looking bairns just as Aunty Kath arrived. As usual they had a tale to tell having played hide and seek, tried to clamber up trees and collected wild flowers but today they had an extra treat. They had watched a squirrel scurrying from branch to branch in a playful mood. Annie had wanted to stroke it and couldn't understand why it didn't come close enough leaving her a little disappointed when it ran down the tree trunk right next to them then darted off in the opposite direction.

The two women, eager to finish dressing for the occasion had listened somewhat impatiently to their exciting experience and agreed it sounded like they had all enjoyed it, though it was hard to tell who had enjoyed the visit the most... the bairns or the adults.

'Well it sounds to me like you have all had fun and games, but might I suggest, Malcolm, as the bathroom is free you start getting ready for the dance otherwise we will be leaving without you!'

'There is no chance of that, it won't take me a fraction of the time you two will have spent titivating yourselves up.'

The women ignored his remark and headed for the bedrooms where Connie styled Kitty's hair first. Just as she was about to leave to do her own Kitty asked as stockings were still an expensive luxury if she would draw a line down each leg for her with an eyebrow pencil. Stepping out of her borrowed dressing gown Kitty looked impressive in her finest underwear and Connie couldn't help but comment.

'My word just look at you in your sexy underwear. It's no wonder Ernie can't keep his hands off you when he's at home.' Being in high spirits Connie was in the mood for fun, but Kitty didn't seem amused. The last thing she needed tonight was to be reminded of Ernie and the fact that he had forced himself on her in a drunken state and made her pregnant again. Unaware of the circumstances that had led up to Kitty's third pregnancy and not wanting to spoil the jovial atmosphere of the occasion Kitty brushed Connie's remark to one side without comment.

'How about a fancy zigzag line if I make sure both legs look identical?' she kidded.

'Don't you dare and make sure it's a straight line while you're at it,' she ordered Connie who she knew was quite the expert having done it so many times in the past. She stood perfectly still while Connie's steady hand drew two perfectly straight lines.

'Job done, Kitty. Now go and take a look in the long mirror in our bedroom to see if you approve.'

'Perfect,' she said, 'now I can get dressed,' and carefully lifted her dress from the bed.

'Are you two not ready yet? Everyone is waiting to see what you look like and if you don't get a move on the

306

dance will be nearly over by the time you get there,' Malcolm called up to them from the bottom of the stairs.

'We'll have less of your cheek, Malcolm Ferguson. We won't be long now. We're just about ready and we'll be straight down.'

'Not before time, you've been up there for ages,' and he returned to the room to await their grand entrance.

Tapping on the living room door Connie shouted from behind, 'Are you ready? We're coming in.'

Slowly she turned the handle and peeped around the door. The three adults, her mam with Jack on her knee, her dad with Annie on his and Malcolm standing behind, looked as though they were awaiting the opening scene of a grand stage performance.

'Ta dah,' Connie shouted as she paraded into the room arms outstretched followed by the more sedate Kitty who was feeling slightly embarrassed. Gasps followed and Annie leapt from Uncle George's knee and ran towards Kitty almost knocking her over. 'Mammy you are so beautiful; you look like a princess,' she said hugging her tightly

'You like my new dress then?'

'Oh, Mammy, it is beautiful and Aunty Connie's as well. You look like two princesses going to the ball like Cinderella.' She looked admiringly at them then after a bit of thought excitedly asked, 'Can I have a dress like that pleaseeeeeeee?'

'You'll have to ask Aunty Connie nicely if she will make you one sometime.'

'Will you, Aunty Connie?' she asked looking up at her

with her winning smile.

'Well it won't be tonight, darling, but I'll see if there are some oddments of material left and I'm sure I can manage to make something for you.'

Seemingly content with Connie's reply she went back to sit on Uncle George's knee. The others had sat back in silence letting Annie enjoy the moment while they looked on with pride. Their faces spoke volumes as they admired Connie's handiwork and it brought back memories for George and Kath of when the two friends were much younger heading for a night out at the dance, but it was Malcolm who commented.

'Well all I can say is I'm glad I'll be alongside my wife tonight as I'm sure there could be quite a few men out there asking her to dance if she were there on her own. And as for you, Kitty, well I reckon we'll have to be keeping an eye on you. I tell you what, Ernie Cartwright doesn't realise what a very lucky man he is.' Nodding his head at her outstanding beauty he added, 'He would certainly be telling you that you are even more beautiful now than when he first fell in love with you.'

'Oh stop exaggerating, Malcolm. I appreciate your compliments but that's going a bit too far.'

'It's not, Kitty and I have to agree with him.' George butted in sharply. 'You look beautiful, you both do and I am very proud of my two girls. You'll steal the show for sure tonight won't they, Kath?'

'Without a doubt, they both look stunning in their new dresses and fancy hairdos.' Then pointing to their feet she added, 'And of course the expensive footwear will be getting a bit of a hammering tonight as they skip the light fandango across the dance floor, and listen to me for a minute, especially you, Kitty, I want you to make sure you have a wonderful night and don't even think about what is happening here because everything will be just fine.'

Kitty wasn't quite listening to all Aunty Kath was saying as her thoughts had drifted to her parents. Their hardheartedness came to mind when Uncle George spoke of how proud he was of his two girls. She had never heard either of her parents say they were proud of her. 'Yes proud of Vera of course they were, but never me,' she thought. Crossing the room she hugged Uncle George and Aunty Kath thanking them for helping to make tonight possible. Kissing Annie and Jack she asked Jack to be a good boy telling him she wouldn't be gone long.

'He'll be no bother, Kitty, you'll see. Now I think it's time you were making your way over to the village hall that is if Malcolm has remembered to put the tickets in his pocket of course?'

He tapped his chest pocket indicating he had. Hugs and kisses were exchanged all around and they set off waving all the way across the green until they saw the front door closing.

Malcolm was cock a hoop. Who wouldn't be with two beautiful young ladies linking him one at each side and by the expression on his face he looked like the cat that got the cream.

'Tonight is going to be one of our best nights out in ages,' he said, 'especially for you two having had to wait so long to have a night out together. It's going to be a night you'll both remember for years to come.'

'It will be because we'll be making sure of that won't we, Kitty?' Connie said raising her eyebrows and smiling for confirmation.

'We will, Connie, I promise,' she said thinking, 'I hope it will be remembered for all the right reasons and nothing else.'

Leaning against the doorway as she half expected, smoking a cigarette and looking very suave in his new outfit was Tom Watson the farmer's son. After missing National Service he chose to leave the farm for a couple of years to learn a trade in the army and is now known in these parts as the farming soldier. The minute Kitty set eyes on him he was neither a farmer nor a soldier. Tonight he was none other than her very own Prince Charming.

Chapter Twenty

Alice was determined that nothing would stand in the way of her seeing Tom on Saturday night even if it was only to discover who the mystery person was whose invitation he had accepted. Convinced she could still win him over she exceeded even her own expectations and made herself up to look her most attractive. Joining her sister Esther and boyfriend Bobby all three set off eagerly for the dance, Alice promising she would not spend the entire evening in their company. 'I've arranged to meet Tom inside the dance,' she lied without the slightest hint of guilt. She had no reason to doubt that Esther would not believe her and she continued her deceit. 'He's not sure exactly what time he'll arrive as he's coming with his brother Jim who is bringing along someone Tom's not met before.' Completely deluded by her own foolish longing she spoke so convincingly it was obvious she almost believed it was the truth.

The music was in full swing when they arrived and already several people were on the floor dancing to the sound of the popular local Dave Scott Band. Dave had formed the 5 piece band with some of his pals in the late 1940s, playing all types of music from the 1920s, 30s, 40s and now the early 50s in order to please everyone. Their popularity had grown very quickly around the area, as their variety of music from ballroom to swing, square dancing to lindy hop and of course the all time country favourite the barn dance meant everyone could enjoy dancing to their favourite music. During the barn dance everyone changes partners and Alice was desperately hoping Tom would partake giving her the opportunity to speak to him if only for the couple of minutes before they move on to the next partner.

With the room quickly filling up she searched for Tom but as he was nowhere to be seen she took her seat alongside Esther and Bobby offering to buy their drinks. Bobby politely refused saying the drinks would be on him and headed to the makeshift bar, leaving the two sisters deep in thought. Although excited about the dance, Esther hadn't wanted Alice to join her and Bobby that night and only agreed she could on the understanding that Tom would be there and she would join him and his brother with the mystery person, and like Alice she found herself searching the room in the hope that they had arrived so she could be alone with Bobby.

'Well, it doesn't look like they're here yet,' she said to Alice with a clear hint of disappointment in her voice.

'They shouldn't be long now, and as soon as they arrive he'll be straight over for me you'll see.' Alice spoke in anticipation rather than truth, still stupidly believing Tom might have a change of heart. The words had hardly left her lips when she suddenly spotted Jim.

'Oh he's got to be here somewhere… I can see Jim talking to a crowd of his mates so Tom's sure to be there as well.' Pretending to scrutinise the group she screwed up her eyes. 'That's strange I can't seem to see him.'

'Well there's sure to be lots of people wanting to have

a chat with him as he's been away for so long so you'll just to have to be patient, he'll be over to see you as soon as he can'. Esther spoke with sincerity yet she knew her sister well enough to suspect that with Alice it was probably all a pipedream. She knew Tom hadn't been seen around the place since he arrived home, and of course she knew nothing of Alice's visit to the farm and Tom's angry rejection which she had intentionally kept to herself. Not wanting to disillusion her so early in the evening she decided she would continue to play along with her for a while. 'The night's very young so stop fretting. If he said he would meet you then I'm sure he will.'

Alice didn't respond, she knew she had lied enough already. Deep down she had a gut feeling that Tom would be arriving with a girl and if that turned out to be the case then she was already scheming up what she could do to spoil their night.

Bobby returned with their drinks but with still no sign of Tom after a short while Alice left them to go in search of him. Esther was relieved and it gave her the opportunity to confess to Bobby that she didn't believe for one minute that Alice and Tom had made arrangements to meet that night.

'I know she has gone out of her way to look her most attractive for him, and I have to say she does look lovely tonight, but I'm convinced she has made the whole thing up. I've never believed that there was anything between those two, but sadly for Alice she has always wanted more from Tom than he is willing to give. One thing I am

313

certain of she has never received any letters from him while he has been in the army which to me speaks for itself.'

Bobby gently slid his arm around her shoulders and drew her close. 'Never mind worrying about her, Esther, we came out to enjoy ourselves and even if Tom doesn't join her there'll be plenty of locals who know her very well so she won't be on her own. There's bound to be someone who will ask her to dance.'

'You're right, Bobby,' she said and moved her chair closer to him then stretching one leg across, she gently pushed Alice's chair away from the table making it available for someone else in the hope that she couldn't rejoin them.

Outside Tom waited nervously for the small party to arrive and when he eventually spotted them he couldn't take his eyes off Kitty. The closer she got the more he admired how beautiful she looked and he knew without a measure of doubt that he was in love with her.

Formalities over, Malcolm led the way into the dance where he handed their three entry tickets to Charles Campbell, a local business man who the family had come to know quite well since moving into the village and who was volunteer ticket collector for the evening. Connie introduced him to Kitty explaining she was her old school friend from the North East, but while doing so for some reason Tom suddenly felt a little uneasy and discreetly stepped to one side.

'Nice to meet you, Kitty and this must be…,' he said glancing across at Tom who had partially turned his back to him and who Charles had assumed was her husband. After taking a closer look he recognised Tom. 'Oh I'm sorry I thought you were all together when you arrived at the same time but now I see it's young Tom Watson from Low Ellerton Farm so I guess I must be wrong.' He looked slightly embarrassed by his mistake and offered Tom his hand which he eagerly accepted giving him the opportunity to move towards Kitty.

'Young Tom Watson,' he paused, 'though not quite so young now are you, lad? Every young lass's dream is our Tom,' and for some reason he directed his words at Kitty along with a mischievous wink. 'Trouble with Tom is he never gives them a chance… doesn't know what he's missing not having a lovely young lass on his arm.'

'Who knows? Maybe one day, Charles, just maybe, I might surprise you. I'm pretty sure the right one will come along eventually,' and as he edged even closer to Kitty she avoided eye contact for fear of blushing and giving something away. She knew he was referring to her and he confirmed it by moving next to her and when he knew no one would notice slid his hand in hers and squeezed it tightly.

'I'm assuming you have a ticket, Tom,' Charles asked as having been so engrossed with Kitty he had completely forgotten about it.

'And here's me thinking you might let me in for free seeing as I've not been home for months but it seems like there's no chance of that happening!' He smirked as he removed the ticket from his shirt pocket and handed it to Charles.

'Good lad, now get yourself in there. You never know, the love of your life might just be waiting for you,' and nodded in the direction of the dancehall. 'It's filling up already and with plenty to eat and drink and the great Dave Scott Band for your entertainment you're sure to have a good night.'

'Little does he know but I've already found the love of my life,' Tom thought as the four of them made their way together through the double doors leading into the hall.

After finding a table the two men headed to the bar for drinks and it was then that Alice spotted him. Hoping the man with Tom was the mystery person her eyes never left them, but with two drinks each she felt sick inside when she watched Tom hand one of his drinks to a young woman she didn't recognise. The other couple she wasn't sure if she knew them or not but it was obvious they had come as two couples and without any doubt Tom was with the one in the red and white dress and she wondered where he had met her. 'I'm pretty sure she's not from around here,' she pondered for a moment unable to take her eyes off them and reluctantly had to admit they made a handsome couple. As her jealousy gradually turned to anger she began scheming up how she could come between them. 'I'll bide my time but I'll think of something before the night is over.' Finally turning her eyes away from the happy foursome, feeling enraged, she strutted across the room to join Esther and Bobby almost knocking the drinks from someone's hand but rudely failing to even stop and apologise.

It wasn't long before Malcolm and Connie took to the

floor for their first dance, leaving the besotted Tom with a rather nervous Kitty. Pulling his chair closer to her he looked into her eyes and she knew immediately he was about to try and win her heart.

'Kitty there is something I must tell you, and please don't try to stop me. Even before I saw how beautiful you look tonight I can't let you return home without you knowing how I feel about you. I not only want to be with you tonight, but forever and please tell me you feel the same?'

'I can't, Tom… I won't deny I'm very fond of you but you seem to forget I'm married and besides, you wouldn't just have me but you would have Annie and Jack as well and why would you want to take on someone else's bairns when you could marry and start a family of your own?'

'I would be more than happy to have you as my wife, Kitty and to bring Annie and Jack up as our family. They're two lovely kids and you know how fond I am of them.' His hand reached out for hers. 'You have already told me how Ernie hardly bothers with them and be honest they deserve a father who will give them plenty of love and attention and I promise you I would do that.'

Kitty knew he was sincere but her heart felt heavy. Deep down she wanted to return his love but it wasn't possible and she thought it might perhaps be better to tell him about the baby then surely he would think differently. She pondered for a moment but decided against it. If she did cut short her holiday and return home as early as next week then there would be no reason for him to know. 'Once I've returned home and

317

he returns to base we will soon forget each other and put it all behind us,' she decided. 'It's just a very short chapter in the lives of two people and nothing more.' Trying to convince herself wasn't easy and with Tom pulling at her heart strings she had a few misgivings.

'Penny for them,' Tom asked.

'Oh it's nothing.' Kitty snapped back to reality.

'Kitty you do understand I have never felt this way about anyone before, that's how I know…'

The sound of Connie's voice brought their conversation to an abrupt end. 'I thoroughly enjoyed that, Malcolm. It's ages since we danced and now it's your turn, Kitty. Remember you promised me you would.'

'I know I did and I will I promise, but later when I have got used to being amongst so many strangers. You have to remember it's a long time since I went out socialising with friends.'

'And when you do I hope you haven't forgotten I'm having the first dance with you so you choose the dance and I'll sweep you off your feet,' Tom reminded her.

'Now there's a promise if ever I've heard one,' Connie commented, 'but mind you be careful with her. It's a few years now since she took to the dance floor.'

Kitty's heart skipped a beat. For a second she was sure Connie was about to tell him about the baby. Relieved she hadn't, she responded quickly. 'Oh I'm sure I won't have forgotten how to dance, Connie, after all we did plenty of it when we were younger.'

'Don't worry I'll keep you right, Kitty. I'm quite good on the dance floor you'll see but don't keep me waiting all night or I might have to find some other attractive young lady to take to the floor.'

Kitty knew different and began sipping her drink as the band increased the tempo. She watched as couples took to the floor and could feel herself getting into the mood and feared that if her Prince Charming was ever going to win her over it might easily happen tonight.

The band played several requests and the floor was filling to almost overflowing but Kitty still refused to grant Tom his wish. Unbeknown to Kitty he had secretly requested a song and when they began to play he offered her his hand insisting this time she must dance and thankfully she finally accepted. Acting like a professional he led her on to the dance floor and with one arm gently around her waist he drew her close. She placed one hand on his shoulder and with her other they entwined hands as they waltzed romantically to the tune of 'You look wonderful tonight'.

'I requested this especially for you, Kitty,' Tom whispered softly in her ear.

'I don't believe you, Tom.'

'Well you can always ask Dave if you don't believe me. He said he could understand why when I showed him the young lady I was with tonight.'

Kitty didn't quite know what to think. It was a lovely compliment but another tactic in his attempt to win her over.

Connie and Malcolm watched them almost in disbelief. 'I can't believe Tom can move that gracefully across the floor being such a strong tough looking lad. I would never have expected him to enjoy ballroom dancing but he's certainly enjoying this one.' Connie sounded truly amazed.

'I guess he must have known with Kitty being quite reserved she wasn't likely to dance to the more up-beat hip hop tunes so he really had no choice other than choose a slow dance, and I can see what he meant when he said he would sweep her off her feet!'

'Well looking at them they certainly seem to be enjoying every minute of it.'

'I might be completely wrong, Connie, but I rather suspect Tom has other ideas than just wanting to dance with Kitty.'

'I have to admit it, Malcolm I think you could be right but I'm afraid if he has then he is going to be sadly disappointed. I've had my suspicions for several days now but thought he wouldn't be stupid enough to be interested in a married woman with two bairns and another on the way. Besides there would be no sense in it, she's going back home in a couple of weeks and he is returning to base so any interest he has in her will soon fizzle out. Never mind, let them enjoy the moment, she deserves a little bit of attention. She gets very little if any from Ernie these days except when he is at home which isn't very often. She doesn't tell me everything but I'm not stupid. I have known her long enough to know when she is trying to pull the wool over my eyes and I know she is not as happy as she tries to make out.'

'Well it's really none of our business but if the expression on her face is anything to go by I think she is enjoying his company just as much as he is hers. I just hope she doesn't do anything silly.'

'She won't. She's not so stupid as to get involved with someone else especially in her condition and if Tom knew he would probably run a mile.'

Meanwhile as the dance continued, Tom drew Kitty close enough to feel her body against his and whispered that he chose the song because that's how she looked tonight and he had never felt happier. Kitty had not felt this happy in years either and as the music came to an end and they made their way back to their seats Tom held on to her hand and secretly she felt she would like him to hold her forever.

'Well I have to say you looked like a couple of professionals out there,' Connie complimented their dancing.

'That's because he led me around the floor like he was a professional. He was right when he said that he was quite good, yes you certainly surprised me, Tom, thank you.'

'Well don't be sitting down and making yourself too comfortable there's plenty more where that came from and the night is still young. Now is anyone ready for another drink?'

'Good idea, Tom. I think we're all ready for another one, it's so hot in here,' Connie suggested accepting his offer on behalf of everyone.

Halfway through the evening the drummer gave a long drum roll then Dave made an announcement for everyone to take their partners for the barn dance. 'Come along now, everyone and I mean everyone. I don't want to see anyone sitting this one out, so let's have you all up on your feet.'

Just what Alice had been waiting for! 'At last,' she thought, 'my chance to dance with Tom,' and she quickly crossed the floor, grabbed the hand of middle-aged Joe Jackson who lived alone but enjoyed nothing better than to go to the dances where he would sit and admire the women.

'Come on, Joe, I know how much you always like to do the barn dance so you can have a cheeky word or two with the women.'

'Aye, lass, I do that,' and he rose slowly to his feet, unaware that the real reason for Alice asking him to dance was for her own personal gain.

Intentionally she pulled Joe to within about a dozen couples' distance from Tom but enough to ensure the length of the dance would mean she would get her turn to dance with him. Dave tapped his feet, clapped and shouted, encouraging everyone to take to the floor, guiding them through the dance he called every time they had to change partners. The floor was bouncing, there were smiling faces everywhere especially Alice's who was almost beside herself with joy when it was finally her turn to dance with Tom. Much to her disappointment he held her at arm's length and never spoke a word.

It hadn't worked out as she had planned but she refused to give up. She would think of something else to do to spoil his night.

A couple of hours into the evening and Kitty began to

feel a little lightheaded. The room was extremely hot with so many people and so much activity; she needed to go outside for some fresh air.

'I'll come with you?' Connie offered.

'No I'll be fine thanks, Connie. I'll only need a few minutes outside then I should be alright.'

Fearing raising suspicion Tom managed to refrain from immediately grabbing the opportunity to go with her and instead said he would pop to the bar and fetch a glass of water leaving Kitty to make her own way out of the hall. She was surprised to find several people gathered outside but not knowing anyone she walked around to the side of the building where she stood alone filling her lungs with the cool evening air. It had turned dark, the moon and stars shone brightly and as she leant against the wall staring up into the night sky her feelings for Tom were foremost in her mind. 'Are you alright, Kitty? I've brought you a glass of water.' Immediately she recognised Tom's voice.

'Thanks, Tom. I will be soon. I found it a bit too hot in there and I just needed to come out for some fresh air,' and took a drink from the glass. 'I'm not used to being in such a crowded room and I began to feel a little overwhelmed.' Her mouth was still dry and as she sipped from the glass she could feel the warmth of his body as he moved closer towards her. He desperately wanted to hold her in his arms and tell her just how much he loved her. Right there under the stars with no one else in view he knew he had to grasp the opportunity to show his feelings before having to return indoors, but Kitty said she had something he should know. Immediately he placed his finger over her lips to silence her, gently removed the glass from her hand and placed it on the ground. Within seconds she felt his strong arms around her, warmth radiating from his body, and his breath hot on the curve of her neck. He whispered his intense love for her sending a shiver of excitement down her spine. She tried to resist him but with all the will in the world she couldn't. Passionately they held each other as his lips caressed her face and neck then she felt his mouth closing over hers and at that moment she knew their feelings were mutual. Every part of her body cried out for him to make love to her even though she knew it would be wrong. They continued to caress each other gently, lovingly, longingly when out of the blue images of Ernie, her bairns, and the new baby appeared before her eyes and instinctively she pushed him away.

'I'm sorry, Tom, really sorry. Please forgive me. I shouldn't have encouraged you, I...' She was lost for words.

Tom didn't speak for few seconds but after composing himself he again wrapped his arms gently around her and tenderly kissed her neck. 'It's alright, Kitty. We both know how we feel about each other. I'll wait as long as I have to. If we are meant to be together then nothing will stand in our way.' For a long time they held each other close, Tom promising their love would remain a secret for as long as was necessary.

Unbeknown to them the envious eyes of Alice Watson, the enemy in their midst, had watched their

324

every move. She was planning what she could do next but there was nothing in the world she could do to tear Tom and Kitty apart.

As they returned to the dancehall they were unsure what their future held but for now the night was not quite over and they were determined to enjoy every precious moment they had together before facing the many challenges that lay ahead.

Arriving back at the table the guilt in Kitty's eyes met the unease in Connie's and she feared Connie was about to ask questions but she had no need; Connie knew without asking that her suspicions had been confirmed.

The remainder of the night went as planned, with lots more dancing, food and drink and everyone having a great time right up until the last waltz which came around far too quickly. The dance floor soon filled up and as Tom and Kitty danced their last dance he promised her he would wait forever if he had to.

The four friends left the hall together, embracing the cool night air as they walked a short distance along the road before it was time to say goodnight to Tom. It broke his heart to have to leave Kitty but he was happy believing their feelings were mutual and that one day they would be together.

Chapter Twenty-one

Kitty had tossed and turned most of the night; all she could think about was Tom, how caring and considerate he was compared to Ernie. Completely exhausted, sleep eventually prevailed, but after just a couple of hours she was awakened by what sounded like a motorbike engine ticking over and she couldn't resist checking to see what it was so early in the morning. She jumped out of bed, cautiously stretched over Annie's bed so as not waken her and pulled back the curtains. Shocked to see a Post Office Telegram Delivery boy she felt anxious as he opened the gate leading to cottage then knocked quite loudly on the front door. She listened nervously, a couple of minutes passed and when no one responded she heard him knock a second time. Guessing Connie and Malcolm must still be sleeping she wrapped a cardigan around her shoulders and ran downstairs to answer the door before he had time to knock a third time. Everything imaginable that could have happened back home passed through her mind as she slowly opened the door confident the telegram must be for her. Was it bringing bad news about Ernie, her parents, or even Peggy? Her breathing became shallow, and her heart pounded deep inside her chest as she greeted him with a solemn, 'Good morning.'

'Good morning, madam, telegram for a Mrs K Cartwright.'

'That's me,' she said, her hand shaking as she accepted

the envelope with its large POST OFFICE TELEGRAM letters printed across the top and the address handwritten below to Mrs K Cartwright, C/O Rose Cottage, Calderthwaite, Cumberland.

By this time Connie had appeared on the stairs. 'Who is it, Kitty? What's happening, are you alright?'

'Yes I'm fine,' she lied, thanked the telegram boy then turned to Connie who immediately noticed how pale she looked and that she was holding a brown very formal looking envelope in her hand.

'Kitty that's a telegram.' She said with a gasp after spotting the large lettering on the top of the envelope and she knew immediately it could only be for Kitty. 'I think you'd better sit down before you read it.'

'Oh, Connie, what do you think has happened and to who? I always expect bad news whenever I see those telegram boys tearing along the road on their little red bikes delivering urgent messages.'

'They do deliver good news to people as well you know,' Connie responded in an attempt to try to relieve her of her worries but secretly dreaded who it was from and what the message would say.

After opening the envelope Kitty carefully withdrew the telegram. 'It's from Ernie,' she said and showed it to Connie. It read simply: RETURN HOME IMMEDIATELY STOP

'Well at least you know he is okay otherwise it would have been the police knocking at the door not the telegram boy so there is no need to worry too much about him. Now let's get the kettle on and have a cuppa before the bairns get up, I certainly don't want them to see you in this state and we can discuss what is so urgent that he wants you to go home immediately and what arrangements we need to make.'

By the time the kettle had come to the boil Malcolm who had been disturbed by their voices guessed that something was wrong and decided he must go down and check. Like the two women he was surprised at the sudden urgency for Kitty to have to return home and wondered was this just Ernie controlling her as usual by making unnecessary demands on her or, had something actually happened to him and he needed her to be with him? The three sat quietly discussing what would be the best thing to do for everyone concerned and they were all in agreement that Kitty should return home that day and to leave the bairns with them in Calderthwaite. Connie suggested she would be happy to take the bairns home after a few days leaving Kitty time to cope with whatever she had to face on her return and to take a well earned rest for a couple of days.

Public transport ran on a reduced service on Sundays and in order for Kitty to make it in time to catch a train to Newcastle a small suitcase was quickly organised into which she put a few essentials and insisted her new dress went with her to prevent it being creased inside the notorious suitcase with everything else. Kitty woke the bairns and explained to them that as Daddy was coming home unexpectedly she had to go to him but she would only be away for a few days and they could stay a little longer with Aunty Connie and Uncle Malcolm. Although

328

Jack seemed a little apprehensive at first, they took the news quite well with only a few tears being shed as they waved their mammy off.

Later that morning Connie and Malcolm took the bairns over to inform her mam and dad of the surprise events and they were equally shocked but agreed with the decisions they had made.

'We all know what a queer beggar Ernie can be but I can't imagine what can be so urgent in his self-centred life that he needs her to go home right away. It's probably for the best that she left the bairns here as who knows what it's all about,' George said being protective of Annie and Jack in the same way he had always been of Kitty and between them arrangements were made to make sure they would be kept well entertained so they would hardly have time to notice Kitty was missing.

It was about 5.00 p.m. by the time a very weary Kitty arrived home. Peggy heard the heavy front door slam shut and listened with bated breath for the footsteps on the stairs assuming it would be Ernie, but they were far too light to be his and she immediately dashed to the door refusing to believe it could be Kitty returning home as there was no sound of the bairns.

'Good heavens it is you, Kitty. I didn't expect you back so soon, but where are the bairns?'

Kitty stopped in her tracks when she heard Peggy's voice. 'I didn't either, Peggy but I received a telegram from Ernie first thing this morning demanding I come home immediately so I've left the bairns with Connie and she is bringing them home one day through the week. You'll see them soon I promise and I'm presuming Ernie must be home seeing as he wanted me back so urgently.'

'He is, Kitty. I heard him arriving around teatime yesterday but I've not seen him since and he wasn't in the flat long, he just dropped off his belongings and left.'

'He never gave you a knock or anything to let you know he was home or to say why?'

'No he just dashed upstairs and was back out again in no time at all.'

Kitty was becoming more suspicious about his strange behaviour and had so many questions she needed answering. 'Did you manage to get a look at him, did he look okay, do you think he was drunk?'

'Well I only got a glance of him as he dashed past the window but he looked alright to me.'

'I tell you this much, Peggy, that telegram gave me the fright of my life when it arrived. Until I opened it I couldn't think what could be so urgent as to need to send a telegram especially first thing on a Sunday morning. Before I opened it I was dreading who it was from. Would it be Ernie, my family or I even thought it could be bad news about you, Peggy. Thankfully there was no bad news about anyone only Ernie's demand that I come home straight away and knowing what he is like, we all agreed it was probably best that I did. Well I'm here now so I'd better get sorted out before he comes home, in what kind of state who knows but I'll prepare myself for the worst and hope for the best and I'll catch up with you sometime tomorrow.'

'I'll be here for you as always if you need anything but I insist on popping up with a nice hot cup of tea for you in a few minutes, you look absolutely worn out.'

'Thanks, Peggy. I'm certainly ready for one I can assure you.'

Kitty unlocked the door to her flat, stepped inside and almost fell over Ernie's luggage which he had just dumped in the entrance. Staring in amazement it was obvious that he hadn't come for a short stay. The amount of stuff packed into two holdalls was evidence he had brought all his belongings with him and would not be returning to the Midlands. Her mind went into overdrive. She kept asking herself what terrible thing must have happened for him to have arrived home so soon. Peggy had said he looked okay so he can't have had an accident. Had he been sacked from his job or was he in some kind of trouble? She wasn't sure what to make of the situation but it was clear he must have left in a hurry as he was not due home for a few weeks. She was dreading learning the truth, but whatever his reason for his sudden change of plans she would soon discover.

Moving their luggage into the bedroom Kitty unpacked her small suitcase and taking her toiletries into the bathroom she freshened herself up before returning to the bedroom. She put away the few items of clothing she had brought with her except for her new dress which she carefully hung outside the wardrobe as a reminder of the wonderful night she had last night and the kindness everyone had shown her in Calderthwaite. As she stood

331

back admiring Connie's handiwork her feelings for Tom returned. She crossed the room and sat on the side of the bed. For several moments she remembered the compliments he had given her as they danced that first dance together and she began humming 'You look wonderful tonight', Tom's request for their first dance, then recalled how under the stars he spoke of his deep love for her.

She knew there were many challenges ahead that she would have to confront, especially the baby she is carrying which during the past week seemed to have been almost forgotten about with so much excitement going on around her. With Ernie still to face especially if he landed home drunk, she was afraid her feelings for him could change after what had transpired between her and Tom. Changing into something more comfortable she set about lighting the fire to warm the flat which felt quite chilly, then filled a hot water bottle as the bed would surely feel cold having been empty for so long. She had just put a match to the fire when Peggy arrived with a hot cup of tea and a few groceries to see her over until she had time to go shopping next morning.

'This'll keep you going until tomorrow. There's a couple of slices of bread, a tin of beans and a couple of eggs you can both share for your tea later as we can't have you not eating properly.' There was Peggy playing mother already and she had barely been home an hour. 'And I hope Connie doesn't leave it until too late in the week to bring the bairns home. I can't wait to see them.'

'I reckon it will most likely be midweek, Peggy. It'll all

depend on how they settle without me. If they're okay she will probably hang on to them for as long as possible. You know how much she yearns to have bairns of her own so she will make the most of having them all to herself for a while,' intentionally avoiding any mention that she would want to keep them in order for her to rest a while to ensure everything goes well with the baby she was carrying.

Leaving Kitty to settle back in Peggy returned to her flat but her parting words, 'When Ernie finally decides to show his face again if he gives you any trouble you just yell for me and I'll be up the stairs in a flash,' had unnerved Kitty and she began to worry about the kind of state he would be in when he did arrive home.

It was around 10.00 p.m. when he finally showed his face and as expected was worse for wear through too much drink. After letting himself in Kitty heard him stumble against the door as he turned to close it, then after recovering his balance he quite aggressively flung the living room door wide open.

'So you've managed to make it back then.' He glared at Kitty, his voice slurred as he staggered into the living room and she knew immediately where the night was heading.

'I didn't expect you'd be home until tomorrow and where are the bairns?'

'Have you seen the time, Ernie? Where would you expect them to be at this time of night?'

'What the hell were you thinkng of putting them to bed without letting me see them?' he yelled at her, his face distorted with rage.

Nervously she began to explain. 'They haven't come home with me, Ernie. I decided to leave them with Connie and Malcolm as I didn't know what to expect when you said I had to come home straight away. I thought you must have had an accident or something and I didn't want the bairns to see you if you had been injured. Obviously I can see you haven't so what has brought you home so soon?'

He stared at her like a madman, then pulled his jacket off and flung it across the room. After yanking at his tie it was next to come off. Opening the top button of his shirt he rolled up his sleeves, acting like a man intent on starting a fight, but much to Kitty's relief he pulled an armchair close to the fire and slumped into it but sadly his tirade of abuse wasn't over.

'I bloody well live here don't I? And I can come and go as I please and I suggest you get in touch with that so-called friend of yours first thing in the morning and have them bairns brought home right away. You had no bloody right leaving them with bloody strangers. They're our bairns not theirs and it's your responsibility to look after them nobody else's!'

'There's no need for all that swearing and besides they're not strangers and they are having a lovely time.' She paused choosing her words carefully so as not to aggravate him further as it was obvious he must had been drinking nearly all day and she was only too aware how explosive the situation was becoming. 'I thought it would be better for the bairns if I got the house warmed through and some shopping in before they come home and besides they are having such fun being able to play outside in the garden and…'

'Oh I bet you've all been having fun,' he said as his head dropped towards his chest. Thankfully he was beginning to look tired, the heat from the roaring fire was making him drowsy and Kitty desperately hoped he would fall asleep but unfortunately he kept fighting it. Pulling his shoes off like a wild animal he flung them one at a time across the room just missing the window. 'While I've been working my fingers to the bone seven bloody days a week to send money home to you, you have had people running after you so you could live the life of a lady.'

'Don't you think it would be better if we forget everything for now, Ernie? It would make more sense to sit down and discuss things sensibly in the morning when you're sober.'

'We have nowt to discuss, Kitty, you have taken advantage of my good nature. I work away to make extra money to pay the rent and feed and clothe you and the bairns and what do you do? You go skipping around the country on fancy bloody holidays.'

The remark about him sending her extra money angered her and she knew she couldn't control her tongue any longer. 'I've never seen a penny of the extra money you earn, Ernie, so I suggest before you say anything else about that, the best thing you can do tonight is to go to bed and sleep off the drink and we'll talk tomorrow when I promise I will do my best to

335

arrange for the bairns to be brought home as soon as possible.' She knew the only thing she would get from Ernie tonight was trouble and that the best thing she could do was to try and get him into bed as quickly as possible. 'I've put a hot water bottle in the bed so it will be nice and warm,' she said holding her breath for a moment hoping this would entice him to go. He didn't answer but got out of the chair and staggered across the room muttering words that made no sense at all and she observed his every move with mixed feelings of both relief and disgust. 'Thank God the bairns aren't here to see him in such a state,' she thought. 'I've never seen him this drunk before which makes me think there is more to his sudden return home than meets the eye. Hopefully I'll learn the truth in the morning when he has sobered up.'

Picking up his clothes and shoes she was just about to follow him into the bedroom when she heard him shouting at the top of his voice. 'Kitty, you bloody bitch. What the hell is this and what the hell have you been up to while you've been away?' She knew instinctively he was referring to her dress and as she entered the room she was astounded to see how furious he was. Like a wild animal he wrenched it from the hanger.

'Ernie no, Ernie please, no. Connie…'

'Never mind bloody Connie. What the hell have you two been up to?' Tearing aggressively at the seams he began ripping it apart. Kitty charged at him a couple of times but was unsuccessful in her attempt to snatch it from his hands and he flung it into the corner of the room. He lunged at her from across the bed and began

336

relentlessly attacking her until finally he pushed her towards the flat door still yelling uncontrollably. 'No bloody wife of mine should be seen out wearing a dress like that, and what the hell you have been up to I can't imagine, but I promise you this much, Kitty, it won't happen again.' At that he released the latch on the flat door, opened it wide then with one almighty shove he pushed her headlong down the stairs.

She landed at the bottom and he stood gazing in horror as she lay completely still. Panicking he went back inside and slammed the door. What had he done? His actions seemed to bring him back to his senses and for several moments he leant against the door. Breathing rapidly he realised the possible consequences of his actions.

Throughout their confrontation, from the comfort of her cosy bed Peggy had listened anxiously to the commotion going on upstairs and when she heard the heavy thud she rushed out and what greeted her was worse than she could have ever imagined. Kitty lay sprawled across the hallway with blood pouring from a head wound and when she spoke to her there was no response.

'Oh my God. I'll get you an ambulance, Kitty,' she said unaware that she was unconscious and couldn't hear a word she was saying. Still wearing her nightdress, she grabbed her coat and the front door key and rushed across the street to Jean's. Relieved to see the lights were still on she hammered on the door with a clenched fist. Colin answered and was taken aback at seeing a breathless and shaking Peggy standing there at that time of night and immediately he knew something was wrong.

'There's no time to spare, Colin. We need an ambulance quickly. It's Kitty. I heard them arguing and it looks like that swine of a husband of hers has pushed her down the stairs and I can't get any response from her… nothing, not even a murmur.'

Colin called to Jean to say he was dashing off to ring for an ambulance and would explain as soon as he got back. After seeing Peggy safely across the road he ran as fast as his legs could carry him to the phone box. Back at the house Kitty was still not responding, so Peggy dashed and got dressed then held her hand until the ambulance arrived speaking words of comfort throughout in the hope she could hear. As they lifted Kitty carefully on to the stretcher the ambulance men did their best to assure Peggy that she would be fine once they checked her over but she had her doubts. She knew how bad a fall Kitty had suffered. Just as they were about to close the ambulance doors Jean appeared. Colin had insisted that she should go to the hospital with Peggy and to stay with her until they knew Kitty was going to be alright.

Nurses and doctors were on hand as soon the ambulance arrived and Kitty was rushed off to accident and emergency. The two women were asked to wait in the waiting room until they could give them some positive information. In the meantime staff enquired about what had happened and when Peggy explained to them what she had heard and how she had found Kitty sprawled out at the bottom of the stairs, the police were called to the hospital and she was asked to repeat the events she heard leading up to the fall. After gathering as much information as possible the police headed off to the house returning within a couple of hours to inform Peggy there was no one at the flat and it looked like Mr Cartwright had done a disappearing act via the back entrance as the door was unlocked and the gate leading into the back lane had been left ajar.

'It seems the argument you say you heard, Mrs Wilson, might have started over a dress which was ripped to shreds and thrown into the corner of the bedroom. The bedcovers were all ruffled as though there had been a struggle between them and it appears to us that it must have been after that that he either pushed her down the stairs or she could have fallen accidently trying to escape from him. The fire was still burning but there was no guard in front of it, so it looks like he made a sharp exit, which leads us to believe it was a push rather than a fall. We're unable to speak to Mrs Cartwright at present but as soon as she is able to talk we will be back for a full statement and hopefully she will allow us to begin the procedure of pressing charges against him if he is guilty of intentionally pushing her and causing her injuries. Until we know the full circumstances of what happened we are not obliged to try and trace him. He may well be innocent, we don't know yet, but I assure you no stone will be left unturned and your neighbour will have our full support.'

Night had turned to early morning with still no news as to exactly what injuries Kitty had sustained. All they had been told was that she was still with the doctors, that she had opened her eyes for a few seconds but was still unable to speak. By this time poor Peggy was worn out and as there was nothing either her or Jean could do they decided it would be best to go home and return later in the day when according to the nursing staff hopefully Kitty would be feeling a little better and may be able to talk to them. Just as they were about to leave one of the doctors appeared.

'We've done all we can for her tonight, the large gash in her head has been stitched and should heal well in a week or two as long as she doesn't catch it. We have thoroughly checked her over and don't think she has broken anything which is a miracle considering the fall she has had but until she is able to speak to us and can point out any specific pain we can't be absolutely sure that she has not sustained any fractures. We will make sure she remains comfortable until the morning when we will be in again to check how she is. The only other thing which I'm sorry to have to tell you is that we will have to get the gynaecologist to check her over first thing to make sure everything is okay as sadly she has aborted her baby. Now if you'll excuse me I'll see if I can catch a couple of hours sleep before I'm needed again.'

'Certainly, doctor and thank you,' they said almost in unison and the moment he turned away the two women's eyes were transfixed.

'You mean you honestly didn't know, Jean?'

'I certainly didn't... did you, Peggy?'

'No not for definite, but I did tell you I had my

suspicions. I figured that was the reason she suddenly took off to Connie's. I know it's very sad to lose a baby but after what he did to her last night it's maybe for the best. You don't know what harm it might have caused the baby and it may have been born with some kind of disability. I just hope Kitty comes to her senses and can see that she would be better off without him the way he treats her every time he's home and I hate to admit it, but I think her parents were right about him all along. Well at least we know she is going to be okay, so let's grab a taxi. I'll pay for it, Jean, to thank you and Colin for your help. I certainly couldn't have coped without you…. Poor Kitty, she doesn't deserve this but I'll be there for her when she wakes up. I love her as though she were my own daughter and I'll be back by her bedside this afternoon to see how she is.'

Chapter Twenty-two

When Peggy visited that afternoon Kitty was still very poorly and sleeping most of the time so she was only allowed to stay for a very short time. When a nurse managed to waken her it was barely long enough for Kitty to ask Peggy if she would let Connie and Malcolm know as soon as possible what had happened and could they hang on to the bairns for her. Promising to do so straightaway she left telling her not to worry as everyone both here and in Calderthwaite would help with whatever was needed.

Leaving the hospital she headed straight for home where she grabbed a pen and paper, scribbled down a few brief words and Connie's address taken from Kitty's letter. From the back of a drawer in her dressing table she lifted out a small Old Holborn tobacco tin containing her small amount of savings and took out a pound note which she slipped into her coat pocket, replacing the lid securely and putting it back in the exact spot she had taken it from. With the piece of paper and the pound note in her purse she left the house and headed straight to the Post Office. As she hurried along her thoughts were with Connie and Malcolm who would no doubt be shocked when a second telegram arrives within two days.

The Post Office was very quiet and on reaching the counter she took the piece of paper and the money from her purse. 'I'd like to send a telegram please. I've written down what it's to say and the name and address of the people it's to go to and it's very important that it reaches them today.' She handed it to the postmistress who much to Peggy's embarrassment had found it necessary to narrow her eyes in order to decipher her writing.

'I'm very sorry but I had to write it down quickly, and I've kept it very brief because I understand telegrams can turn out to be quite expensive.'

'Aye they certainly aren't cheap but a blessing especially in an emergency, and I do hope Kitty gets better very soon,' she said warmly then attempted to read the note again, this time reading it out loud. 'Kitty is in the RVI letter following Peggy.' And then the address to be sure she had read it correctly, then after taking payment for it she assured Peggy it would reach them that evening.

As she was just about to leave Peggy suddenly remembered she didn't have a postage stamp and returned to the counter. 'I really must write that letter and get it in the post tonight to let them know exactly what has happened but there will be no point if I don't have a stamp for it.'

'You're right there it won't reach them without one... and take your time over writing it.' She quickly added the latter thinking she needs to make a better job of it than the note she had been given if these people were to understand it. 'You still have well over an hour or so to catch the post so don't you go dashing about. We don't want you finishing up in the next bed to Kitty do we?'

'Aye that's the last thing I need right now,' she agreed

343

sounding a little forlorn.

She knew the telegram would be sufficient for Connie and Malcolm to keep the bairns, but at the same time they would be desperate to find out exactly what had happened to Kitty. Determined to get the letter in the post that night to be sure they would receive it the next morning, she ignored the postmistress's advice and set off walking home as fast as her weary legs would allow.

With a refreshing cup of tea to help revive her sapping strength, Peggy sat at the dining table and though sending letters was not her strong point she began painstakingly to write.

Dear Connie and Malcolm

By now you will have got the telegram about poor Kitty. I dont no the full story about what happened to her but after a big row with Ernie I found her lying uncontous at the bottom of the stairs. She has had a lot of stitchs to a very bad cut on her head and has lost a baby which I didnt no anything about and she is very poorly and she will have to stay in hospital for a while so she has asked if you will keep the bairns for now. If you are wondring about Ernie well he has disapeared but I don't care about him and the police may be looking for him. Dont worry I will visit Kitty every day. I want to catch the post tonite so I will finish now but will right again and keep you up to date with how she is. Please give Annie and Jack big hugs from there Mammy and me.

Peggy

Reading through the letter she felt proud, being a very poor speller it had taken her a lot of effort to write just a few short lines but she was sure Connie would be able to understand what she was saying. Putting her feet up would have been her first choice but knowing she must catch the post she set off again, this time her first stop being the post-box, then she would call in at Jean's on the way home to give her an update on Kitty.

'If you don't mind, Jean, I won't bother to come in. The lack of sleep is catching up on me so I'm off to get the fire roaring to heat the water for a nice hot bath and an early night. I've been to the hospital this afternoon but was only allowed to see Kitty for a few minutes as she really is quite poorly but she did manage to talk a little. She asked me to let Connie and Malcolm know what has happened and to ask them to hang on to the bairns. I've sent a telegram which they should get tonight and I have just been and posted a letter telling them what little I know and which I hope will reach them in the morning.'

'You've done really well for your age, Peggy, but you look absolutely worn out now so make sure you have something to eat then have a nice long soak in the bath and a good night's sleep. I'll pop across in the morning and make arrangements for us to visit the hospital together.'

'Aye, poor Kitty. I can't help worrying about her but at least they're all in good hands and being looked after properly. See you in the morning, Jean.' Leaving for home she looked a worn out figure with the result Jean was a little concerned that this was all going to be too much for her to cope with.

Connie and Malcolm and their additional family were

345

tucking into dinner when they thought they heard the sound of a motorcycle engine, and within seconds their eyes were transfixed in disbelief when they heard a knock at the door.

'It can't possibly be, Malcolm, not another…?'

He cut her short. 'I think it is, Connie. I'll go, you stay here with the bairns and don't worry it might only be from Kitty to tell us she is already on her way back.'

'Well I hope that's all it is.'

Malcolm answered the door and sure enough facing him was a young telegram boy.

'Telegram for a Mr and Mrs Ferguson this time,' he said with a puzzled look on his face.

'That's us,' Malcolm informed him as he reached out to accept the telegram.

'I can't believe I'm here again it was me who delivered one to Mrs Cartwright only yesterday so I hope I'm not the bearer of bad news.'

'Nothing we won't be able to handle,' Malcolm replied apprehensively. Then added in a more friendly tone, 'Mind don't you be making a habit of coming to us with telegrams. We can do without the worry that always seems to accompany them.'

'Sorry about that, sir, but we do deliver good news as well,' he said with a cheerful smile, left and sped off to his next delivery.

Slightly hesitant and looking nervous Malcolm returned to the room. 'It's another telegram Connie so would you like me to read it first?'

'I'd rather you did. Telegrams always make me feel nervous.'

His eyes flashed rapidly between Connie and the bairns as he opened telegram. 'It's from Peggy not Kitty,' he said sounding and looking completely shocked as he read the brief message.

'Oh no do you think something must have happened to her?'

'She's in hosp…' He stopped suddenly not wanting the bairns to hear and handed it to Connie to read for herself.

'What can have happened? I hope she hasn't lost the baby in which case they will probably want to keep her in for a few days.'

'Let's not speculate, Connie and seeing as Peggy is going to drop us a line straightaway we should hear soon enough. If it was anything really serious you would have been asked to dash across to Newcastle as she really has no one except poor old Peggy and Ernie… well he's not much use when he's at home anyway!'

'You're probably right on all counts, Malcolm.' Then she lowered her voice. 'We must make sure the bairns don't know anything is wrong. They've settled with us better than we could have hoped so let's just carry on as though nothing has happened.'

A little later Connie was just about to take Annie and Jack up to bed and read them a story when there was a further knock at the door.

'Will you go, Malcolm? That'll probably be Mam hoping to see the bairns before bedtime.'

Answering the door he was surprised to find Tom at the other side. 'Oh it's you, Tom. Come in. I hope you're not the bearer of bad news as well.'

347

Tom was lost for words, wary of what bad news they had received since he last saw them.

Connie was taken aback to see Tom and not her mam enter the room. 'Tom!' she said surprised as an excited Jack wriggled out of her arms and ran towards him. 'You're looking a bit washy, are you still getting over Saturday night or has Malcolm told you the bad news?'

'He did say you have received some bad news but not what it was,' and immediately he became suspicious that it must be something to do with Kitty when he noticed only four place settings at the table.

'Malcolm will explain when I take the bairns up to bed, but I reckon I'll have to delay that for a while so they can have a few minutes with you to tell you what they have been up to all day.'

For the first time ever Tom was only half listening to them. His thoughts were elsewhere. Anxious by Kitty's noticeable absence he refrained from asking questions in front of them.

'Time for bed, you two. It's getting late now and I have a lovely story about a little kitten and a ball of wool to read to you tonight so say "night night" to Uncle Malcolm and Tom and you will see them again tomorrow.'

Connie eventually managed to entice them upstairs leaving Malcolm to break the news to Tom who immediately they left the room asked where Kitty was.

'It's quite a long story, Tom. She's had to go back home.'

'Home…,' he gasped, '…but what about the bairns?

Why are they still here? I can't believe she would go without them!'

'It all began early yesterday morning. We were all still in bed when a telegram arrived from Ernie demanding she return home immediately. Everyone agreed that she should go that day and as you can see leave the bairns with us until she found out what was so urgent. The bairns have settled with us no bother and all seemed well until just an hour or so ago when another telegram arrived this time for us. It was from Peggy …she's the old lady who lives in the flat below… to tell us that Kitty's in hospital and that's as much as we know. She is writing a letter with all the details so we are hoping it arrives in the morning. Obviously the bairns will stay with us for as long as necessary.'

Tom looked dumbfounded. Lost for words he stared blankly at the floor. One minute he had her in his arms and now she was gone, gone back to her abusive husband. Not only that but she was lying in a hospital bed somewhere and no one seemed to know what had happened to her. He feared the worst thinking Ernie may have physically abused her but kept his thoughts to himself. He was absolutely distraught and it showed in his stricken face.

Malcolm remained silent to allow him time to take in the news. He had a good idea how he felt about Kitty and the news would be painful to take in. Crossing to the sideboard he took out a bottle of whiskey and two whiskey tumblers and poured a small measure into each handing one to Tom.

'Here you are, Tom, get that down you. I think we could do with this; it has been rather a strange couple of days to say the least.'

Connie returned to the room just as they began to sip their whiskey and suggested she would join them in a small one with a dash of water as the bairns had gone straight off to sleep cuddled up to each other in their mammy's bed.

'I take it Malcolm will have told you that Kitty had to leave quite early yesterday and is apparently laid up in hospital,' she said joining him with her tot of whiskey on the sofa.

'I can't believe it, poor Kitty. I hope she is going to be alright. Have you any idea what might have happened to her?'

'We've no idea but hopefully we'll hear in the morning. We expect to have had a letter by then.'

'Yes Malcolm did say, but tomorrow must seem such a long time away when you're so worried about her. Do you know which hospital she's in so we can ring and enquire?'

'We won't lie to you, Tom, we do know but I think you'll agree it would be better to leave it until the morning, and if Peggy's letter doesn't arrive we'll ring then. Our post usually arrives quite early so we'll just have to be patient, but we're pretty sure if it had been anything really serious then Peggy would have wanted us to go to her straight away.'

Plucking up courage Tom spoke from the heart. 'I would really like to go and see her unless of course you

350

object. As you know my leave will be over before we know it and I feel I couldn't possibly go back without knowing and seeing that she is well again.'

'Your asking doesn't come as a surprise, Tom. Connie and I have suspected all along that you two had become more than just acquaintances. Listen it's none of our business what either of you do, you're both adults, but I'll warn you Ernie Cartwright can be a very violent man and if for one minute he thought Kitty had been up to no good he wouldn't take it sitting down and he would make her suffer. Not only that but he would be after you in a shot.'

'And possibly us as well,' Connie added. 'He would probably blame us for inviting her here in the first place. You know you're a handsome lad, Tom and could choose any woman you want, so why would you want to take on someone who is already married with bairns? Once Kitty is up and about again then you both need to think long and hard about whatever it is that's going on between you both.'

'I realise this must have come as a big shock so I can understand what you must be thinking but I fell for Kitty the minute I set eyes on her; she's so beautiful inside and out. We talked for a long time on the train and she was very open about the state of her marriage, saying it was not perfect but she would stick by Ernie if only for the sake of the bairns. To be honest I have my doubts and therefore told her I'll wait for as long as it takes. She also told me all about her parents and I think they are most likely the reason she refuses to leave him. It sounds to me that they would love to hear the marriage wasn't working if only to throw it in her face that they had been right about him all along.'

'Well it seems she certainly has been very open with you. I have suspected for a long time that things weren't quite as they should have been between them but she keeps a lot of things close to her chest. Regarding her parents they never liked Ernie from the start and were dead against the marriage even though they did attend the ceremony. It seems to me that you turned out to be a good listener, someone she could open up to as you didn't know anyone she was talking about and at the end of the journey you would both be going your separate ways, or so she thought!'

'I'll tell you the same as I told Kitty, that I believe fate brought us together. You may already know that she doesn't believe in fate but why else would she open her heart out to me if she didn't feel some kind of connection between us, and it beats me why on earth she stays if she is unhappy.'

'Believe me, Tom, there are lots of women out there who have to put up with a lot from their husbands but still stick by them through thick and thin.'

'But I don't think women should have to put up with it if there is a way out for them and it can't be healthy for bairns to see their parents battling all the time.' He lowered his head wondering how much more he should tell them and decided there was no point in holding back. 'I think I should tell you everything that happened when we were alone on Saturday night. We agreed our feelings are mutual and to put you in the picture said we would keep it our secret for as long as necessary. I know all this has happened very quickly and it must be hard for you to take in but now she is in hospital I'm sure you'll understand why I would like to go and see her.'

They both fell silent for a few minutes as they contemplated the consequences of this unexpected turn of events. Tom looked and felt uncomfortable but under the circumstances he knew it had to be said and he waited nervously for their response.

'As we have said, Tom, it really is none of our business what Kitty does with her life, but as she has been a dear friend of mine for many years whatever she does I like to think that it is right for her after the way things have turned out what with her parents and now Ernie. It has not been easy for her and I would hate to think she is making a mistake.' She looked across at Malcolm. 'Perhaps another whiskey wouldn't come in wrong. This is all getting a bit too much to take in.'

Malcolm took their glasses and poured another small measure into each, although right now he felt doubles would go down better.

'I know it's wrong and I shouldn't be encouraging it but if it's meant to be then I can only say here's to you and Kitty whatever your futures hold,' and he raised his glass much to Connie's utter amazement. 'Whatever will be, will be, you both have my blessing. It will be a long tough journey you'll have to face but promise me this, Tom… please don't rush Kitty into anything. You have said that you have both agreed to wait until the time is right and that's what you must do for everyone's sake, especially the bairns. Their lives are what's important especially when they are still so very young. Perhaps it's as well you still have several months before you are finished with the army which should give you both plenty of time to think things over thoroughly.'

'If I can get a word in,' Connie butted in, 'I noticed from the start that you two get on very well together, but not only that, you care so much about Annie and Jack and they love you for it, but like Malcolm I insist, please don't rush Kitty into anything especially now that she is laid up in hospital. She must feel her life is in turmoil. You both need to take things a day at a time and with that in mind I suggest we finish our drinks and call it a night. When you call tomorrow I promise if we have received Peggy's letter we will sit down together and discuss what steps to take but right now I need to pop over to Mam and Dad's to let them know what has happened. They would be most upset if I kept them out of the picture, they love Kitty as they would another daughter. Oh and by the way I better warn you, you will find they won't take the news about you and Kitty as lightly as we have so you best prepare yourself for a few strong words rolling off Mam's tongue when you next see her.'

Tom had listened attentively to all they had to say and felt he must express his appreciation for the way they had accepted the shocking news. 'Thank you both for being so understanding. Kitty is very lucky to have such loyal friends who I hope I can say are my friends too.'

'You can, Tom. Whatever happens between you two in

the future, you will always be welcome here anytime. Now if you will excuse me I'll head off to break the news and I'll see you again in the morning.'

Chapter Twenty-three

Four pairs of eager eyes were watching for the postman. Connie, desperate to learn what had happened to her beloved friend waited anxiously on the doorstep in the hope that he would deliver Peggy's letter. Having taken the morning off to support his wife, Malcolm was upstairs watching from the bedroom window playing 'see who spots the postman first' with Annie and Jack.

'There he is,' Annie shouted at the top of her voice the second she spotted him. 'I knew I would see him before you, Jack, and look I think that's Tom over there… look, Jack, look,' and she pointed towards a man riding a bicycle in the distance. 'It is him. Uncle Malcolm, isn't it?' she asked almost pleading for him to agree.

'Oh I'm not so sure it is him,' he kidded her. He had of course seen both the men but he leant his head against the windowpane pretending he needed a closer look. 'Umm I'm still not sure it's him, Annie, but we'll go downstairs and wait to see if anyone arrives.'

She didn't answer but jumped fearlessly from the windowsill. 'Come on, Jack. I know it's Tom,' she said excitedly so convinced in her own mind that she was right.

Malcolm lifted Jack from the sill and as they made their way downstairs he decided Tom's early arrival could turn out to be a blessing. If Peggy's letter did arrive then Tom could amuse the bairns while he and Connie sat down to find out just what had caused Kitty to end up in hospital.

'Morning, Connie, lovely morning again. I've just the one for you today but you'll be pleased to know it's not a bill.'

Reg their regular postman for many years was cheerful as always. On first term names with just about everyone in Calderthwaite and the surrounding villages he never failed to turn up no matter what the weather and always had a cheery smile and a good word for everyone.

Fixing her eyes on the envelope as he handed it to her, Connie felt confident it was the letter they were hoping for and immediately checked the postmark for confirmation before acknowledging him.

'Good morning, Reg, I was hoping this would arrive today,' she said with a smile and as he left to continue his deliveries she wished him a nice day. Desperate to read Peggy's letter she was just about to close the door when she heard someone calling to her.

'Good morning, Connie.'

She recognised Tom's voice and called back to him. 'Morning, Tom. I guessed you would turn up bright and early this morning to see if we'd received Peggy's letter.' She waited until he reached the door.

'I saw the postman leaving, is it the letter you wanted?' he asked anxiously as much for his own peace of mind as hers.

'He did, Tom and seeing as you're here it might be a good idea if you take the bairns straight through to the garden while Malcolm and I sit down and see what Peggy has to say. We won't keep anything back from you but just in case there is really bad news then it might be better if they're out of earshot.'

Connie's hands were shaking as she ripped open the envelope and took out the letter, her eyes scanning the words at rapid speed.

'Never.' she spoke loudly and immediately turned to Malcolm. 'The things Kitty has been telling Tom seem to be true. It appears they've had a big row and Ernie has pushed her down the stairs causing her as we had already suspected to lose the baby but not only that, she's had stitches to a head wound and I wouldn't be surprised if we find out later a few broken bones as well.' Finding it almost too hard to believe, she clung on to the letter needing to read it a second time to make sure she had read it properly and not misunderstood anything Peggy had written.

'It's not good, Malcolm,' she said shaking her head as she re-read the letter before handing it to him to read for himself.

'The bloody swine. Pardon my language, Connie,' he blurted out disgusted that Ernie would go as far as to push her down a flight of stairs knowing she was bound to suffer serious injury. 'I'm just glad we decided to keep the bairns with us otherwise who knows what might have happened to them?'

'And poor Peggy. I can't help thinking it must have been a terrible shock for her finding Kitty lying there unconscious, and I'm wondering what all that is about the police. Do you think Peggy must have reported him?'

'I've no idea, Connie, but if she didn't then most likely the hospital would have if they thought for one minute Kitty's injuries were caused intentionally and her fall wasn't an accident.'

'I really don't know what to think but one thing is certain, Malcolm, the bairns will stay with us until we know she is one hundred percent well enough to look after them.' She pondered for a minute wondering just how serious Kitty's injuries could be. 'Well we better break the news to Tom. He'll no doubt be desperate to find out.'

She was determined the bairns weren't to know that their mammy was in hospital. They were perfectly happy up to now therefore there was no reason to tell them. She asked Malcolm to take treats into the garden for the bairns and to warn Tom that the news was not good.

Tom's face was ashen as he dashed indoors.

'Come through, Tom.' Connie's voice sounded sombre as she anticipated his reaction and asked if he would like to read the letter himself.

As a result of what Malcolm had said and the look on Connie's face he knew it wasn't going to be a pleasant read and prepared himself for the worst.

Connie watched nervously. His expression continually changed as he carefully absorbed every word. Shaken by the extent of what had happened to his beloved Kitty he never uttered a word.

'You okay, Tom?'

No response.

'Tom!'

'I can't believe he could do such a thing especially when… I promise you, Connie, I had no idea. That's one thing she did keep to herself.'

'Of course we all knew she was pregnant. It's the reason we asked her here so she could take things easy for a while, but it wasn't our place to tell you though we did wonder whether Kitty had said anything.'

'I swear to you, Connie, I knew nothing though knowing wouldn't have changed my feelings for her. It certainly wouldn't have stopped me befriending her, she's such a lovely person, and the kids, well they are just great to be around but I would never have...' His voice trailed away.

Connie knew what he was about to say and believed his every word.

With just over a week before he had to return to base he knew he must to go to her. How would he explain not only to his parents who had no idea their son had fallen in love with the young wife and mother, but also Connie's parents when they heard of his intentions?

'It's no good, Connie, I really must go to her. It sounds to me she's in a pretty bad way and you know I don't have a lot of leave left. If the police are looking for Ernie then he must have done a runner which suggests to me he did push her and if that's the case then I don't think I need to worry about him turning up at the hospital. Will you have a quick word with Malcolm and let me know how you both feel about it?'

'I don't think either of us can stop you doing whatever you want, Tom, you're an adult and know your own mind, and from what you have told us, who are we to try to stop you? It's not possible for me to visit as Malcolm is going into work this afternoon and even though I know

Mam would look after the bairns I'm not prepared to pass the responsibility over to her. They're only just getting used to the idea of being here without Kitty. The last thing we want to happen is for Annie to start wondering what is going on; she's as bright as button is that one and she just might pick up that something is wrong.

'That's all the more reason for me to visit, and I can assure you I wouldn't even think about rushing to Kitty's bedside if I wasn't absolutely sure that she will be pleased to see me.'

'I think you might be right, Tom, so I suggest you go as soon as possible, then we can get to the bottom of just exactly what did happen to her when she arrived home on Sunday,' and then they called Malcolm back into the house.

'Do you want to tell him what we've discussed or should I?' Connie asked.

'It's okay, Connie. I'll tell him,' and Tom stood up to meet him as he entered the room with Annie and Jack close behind. 'I was saying to Connie that I would to go and visit Ki....' he stopped himself just in time before saying her name in front of the bairns.

Malcolm looked at Connie to see what her reaction had been to his unexpected request, but she was expressionless. 'What do you think, Connie?'

'I've already told him it is not up to us to tell him what he can and can't do.'

'My thoughts too,' he said. 'We can't change what has gone on between you two but do you think she will be well enough to have visitors so soon, and more importantly, Tom, are you sure she will want to see you?'

'I'm absolutely certain she will otherwise I wouldn't even think about going.'

'It seems your mind is made up so the best thing we can do is agree, and decide the best way you can inform us. How soon are you planning on going?'

'On the afternoon train. I'll pack a few things for a couple of overnight stays, there's sure be a place near to the hospital that will put me up, and then I'll be able to pop in and see her as often as they will allow.'

'At least if one of us has been to visit her then we'll find out exactly how she is. What do you think, Malcolm, I could arrange to be in the telephone box each night at nine after the bairns have gone to bed? Tom could ring and speak to me then.'

'What a good idea, Connie. Seems like everything is sorted then!'

After giving Tom the number of the telephone box she told the bairns he was going back to help on the farm. As expected there were a few moans and groans when they weren't allowed to go with him, but they were promised another visit very soon.

Connie saw him out and as they said their goodbyes in a rather serious tone she asked, 'Promise me just this one thing, Tom, if Kitty decides she doesn't want you there you won't put any pressure on her and you'll head straight back here?'

'I promise I will but believe me she will be over the moon to see me especially after what has happened. I reckon this could be the last straw for her and could be the beginning of the end of their marriage.'

'Don't you count on it, Tom. Kitty has always managed to cope with adversity from whichever direction it came and will probably overcome this one in just the same way.'

'Well we'll just have to see but one thing is certain, time will tell. Now I must be off and make sure you're in the phone box tonight, I'll be ringing you spot on 9 o'clock.'

Chapter Twenty-four

Olive Watson was taken aback when her son returned home so soon. Breaking the news that he was heading to the North East to visit Kitty in hospital, he explained why she had returned home and the real reason why he felt he must go and see her. Admitting she had noticed a change in him since he met Kitty she had never for one minute suspected how close the two of them had become.

'That's the last thing I would have suspected and to be honest I think you need your head looking at, Tom Watson. A lovely lass she might be but she's married with two bairns... and, oh for goodness' sake, Tom, I don't think you understand the consequences of what you are doing!' She jumped up from her seat annoyed to think her son could be so stupid. 'I really don't know what has come over you but whatever it is let me warn you, lad, you'll never turn a city lass into a country lass. Unlike Alice she'll never make a good farmer's wife that's for sure.'

'For heaven's sake, Mam, have I said anything about wanting a wife?' Shocked she was still foolish enough to hope that one day Alice Armstrong would actually become Mrs Alice Watson he calmly tried to make her understand. 'Listen, Mam, Alice will never have a place in my life and when you hear the full story about Kitty and me then I can guarantee given time you will have a change of heart.'

She didn't look at all convinced. 'Well I hope you're

not just feeling sorry for her about whatever it is that she seems to need so much sympathy over, but when you do see her let's hope she isn't too badly hurt and give her our regards and wish her a speedy recovery.'

'That sounds more like my mam,' he said giving her a hug knowing she didn't have a bad bone in her body. It was not like her to be so outspoken and he left without any further discussion.

Throughout the train journey he reflected on the unexpected events that had taken place during his short leave and could hardly believe it was less than two weeks since they met. His feelings for Kitty were so strong he felt as though he had known her for years, and was confident she felt the same way. Amazed how quickly their meeting turned into friendship, he was even more overwhelmed how their friendship turned into love that neither could explain. After all the years without a girl by his side, to find the love of his life already married, with two kids and living at the opposite side of the country seemed beyond belief. Following the horrific events of Sunday night he could only hope Kitty would come to her senses and refuse to return to face more pain and suffering which was all Ernie seemed to have to offer her.

With his mind in overdrive and unable to manage a catnap his journey seemed to go on forever, but he knew once the train arrived at its destination it wouldn't take him long to reach the hospital. Hopefully Kitty would be feeling well enough for visitors, and as he had travelled a long distance, whatever time he arrived at the hospital he felt sure they would allow him to see her straightaway.

365

The train arrived at its destination on time and he headed to the station cafe for a quick sandwich and a cup of tea; enough to satisfy his appetite until after his visit when he would search for accommodation and a decent meal. After jumping into a taxi it wasn't until it pulled up outside the hospital that he began to feel a little anxious. The reality of what had happened to Kitty was just beginning to sink in and he walked nervously into the reception area.

'Good evening. How can I help?' the receptionist asked.

'I understand you had a Mrs Kitty Cartwright admitted on Sunday night. I'm here to visit her so could you tell me which ward she is on?'

'I will check but visiting is only between 7.00 p.m. and 8.00 p.m. so I'm afraid you'll have to wait until then.'

'But I have just travelled all the way over from the North West where she was staying with friends when her husband sent for her to return home immediately and since arriving home she has had an accident which has resulted in her ending up here. She has left her two bairns with her friends and of course they are anxious to find out how she is and I have come on their behalf.'

'Then in that case Matron's sure to allow you to see her outside of visiting times. I'll check which ward she is on then call her to let her know who you are and that you are on your way up.'

'Thank you,' he acknowledged her, relieved that the visit could go ahead immediately.

'It's on the fourth floor, Ward 41 to your right. There

are lifts further along the corridor or stairs should you prefer them.'

After thanking her again he didn't need to be told twice and took the lift. Matron, a portly lady with a rather stern expression but who turned out to be the very opposite to what she portrayed was waiting to meet him and took him straight to Kitty. She was lying on her side in what looked to be a deep sleep.

'Kitty I've brought along a visitor to see you.' Matron leant over and spoke directly into her ear but she didn't move. Tapping her shoulder very gently she tried again. 'Kitty you have a lovely young man here to see you. Are you going to open your eyes?'

She began to stir and eventually turned on to her back, half opened her eyes, but immediately turned back onto her side.

'Would you like to try speaking to her?' Matron asked, stepping to one side.

'Kitty it's me, Tom. Are you going to wake up and talk to me? I've come all this way specially to see you.'

Rubbing her eyes she could hardly believe it when, through blurred vision she eventually recognised him and instantly stretched her hands out towards him. Matron knew it was time to take her leave when she managed to sit up and Tom held her close.

'Oh, Tom, Tom I…. Oh I don't know what to say. What are you doing here? Did Connie and Malcolm tell you I was in hospital and do you know how the bairns are? I miss them so much.'

Positioning her pillows so she could sit comfortably

Tom pulled a chair up to the bed, and took her hand in his. 'Just take things slowly, Kitty, we have plenty of time to talk about everything. I'm not dashing off anywhere. Now listen, I saw Annie and Jack this morning and they are fine. They couldn't be in a happier place without you but more importantly how are you feeling?'

'A bit sore in places as you would expect, especially my head but nothing the doctors have told me that won't heal through time.'

'So are you going to tell me what happened to cause you to finish up in a hospital bed?

'There's nothing much to tell, Tom, other than I slipped and fell down stairs from top to bottom.'

'Really? Well that's not what Peggy said in her letter to Connie.'

'She has written to them already?'

'She has. They received a telegram from her yesterday saying you were in hospital then a letter arrived this morning giving them the details and that's when I knew I had to come straightaway to see you. Tell me the truth, Kitty. Did Ernie push you down the stairs?'

'Is that what Peggy has told them?'

'No, but she did say she had heard you having a big row so I'm just assuming from what you have told me about him physically abusing you that there may have been a struggle and he has pushed you down the stairs.'

'We did have a row. He was drunk as you will have probably guessed, but he didn't push me, Tom. He had gone to bed and I was dashing down to Peggy's to apologise about the noise when I slipped and that's all

368

there was to it. I'm too weary to tell you everything now but I'm sure you will find out one day.'

It was obvious she didn't want to discuss it, whether it was because she was too weak or she was lying to protect Ernie he couldn't be sure, but right now wasn't the time to try to get the truth out of her or to mention anything about her losing the baby. What did concern him though was why Ernie had done a disappearing act if he wasn't guilty of anything other than verbally rowing, but their short time together was far too precious to waste asking questions which he knew would be answered in due course. All he wanted right now was to know Kitty was pleased to see him and to assure her that Connie and Malcolm were more than willing to keep the bairns until she was well enough to look after them herself.

When visiting began he was hoping he would still be alone with Kitty but it was not to be. Jean entered the room carrying a bunch of flowers but took a step back in shock when she saw a man, who she knew couldn't be Ernie, sitting at the bedside. Approaching warily she thought she recognised him but needed to take a closer look to be sure.

'Tom… yes it is isn't it?' She frowned as she wasn't a hundred percent sure having only met him fleetingly and he was wearing his army uniform at the time.

'It is, and you're Jean. See I remember, and I can understand why you're looking surprised to see me.' He stood up and gestured for her to take his seat.

He could see by her expression she was desperate to know what he was doing there but refrained from asking.

Accepting his offer she sat down and began talking to Kitty who by this time was looking very tired and Tom decided it was a good time for him to leave.

'Please don't go, Tom, Jean won't mind. I feel a little tired but I'm alright!'

'Listen I plan to stay in a B&B for a couple of nights so it might be a good idea if I leave while the night is still quite young to find somewhere. I'll be back in tomorrow to see you I promise and I think Matron will most likely allow me to come in outside of visiting hours seeing as I don't live local.' He leant over and squeezed her hand. 'I've arranged to ring Connie at 9 o'clock to see how the bairns are and to let them know how you are. You enjoy your chat with Jean. No doubt you will have plenty you want to tell her and make sure you have a good night's sleep so you will have lots of energy to talk to me tomorrow.'

'Thank you for coming, Tom. You'll find there are plenty of B&Bs nearby and I'll look forward to seeing you tomorrow,' and with a tear trickling down her cheek added, 'and tell Connie to give the bairns a hug from their mammy.'

'I will,' he said as he gave her a wink, but she couldn't bring herself to smile, she was missing Annie and Jack so much and now she felt disappointed to see Tom leaving so soon.

With Tom out of the way Jean was desperate to find out what was going on.

'Well that's certainly a turn up for the books. Now are you feeling well enough to put me in the picture about what on earth he is doing here?'

'By a rather strange coincidence Tom lives on a farm

370

only a couple of miles from Connie and Malcolm and they were already friends before we met him. Oh really, Jean, there's so much to tell you but I don't feel well enough yet. Let's just say Tom has come instead of them as they are looking after the bairns for me and of course they have work commitments as well.'

'I hope that's the only reason he's here. He seems very keen to stay within the vicinity of the hospital so he can keep popping in to see you.'

She could hardly believe she was lying to the very people who meant so much to her, but her condition meant she was too weak to argue and found it easier to ignore Jean's curiosity until she was fit and well enough to explain everything.

As her eyelids were beginning to droop and she looked to be in a bit of pain Jean decided it would be best to leave her to rest for the night.

'I'll find a nurse on the way out and ask her to bring you some painkillers and I'll pop into Peggy's to let her know how you are.'

'And be sure to tell her about Tom won't you?' Kitty said almost sarcastically knowing only too well that she would be breaking her neck to do so.

'Of course I will as chances are she is bound to bump into him during visiting tomorrow and forewarned is forearmed as they say.'

Waiting in the telephone box on the edge of Calderthwaite village green the phone rang at exactly 9.00 p.m. and immediately Connie picked it up.

'Is that you, Tom?'

'It certainly is, how's everything in Calderthwaite?'

'Fine. The bairns have been no bother and they're both tucked up in bed. Now tell me how is she and was she pleased to see you?'

'Yes she was pleased to see me. She was sleeping when I arrived but after several attempts to waken her she opened her eyes. She was shocked of course but her immediate concern was how the kids are.'

'You told her they're fine.'

'Of course and that they would be staying with you for as long as necessary. She's too weary at the minute to take everything in but she knows they're happy with you and Malcolm.

'Did she mention anything about Ernie?'

'Not really, only that he was drunk and went to bed. She said she was on her way to apologise to Peggy for the noise when she fell down the stairs. I asked her outright if Ernie had pushed her but she flatly denied he had anything to do with it, but I'm not convinced. She's not well enough to talk for very long but she did say we would find out one day what happened.'

'How long do you think they will keep her in?'

'I've no idea. Maybe two or three days. Listen, my money is about to run out. I'll ring you at the same...' The call ended abruptly but he had passed on enough information for now.

After finding a comfortable B&B he was feeling quite tired but popped back out to a late night snack bar where he tucked into pie, peas and chips and a large mug of tea. When he finished eating the owner came over to speak to him.

'I take it by your accent you're not from these parts?'

'That's right I'm just here for a couple of nights so I'm staying at The Claremont just up the road.'

'Well you'll be pleased to hear I'm open every day 8 in the morning till 10 at night so call in and I'll make sure I serve you a plate of food the likes of which you've never tasted in your life before.'

'Well if the pie, chips and mushy peas are anything to go by I think I'll take you at your word, but I'm done for today. It's been a long one and I'm ready to hit the sack for a good night's sleep.'

He let himself into the B&B where after a relaxing bath he was soon in bed. He closed his eyes and was imagining Kitty had accepted Ernie was never going to change and decided to finally leave him so they could begin a new life together.

'It will definitely happen one day. I'll just have to be patient; common sense will prevail and she will realise that there is more to life than putting up with an abusive marriage and leave.'

How he could be so sure was uncanny, but somewhere deep in his psyche he was confident that day would come.

Chapter Twenty-five

Thick blue damask curtains completely blocked out the daylight causing Tom to fumble for the bedside light in order to get his bearings. Remembering why he was sleeping in a strange room he leapt out of bed and flung back the curtains. It was a little after 8.00 a.m. but with breakfast being served until 9.00 a.m. and with no need to rush he decided to have an extra half hour before going down to eat. Stretching out on the top of the covers he planned his day. First stop would be the florists for a bouquet of flowers, then onto the greengrocer for some fresh fruit for Kitty then if she was feeling well enough to take her for a stroll in the hospital grounds. The fresh air would do her the world of good and hopefully, still convinced Ernie was responsible for her fall, once they were alone he would learn the truth about the terrible events of Sunday night.

Making his way down for breakfast the delicious aroma of bacon whetted his appetite and with thoughts of Kitty foremost in his mind, he hoped she was eating sufficiently to build up her strength so she could leave hospital and return to Calderthwaite before he had to return to barracks. After acknowledging a couple of guests who were already tucking into their breakfast, he chose an empty table by the window where he fidgeted nervously with the place settings.

'You're looking very worried this morning, Mr Watson. I hope it's nothing as bad as must have been the case for the poor fella mentioned in the late headlines of this morning's newspaper.'

'Nothing so worrying that it will stop me eating a good healthy breakfast to set me up for the day.'

'I guess that'll be the full works then including tea and toast,' she said placing the newspaper on the table. Tom's eyes were immediately drawn to the large bold headlines in the left hand column of the front page.

LATE NEWS HEADLINES

Last night after several failed attempts to discourage him, a man in his mid twenties leapt from the Tyne Bridge. His body has been recovered but it was too late to save him. His identity is being withheld until his family have been informed.

Guessing this must have been who Mrs Jefferies was referring to his thoughts went out to the poor family who were about to hear the devastating news. He tried to comprehend how someone's mind can become so disturbed that it drives them to do such a thing and saddened by what he had read, he folded the paper and placed it back on the table.

'There's no need for you to go dashing out if you don't need to,' Mrs Jefferies told him as she placed his breakfast on the table, 'and you're quite welcome to use the sitting room anytime. It's there for your comfort should you feel the need.'

'That's very kind of you, I'll see how the day goes and I might just take you up on that.'

'It wouldn't be any trouble to me as the place is pretty

375

quiet at the moment and you have a key so you can come and go as you please.' She was just about to leave when she remembered about the news headlines. 'Incidentally did you read about the poor fella who jumped from the bridge last night? His poor family must be in a terrible state. I guess something really bad must have happened to drive him to do something so desperate!'

'I did read it, and you're right it's a terrible tragedy not just for him but also the family he has left behind,' he said picking up his knife and fork, 'but if you don't mind I'll get stuck into my breakfast while it's hot then I'm heading off to visit a friend in hospital. I promised I would go and see her this morning so she will be expecting me and I don't want to disappoint her.'

Grateful that he had somewhere to put his feet up if the hospital did restrict his visiting he left the B&B around 10.30 a.m. Calling at the greengrocer and florist he bought fruit and flowers to take in with him then walked the short distance to the hospital hoping they would allow him to see Kitty before lunchtime. Unnoticed by the receptionists who were busy attending to a queue of people he headed straight up to the ward but as he approached the closed doors he was stopped by a young nurse who explained that visitors weren't allowed in until the afternoon. Once he had enlightened her who he was she assured him that Kitty had a restful night but that she would need to speak to Matron before allowing him on to the ward.

Waiting anxiously for an answer, he was greeted by a sombre looking Matron.

'I'm really sorry but it's not possible for you to see Kitty at present,' and guided him towards a small waiting area nearby.

Desperate for answers he hardly stopped to take a breath and asked, 'Has something happened to her? Has she taken a turn for the worse? The nurse told me she had a restful night.'

'She did have a restful night but... listen I'm not sure how much you know already, but the police are with Kitty as we speak. We had to call them the night she was admitted as we were made to understand there had been a terrible row between her and her husband but we couldn't allow them to question her until she was feeling a little better. I can't tell you any more than that as it would be up to Kitty or the police to give you more information. We have moved her into a side room for privacy but I can't let you see her until the police have completed their interview.'

'Does anyone have any idea exactly what did happen to her?'

'Only her neighbour who apparently lives in the flat below. She's the lady who heard Mr and Mrs Cartwright having a row but doesn't know for sure if Kitty fell or was pushed down the stairs. When the police left here they went straight to the flat but it was empty; it seems her husband had already left. I'm really sorry I can't say any more than that as it's not our place to speak to family and friends when there is an ongoing police investigation.'

'That's okay, I understand. I'll wait here until they've

finished their interview, but I'm sure Kitty must be feeling pretty distressed and she is expecting me.'

'I'm sure she is, Mr… er sorry I didn't get your name.'

'It's Tom. Tom Watson, but just call me Tom.'

'Is there anything I can get you while you're waiting?'

'No thanks, it's not long since I ate breakfast.'

Food or drink was the last thing on his mind, Kitty being his only concern. All that was going through his mind was what had taken place on Sunday night that the police had to be involved.

Some twenty minutes or so later Matron reappeared with two police officers, the older being male and as is often the case in these situations, his colleague a female officer. Drawing up seats next to Tom the male officer took the lead by enquiring what his relationship was with Kitty.

Tom hesitated for a moment before answering. He needed to choose his words carefully so as not to jeopardise his chances of being able to see her and hear exactly what had happened. 'Kitty's a very good friend of friends of mine who live in the North West. She was staying with them when a telegram arrived from her husband telling her to return home urgently. Not knowing what could be so urgent they agreed she should do as he asked but to leave her kids with them… but I'm sure you'll know this already.'

'Carry on, son, it's just we need to be absolutely certain who we are passing information on to.'

'I'm here on behalf of the friends who are looking after her kids as they don't want them to know that their mammy is in hospital. It's very kind of Kitty's neighbour to be prepared to visit and keep them informed but as she is quite elderly we decided it was a lot to expect of her to visit every day and write letters, and as I'm home on leave at the minute I could spare the time. It made more sense for me to travel across to find out what was happening and keep them informed of her progress.'

'What do you think, Matron, should we let him see Mrs Cartwright and if she agrees... and only if she agrees we can then enlighten him as to what happened last night?'

'Last night!' Tom retorted more confused than ever but no one responded.

'I'll pop along and see how she is but after hearing such bad news she's deeply shocked and may not be ready to face visitors.'

Tom eyes searched their faces trying to perceive what could have happened last night that would cause Kitty to be in such shock, but he refrained from asking questions and all three waited in silence for Matron's return.

'She is in a very bad way but said she would like Mr Watson with her.'

As they walked to the room Tom's mind flashed back to Calderthwaite. He was certain it couldn't be anything to do with Annie or Jack as they were fine last night when he spoke to Connie and decided it had to be something to do with Ernie. Had they found him and arrested him on suspicion of causing her grievous bodily harm? If they had then they may be here to see if she wanted to press charges against him. His mind was working overtime but

379

he needed to stay calm; he didn't want to upset Kitty any more than she already was.

The male officer stood by the end of the bed suggesting Tom take the seat nearest to Kitty. Shocked to see her looking ghostly white with red swollen eyes he held her hand until eventually between sobs she managed to speak.

'Thank you for being here for me, Tom. I really don't know what I would do without you.'

Matron and the female officer exchanged glances as they stood by leaving the male officer to again take command of the situation.

'Would you like me to explain to your friend why we are here?' he asked Kitty.

'Yes please, officer, he will have to know sooner or later.'

'I don't know if you have read this morning's local paper but the late headline reports of a man jumping from the Tyne Bridge last night?' Even before he had finished the sentence Tom's expression had changed and the officer guessed he must have already put two and two together.

Tom nodded slowly in response. Seeing Kitty in such a terrible state he suspected the man they were talking about was none other than Ernie Cartwright.

'We understand several passers-by tried to talk him down while waiting for the police to arrive, but it was in vain. He jumped before any of my colleagues reached the scene. All the necessary procedures were carried out, divers were called in but he couldn't be saved.' He waited a moment before continuing. 'It's been our duty this morning to break the terrible news to Mrs Cartwright that it was her husband.'

Struggling to maintain his composure Tom squeezed Kitty's hand firmly in a reassuring gesture as he tried to make her feel everything would be okay, but he knew it would take more than a firm hand squeeze to help her cope with such devastating news.

'Before we take our leave is there anything else you think Mr Watson should know?'

'There's no point in holding anything back from him...,' Kitty replied. Struggling to speak she continued nervously. 'And my friends need to be told as soon as possible as you know they have my bairns....'

'There's no need for you to say any more, Mrs Cartwright, I'll explain everything. There was a note sealed inside a plastic bag in the pocket of his trousers. On it was written his brother's address asking whoever found it to contact him. There was no mention of a Mrs Cartwright. Two of his brothers identified him and they gave us his home address but it seems they knew nothing about an accident. After they identified him the Chief Station Officer recognised the Cartwright name and checked their records to see if his home address corresponded with the one the police had visited on Sunday night and of course it did. We will be calling at the flat again looking for any clues as to what caused him to take his own life but for now thankfully, we have no need to ask Mrs Cartwright any further questions and we can leave her to get some rest. Once we're back at the station further procedures will be set in motion for an officer to call on Mr and Mrs Ferguson as they are the children's guardians at the moment and will need to be kept informed. Mrs Cartwright has already given us their address, so unless there is anything either of you would like us to pass on to them, then we'll take our leave.'

'There's just one thing, will you tell them...,' Tom turned to face Kitty, '...tell them I will stay here for as long as is necessary and that I will ring Connie... that's Mrs Ferguson at 9.00 tonight as we previously arranged.'

Shaking the hands of the officers he thanked them on Kitty's behalf, then as everyone left the room Matron said she would send someone along with refreshments. Under the circumstances Tom was allowed to stay for as long as Kitty wanted him there, and she was to remain in the side ward until she was discharged hopefully in the next couple of days if she was well enough.

Tom's feelings for Kitty intensified. How much more suffering could she endure? With her precious bairns miles away and her body beaten and bruised by a husband who has taken his own life he was certain of one thing: he would do everything he could to try to ease her pain.

'Did you manage to speak to Connie last night?' Kitty asked, her voice weak from exhaustion.

'I did and everything is fine.'

'Tell me, Tom, how am I ever going to explain to the bairns what has happened to their daddy?'

'They're far too young to understand, Kitty, so there's no need to even try to explain. They can learn the truth when they are older and not before. Listen Connie assured me they are perfectly happy so you have no need to worry about them. I know you are bound to be missing them but they are in good hands and hopefully you will be out of here and back with them in a few days.'

'I don't think I can face going back into that flat just yet, not after all that has happened. It will hold too many unhappy memories for me, and poor Peggy what will she make of all this when she hears?'

'Stop worrying, Kitty. Let's just take one thing at a time and we'll get through this together.'

'Oh, Tom, how will I ever be able to face everyone again?'

'You will, when you feel stronger. Everyone knows you have had it rough with Ernie at times so stop worrying. No one is going to think any less of *you* because of what *he* has done.'

The two talked for a short time until Tom decided she must rest before lunch arrived. He doubted if she would want to eat after all she had been through which suddenly reminded him the fruit and flowers were still in the waiting area. The large bouquet of flowers and the basket of fruit brought a smile to her face for the first time that morning which meant so much to them both.

'Oh, Tom, you shouldn't have but thank you, you're so kind. I can't remember the last time a man bought me flowers,' and she reached out towards him. He leant towards her and in the privacy of the small room they embraced like young lovers.

'Now I must let you get some rest. Peggy will coming in this afternoon and though she is in for a terrible shock if she thinks you are managing to cope then it may be easier for her to accept.'

'You're right, Tom, but you will be coming back in after dinner won't you?'

'Silly question, Kitty, of course I will.' After an affectionate hug, they held hands and gazed into each other's eyes but no words were spoken, they both knew now was not the right time to be talking about the future.

Kitty was given a light sedative to hopefully relieve her anxiety and help her sleep a little but when Tom returned he found her awake and still badly shaken by the morning's events. Understandably her heart felt as though it had been ripped apart. To learn she had lost Ernie forever and in such tragic circumstances then to have another man at her bedside, holding her hand to comfort her all in the same day was almost too much to bear. Little did she realise that the compassionate and caring man who entered her life less than two weeks ago would prove to be her strength in her time of need.

Peggy arrived for afternoon visiting and made straight for the main ward where she was shocked to find Kitty's bed empty. One of the nurses explained to her that she had been moved to a side room and pointed her in the right direction. Puzzled as to why they should move her, Peggy assumed she must have deteriorated and as she nervously entered the room she wasn't altogether surprised to find a young man sitting by her bedside. Jean had informed her about Tom and she was prepared for him to turn up at some point during visiting, but not *before* she had arrived.

Hearing the familiar sound of Peggy's slow footsteps treading wearily across the floor Kitty quickly withdrew her hand from Tom's. He immediately turned to see who it was and guessing it was Peggy he politely stood up to greet her.

'I take it you'll be Peggy, Kitty's neighbour?'

'I am, and from what Jean has been telling me you must be Tom, one of the young soldiers who helped her on the train?'

Kitty looked on nervously unsure how Peggy would have taken the news about Tom and decided with trepidation to formally introduce them.

'Peggy, meet Tom, my knight in shining armour,' she bravely added. 'Tom this is Peggy who unofficially adopted me when I moved in upstairs.'

The two strangers shook hands and Tom offered Peggy his seat which she gratefully accepted.

'Would you like me to leave you ladies on your own for a while?'

'No you're alright, lad. Pull yourself another chair up there's no need to disappear. I know you've come a long way to see Kitty and besides I'd like to get to know the young man who I hear kindly helped her and the bairns and I understand, lives near her friend Connie. It's quite a coincidence I have to say, the chances of that ever happening again must be very slim.'

As her tone was cheerful, they both assumed she had accepted that Tom was there for no other reason than it would be difficult for Connie to come when she was looking after the bairns. 'First hurdle over,' Kitty thought, but there were a few more to jump before this unprecedented situation could be explained.

'So how are you feeling today, Kitty and why have they moved you out of the big ward?'

'I'm feeling better already just for seeing you, Peggy.' She smiled. She loved Peggy dearly and was genuinely pleased to see her but felt uneasy about breaking the shocking news to her.

'Well looking at you I'm not quite so sure. You look very tired and a bit red around the eyes,' then went into her handbag and brought out an envelope. 'Now I don't know whether I've done the right thing or not but this letter came for Ernie this morning so I thought I would bring it in seeing as he's still not turned up at home. It has a Midlands postmark so I thought it might be something urgent to do with his job.'

Kitty took the letter from her scanning the envelope suspiciously. Addressed to Mr Ernie Cartwright the postmark showed it had been posted the day before. Puzzled as to what on earth it could be and not knowing why Ernie had returned home unexpectedly with all his belongings, she turned to Tom for advice.

'What do you think, Tom? Should I open it now or leave it until later?'

Peggy's eyes darted suspiciously between the two of them. Having no idea how much Kitty would be relying on him in the coming days it was understandable. She questioned what gave Tom the right to interfere in Kitty's decision making, and feeling rejected she pulled her shoulders back and curtly suggested, 'Well if Ernie doesn't mind you opening his post and nobody seems to know where he is then I can't see that it will matter.'

Kitty again turned to Tom, her eyes pleading with him to help her decide.

'I can't tell you what to do. It's up to you, Kitty, but if you feel strong enough to cope with whatever it has to say then open it now. Who knows? You might even find out why he arrived home unexpectedly.'

'I'm not sure. I think I'll leave it until later. I've had enough to cope with today already.'

Peggy sat rigid rubbing her hands together, she looked completely baffled. 'Are either of you going to enlighten me as to what is going on? You look as though you have been crying a lot, Kitty, so are you going to you tell me what has caused you to be so upset?'

'The police have been in to see me this morning, Peggy, that's why I've been moved to the side ward…' but before she had chance to say another word Peggy butted in.

'Well, I expect you told them the truth about what happened on Sunday night. They need to know, Kitty, it's no use you trying to protect him and it's about time he was put in his place the way he treats you when he's been drinking. I'm sorry, Tom, but I do get so upset by the way he treats her. I've seen and heard it too many times.'

'That's okay, Peggy. I know how much Kitty means to you but she could do without any more grief at the minute. What she was about to tell you is that she had a terrible shock this morning.'

'I'm sorry, Kitty, I don't mean to upset you but I think

you should know that I'm pretty sure he's never been back to the flat so have the police been to say they've found him and arrested him?'

'They've found him alright, Peggy,' she assured her but could not stop trembling, and began sobbing loudly. Tom took her hand.

'Would you rather I...?'

'Would you, Tom?'

'They came to inform her that Ernie was pulled out of the river last night, apparently he had jumped from the bridge. Passers-by at the scene had tried but were unable to stop him.'

The colour drained from Peggy's tired face and she seemed to struggle to breathe.

'Would you like me to get you a drink?' Tom asked worried what the shock might do to her.

'I'll be okay, just give me a minute but I'm so shocked. I really don't know what to say to you Kitty, other than I would never have expected Ernie to do anything like that.'

Kitty reached for her hand. 'Don't worry, Peggy. It has come as a terrible shock to us all, but thankfully Tom has been here for me most of the time.'

Tom decided to interrupt again concerned it was all getting too much for Kitty to go over it all again. 'I think you should take it easy for now, Kitty, so let me explain to Peggy. The local police are arranging for Cumberland Police to call on Connie and Malcolm later today to let them know what has happened. Thank goodness they kept the bairns as at least Kitty needn't worry too much

388

about them. I spoke to Connie last night and they're having a lovely time and they don't need to know that their mammy is in hospital. We'll all be doing our best to make sure they are back together again at the first opportunity so I've arranged to ring Connie every night while I'm here to let her know how things are progressing.'

Tom could see Peggy was becoming agitated. She wasn't happy that he was so involved in Kitty's life, and in an effort to make her feel better he reassured her she still had an important role to play.

'Don't feel you shouldn't write to Connie as you planned, Peggy. She will love to hear from you and so will Annie and Jack.'

'Well I suppose it is better that you can contact her by telephone that way she will find out straight away what's happening every day, and yes I will still write to her when I get over the shock. Have you any idea how long you intend to stay in Newcastle? I understood from Jean that you are only home on leave for a couple of weeks so you can't have much of it left?'

'I don't go back until early next week and I'll only stay here for as long as Kitty wants me to.'

Kitty wiped her eyes and looked directly at Peggy. 'I don't know how I'm ever going to face going back into the flat, Peggy, not after what happened in there on Sunday night. The memory of it will stick with me forever.'

'I know it was bad, I heard most of what was going on. So did you tell the police that he threw you down the stairs?' Peggy quizzed her, still curious to learn the truth.

'It's immaterial now, Peggy, he can no longer be punished for anything he has done and the police didn't seem interested in what took place on Sunday night any more. I'm the only one who will ever know the truth about what happened so I think it best if we just leave it at that.'

Tom could see Kitty was getting very emotional again and suggested to Peggy they leave so she could rest for a while.

'I think you're right, Tom. I'll head off for home and break the terrible news to Jean and suggest she doesn't visit tonight. No doubt you will be popping in again later and by then she will have had enough visitors for today.'

Kitty thanked them for coming and waved them off, placed Ernie's suspicious letter under her pillow and slid down between the covers. She needed to shut the terrible events of the past few days out of her mind and the only way she knew she could was to try to get some sleep.

Chapter Twenty-six

Tom intended to have a catnap before returning to the hospital but unable to rid his mind of Kitty and the tragic news of Ernie's death, sleep eluded him. From what she had told him about her blood relatives, he doubted if any of them would be prepared to support her and believed being back with her loyal friends who would be more than willing to help her through the difficulties that lay ahead in the coming days and weeks, would be the perfect answer. His one regret was that he had only just over a week's leave left then he wouldn't see her again until he completed his army service, but throughout that time he would look forward to them keeping in regular contact. After giving her situation serious consideration he decided an early discharge to enable her to return to Connie's would help her recover quicker and decided he would discuss it with Matron when he returned. If she was well enough to travel then he would mention it to Connie when he rang that night. The news of Ernie's death would have reached her by then and he felt sure that more than anything in the world, her family would want Kitty with them so they could help her through this, the most traumatic chapter of her life.

It was just after 6.00 p.m. when he arrived back at the hospital and before checking on Kitty he briefed Matron about his plan to take her back with him to the North

West. With only the elderly Peggy to help care for her at home he assumed she would agree it would be the best place for her.

'I'm afraid it's not up to me to make that decision. I will have to have a word with Dr Blewitt who I do believe may have left for the day, but I'll make enquires and get back to you as soon as I can.'

'Thank you, Matron. Do your best, I know how desperate Kitty is to be back with her bairns.'

'Oh I'm sure she is but it's completely out of my hands. It's entirely up to the doctors to say when a patient can be discharged.'

'I understand but I'll be keeping my fingers crossed for her anyway.'

As he entered the room he was delighted to see Kitty sitting by the bed looking a little more cheerful. She had slept for a couple of hours and eaten the majority of her evening meal which pleased him, knowing that she would not be allowed to leave unless she was eating properly.

'It's great to see you looking much better than when we left and with a bit of luck I'll have some good news for you very soon. I've had a quick word with Matron about trying to get you discharged as early as tomorrow.'

Her eyes lit up. 'Oh, Tom, what did she say?'

'She can't authorise your discharge, only the doctor can do that and unfortunately he may have left for the day so don't build your hopes too high. If she does manage to catch up with him and he agrees you can leave, do you think you would be strong enough to travel tomorrow?'

'I'd go tonight, Tom, if they said I could. I can't wait to get out of here but I have to admit I am worrying about going back into the flat. I don't think I will be able to face up to it so soon after what has happened.'

'You won't have to, Kitty. I intend to take you back to Connie's if they agree you're well enough to travel and besides, no one in Calderthwaite would expect you to return to your flat so soon or for Peggy to look after you even though there is probably nothing she would like better.'

'I'm desperate to see the bairns but the flat is not the place for them either at the minute. You have no idea how much I long to hold them, Tom. They're all I have left in my life now and we need to be together to help us come to terms with losing Ernie… but there is something else bothering me, Tom. Do you think I'll have to identify Ernie's body as well as his brothers because I really don't feel I could face up to that either?'

'What you've been through in the past few days, Kitty, most people never have to face in a lifetime, and as he has already been identified by his brothers then I think you should stop all this…'

'But you don't seem to realise…'

'So, Kitty, what's this I'm hearing about you wanting to leave?'

The sound of the doctor's voice came as a welcome interruption. 'Matron tells me you would like to leave as early as tomorrow morning but I don't think you quite

393

understand the terrible trauma you have been through these past few days. Not only have your injuries been pretty serious but losing your baby and then the tragic news of your husband's untimely death is an awful lot for anyone to have to cope with in such a short time.'

'I understand what you are saying, doctor, but I know I'll recover much quicker if I have my bairns around me. They're being looked after by friends who I know will be more than willing to have us stay with them until I feel ready to return home and deal with all the legal issues that will need sorting out. Tom has offered to see me back safely so please say I can go!'

'Well not before I give you a good check over so if you wouldn't mind leaving the room, Tom, I'll have a good look at her and see if it's at all possible.'

Tom was happy to leave so he could focus on his next move if Dr Blewitt allowed her to leave next morning. This would entail dashing over to Kitty's flat to collect what she needed to take with her but if it meant she would improve quicker then he would do whatever was necessary. Thankfully he didn't have to wait long for an answer.

'Well, it's good news, Tom, but only on condition you promise to carry out my instructions. I'll allow Kitty to leave tomorrow provided you make sure she is transported from A to B. I don't want her walking very far at all as it could set her back quite a bit and I'm sure you'll understand she will need lots of support both physically and mentally after all she has been through.'

'There will be no shortage of that where she is going,

Doctor Blewitt, I can assure you.'

'Then in that case I wish you well, Kitty. Any problems once you leave here then get in touch immediately with one of the local doctors.'

'I will and thank you so much, Doctor Blewitt.'

As she turned to follow the doctor from the room, Matron's smile matched that of Kitty and Tom. 'I'm really happy for you, Kitty but I must have a quick word with doctor so I'll pop back later to say goodbye. I finish at ten tonight and won't be back in again before you leave.'

Kitty looked at Tom her glazed eyes expressing the various emotions she was feeling. 'I feel so relieved, Tom but I really owe you an explanation about the baby.'

'There's no need to explain, Kitty, what's more important is how you feel about it though I have to admit it did come as rather a shock… I had absolutely no idea at all.'

'No one knew except Connie and her family of course. It's the reason I went to stay so she could help me with the bairns during the early stages. Yes it is heartbreaking to have lost my baby although under the circumstances, and I hate to say this but I'm beginning to think it could be for the best. I reckon I'd struggle to bring up three bairns without a husband and no money coming in.'

Tom longed to tell her that there was nothing he would like better than to step into Ernie's shoes but he knew now was not the time to talk of a future together and quickly changed the subject.

'How would you feel if I popped over and asked Peggy to sort out the things you'll need to take back with you rather than you having to go into the flat in the morning? That way we could go straight to the railway station from here which will cut out some travelling time and hopefully we'll make it in time for the mid morning train. What do you think, Kitty? If I head off now I should make it back here before visiting is over?'

'Oh I don't know if I want you to see what happened in there, Tom... you see...' She felt she couldn't bring herself to enlighten him and buried her face in her hands.

'What is it, Kitty? What happened that you don't want me to see?'

'Everything, Tom, but mainly the dress, the dress Connie made that I wore for the dance.' She hesitated again, her eyes glistening with tears. 'I brought it home with me and when Ernie saw it he began tearing at the seams.' She began to tremble. Clasping her hands to try to control the shaking, she sounded afraid as she struggled to continue. 'He was furious with me because I had left the bairns at Connie's then when he saw the dress hanging outside the wardrobe he went into a rage and wrenched it from the hanger. I tried to stop him but couldn't and that's when... Oh, Tom, how am I ever going to explain to Connie after all the hard work she put into making it for me?'

'Kitty your blood pressure will go through the roof if you don't try to calm down and then they won't let you out tomorrow. Let's try looking at things more logically shall we? First of all, I'm sure Connie will be very understanding about the dress and secondly there will be nothing in your flat that will upset me. All that matters to

396

me is to see you getting better then eventually everything else will take care of itself. Now are you going to give me the address or am I going to have to watch you suffering when you go into your flat in the morning?'

Finally agreeing that it would probably be for the best she gave him the address along with a list of things she needed and where Peggy could find them.

'Tell Peggy I'm really sorry for all the trouble I've caused and explain why I can't return to the flat just yet and that I will keep in touch with her by letter.'

After giving her a reassuring hug he left for 'Hazeldene' where Peggy was completely taken aback when she opened the door to find him standing at the other side.

'Whatever brings you here, Tom? Please don't tell me Kitty has taken a turn for the worse?'

'It's nothing to worry about, Peggy; Kitty is going to be okay. The doctor has been in to see her tonight and has said she can leave hospital in the morning so I've come to collect a few things for her. She has written a list of what she needs and asked if you will sort them out for her.'

'What on earth does she need all these for if she is coming home?' she asked puzzled by the number of items listed.

'She's not coming home, Peggy, I'm taking her back to Connie's. She's desperate to see Annie and Jack and can't face coming back into the flat just yet, I'm sure you'll agree it will be better for her to be with them. They'll take care of her until she is well and ready to come back.'

'You're right, Tom. She's going to need a lot of looking after so I best get used to the fact she won't be home for a while. I guess I better pop in and pick up her key then we can get cracking and sort out the things she needs.'

Peggy entered the flat ahead of Tom and it was obvious a disturbance had taken place. Walking into the bedroom she was shocked to see the state of the room and as she headed towards the chest of drawers she spotted the crumpled dress in the corner by the window.

'What on earth…' She gasped as she went to pick it up.

'I wouldn't if I was you, Peggy, you best leave it where it is. With a police investigation ongoing they may be calling back and will expect the room to have been left untouched.'

Reluctantly she left it and much to Tom's relief didn't ask if Kitty had explained to him what had actually taken place on Sunday night. As she packed the small suitcase memories of the 'notorious suitcase' came flooding back. She wondered if Kitty had told Tom about the many laughs they had the morning she left, but held back from asking as she felt now was probably not the right time for humour. Handing him the suitcase she locked the flat with its dark secret believing only Kitty held the key to the truth of what had taken place between husband and wife.

Before leaving Tom passed on Kitty's message and she became a little tearful. Feeling so emotional she could only manage to mumble a few kind words of comfort in return.

'Don't worry, Peggy, you'll see her again very soon. She'll have to come home to make arrangements for Ernie's funeral but it may take a while until she is well enough to cope on her own and ready to return for good.'

Deep down of course Tom was hoping she would never return. His wish was she would find a place near to the farm where, in the not too distant future, they could be together.

'I hope it won't take her too long to get over the shock of everything. I do miss her and the bairns so much but I suppose I'm being selfish expecting her to come home before she's ready.'

They said their goodbyes, leaving Tom just enough time to see Kitty before visiting ended.

Chapter Twenty-seven

Tom had no intention of telling Kitty of his immediate reaction when entering 'Hazeldene'. Taken aback by the cold unwelcoming atmosphere and the steep staircase leading to her flat, had sent a shiver down his spine. He imagined the terror she must have experienced as she tumbled headlong from top to bottom. Whether Ernie had pushed her or she had fallen accidently made no difference; witnessing the scene for himself had been gut wrenching.

'Did you manage, Tom? Was everything okay? What did Peggy have to say?' Kitty, desperate to know what had happened, blurted the questions at Tom before he had even placed the suitcase by the side of her bed.

'I could see she was still curious to know exactly what had happened but didn't ask any questions, and I made sure we didn't touch anything we felt we shouldn't, though at one point Peggy was about to pick up your dress when I managed just in time to stop her.'

'That sounds typical of Peggy. She was probably going to start tidying up rather than being nosey... but then again...' She smiled but kept her suspicions to herself. After all Peggy had done for her over the years, if anyone deserved an explanation she most certainly did. 'One day I will tell her everything, Tom, but now's not the time.'

'I'm sure you will, and by the way she's hung on to the

key just in case the police need to go in again, but I'm pretty sure she won't be joining them.'

'That's okay, Tom, it's just as well she has. As you say the police are nearly sure to need to go in again at some point.'

'When I broke the news that you were going to Connie's she looked quite upset. I think she expected you to go straight home from hospital but once I'd explained the benefits of you returning to Calderthwaite for a while she agreed it was probably for the best.'

'Bless her she does miss us but it's going to take a week or two before I'll be able to face going back to stay and although I do feel sorry for her being in the great big house on her own, she'll get used to it and I know Jean will be keeping an eye on her. I only hope Connie and Malcolm are as happy as you say they are about us staying with them longer than planned.'

'I think you know better than to doubt that, Kitty,' he said checking the time on his watch. With only fifteen minutes visiting time left he asked if she had solved the mystery of Ernie's letter.

'I haven't, Tom. I've had enough shocks already and decided it might be better if you were with me when I open it. I have been thinking about it though and I've worked out if it's from his employer then surely it would be addressed to Mr Ernest or Mr E Cartwright giving him his proper title rather than Ernie which seems very unprofessional for a business letter. If I'm right then it can only be from his landlady but why would she need to write to him?'

'Good thinking, Kitty, but the only way you're going to find out is to open it!'

Reluctantly her hand crept under the pillow and she withdrew the still unopened envelope. Looking at the handwriting the style seemed to be more male than female and she hesitated again. It took further encouragement from Tom before she eventually plucked up the courage to remove the letter, and immediately she recognised the address at the top of the page.

'Well it's not from his employer,' she said her hands shaking slightly and handed it to Tom. 'Will you read it first, Tom? It's from the people he has been lodging with but I can't imagine why on earth they would write to him at home; they have never had reason to do so before!' Remembering Ernie had brought extra luggage home this time she watched Tom nervously. 'I have a strange feeling this is going to be more bad news. Something must have happened and he has had to leave!'

Tom didn't answer preferring to read the few brief lines written by a man just as Kitty had suspected. It was signed by a Victor Robinson informing Ernie that, as a result of his affair with his wife Joyce Robinson, he was petitioning for divorce and was naming him as the co-respondent. A letter from his solicitor would be arriving within a matter of days. Shocked by what he had read he scanned the words a second time but could not bring himself to read it to Kitty. Another terrible blow was about to rock her world and he was concerned that more bad news would set her back and she wouldn't be well enough to leave next morning.

'What is it, Tom, what does it say?' She could see by his blank expression that it must be more disturbing news. 'Listen, Tom, nothing can upset me any more than I already am so please read it to me or give it to me and I'll read it myself.'

Unable to bring himself to read it aloud he handed her the letter. Watching intently for her reaction he was surprised she seemed quite calm. It didn't last; out of the blue she screwed it into a ball and flung it angrily across the room.

'Well I said nothing else could shock me but I'm furious, and why has this man gone to the trouble of forewarning Ernie? You must agree, Tom, it seems a very strange thing to do?'

'Maybe he was trying to protect you by warning Ernie in advance of his intentions and giving him the opportunity to confess to you before the solicitor's letter arrived.'

'Do you think that's the reason he jumped from the bridge, Tom, because he knew I was bound to find out sooner or later and riddled with guilt he couldn't face the consequences?'

'More likely a combination of his adultery and what he did to you,' Tom thought but said nothing.

'Answer me, Tom. What do you think?' she pleaded with him.

'I didn't know him, Kitty, so I can hardly pass judgement and does anyone other than the person themselves know what drives them to such desperate lengths rather than face up to their demons?'

403

She stared almost mesmerised at the crumpled ball of paper which had landed near the door. 'I think I need to read it again, Tom, if you wouldn't mind fetching it for me.' After straightening it out she re-read Victor's words almost in disbelief.

Joyce Robinson had been Ernie's landlady for over two years and Kitty had never suspected anything inappropriate might be going on between them. Ernie spoke very little of her, other than how well she looked after him and how nourishing the meals were she cooked for him. Obviously after reading this, it explains why he preferred not to talk about her. She was looking after him alright and far beyond the expectations of a normal landlady.

'Well I suppose there's nothing I can do about it now, but I really can't imagine how hard it would have been for me to accept if Ernie was still alive. I would never for one minute have thought that he... Oh this entire horrible business doesn't bear thinking about!'

'You're right, Kitty, there is nothing anyone can do about it now so why don't you settle back into bed and try to have a good night's sleep? It will be a long day for you tomorrow. Remember you are innocent in all of this and when the solicitor's letter arrives all you need to do is return it to them explaining briefly what has happened. There's no need for you to reply to Victor Robinson's letter; his solicitor will deal with that.'

Kitty knew he was right and she looked at him approvingly. 'When I write to Peggy I'll ask her to forward my mail on as soon as it arrives and when the solicitor's letter reaches me I'll reply to it straight away. Oh I don't know, Tom, I seem to have made such a mess of my life. Marrying Ernie against my parents' wishes who, unfortunately seem to have been right about him all along and now after taking his own life I'm left to bring up our bairns without him being here to provide for them. I know him having an affair was wrong but he didn't have to end his life because of it. I'm sure over time I would have forgiven him.'

'I'm sure you would, Kitty,' he responded through gritted teeth, believing that's exactly what she would have done. 'You don't have to worry though you won't have to face the future alone. Like Connie and her family I'll always be there for you.'

'I know, Tom, but it wouldn't be right. Let's be honest we hardly know each other and I appreciate the bairns think a lot of you but they'll never forget their daddy, especially Annie being that little bit older than Jack. My mind's all mixed up right now and it's going to take me months to get over the torment of the past few days.'

'Of course it will, Kitty and there's no need to rush into anything. Now I think we've probably done enough talking for one night as you'll need to have a good night's sleep to be well enough to travel tomorrow. I'll ring Connie at the usual time and will let her know we'll be arriving tomorrow afternoon. She'll be over the moon and so will the bairns when they wake up in the morning to be told their mammy is on her way back.'

She couldn't help but smile when she heard Tom call Annie and Jack 'bairns' instead of 'kids' and spontaneously reached out to him. Not a word was spoken as they clung to one another, both aware that neither wanted to let go. Tom took the liberty of kissing her gently on the lips. She didn't reject him but she knew a future together from her point of view was very unlikely.

Spot on 9.00 p.m. with the telephone receiver close to his ear, Tom pressed button A. Connie barely allowed the phone to ring once before she answered.

'Is that you, Tom?'

'Yes it's me.'

'Oh, Tom, I can't believe it, the police called earlier to break the news. How is she? I honestly don't think she can possibly take much more.' Her voice sounded fraught.

'She's coping quite well considering and I actually have some good news for a change. I've arranged for her to be discharged in the morning.'

'Oh she can't go back to that flat, Tom, not right now!'

'I know that, Connie, and I can assure you she's not. With Peggy's help we've sorted out what is needed for her to leave hospital and I am bringing her back with me to Calderthwaite in the morning.'

'Oh thank goodness for that. We'd already decided she must come to us as soon as she is ready to leave hospital.'

'That's good. So everyone is happy then. We'll be travelling back on the mid morning train, I'm arranging a taxi from the hospital to the station and again from the station to Calderthwaite as her doctor has insisted she has to do very little walking.'

'You do whatever you have to, Tom and don't worry about the expense. We'll square up with you once we have Kitty settled back here.

'Don't even think about fares. To see Kitty's face when she walks through the door and sees Annie and Jack again will be worth every penny. Let's leave it at that for tonight, Connie and don't worry, I'll take good care of her and we'll look forward to seeing you all tomorrow.'

'I can't wait to tell everyone and thanks for all you've done. Goodnight, Tom, see you both tomorrow.' After placing the receiver back on its rest she raced home to break the good news.

With so much on his mind Tom hadn't realised just how hungry he was until he called into the little snack bar, took a seat and began reading the menu.

'You've left it a bit late for that, son, I was planning on closing just now. Not had a soul through the door for nearly an hour and didn't look like I was going to get anyone else in tonight, but seeing it's you I'll take a look and see what's left that'll help fill your belly till morning.'

'Sorry I've left it so late but if you're sure it's no trouble, anything will do as long I have something to eat to see me through till breakfast.'

A few minutes later he returned with an unappetising plate of what looked like left over warmed up greasy chips, a couple of fried eggs, a serving of dried out baked beans, and a couple of slices of bread and margarine. 'It's the best I can offer you tonight I'm afraid but I'll not charge you much, and it's better in your belly than finishing up in the waste bin.'

Tom wasn't quite so sure about that. The meal in front of him had done nothing to whet his appetite, however he knew he must eat something and at the present moment it was better than nothing.

A few minutes later the owner returned. 'There's a mug of tea, son, I'll throw that in as well. You'll need it to help wash down your meal.'

'Thanks, it's much appreciated.' Tom acknowledged him with a forced smile, it certainly hadn't been the best meal he'd ever had placed in front of him.

After rushing his meal so the owner could close for the night he happily paid the reduced price. 'I'm heading home tomorrow so I won't be in again but if ever I pass this way again I'll pay you a visit.'

'It's been a pleasure, lad and have a safe journey home.'

Tom, being mentally worn out, slept right through until 7.30 a.m. A little after 8.00 a.m. he went down for breakfast and informed the landlady that he would be leaving that morning. After settling his bill she allowed him the use of the phone to arrange a taxi from the hospital to the railway station in time for the eleven-thirty train.

When he arrived at the hospital Kitty was as he had hoped up and dressed. 'Morning, Kitty. How are you this morning?' he asked as he leant towards her giving an affectionate peck on the forehead.

'Raring to go, Tom... well maybe not quite. The mind is but I'm not so sure about the body but as far as anyone in here is concerned I'm feeling really well and strong enough to travel, because believe me nothing is going to stop me getting on that train this morning. That's of course if Connie said she is happy for me to be going back there.'

'Of course she is, they have all been very worried about you and said they wouldn't expect anything other than for you return to them while you recover. Now if you have everything ready I'll find whoever is standing in for Matron and let them know we are about to leave. I've already arranged a taxi so we can take our time getting down to the entrance.'

After saying their goodbyes, they took the lift to the ground floor where Kitty refused to use a wheelchair insisting on walking to the taxi which was already waiting for them.

'Taxi for Watson?' the driver asked.

'That's us,' Tom replied, and assisted Kitty into her seat.

'Central Station I understand?'

'Yes please,' Tom responded enthusiastically but his feelings were a mixture of joy and apprehension. Taking Kitty's hand in his he reassured her that everything would be fine once she was back with Connie and the bairns, but her response told him she thought differently.

'I guess it will, Tom, but until this journey is over I won't relax. I feel quite guilty about not staying in Newcastle, and I'm pretty sure the gossipers will be having a hay day accusing me of running away from my responsibilities, but I know I'm doing what's right for me and the bairns. You will have noticed that no one from

409

Ernie's family has made any attempt to get in touch which in a way doesn't surprise me, and whether my parents will have heard anything or not I couldn't say, but word soon gets around and you would expect by now everyone who knew Ernie will be talking about him.'

'If your parents have heard, Kitty, then they'll no doubt be feeling very guilty. If it's any comfort to you I'm sure their thoughts will be with you and they will be wondering what to do to be right, but to be honest you have enough to think about at the minute without worrying about them.'

Arriving at the railway station Tom found Kitty a seat while he headed for the ticket office. While she waited for him to return, memories of being in this very same place less than two weeks earlier came flooding back. She recalled Annie yelling at the young soldier who she thought was her daddy and wondered how on earth she was going to explain to her that he would never be coming home again.

Tom returned smiling and waving the tickets. 'Train's already in, Kitty so we'd better head over and just think, we'll be back in Calderthwaite before you know it!' She understood Tom's enthusiasm; he was doing his utmost to try and lift her spirits but as they headed towards the train she became a little fretful. Certain Tom was looking on this as a re-run of his failed attempt, she felt this time he was looking at it as the start of their future together.

Once they were settled on the train Tom put his arm around her shoulder and continued trying to reassure her that eventually she would pick up the pieces and move on. He reminded her of happier times, how they met on this very same journey, their meal with Connie's family, visits to the farm where he entertained Annie and Jack, and of course the all important dance. Throughout she struggled to respond with even a smile which worried him. He was concerned that maybe he had encouraged her to leave hospital before she was well enough to face the future.

She had only half listened to what he said convinced he still believed it was fate that had brought them together. 'If fate is in the lap of the gods then they have dealt me a very cruel blow in order for Tom to have his wish fulfilled.'

'Penny for them,' Tom asked seeing she seemed a little agitated.

'Oh it's nothing really, Tom. I was just thinking how you once said that it was fate that we met and if you remember I told you I've never believed in it. I'll never accept that the three of us are victims of fate. Ernie's death was of his own choosing not fate, nor will I ever believe it happened so that we could be together. It was pure coincidence that you arrived on the scene before I was about to face the most challenging time of my life. I really don't know what to think any more, Tom and who is to say where I'll end up but one thing is certain, my bairns will always come first and we'll return to Newcastle as soon as I am well enough because it's our birthplace and where we belong.'

'You're such a deep thinker, Kitty, why don't you just try to take one day at a time? At present your health is

411

more important than anything else and who knows, once you've recovered and start to come to terms with losing Ernie, what will happen?'

An uncomfortable silence followed. With more than half an hour travelling time before they reached their destination Kitty rested her head on Tom's shoulder and finally began to relax. Very soon she would be back with her bairns and have the love and support of her very dear friends to help her through this terrible time. Feeling a little more relaxed she managed to doze off in his arms.

'Wake up, Kitty, we're here.' Tom shook her gently as the train slowed down ready to make its way steadily into the station. 'Not long now and you'll have the bairns in your arms again.'

'For a minute I'd almost forgotten where I am,' she said, tears of joy trickling down her cheeks. 'Not long to go now, Tom and I'll see my precious bairns again.'

'You're right, Kitty, the waiting is nearly over and with a taxi to take us to Connie and Malcolm's we should be back at Rose Cottage around threeish.'

'I can't wait to see everyone, Tom. These past few days have been a living hell for me.'

'Well some of your pain will be over soon. I know you still have lots to cope with but at least we managed to get you out of hospital and back with your loved ones.'

'In that respect I am so lucky to have such good friends,' she said speaking from the heart.

It was a very emotional welcome back. Connie opened the door with outstretched arms while Annie and Jack ran around frantically trying to reach their mammy.

With tears in her eyes Kitty reached for her bairns. Her joy was so overwhelming it was as though she hadn't a worry in the world.

'Where's Daddy?' Annie asked looking puzzled. 'That's Tom not Daddy. You said Daddy was coming home that's why you left us with Aunty Connie to go and get him.'

Completely taken aback she glanced across at Connie and then at Tom, who both like herself, looked dumbfounded. There was an uneasy silence for a second or two, broken only when Kitty after taking a deep breath began to explain.

'I'm sorry, Annie but Daddy has gone away for a long time so I've brought Tom to see you instead.' She tried to sound cheerful but deep down her heart was aching.

'But why, Mammy? You said Daddy had come home.'

'He did, darling. I'm sorry but he couldn't stay long. One day when you're a big girl I will explain everything but for now are you going to let me sit down so I can take a good look at you both. I've missed you so much and I can't wait to hear what you have been doing while I've been away.'

Both the bairns climbed on to her knee wrapping their arms around her hugging her tight. 'Are you sad that Daddy had to go away again?' Annie asked stroking her mammy's hair.

'Of course, Annie, I'm very sad, but I'll always have you and Jack.'

'And your mammy will always have me, Annie,' Tom interrupted though whether to convince everyone present or himself, Kitty couldn't be sure. She looked up at him and her gut feeling told her he was probably speaking the truth even though now was not the time to be talking about promises he had made earlier.

'Does that mean we can live here forever, Mammy, because me and Jack love being at Aunty Connie's and Tom can take us to the farm every day can't you, Tom?'

Kitty squeezed her tightly. Little did she realise that not only her dream of going to the farm every day could be fulfilled, but the lifelong wish of the two friends to live close by could possibly come to fruition in the not too distant future.

Connie, still standing by the living room door, was lost for words as she observed how tenderly Kitty gazed into Tom's eyes proving to her that what he had told them before leaving for the hospital must be true. Feeling slightly shaken by the extraordinary events that had occurred during the past two weeks, she wondered, should today be a day of sadness or a day for celebration? Kitty on the other hand, free from her abusive marriage, knew her future lay with Tom but at this moment in time with a heavy heart her thoughts were with Ernie who, when they married, changed her life forever. As the father of her bairns he would never be forgotten but she wondered, after all the pain and suffering he had caused did he really deserve anyone to mourn his death?

Three feet of Lightning

by

Rita Wilkinson

Muriel sobbed relentlessly for what seemed like hours but finally managed to drag herself from the bedroom chair and cross to the window. The clouds had darkened and she could hear the wind whistling around the farmhouse as she watched the trees swaying violently from side to side. She checked the time. It was past midday and her thoughts went back to the three men, knowing how hazardous it would be up on the fell. 'Hopefully they should be on their way down before it gets much worse,' she told herself as she turned away from the window wishing they had never had to make the journey at all that day.

She was shocked to hear Shelia's car coming up the track, having completely forgotten about inviting her for lunch as she relived the memory of the terrible day when the tragedy occurred. She could hear Bess barking to warn her that someone was approaching and tried to reduce her swollen eyes by splashing them with cold water; then brushed her hair which was damp and unruly from running her tear-drenched fingers through it so many times. By the time she reached the bottom of the stairs Sheila was calling to her as she opened the door.

'It's just me I'm here at last,' but on seeing Muriel she was taken aback and her tone of voice changed. 'Oh, Muriel, whatever is the matter?'

'It's nothing, Shelia. I'll be okay in a few minutes.'

'I knew there was something wrong when I spoke to you earlier. Even Brenda could tell by my voice that something was wrong. She knew I needed to check on Tia but that I wanted get to you as soon as possible and suggested I finish a little earlier.'

'I'll be alright, Shelia, but as you can see I haven't made our lunch yet. I happened to pick up Michael's photograph to dust as I do most days, but for some reason today I got really upset remembering that terrible day. Perhaps I shouldn't tell you this....'

Shelia was anxious to know what was going on in her friend's head. 'You shouldn't tell me what?'

'Oh nothing it's probably me just being silly and imagining things.'

'Muriel I need to know what is worrying you if I'm to be of any help. Seeing you so distraught, you can't expect me to just sit here and not do anything to help.'

Published by and available from

Hayloft Publishing Ltd
Kirkby Stephen
Cumbria

ISBN No 9781904524892-02

Also available as an e-book on Amazon

Lightning Source UK Ltd.
Milton Keynes UK
UKOW02f0319131216
289864UK00002B/21/P